To a special sister,
Ann —
A dream is a 8
into your soul.
Fondly,
Anna A Garr
11/5/18

Apollo's Raven

LINNEA TANNER

BOOK ONE IN THE APOLLO'S RAVEN SERIES

Apollo's Raven
An Epic Celtic Tale of Love, Magic, Adventure, Intrigue and Betrayal in Ancient Rome and Britannia
by Linnea Tanner

©Copyright 2017 Linnea Tanner

ALL RIGHTS RESERVED
With certain exceptions, no part of this book may be reproduced in any written, electronic, recording, or photocopying form without written permission of the publisher or author. The exceptions would be in the case of brief quotations embodied in critical articles or reviews and pages where permission is specifically granted in writing by the author or publisher and where authorship/source is acknowledged in the quoted materials.

Although every precaution has been taken to verify the accuracy of the historical information contained herein, the publisher and author assume no responsibility for any errors or omissions. No liability is assumed for damages that may result from the use of information contained within.

Books may be purchased by contacting the publisher or author at:
www.linneatanner.com or
linneatanner@skybeam.com

Cover Art, Cover Layout and Interior Design: Nick Zelinger, NZ Graphics
Maps: D. N. Frost, maps@DNFrost.com
Editor: John Maling, Editing by John
Book Consultant: The Book Shepherd; Judith Briles
Publisher: Apollo Raven Publisher, LLC

Library of Congress Catalog Number: 2016920018
ISBN: 978-0-9982300-0-9 (softcover)
    978-0-9982300-1-6 (hardcover)
    978-0-9982300-2-3 (e-book)
    978-0-9982300-3-0 (audio-book)

1) Historical Fiction   2) Fantasy   3) Ancient Rome and Britannia   4) Celtic Mythology

First Edition: Printed in the USA

Book One

🐦🐦🐦

Apollo's Raven

An Epic Celtic Tale of Love, Magic, Adventure, Intrigue
and Betrayal in Ancient Rome and Britannia

Britannia

- River Wensum
- Iceni
- Great Ouse River
- Corieltauvi
- River Trent
- River Avon
- Catuvellauni
- Camulodunum
- Verulamion
- Trinovantes
- River Scour
- Durovernum
- Cantiaci
- Cantiaci Cliff
- White Fortress
- Cliffs
- Gaul
- Dobunni
- River Thames
- Atrebates
- Calleva
- River Medway
- River Arun
- Belgae
- Regni
- Noviomagus
- Temple of Apollo
- River Severn
- Silures
- River Avon
- Durotriges

© D.N.Frost

I

RAVEN'S WARNING

*"What if Father learns that I've taken this next step?
Will he punish me for disobeying him ... for ignoring his warning?"*

24 AD, Southeast Coast of Britannia

Princess Catrin reined in her horse at the edge of the precipice overlooking the sea below to study the pattern of her raven's flight, seeking an omen. Her dream of the skull-faced moon, bleeding crimson, still plagued her. It was as if she had glimpsed both into her soul and into the future, yet she did not know how to interpret it.

The raven shot like an arrow into the thickening mist partially obscuring the sun when the sudden nip of a cool, salty breeze made her shiver. Longing for the disappearing sun's warmth, she nestled into her plaid cloak and focused on the bird's aerial acrobatics, first diving at the sheer cliff, then darting up. This close to the edge, one misstep of her horse could dash them both onto the jagged rocks below. Only her raven, a divine messenger, had the power to overcome such a fall and rise into the heavens to soar with the gods.

The raven disappeared into the fog and suddenly, out of the haze appeared the red-striped sail of a flat-bottom ship. Driven mainly by oars, it thrust to and fro in the turbulent water; it was unlike the deep-hulled vessels of seafaring merchants powered by air currents over their sails. At the bow of the ship was a strange looking beam shaped like a bird's beak.

Catrin's eyes followed the raven's movement beyond the white cliffs where more striped sails were emerging from the mist. She counted ten, but there might be more. A chill feathered up her spine.

Warships!

From the distance, she could not determine the total number of ships or the country of their origin. She needed to see through her raven's eyes for that. To do so, to meld her thoughts with the creature's, she had to be alone. Uneasy that her sister, Mor, and their companion, Belinus, might disrupt her connecting with the bird, she scanned a clump of brambles, some distance down the grassy slope, where she had left them. The couple met at Beltane's spring festival, a few weeks back, and had become intoxicated with each other.

Catrin was still rankled that Belinus had tricked her into weapons training. His real purpose came to light the evening before, when he told her to wait on the hillside, so he could finish practicing with Mor. A warm blush spread across Catrin's face as she imagined their legs entangled around each other. Did they think she was deaf and blind? That she was too stupid to understand what they were doing? The king would not think kindly if one of his trusted warriors charged with training his daughters for battle was "gallivanting" with one of them.

Now barely discerning the couple through the thick brush, she surmised they were again fully occupied with each other. That left ample time to take the next step with her raven before they joined her.

She dismounted and raised her sword, a signal for her raven to return. The large bird swooped toward her like a dark shadow. She lifted an arm on which the bird landed, its midnight-black plumage contrasted sharply with her fair skin and gold braided hair. On the threshold of womanhood, she felt closer to this creature than to many of her own kind. Still, she hesitated connecting with the bird.

A few years back, she told her father of her ability to see the present and future through the raven's eyes. She desired to be a

Druidess. He denied her request to be trained in the spiritual order, saying, "I have decreed that no one in my family can use the powers of the Ancient Druids."

When she asked why, he responded with a grim frown, "The magic is too unpredictable and often alters in deadly ways. Foresight is not a gift, but a curse in our family."

Her father's answer bewildered her, yet she dared not defy him openly or get caught when she secretly practiced this new mystical ability the raven showed her. *The raven first sought me out,* she reasoned, in favor for now using her newly discovered powers. *I must heed its warning. And if I am to assess the danger the ships pose, I need to study them up close.*

She had to hurry, though. The fire stoking between her sister and Belinus would soon cool.

Catrin lifted her arm and looked to the raven, considering her decision. "What do I have to fear from you? I am a Cantiaci warrior."

The raven cocked its head and gawked at her, as if ready to answer her question. She asked, "Did the sun god send you a sign about the ships near the coast?"

When the raven mumbled some gibberish, she tapped its beak. "What does that mean?"

The raven screeched, bobbing up and down. She smoothed its ruffled feathers. "Were those warships offshore?"

The raven then grew still on her arm. She winced, recalling the image of the blood moon in her dream. "Should my father beware of the warships, if that is what they are?"

The raven nodded excitedly, as if in response. Encouraged, she asked, "If I saw through your eyes, could I learn the true reason of who they are and why they are here?"

The creature tilted its head sideways, the signal for her to enter its mind. She paused. "What if Father learns that I've taken this next step? Will he punish me for disobeying him … for ignoring his warning?"

The raven shrieked and arched its wings. She chuckled, "That is right. He did say to study the enemy before each encounter, but never hesitate in battle. That is what I'm doing—doing exactly what my father expects. I am finding out if enemies are aboard the ships, but to do so, I must see through your eyes."

Catrin again hesitated. Once before, when she had melded and then disconnected from her raven, she lost consciousness. It took awhile for her head to clear after that episode. If that happened again, it could spell disaster so close to the precipice.

She stepped away from the cliff's edge and stared into the raven's eyes which were glowing like amber gems. The bird's talons emitted a bolt of electric heat into her arm. A light flashed in her mind, and the raven's essence permeated her core being. She knew then that she had entered the raven's prescient mind.

At first, the landscape appeared blurry until she adjusted to the raven's eyesight. Then brightly colored wildflowers dazzled her with purple hues that she was unable to detect with her human eyes. A thrill rushed through her as she sensed the bird's breast muscles contracting to flap its wings. When the raven began its thrust into flight, she felt the misty air lift the bird's outstretched wings.

When the raven flew into the sky, she could see her human form that stood as motionless as a statue on the emerald hilltop clasped to the jagged precipice. The sheer cliffs below formed an impenetrable wall against the crashing waves. Beyond the cliffs was a sparsely vegetated shoreline toward which several ships were sailing and where other vessels were moored. Armored infantrymen had disembarked, waded to the shore and were marching across the beach. On higher ground, soldiers had set up tents in a square encampment. One of the guards had a lion's head covering his helmet. In his hands was a pole with a silver eagle on top. She assumed it meant powerful animal spirits were guiding them.

A palatial tent in the center of the encampment caught her eye. Its outside walls were made of twined linen sheets, violet and red, brocaded with eagles. Surrounding the central structure were crimson banners, each emblazoned with the sun god in a horse-driven chariot. At the tent's flapped entrance were two foreign noblemen attired in purple-trimmed, white togas. Another man, towering over the foreigners, wore a rustic toga and plaid breeches, garments that nobles from her kingdom typically dressed in. From the back, he looked familiar, his thick coppery hair draped over his shoulders like a lustrous wolf pelt.

Why is he here?

To confirm her suspicions that she knew this tall, brawny man, Catrin directed the raven to circle around, so she could get a closer look. When the man's ghostly, disfigured face came into view, her heart wrenched when she recognized her half-brother, Marrock.

Grotesque images of ravens pecking tissue out of his face flashed in her mind. For seven years, she had believed herself safe from him, but there he was—a specter arisen from the cold ashes of her nightmares.

What does he plan to do with the foreign army?

A sense of doom crawled over her when Marrock's head tilted back, as though he knew her essence was flying overhead. His blue-green eyes began glowing and then changed to the same amber-gem color as her raven whenever she harnessed its magical power. The raven's muscles suddenly paralyzed, freezing the wings. A strong force pulled her through a crevasse in the raven's mind and sucked her into a tunnel of brilliant gold light. She then plummeted, tumbling out of control, toward a black portal in the center of a rainbow-colored arch.

2

SECRET MAGIC

"What was wrong with you? You appeared frozen; your arms twisted over each other like broken wings. It was as if you had left this world and became something else."

A split instant later, just before Catrin burst through the portal, she found herself lying on familiar, yellow-flowered grass on the cliffs. Above her, the raven's wings disappeared into a gray haze. A shiver of panic as sharp as needles prickled down her back.

Was this what my father meant about the magic being unpredictable?

The landscape settling around her, she inhaled the briny air and felt her own world again. Still, a burning tingle lingered in her arm as questions barraged her mind.

Did Marrock do this to me? Did he somehow sense I was spying on him by using my raven's eyesight? Did he put me into another world? Is this the deadly magic my father warned me about—the double-edged blade that others who detect my raven-sight can do me harm?

A woman's shrill voice startled Catrin out of her troubled thoughts. She rolled on her back to find her sister, Mor, looking down at her, the reins of her bay horse in hand. Gusty wind swirled Mor's ebony tresses around her face etched with concern.

"What happened to you?" Mor asked. "Your horse was loose. From a distance, I saw a raven on your shoulder. Then you collapsed."

"I slipped and fell," Catrin said, trying to wrap her mind around what just happened. "Help me up." She grasped Mor's extended hand and pulled herself up. Woozy, she teetered while brushing the chalk of the cliff stones off her leather chest armor.

Mor asked, "What was wrong with you? You appeared frozen; your arms twisted over each other like broken wings. It was as if you had left this world and became something else. A wraith, a soulless corpse comes to mind. Did the raven do that to you?"

Ignoring Mor's comment, Catrin glanced around, thinking it odd that her sister was there without Belinus. Assuming he was nearby, she looked beyond Mor, but there was no sign of him.

"Why don't you answer me?" Mor snapped. "This is the second time I've seen this happen to you this week. You know what Father said. You are not to do magic with that raven."

"I don't need you to remind me," Catrin muttered, her thoughts racing to Marrock and the ships offshore. She blurted, "There is something offshore that concerns me."

Mor gave her a befuddled look. "What ships? I thought we were talking about your raven."

Catrin pointed to the ocean channel. "The warships that are out there!"

Shaking her head, Mor walked to the cliff, peered over the edge, and looked back at Catrin. "What exactly did you see?"

Words darted out of Catrin's mouth. "Striped sails, oar-driven warships, foreign soldiers landing, and Marrock!"

"Whoa! Slow down," Mor said. "Where did you see this?"

Catrin gestured northward. "Beyond the cliffs."

Mor shielded her eyes with a hand to search again. A few seconds later, she gave Catrin a dubious frown.

"I can't see anything from here, too much fog. When did you see Marrock?"

"A bit ago—" Catrin suddenly realized it could have been quite some time since being in the raven's mind.

Mor gripped Catrin's arm and pulled her closer. Catrin stared into Mor's chestnut-brown eyes as her sister continued with the hard questioning. "Is something else going on with you? Is that crazy raven casting spells on you? You know what people say, that creature will make you go mad."

Catrin bristled. "Nonsense! It is nothing like that. I only connect to it when I need its help and have complete control over it."

Seeing Mor's jaw drop, Catrin realize her secret had slipped out and bit her lower lip, making it bleed. It was too late to take the words back. Considering it further, she didn't know how to convince Mor of the threat posed by Marrock and the foreign army unless she disclosed her use of forbidden magic. She finally said, "I need to tell you something, but you must promise not to tell Father."

Mor's eyebrows arched. "What have you done now?"

Catrin's throat felt parched as she stumbled through the explanation, her voice sometimes cracking. "Whenever I need help—like … like seeing something in the distance—I can enter the raven's mind. Once in, I can see through its eyes."

"What do you mean by 'once you are in?' You transform into a raven?"

"No … not that." Catrin again fumbled for the right words. "My human vision turns off when I switch to the raven's eyes. I can see below me when it flies. The raven also sends me dreams of the future. Last night, I dreamt the moon turned into a bleeding skull. I took this as an omen that our kingdom is in grave danger. When I saw Marrock with a foreign army, I knew this was true."

Mor paused, as if trying to absorb what Catrin had just described. "Merchant ships are always sailing near the coastline. How could you even tell they were warships from this distance?"

"They were not like merchant ships and soldiers were disembarking from them beyond the cliffs—"

Mor interrupted. "You can see that from here? I doubt it."

Catrin blazed. "Let me finish!"

Mor's lips clamped, finally allowing Catrin to continue. "Hundreds of soldiers are setting up camp near the shore north of here, in the bay. That is where I saw Marrock!"

"I find this incredibly hard to believe," Mor said, lifting her eyes in disbelief.

"It is true, Marrock was there," Catrin insisted. "Omens do not lie. Soldiers would not be with him unless they plan to attack. We need to warn Father."

"Warn him of what?" Mor said, still appearing skeptical.

Growing impatient with Mor's questions, Catrin said sharply, "Marrock has come back. He is conspiring with foreign troops. Remember, sister, he swore to kill everyone in our family when Father banished him."

"That is quite a bold accusation," Mor exclaimed. "I have never seen Marrock and, for that matter, I have never seen any warships. What if you're wrong? You don't have any proof that he is plotting to attack our kingdom. I don't want to look stupid telling Father something that is not true. He will be angry when he finds out you used your raven's magic. Besides, I want to stay here and finish training with Belinus."

Catrin's face burned. *Train with what, his sword?* She pointed to herself. "I'll accept the blame if it turns out wrong, which it isn't. We need to get back now!"

Mor put hands on her hips. "I'm not leaving until I see these soldiers and ships with my own eyes."

Catrin, noticing her sister suddenly glance up, turned and spotted Belinus waving from the adjacent hilltop to signal weapons had been setup for practice. The last thing she wanted was for Mor to persuade him to stay, so they could finish their tryst before slinking back home. Catrin fumed that Mor had lost all sense of propriety behaving as she had with a common warrior.

Of all days to practice! I should be warning Father.

When Mor pulled the reins of the bay and began walking away, Catrin yanked her by the arm to halt her. "What are you doing?"

Mor spun toward Catrin. "Belinus is set to go. I'm getting your horse ready, so you can practice spear throwing."

Catrin shook her head in disbelief. "Didn't you hear what I just said? We need to go now and tell Father what we have seen."

Mor shot a seething glare. "I don't take orders from someone who practices black magic with a raven. You see things nobody else can."

Catrin ripped the reins from her sister's fingers. "I don't care what you think. I'm going. If Father asks why you're not with me, I will tell him about your little meeting with Belinus."

"And what do you mean by that?"

Wordlessly, Catrin mounted her bay and stared at her red-faced sister.

Mor shouted, "Answer me!"

Struggling to remain calm, Catrin pointed to the spear on the grass. "Hand me that lance. I'll tell Belinus about what I saw. You can load up your weapons and join us."

Mor angrily flung the spear up to Catrin. She adjusted the weapon and kneed her horse into a gallop. Gales from the sea stung Catrin's eyes as she drove her horse near the cliff's edge and up the ridge to where Belinus was waiting. With thoughts running wild about a possible attack by Marrock, she ignored the perils of the precipice and the rocks below. With spear in hand, she clamped her legs against the horse and threw it.

The metal tip pierced the raven's image on a shield that Belinus was holding. Clad in leather breeches and chain mail, he yelled, "Why did you do that? I wasn't ready."

Catrin halted in front of him. "We need to get back! Warships have landed; Marrock is leading them!"

Belinus gave a shocked look. "Marrock? Warships? Where?"

Catrin pointed northward. "In the nearby bay."

Hearing horses approaching, Catrin turned; it was her sister riding the black stallion and leading a pack horse.

Mor huffed. "Why didn't you wait for me? You are lucky I don't have to scrape your smashed bones and flesh off the rocks."

"No time to argue!" Catrin said, then looked at Belinus and ordered, "See to the weapons. I will explain everything on our way back to the village."

Mor blazed at Catrin as Belinus packed the weapons. After he mounted his horse, he told Catrin, "With the coming fog, it may be difficult to see the ships on our way home. Ride with me and tell me more about what you saw."

Catrin rode with Belinus on the pathway while Mor followed them. As they descended the grassy hilltop, Catrin told Belinus of the warships and of Marrock's return. Unlike Mor, Belinus appeared agitated, glancing all around. He asked Catrin more questions and suggested they take a closer look at the seashore.

They veered their horses into a darkening forest in the valley. When they rode out of the woods and approached the beach, thick fog was swallowing the ships in the bay and marching out of the haze were soldiers heading their way.

Catrin glanced back at Mor. "See … there is the danger."

Mor's shoulders stiffened. "Keep riding."

Belinus rode ahead and kept his hand on his sword's pommel. "Follow me. Don't look scared. These are Romans!"

3

ROMAN DEMANDS

She seethed. This is brazen betrayal. Marrock cannot become king! He will destroy everyone in my family!

Catrin watched for any untoward movement from the marching Romans as she followed Belinus, with Mor trailing her. They wove their horses around some infantrymen laden with heavy gear. Some of the soldiers glared at them while others grumbled among themselves.

Passing the troops, Catrin wiped some cold sweat from her brow and looked down at her ragged trousers. She twitched a smile. She remembered the queen's instructions for her to dress more befittingly of their family's noble status at the feast to be held that night. Curious she would think of that now, she groaned at the thought of wearing a skirt.

Belinus must have heard her. He looked back at her and grimaced. "I don't like the looks of those soldiers. They look hungry for battle."

The comment from one of the most renowned warriors in the kingdom reinforced Catrin's trepidation. She added, "It looks like Marrock is behind this."

Belinus rasped, "We need to get back and tell your father."

Mor bellowed from behind, "What are you two jabbering about?"

Belinus glanced back. "The Romans! Now get up here, so I don't have to yell."

After that, they trotted their horses through a pine forest, then onto a pathway between farm fields that led to Durovernum, the

Cantiaci capital. There, they urged their horses up the steep hillside encircled by two concentric ditches. On top of the fort hill, they entered the fortressed settlement through the main tower gate. On the other side, heavy stench from nearby cattle corrals and smoky dome-clay furnaces racked their senses. Farmers and tradesmen, appearing agitated, were streaming toward the town's center on the central thoroughfare.

A foreboding dread overcame Catrin as she pressed her horse through the congestion, weaving between the thatch-roofed structures, until she reached the entrance of the stone wall palace. At the entryway, commoners were cursing and shoving against the king's guards, who held firm to prevent them from entering. Catrin's heart quickened. This was a bad sign that the omen of the blood moon would soon occur. Of what, she was yet uncertain.

She halted her horse and waited for the king's commander, Trystan, to order the rabble back. Unlike the scruffy commoners, he was clean-shaven, his military chain mail and a gold-pin clasped cape distinguishing him as a noble warrior. He shot a surly frown at Belinus and yelled, "Why are you late from training? King Amren has begun introductions."

Belinus shouted, "With whom?"

"Roman agents," Trystan shouted back. "He wants his daughters inside now!"

The commander's announcement alarmed Catrin. She dismounted her horse and gave the reins to a stable boy. The sisters trailed Belinus and Trystan into the reception hall jammed with the king's guards and scurrilous villagers. The stifling chamber stank like gutted cattle, most likely from a couple of butchers standing nearby, still wearing brown-smeared aprons.

Catrin knew the crowd's presence meant that her father was ready to make a major decision. She again pondered if the blood moon in her dream portended dramatic changes to the kingdom as a result of a rebellion? She felt her stomach drop like a hung corpse when she heard her father's gravelly voice echo off the room's stone walls.

"Mor and Catrin, come in here now."

Belinus and Trystan rammed Catrin through the masses to the front of the elevated thrones where her parents were seated. King Amren appeared calm, the gold torc around his thick neck reflecting his status and wealth. Sitting next to him was Queen Rhiannon elegantly attired in a burgundy dress and a black wolf pelt. The commoners usually held the king in reverence as a generous ruler who shared his plunder from rival kingdoms. Today, however, they were ready to riot.

When her father rose from his throne, Catrin rushed up three stairs to the platform and into his arms. "Father, what is happening here?" she anxiously asked. "Did you know Marrock has returned with a Roman army?"

She could smell her father's musky scent as he hugged her. "I am aware of this. Don't worry. Just stay close to me while I calm the situation down."

Catrin watched Mor climb the stairs to stand between her mother, still seated, and her other sister, standing erect. Staying at her father's side, Catrin warily scanned the high-vaulted chamber to assess the assemblage. A caped Roman commander with a disfiguring facial scar and his soldiers stood at attention near the central hearth. Crammed near the entryway were the king's warriors and commoners, squeezed in like fish caught in a net. Belinus and Trystan, both speakers of Latin, joined two Roman diplomats standing near the royal dais. The elder statesman reminded Catrin of a boxer with a thick neck, square jaw, and eagle-beaked nose. Next to him was a striking young Roman attired in a scarlet-edged, white toga. A few years older than her, the young man had short curly hair that gave him a boyish charm, but she could almost feel his licentious eyes wandering over her hips.

No man from the village would dare look at her that way!

A seething confusion boiled into her heart as she drank in the nobleman. The danger of galloping off a cliff now seemed tame. Her father also seemed to notice the Roman's salacious mien. The young Roman, appearing aware of the king's glower, turned to the elder statesman.

King Amren then stepped away from Catrin to the front edge of the dais. He raised a hand for quiet. Silence fell over the chamber as he addressed the audience in Latin, a secondary language that Catrin could speak and read.

"Welcome, Senator Lucius Antonius, noble descendant of the legendary Mark Antony. I recall our meeting as young men in Massilia, Gaul, where I was educated by your mentor. I assume the young man beside you is your son."

The revelation that her father knew the senator surprised Catrin. She could not keep her eyes off his imposing son as the senator introduced him in a commanding voice.

"This is my youngest, Marcellus Antonius. He is training to be a diplomat and has journeyed with me to learn about your customs."

The young noble's name resonated like a song in Catrin's mind. *Marcellus Antonius.* He acknowledged with a nod, his eyes consuming her as they flamed in the torch light. She smiled shyly into his fiery grin. Heat flushed over her face as she looked again to her father, now presenting the queen.

"Beside me is my beloved wife, Rhiannon. As queen, she stands as my equal."

Catrin noted the senator's dismissive sneer while Marcellus leaned forward with interest. Her father then proudly introduced Vala, dressed as a warrior in a chain mail shirt, gray trousers, and variegated cape.

"This is my eldest, Vala. As you can see ..." —the king rubbed his lips, as if trying to restrain a chuckle— "she took height away from her younger sisters to see eye-to-eye with any opponent."

Catrin smirked, knowing Vala had soundly defeated every one of her challengers in single combat.

The king gestured toward Mor. "Next to Vala is my middle daughter, Mor. She is a mirror image of my queen at a younger age."

Unlike Vala, Mor wore leather chest armor over a knee-high tunic and piqued the interest of many men in the kingdom. The king had recently negotiated a dowry for her to marry the son of the rival Catuvellauni king. Only Catrin knew Belinus was Mor's true love.

Lastly, King Amren affectionately wrapped his arm around Catrin. "This is my youngest daughter—the runt of the litter. Like me, she has bandy legs. Perchance …"—he peered at her trousers—"that is why her breeches are torn."

Hot sweat flooded all over Catrin's face as she squirmed under her father's comment. She glanced at the big rip in her plaid trousers and looked up to find Marcellus grinning with amusement. At that instant, she wanted to hide in a cave and disappear into its walls.

The king continued jesting, "Don't let size fool you. Catrin is the bravest of my daughters. She is—"

Senator Lucius Antonius interrupted. "What of your son?"

"My son?"

"Marrock."

Catrin could feel her insides tumble when she observed her father's smile sour. The chamber stilled like a moonless night before a tempest. She again pondered why Marrock had returned, another harbinger of potential conflict.

King Amren finally proclaimed, "Marrock is no son of mine! I renounced and banished him almost seven years ago for his treacherous acts."

The senator remained adamant. "Rome only recognizes the birthright of your eldest male heir, not the queen or your daughters."

"Marrock!" Amren growled with contempt. "Why would Rome support him?"

"Cunobelin, the king of the Catuvellauni, claims your son is the rightful heir."

The senator's disclosure shocked Catrin; she could feel her heart pounding in her chest. Even though her father and Cunobelin had been bitter rivals, they had recently forged a truce. Obviously, Cunobeline had offered her father a hand of friendship while stabbing him in the back by championing Marrock's claims. She seethed. *This is brazen betrayal. Marrock cannot become king! He will destroy everyone in my family!*

When Catrin's noticed her father's clenched jaw, she assumed that he had also reached the same conclusion. She had seldom seen him lose control of his steel-edged demeanor, but his face blazed like molten metal. A battle-hardened warrior, he might lash out. Her mother must have also seen this, because she rose to calm him with a soft touch. It seemed to work, as her father appeared to relax, his face returning to normal color. He looked at the senator and said in a more tempered voice, "How did you hear of Marrock's claims?"

The senator pulled at his toga. "From the mouth of the Catuvellauni king himself in Rome. Last fall, he presented your son's case to Emperor Tiberius."

Every new disclosure by the senator grated on Catrin; nothing made sense. Why would the mighty emperor support her half-brother's claim to the throne if he had seen his monstrous face?

She then overheard her father grumble in Celtic, "Cunobelin, that treacherous dog." Her mother again nudged him and shook her head. This time, the king made no attempt to hide his rage.

"Why should Cunobelin's support for Marrock matter to Rome? This is a local tribal issue that has no impact on the empire. For that matter, neither does it affect the Catuvellauni."

"I beg to differ," the senator replied. "Cunobelin accuses you of blocking Roman merchants from traveling through your kingdom to trade with the Catuvellauni. Marrock promises to open trade ways through your territory."

"Where is Marrock now?"

"Under the protection of the Catuvellauni. Marrock is married to Cunobelin's eldest daughter."

Shocked, Catrin gaped at the senator. How could Marrock have gained so much influence with Cunobelin without her family knowing? With the tensions escalating in the chamber, she intently studied each person's stance and reactions as the bitter discourse continued.

The king jabbed a finger at his own chest so hard that Catrin feared he would break a rib. His voice rose like a thunderstorm as he said, "Cunobelin should have consulted me before giving Marrock safe harbor. Rome should only deal with me about issues in my territory. Our treaty with Rome is separate from the Catuvellauni. Again, what does Rome hope to gain by declaring its support for Marrock?"

The senator matched the king's fervor. "Marrock promises to recompense sums still owed Rome from treaties bartered by your forefathers and Julius Caesar, almost eighty years ago. He also agrees to pay additional tribute in exchange for favorable trading and peace with Rome."

"What tribute?" Amren asked incredulously. "We have always met our obligations."

Each of the senator's demands now rumbled through the chamber: "One thousand gold coins; fifty horsemen to serve in the empire's auxiliary; one hundred slaves, including captured warriors to fight as gladiators."

"We never agreed to these in our treaties with Rome," Amren said through gritted teeth. "How can you expect us to supply you with gladiators when our kingdom is at peace?"

Trystan interrupted and shouted in Celtic to the crowd in the rear, "That slimy leach, Cunobelin, has turned on us. He demands that Marrock be declared heir to the Cantiaci throne. The next rightful heir is Queen Rhiannon, not that child murderer, rapist, and traitor! Rome wants our warriors to die in their legions ... or be sold as gladiators."

From the back of the hall came a staccato of cries. "Never ... never ... never!"

Of all the people in the room, Catrin had the most compelling reason to hate Marrock for what he had done to her, for abandoning her as a child to die in the forest. Nonetheless, Trystan's inciting outburst was both reckless and stupid. Even worse, it was open defiance to the king. She looked to her father, expecting him to take control of the situation.

King Amren roared, "Quiet! Let me deal with the Romans."

Trystan stomped closer to the platform. "My Lord Amren, I refuse to bow to this Roman boar's demands. Every warrior has sworn to cut off Marrock's balls!"

"Stand down, Trystan," the king ordered. "You forget your place! I negotiate for my people."

Trystan scowled and reluctantly stepped back.

Catrin shifted her attention to the senator, whose eyes flitted between Trystan and the king. The elder statesman finally asked, "What did your guard say?"

"The truth," Amren answered in Latin. "Cunobelin intends to steal our lands through treachery and deception. He has negotiated from both sides of his face. He promised to forge an alliance with me through the marriage of my daughter to his son. Yet today, I've learned he has already married his daughter to Marrock, and behind my back has crawled to Rome pleading for support of Marrock's treacherous claims. How can I trust Cunobelin? He threatens to tear my kingdom apart by using Rome to secure Marrock as the next king. Now you make new demands for tribute. My people will never accept this!"

The senator fidgeted with his unraveling toga. "Remember, Rome's reach extends far into Britannia. A cohort of expeditionary forces is now ashore to make sure you meet all the emperor's demands. You must bend to Rome's rule if you want favorable position as our client king."

The king roared, "Not if Rome chooses the wrong side!"

When Belinus suddenly pulled a knife and pressed the blade against Marcellus' throat, Catrin's heart seized. The young Roman gasped as the blade cut into his throat and blood seeped from the wound. Trystan then clutched the senator by his toga. The fear-stricken statesman cried out, "Amren, remember your pledge. No harm must befall me or my son."

Catrin glanced all around. The loud clamor of shuffling feet and clanking swords rumbled throughout the room as both sides became restless. Warriors, appearing incited by the reckless actions of Trystan and Belinus, encircled the Roman soldiers. Amidst the commotion, Catrin could hear her rapid heartbeat in her ears. When she looked at Marcellus, he appeared deadly calm, even with a knife to his throat, as he rasped, "Easy, let us not get excited."

Even so, Catrin's throat constricted from angst that he might be killed. Why hadn't her father stopped Belinus? He must know harming a Roman diplomat would incite a bloody brawl. Fearing that anarchy would break out, she reached for her father's hand. "Don't let Belinus kill him!"

Her voice sounded puny against the deafening noise in the chamber. The king's icy stare and silence seemed to sanction the young Roman's doom. Catrin turned to her mother for help. "Do something!"

The queen reached for the king's arm. "Stop this! Or you will start a war."

The king wrenched her hand away. "Let me handle this, woman!"

The queen stepped closer, eyes ablaze. "Then act like a king! Control your warriors."

When the king glowered at the queen and his lips pressed into a firm line, Catrin knew then that she had to act now to stop a bloody conflict. She squared her shoulders, stomped her foot, and ordered Belinus, "Release that man now!"

This time, her voice resonated around the chamber.

4

APOLLO'S RAVEN

The massive outer door rattled and crashed open in a roaring wind. Red embers popped out of the hearth and choking soot rained on the chamber. Out of the billowing cloud of smoke, a raven swooped through the chamber.

Catrin thought the next moments would be etched in her memory for a lifetime. Her bold action of ordering Belinus to release Marcellus had the impact she had hoped for. Stillness pervaded the chamber as Belinus pulled his knife away from Marcellus's throat. All the stunned faces locked on Catrin, but what she believed had been her defining moment dissipated when the king's hand clenched her shoulder and yanked her back.

"Enough!"

Not only did Catrin's shoulder stab with pain, but her heart stung from the humiliation of being publicly reprimanded. Her chagrin compounded when the king roughly whirled her into the arms of the queen. "Deal with her! Now!"

The queen exacerbated Catrin's humiliation by dragging her behind the elevated thrones for a scolding. "Never overstep your father! I repeat, never ... never!"

Catrin tried to argue, "But ... but you told Father to stop—"

"Shhh! Not another word."

Catrin seethed under her mother's raised brow. She looked down at the rip in her trousers and bit her lower lip, tasting blood. The sudden grip of the queen's hand about her arm reinforced the warning. "Stop it! Or I'll have you strapped."

Forced to the side of the platform by the strong grip of her mother's fingers around her arm, Catrin continued to simmer under her father's scowl.

This is not fair! I should be praised, not shamed!

The king became stone-faced, stepped to the front of the platform, and lifted his hand to still his people and warriors. "Everyone, calm down! Put your weapons away. We have more honor than to attack our guests!"

With sword in hand, Trystan shook his head in defiance. "I refuse. These Roman pigs have threatened us with their army."

When Catrin saw Belinus again press the knife against Marcellus's neck, she felt as if her heart had leapt into her throat. She gasped and held her breath.

The king bellowed, "Put your weapons down. Now!"

Grimacing, Trystan sheathed his sword, his hand still ready on the hilt. Belinus and other warriors followed suit, also putting their weapons away. In turn, the senator signaled for his Roman soldiers to sheathe their swords.

Exhaling relief, Catrin looked at Marcellus, whose eyes reflected the hottest of blue flames. She admired his courage. He had stayed calm, never flinching, even with a blade to his throat. He met her eyes as if thanking her. She bubbled with pride that, indeed, her bold action had made her father pause and reconsider his next moves. In truth, she had stopped the conflict and saved the handsome Roman. She smiled demurely at him.

He returned the smile.

With order returning to the chamber, Catrin closely watched her father to see what he would do next. Though his face was still flushed red, he nonetheless addressed the Romans with a more even voice.

"Lucius, I will honor my pledge that no harm will come to your son. I do this despite my people's anger over your unreasonable demands. To soothe hostilities, I propose you and I talk off-site with Cunobelin to discuss new terms for a marital pact between my daughter and his son. That way, we can settle our political differences through the alliance this marriage will forge. This would be in everyone's best interests, including Rome's. Let me be clear," the king said, hardening his stare, "I will never accept Marrock back as heir to my throne."

The senator grimaced. "What do you expect from me in return?"

"Arrange a secret council between Cunobelin and me. You can act as arbitrator to insure a fair outcome. As a good faith measure, I propose your son, Marcellus, stay as my family's guest until we reach a settlement."

The proposal pleased Catrin, her belly tickling with delight at the thought that she might get to know Marcellus better. *After all,* she again extolled herself, *I did save his life. And he has a charming smile.*

The senator did not embrace the proposal. "What? Are you mad? Are you suggesting I leave my son as a hostage? I cannot agree to such a thing!"

"No, I am quite sane," King Amren retorted. "I ask no more of you than what Rome required of my father for assuring his yearly tribute. I was held in thrall during my earlier years when I learned your customs. Likewise, Marcellus will be retained to assure no harm visits me during our talks with Cunobelin in his territory. Then you can see the advantage of Marcellus learning our ways."

The king's maneuver reminded Catrin of a fox tricking a rival predator to settle for other hunting grounds. Yet, when she studied Marcellus, he appeared stunned as his father leaned over to whisper something to him. The senator turned to the king and demanded, "Tell everyone to leave us, except for your advisors and family. I will entertain your terms, but matters such as these must be brokered by rulers, not by the whims of plebs."

The room seemed to swelter as Catrin anxiously wiped her sweaty palm on her breeches. She regarded Trystan's scowl. If her father insisted he leave, Trystan would take it as an insult. The king could also anger other noble warriors in the chamber who had pledged their fealty to him for a small say in his realm. Her father must have also considered this; he quietly conversed with the queen before turning to the senator.

"I agree on the condition you order most of your soldiers back to the ships. Only your advisors and a few guards are welcome to stay."

Again the senator hesitated, then threw out his final condition. "My son, tribune, and six guards will remain here. You must do the same with your warriors."

The king nodded.

The noise rose in the chamber from the commoners, most of whom were unfamiliar with the Roman tongue. Catrin assumed they were agitated as a result of their confusion about what her father had agreed to.

The king extended both arms, as if embracing his people. He announced, "No need to show further hostility toward our Roman guests. I ask everyone to go outside where a cauldron of wine is waiting for your drinking pleasure. My queen and advisors will represent everyone in this room as we confer with the emperor's agents. Before we make any final decisions, my Druidess will offer a sacrifice to the gods and ask their favor on all agreements made today."

A cool breeze emanating behind the platform suddenly made Catrin shiver. She looked over her shoulder. When a wolf appeared to float out of a dark corner, she blinked with disbelief. She recognized Agrona's eyes peering through the jaws of her wolf headdress. A black pelt was draped over her shoulders, wolf claws curled down her wrists and over her fingertips, and tattooed wolves appeared to creep down her arms.

King Amren waved Agrona forward and introduced her to the Romans. "This is my spiritual advisor, Agrona. She will seek the blessings from the gods on our meeting today."

Agrona removed her headdress and climbed the stairs to join the king and the queen. The king once told Catrin that he believed Agrona bestowed strength and courage on any warrior she touched. He insisted that no one knew his enemies as well as she did. Nonetheless, Catrin felt wary of the Druidess. Her eyes switched from fiery green to amber-gold in the light of the silvery moon—a mark of a sorceress.

Catrin studied the Romans' reactions to Agrona. The senator was expressionless, except for a rise of his brows. Marcellus gaped at the Druidess, as if she were an apparition from the Otherworld. The Roman soldiers remained at attention, their shoulders squared and eyes fixed straight ahead. This was a show of discipline that her father's commanders had not demonstrated when they threatened to kill Marcellus.

The king then ordered Trystan to escort the commoners out of the chamber and return with his most trusted guards. Catrin could sense the Romans' growing uneasiness when Trystan returned with other warriors. Marcellus and his father joined the tribune and his soldiers at the central fire where they spoke in hushed tones. After that, about half of the Roman guards left, leaving five of them in the chamber. Trystan, Belinus, and several king's guards scattered across the room, their hands on sheathed weapons. The chamber quieted except for the scampering of rats along the walls, their vermin eyes aglow from the fiery torches.

The hairs on Catrin's neck prickled when she noticed Agrona's eyes glowing like the rats, her lips twisted in a wicked grin. The next instant, Catrin felt a stabbing pain in her chest and tingling on her arms. She sensed her raven and looked up at the wooden rafters.

There was nothing there.

Heart racing, she again focused on her father as he told the senator, "So we can negotiate on friendlier terms, I propose that we offer a sacrifice to our gods and ask their favor in the outcome of our meeting."

Senator Lucius Antonius interjected, "The offering must be to a Roman god."

"Proclaim your god, then."

The senator lifted his left hand to reveal a gold signet ring on his finger. "Apollo, almighty god of the sun and divination and my family's patron god."

The king lifted his arms toward the ceiling. "I also offer blood to our sun god, Bel, and his consort, Belisama—goddess of fire and light." He then gestured to Agrona. "Prepare a suitable sacrifice to appease the gods."

Curiosity piqued about the ritual, Catrin intently watched Agrona descend the stairs, stride through the chamber, and disappear through the entryway. A little later, she reappeared in the doorway alongside a Druid, dressed in a white robe with a cowl shrouding his face. His hand was clenched around the curved horn of a struggling ram. Bleats of terror echoed throughout the chamber as Belinus helped the Druid drag the resistant ram into the chamber. A guard slammed the massive entrance door shut to prevent the animal from escaping.

Most of the Romans turned to watch the struggle between the men and the ram. Marcellus alone appeared unrattled by the commotion. When he again met Catrin's gaze, his blue eyes shimmered like a crystal lake at sunrise. She blushed and looked down, her heart pounding rapidly.

Why do I feel this way?

She had always had the mettle of a warrior with no fear of death. Yet this foreigner disarmed her every time he gazed at her. How could she resist her growing attraction for him and not plunge headlong into his fire?

Loud drums shook Catrin from her longings. She watched Agrona dance around the ram, twirling one foot over the other, the tattooed flames on her leg flashing through a slit in her leather dress.

When she quickened her steps, her hair flung wildly. Entranced warriors around her crouched, howled, and swiped at her bare leg to capture the wolf's cunning, strength, and fierceness. Some Roman soldiers smirked while the mouths of others cracked open in awe as they watched the ritual.

Agrona drew a knife from a leather strap tied to her thigh and approached the animal with the blade held close to her side. She stopped a few feet from the ram and shouted in Celtic, "Bel, send us your sun to shine on today's truths. Belisama, send us water to reflect past, present, and future." Her voice wailed above the drum's pitch as she prayed in Latin. "All mighty Apollo, god of sun, Romans and Cantiaci beseech you, accept our blood offering. Feast on this unblemished ram's tissue and bones. In return, we humbly request …"— the sorceress looked at the metal-rimmed oak door—"your blessing."

The drum beats rumbled throughout the chamber. Catrin, becoming feverish with anticipation, sensed the approach of the climax as Agrona slowly circled the bleating ram and lifted her ceremonial knife. The blade glimmered in the torchlight as she waved it over the ram's head. She cried out, "Apollo, reveal your divine messenger."

With a flick of her wrist, she slit the creature's throat. Blood spurted over the ram's pristine wool and the animal collapsed on the floor. A crimson puddle formed beneath its head.

The massive outer door rattled and crashed open in a roaring wind. Red embers popped out of the hearth and choking soot rained on the chamber. Out of the billowing cloud of smoke, a raven swooped through the chamber. Invisible behind the smokescreen, Agrona raised her voice above the clamor. "Behold, the raven rises out of Apollo's flames."

5

SPIRIT WARRIOR

"No matter what you see during the ritual, reassure my people and the Romans that Apollo will favor our decisions today. Do you understand?"

Catrin recognized the shadowy creature hovering over the thrones as her raven. Dumbstruck, she watched it land at her feet and then looked to her mother. The queen's eyes were frozen in terror at the raven.

Agrona declared, "Apollo sends his messenger to reveal the fate from today's decisions."

Catrin's mind whirled about what the Druidess had just proclaimed. It seemed nonsensical that the Roman god, Apollo, would use her raven as his messenger. The creature had never revealed any divination from the sun god.

Or had it?

On the white cliffs, earlier that morning, the raven had shot like an arrow across the sun's fiery glow. Catrin remembered a tale told by a Greek merchant that Apollo had slain a Cyclops with an arrow. The sun god asked the northern people, the Hyperboreans, to hide his arrow in a winged temple. Perhaps, indeed, Apollo did send her raven as his messenger.

Through the lingering haze, she could see shadowy images shuffle near the entryway where the ram had been sacrificed. A cacophony of shouts rumbled into the chamber.

One man yelled, "What has happened?"

A woman shrilled, "A raven, I saw a raven fly in!"

"The gods are cursing us," said others.

Catrin's eyes began to burn from the acrid smoke. She closed them and rubbed her eyelids to soothe the irritation. Amidst the loud coughing, she heard a man's gruff voice yell, "Protect Lucius and Marcellus," which was followed by stomping boots.

Alarmed, Catrin forced her eyes open to find that Roman soldiers had encircled Marcellus and his father, forming a shield wall to protect them. She could barely see the senator's face when he said, "We will not begin the meeting until Apollo has sent us a favorable omen."

The king said in a firm, reassuring voice, "There is no reason for concern, Lucius. Agrona will speak to my people and assure them the gods have sent a favorable omen. She will inspect the ram's entrails on an altar outside for a sign from Apollo. Meanwhile, you can wait in here until a table has been set with food and wine for your enjoyment."

The senator said, "Arrange for it."

Catrin watched Agrona exit the chamber. From outside, her words, which were meant for the commoners, drifted back into the receiving hall. "My people, you have nothing to fear. Rest assured that the sun god accepts our offering. The bright one sends his raven to proclaim that Catrin will deliver his message. Clear a pathway. I must complete the ritual with her to appease the Roman sun god, Apollo, so he will favor any decisions made on this day."

Agrona's pronouncement stunned Catrin. Why had the sorceress drawn attention to her?

The white-robed Druid then dragged the ram through the doorway, the animal's head thumping on the door jamb. Lips quivering, Catrin did not know what to do. Should she join him or stay? She looked to her parents for direction.

The queen's face was aflame when she gripped the king's arm. "That raven is a bad omen, a curse!"

From their mumbling and grim faces, Catrin could tell her parents were in a heated argument. She bit her lip. Why did her mother say the raven was a curse? Disconcerted, she stepped to the back of the dais.

The king glanced at her, seemingly aware that she was anxious. He walked over and kissed her gently on the forehead, then wrapped his arms around her and said in a hushed voice, "I know you don't understand what is going on. Trust me, and do what I say. No matter what you see during the ritual, reassure my people and the Romans that Apollo will favor our decisions today. Do you understand?"

A foreboding shiver ran down Catrin's spine. Nevertheless, she reluctantly nodded, affirming her understanding.

King Amren nudged her toward the raven waddling near her feet. "Take that creature out of here and do what Agrona says. Later, we'll talk about what I expect of you."

The words "expect of you" chilled Catrin. What more could her father ask of her? Did he know that she had already harnessed the raven's powers? The only words she could utter to him were, "Oh, yes." Then she knelt and coaxed her raven onto her arm. A burning sensation discharged from the raven's claws.

The next instant, different colors of light circling each person like sparkling gemstones bedazzled Catrin. Head spinning, she wondered if she had entered a dream as she instinctively began dancing at the beat of her heart. Her feet felt as light as clouds as she floated through the midst of Romans near the hearth. The soldiers seemed wary and backed away, except for the tribune. His hawk eyes peered through clashing orbits of bronze and indigo light around his face.

Catrin's gaze landed on Marcellus, standing behind the tribune. Heated by the flames of the hearth, she circled him, swaying her hips and drawing closer and closer. She felt his hand brush her hip and the touch shot through her. He met her gaze in a magical moment where time seemed to stand still.

Suddenly, a blue light snaking around the senator, then entwining Catrin, made her recoil. She blinked hard. Opening her eyes again, she beheld fire-breathing eagles, red shield walls, and human skulls hovering over the Romans.

Terrified, she scurried out of the chamber, the raven bouncing on her arm. She told herself, *Do not trust the Romans.*

In the courtyard, she found people of all ranks holding hands with each other and chanting, "Show us the light. Show us the light." In the center of the courtyard was a stone altar on which the limp ram lay. Beside the altar, Agrona extended her arms over the sacrificial animal. A shadow webbed around the Druidess, making it difficult for Catrin to discern her face, her true purpose. One end of the human circle opened, allowing Catrin and the perched raven on her arm to enter the inner sanctum. Agrona acknowledged her with a sweeping arm gesture. "Welcome, spirit warrior."

The people repeated with monotone voices, "Welcome, spirit warrior."

Agrona threw her head back like a howling wolf and cried out, "Ancestors, come into our circle of life. Give spirit warrior the eyes to see truth today … and time forward." When she lifted the ceremonial bone-handled knife, a shimmer shot from its surface into Catrin's eyes.

Catrin stepped sideways to avoid the blinding glare.

The Druidess sliced the ram's belly open, and the intestines oozed out like slimy serpents. She scooped up the entrails and draped them around her body. Nose upturned, she crouched near Catrin and pawed at the air. "Raven, give warrior spirit the foresight of Apollo."

The raven took flight and landed on the ram's head. Its beak gouged out an eyeball. As the bird gawked at Catrin, it gobbled the eye down whole. Then the raven fluttered over the heads of the humans.

Agrona poked out the ram's other eye with a knife and cut it in half. She handed the pupil-end piece to Catrin, saying, "Warrior spirit, eat. Let Apollo light the truth, the future."

The only future Catrin could foresee was her stomach puking the eyeball onto the circle of worshipers. With all her resolve, she bit down on the raw eye and gagged it down. The slimy thing ripped at her stomach. As directed by her father, she raised both arms and proclaimed in Celtic, then Latin, "Apollo has divined his favor on all decisions made today."

The ram's eyeball rumbling in her stomach told Catrin otherwise.

6

CELTIC RESCUER

"You have dealt with these barbarians before," Lucius said. "Do they plan to kill us?"

Marcellus rubbed his injured neck as he waited for the bizarre ritual to finish outside. He looked at his fingers, tinged reddish-brown from scratching at the dried blood. The cut was deeper than he had first realized. The image of the ram's slashed throat made him recall his terror when the sun-tattooed warrior pressed a blade against his neck. He spat on the wooden floor.

Barbarians!

Again he spat.

Savages!

A biting cold penetrated the stone walls and made him shiver. Looking at the painted Celtic warriors around him, he feared the great adventure with his father would soon come to an untimely end. The sacrificial ceremony was macabre, even by Roman standards. In Rome, priests sacrificed hundreds of animals in holy temples, not in receiving chambers where human skulls on the walls welcomed guests as they entered the chamber. The raven's blasting through the smoke was the most foreboding sign of the ritual. Trying to make light of his grim situation, he chuckled.

Nothing like a bloody sacrifice to lift everyone's spirits. Thanks to Apollo for sending his Celtic rescuer.

Marcellus whispered to himself, "Was his rescuer's name Cātacā or Catrin?" He struggled with Celtic names and could not understand the awful sounding guttural language. The bold actions of the foreign princess, garbed in warrior leather armor, confounded him. Why would she intervene to stop a deadly clash from breaking out— a move that saved his life?

He grinned.

Most likely, she has more than a passing interest in me.

The coy smiles the princess directed at him suggested so. After considering the options of saying her name, he decided on *Catrin*. *Cātacā* was too harsh for an exotic princess on the threshold of feminine adult beauty. With her multi-braided flaxen hair, she would be the envy of any Roman noblewoman. Her pale blue-green eyes reminded him of the sea shallows near Massilia. Through her torn breeches, he could see a shapely leg. She shared her father's fair skin and comely looks. Perhaps their common features might explain the king's obvious favor toward her.

Although the princess had been a bright moment, he groaned from the more poignant memories of his miserable expedition to Britannia with its myriad mishaps. Not one friendly word had passed between his father and him. In Gaul, they suffered in hostelries populated with dog-sized rats and lice-infested beds. While there, they had been robbed of their horses from the stables, forcing them to buy inferior mounts.

Most of all, Marcellus missed the public Roman baths where he could fritter the afternoon away with friends before their drinking bouts at night. Why did his father even bother to take him to Britannia? Surely his older half-brother would have been more amiable company.

He suspected his "old man" had designs on correcting his wastrel behavior on an island across a monster-filled sea. So far, the only monsters he had seen were the tattoos besmearing the Cantiaci warriors ready to fight in a free-for-all brawl—all because of his father's bungled negotiations with King Amren. Not only did his father lack the skills to barter rates for acceptable accommodations in Gaul, he was a buffoon in his debates with the king. His father, the pompous Senator Lucius Antonius, demonstrated a dearth of finesse in garnering political advantage. Current proof was his apparent eagerness to incite King Amren, almost costing them their lives.

Suddenly, bellowing carnyx war horns and drumbeats poured disharmoniously into the chamber. Growing uneasy, Marcellus looked at the entrance, wondering how much longer the ritual would last outside. He hoped the wolf sorceress and the princess would soon return inside and proclaim Apollo's favor. The negotiations could then begin. After that, he prayed that Minerva would give his father enough wisdom to leave this isle inhabited by painted warriors and animal worshipers.

The tribune's graveled voice jolted Marcellus out of his grim thoughts. "Come here. We need to talk."

Marcellus joined his father and Decimus Flavius, a tribune cursed with a disfiguring scar, a reward for his service in the Roman Legion. The tribune's service to his father left no doubt in Marcellus's mind that he was a loyal, ferocious guard dog. Also to their advantage, Decimus knew the Celtic mindset.

Lucius looked to Decimus. "Where are the soldiers you ordered away?"

"Just outside the fortress gate. I dispatched a courier to gather more soldiers from the encampment. There may not be enough time."

"You have dealt with these barbarians before," Lucius said. "Do they plan to kill us?"

Decimus shook his head. "They usually honor their truces. Yet, after what I have seen today, I'm no longer sure. The king understands the consequences. His people may not."

The tribune's words did not reassure Marcellus. He scowled at his father. "Why didn't you at least offer the king and his people a gift of wine, before ranting off with your demands? They might have been in a better mood to listen."

Marcellus could almost feel his father's face invade his.

"Stupid boy!" Lucius spewed with disdain. "You know nothing about treaty-making! You are here to learn and keep your mouth shut."

Marcellus retorted, "I hope I have a chance to learn before those warriors paint their bodies with our blood."

The tight grip of his father's hand around his arm made Marcellus flinch. "Enough!"

Decimus now interceded. "The enemy is just over there, not here. We need a plan."

The pressure eased on Marcellus's arm when his father turned to Decimus and said, "What do you propose?"

Decimus suggested, "Give Amren what he wants."

"And that is what?"

Decimus scratched his head. "Marcellus may need to stay here as a hostage to calm the hostilities. King Amren needs assurances we will honor our truce while you help arbitrate a settlement between the two rival kings. Amren perceived Cunobelin's support of Marrock as betrayal. We may not get out of here alive if he also suspects treachery from us."

"No! I will never concede to that barbarian," Lucius said adamantly. "We hold the stronger ground."

Decimus frowned. "Look around. We are outnumbered and at their mercy. Hostage exchange is standard protocol to assure peace while disagreements such as ours are settled. It was not our commission to start a war, but to assess the political situation here and demand more tribute."

Marcellus glanced at the king's warriors, who were positioned under human skulls on the walls. Imagining his bloody head spiked alongside the other skulls, he rasped, "What guarantee is there that I won't be butchered?"

"Cantiaci honor. They must keep their word. In return, we need to demand a hostage as surety that they will not harm you regardless of the outcome between the Celtic rulers, someone close to Amren's heart … perhaps his youngest daughter."

Decimus's stratagem did not reassure Marcellus. Why should he be the sacrificial ram to assure the truce? Before Marcellus could say anything about his reservations, shouts of *"bleidi aurinia"* resonated throughout the chamber. He turned to the direction of shuffling feet at the entryway where the wolfish sorceress and Catrin had just appeared.

Decimus nudged Marcellus. "Are we in agreement that you might need to stay?"

Marcellus hesitated. "I will do it. But only if there is no other way." He looked for concurrence from his father, but the chanting warriors gathering around the sorceress distracted him. The wolf sorceress rinsed blood from her face and arms.

Catrin walked from the entryway and halted beside the Romans at the central hearth. She raised her arms and declared in Latin, "Apollo has granted his favor on the meeting today."

Though a nonbeliever of priests' divining omens by inspecting the entrails of an animal, Marcellus was nonetheless relieved by the announcement. Decimus, a highly superstitious man, also seemed more at ease. Marcellus could not read his father's expression.

As Catrin passed Marcellus, she appeared dazed and in pain. He wondered if anything more bizarre had happened in the ceremony as she joined her mother and sisters in front of the elevated thrones.

Then King Amren heavily descended from the dais, a sign that he was ready to talk with the Romans on an equal footing. The wolf sorceress joined Amren, and they walked over to Lucius. The king grasped the senator's arm in an obvious display to show his power.

"Time we settle. Omens are good," King Amren said, his voice resonating throughout the chamber. "We will dine in another chamber where we can finish our talks. There is only enough room for three Romans. Your guards will have to wait here."

Lucius frowned but acceded and waved for Marcellus and Decimus to come with him.

7

ROMAN HOSTAGE

Challenged to do likewise, Marcellus impulsively stood up and blurted, "I also agree to stay here as a hostage."

Marcellus braced himself for terse negotiations as he followed his father into an open chamber at the right of the elevated thrones. Inside the room was a pentagram-engraved table that had been set with a flagon of wine, goblets, and plates piled high with cheese, bread, and dried meats. The windowless chamber had no circulation and smelled musty from moss growing in the cracks of the gray wall.

Now appearing calmer, King Amren sat down first in a massive chair nearest the opening. Marcellus had been told that Amren was an ignorant savage, but the king spoke Latin as eloquently as any Roman.

Marcellus seated himself on one side of his father, Lucius, while Decimus was on the other. Unlike the calm demeanor of the king, his father's jaw clenched with obvious irritation. He could never read Decimus who wore a permanent grimace on his fissured face.

Queen Rhiannon and her eldest daughter sat on each side of the king. Undoubtedly, these tall women were the equals to their male counterparts. Marcellus found the queen fascinating, unlike his father who openly displayed his disdain for her. She exuded confidence by the way she held her head high. Though she had remained quiet during the tense discourse, the king frequently looked to her as though he was seeking direction.

Catrin was last to enter the chamber. Marcellus was intrigued by how divergent her features were compared to her oldest sister. Vala had a soldier's demeanor that quietly announced her ferocity. She was uglier than a Molossian guard dog with her square chin and pronounced overbite. With frizzled dark hair, Vala was as different from Catrin as a moonless night and a golden morning. Catrin was precocious, risking her father's wrath by blurting out the words that saved his life. Vala kept her mouth shut like a muzzled hound.

Marcellus then noted the commander, Trystan, and the wolf sorceress taking their places behind the king's ornate chair. She acted strangely, sniffing the air like a dog on a hunt. Depending on the wavering torch flame, the color of her eyes changed from brown-speckled green to shiny amber. Catching a waft of foul odor from the direction of the sorceress, Marcellus scrunched his nose. Brownish tissue still clung to her dress, probably as a result of disemboweling the ram.

Trystan worried Marcellus the most. The snarl on this warrior's face left no doubt he wanted to spill Roman blood; his hand looked too busy on the dagger's thumb rise.

The meeting chamber darkened when Catrin drew a curtain, partitioning off the room from the receiving chamber.

Adjusting his eyes to the dimmer light, Marcellus could see Catrin gazing at him. Her turquoise eyes shone like beacons beckoning him to explore her mysterious shores. Though everyone else in the room had pincer scowls, she gave him a demur smile. His heart quickened.

Sweet Venus above, she is beautiful!

Marcellus smiled at Catrin, but becoming aware of the king's glare on him, he swiveled his eyes to his father crunching on an apple and his face grimacing in disgust as he spat out what looked like a half-eaten worm. Marcellus rubbed his lips with a of couple fingers to hide his amused smirk. His father then wiped his mouth and leveled his dark eyes at the king.

"Why is your youngest daughter in here?" asked Lucius.

The king's face hardened. "Apollo delivered his message through her. Do you want to risk your god's wrath by not having her stay?"

Marcellus could tell by the disdain on his father's face that he wanted to throw the wench out. Decimus wisely shook his head, warning him not to confront the king.

"So be it," Lucius grunted. He pushed the flagon across the table toward the queen, as if she was a lowly servant. "Pour me some wine."

The queen barked, "Pour your own."

An abrupt move behind the king's chair caught Marcellus's eye. He flinched when he saw Trystan draw his dagger. The warrior's face flushed as red as a flame when he stared at the queen. She blazed back, shaking her head.

Alarmed by the sudden show of hostility, Marcellus gripped the table and prepared himself to lunge at the warrior if he made any untoward move.

Decimus also seemed to wake up to the danger; he placed a hand on his gladius.

King Amren regarded Decimus, then turned to Trystan and barked some Celtic orders. The wolf sorceress gripped Trystan by the arm and swatted the curtain back for the two of them to leave.

Marcellus leaned back in his chair to mark the king's next actions. Amren picked up the flagon and smiled at his wife. "Let me do the honors." He filled the goblets, handed one to each person, and offered a toast: "To Apollo."

After the toast, everyone then seemed to relax around the table. The king initiated the conversation by amiably asking Lucius, "How was your journey?"

Lucius stared at his goblet of wine for a moment and said brusquely, "The brackish air on the sea voyage made my stomach roil. I had to ruminate on spoiled meat before swallowing it down again."

Amren's stare froze on the senator as he took a bite of cheese.

After a couple of sips, Lucius set his goblet down with a bang. "Enough of the pleasantries! Let me get to the point. I do not want to belabor the terms for arranging a private meeting between you and Cunobelin. Know this! I will not accept the condition that my son stays as hostage to assure your safety during the talks," he said, leaning back into his chair and staring at Amren, "unless you also offer someone of equal value for me to hold as hostage."

"Who do you propose?" asked Amren with a grated voice.

Lucius took another sip of wine and smiled. "I want your youngest daughter."

The king gulped the wine in his mouth and slammed his goblet on the table. "No ... never."

"Then who?"

When Marcellus regarded Catrin, the air seemed to suck out of the room and the chamber darkened. He could see fear in her big beautiful eyes. Though he should not care about what happened to her, he could not bear the thought of sex-hungry soldiers harming her at the camp. The chamber fell into a deadly silence.

Then Vala slowly scuffed her chair back, stood, and pointed to herself. Though she spoke with a strong accent, her message was clear. "As firstborn daughter and king's champion, I will do it."

Challenged to do likewise, Marcellus impulsively stood up and blurted, "I also agree to stay here as a hostage. And let that be an end to this bickering." He puffed out his chest with pride until he turned to his father, who was ready to pounce on him as he mouthed: *You imbecile!*

Only once had his father called him an imbecile. It was the time when he came home drunk and reeked of perfume from a married noblewoman he had bedded. He remembered thanking the gods that his father believed that he had been with a harlot. The rift with his father would have widened even further if he had found out the noblewoman was the consul's wife.

A loud slap on the table shook Marcellus out of his thoughts.

"Agreed," declared King Amren, then beamed at Vala and said, "Daughter, you bring me great pride by volunteering to take Catrin's place."

"Good," Vala said, squaring her bull-sized shoulders.

But Lucius had the last word. "I will not have my son stay as prisoner. One of my commanders can stay here instead."

The king raised a hand. "Marcellus will not be treated as a prisoner, but as a family guest. He can sleep in our family's quarters. My youngest, Catrin, can escort Marcellus around our village. She is fluent in your tongue. I commend your son for volunteering to stay with us, as I do Vala for agreeing to go with you. I consider this an equal exchange."

Though his face was crimson, Lucius said with a gruff, steady voice, "Allow me a word with my son before I agree."

Marcellus apprehensively rose from his seat and followed his father to a corner. Lucius leaned over and blasted hot air into his ear. "Imbecile! You can wallow in your own shit for overstepping my authority! We will have words about this later!"

Lucius pivoted on his heels to face the king. "My son has made the decision to stay as hostage. He can abide with it."

"Then it is settled," King Amren said, rising from the chair. "Stay for a feast that we have prepared in your honor."

Lucius bumped his shoulder into Marcellus, then said, "I have other duties to attend. For now, Marcellus will leave with me to gather his belongings at the headquarters, but he will return to honor the feast. Tomorrow we can discuss our next steps in private."

Lucius clicked his fingers at Marcellus as if he was summoning a mongrel pup.

8

RHAN'S CURSE

*"The gods demand the scales be balanced for the life you take.
If you deny my soul's journey to the Otherworld by beheading me,
I curse you to the same fate as mine."*

Conflicting emotions whirled inside Catrin as she watched everyone leave the chamber. Although tensions had eased with the Romans, the foreboding images she had seen at the sacrificial ritual still plagued her. She did not trust any of the Romans, yet, when Marcellus passed her as he followed his father outside the chamber, an excitement fluttering in her belly bewildered her. Marcellus looked over his shoulders and gave an impish grin. Feeling as light as a butterfly, she stepped toward him with the hope they could exchange words, but a heavy hand on her shoulder stopped her.

"Follow me," the king ordered. "I want to speak with you in my chambers."

Catrin glanced at the entryway, but Marcellus had already left. She nervously followed her father into a musky chamber sparsely furnished with a candlelit table and two chairs. Anticipating hard questions, Catrin wilted under her father's burning glare as she sat across from him.

"What were you thinking to challenge my authority?" he demanded.

Lowering her eyes, Catrin feigned she did not understand what was causing his ire. "What authority?"

Amren slapped the tabletop. "You know damn well what I mean!"

Catrin flinched and stared at her father's fingers drumming the tabletop.

"Not only did I have to deal with the Romans and their unreasonable demands," he said, voice grating, "but I had to prevent a revolt from my own guards. And here is my rebellious daughter bent on saving a Roman with eyes all over her!"

Gripping the table's edge, Catrin struggled to balance herself on the wobbly chair. "I only did this to stop a conflict which I foresaw in omens."

"What omens?"

"I ... I ..." Catrin looked down, suddenly hesitant to answer. Her father might become enraged if he knew of her newfound powers. She could feel his eyes on her, demanding the truth.

"I'm baffled by your behavior," Amren finally said. "For the first time in your life, you have overstepped my authority. Our kingdom is at stake. We need to present a united front. What did you see in your omens to make you do such a thing?"

Catrin took a deep, calming breath before responding. "The first omen I saw was the blood moon last night. This is a sign of great changes to the kingdom as a result of a bloody battle. This morning my raven shot across the rising sun warning me that danger approached from the sea. When I saw Roman warships landing offshore, I came back to warn you about this, but it was too late. The Roman envoys were already here. When Belinus threatened to slit the young Roman's throat, I feared his act would incite war with the Romans, and the omens would be fulfilled."

"Was that your raven that swept into the chamber during the ritual?"

Catrin's voice quavered. "Well ... it might have been."

Amren regarded Catrin a moment and his eyes turned upward, as if seeking an answer. Then his face became ashen and his eyes grew big. His brooding silence confused Catrin; the king was normally a man of action and words.

"Father, what is wrong?"

He tapped his fingers and muttered, "The raven. The curse. Is it possible? Has it begun? Why did I not see this? Agrona should have known. Oh, gods! Oh, gods below—" His words crumbled into broken mumbles.

The sudden anguish on her father's face disquieted Catrin about her raven. Not sure why it had provoked such a strong reaction, she blurted, "Is my raven a curse? At the ritual today, Mother said it was."

Amren gripped the chair's armrest as if reining in some troubling thought, and he said, "Something happened many years ago, which I never discussed with you. Someone cast a curse on me. I thought the gods had sent a favorable sign that the spell had been lifted, but after witnessing what happened at the ritual today, I'm not so sure."

A heavy pain hooked in Catrin's heart when her father sunk his head into the palm of his hands.

"Oh, Father ... I never asked for the raven's powers."

Amren jerked his head up, "What powers?"

Catrin looked at her shaky hands, afraid to alienate her father if she revealed the magical forces she culled from her raven.

Amren lightly touched her arm. "I'm not angry with you. Tell me what the raven has shown you."

More reassured, she replied, "My raven reached out to me. I can sense everything it sees and hears. When it flies over the white cliffs, I see the grassy hilltop and ocean beneath me. It was through the raven's eyes I observed warships moored in the bay beyond the cliffs. Hundreds of soldiers were settling into camps. This is where I observed Marrock talking with the Roman envoys. The raven warned me they were conspiring to attack us. It is difficult to explain how I sensed this. It was as if I entered its mind and could see things more clearly. Sometimes I'm not sure if I am dreaming or not."

"Explain what happens when you enter this creature's mind."

"A burning pain shoots up my arm." Catrin grimaced and stroked her forearm. "Then a light flashes in my mind. After that, the world looks different to me. I can see all around, not just in front of me. There are purple hues I've never seen with my human vision. Once I visualized falling into a crevice where a strong force pulled me into a light tunnel. Then I plunged toward a rainbow arch where animals and humans appeared and disappeared on its surface. In the middle of this arch was a black portal. Just before I burst through it, I leapt out of the raven's mind."

"How do you know this is a portal?" the king asked.

Catrin shrugged. "I … I never thought about it. I just knew that, if I broke through this, I would enter into another realm. I might not get back to my world."

Amren quietly rubbed his chin for a moment. "This place was also described by a Druidess."

"Agrona?"

"No, my former queen, Rhan. Did Agrona teach you how to summon the raven's magic?"

"No, the raven showed me."

Amren narrowed his eyes and frowned. "You are dealing with divine forces from the Otherworld. Rhan told me she summoned her magic from the other side of a portal, but she never told me how. She could prophesy, shape-shift, and call on nature's forces to help me overcome my enemies. Once, when I was nearly defeated in battle, she summoned Taranis to hurl lightning bolts at my enemy. My rival was struck down dead along with several of his warriors. His remaining troops fled and I won the battle. Alas, Rhan abused these powers."

The wrinkles around Amren's eyes crinkled deeper, as if he had dredged up a demon from his past.

A twinge of panic hit Catrin that she could release some unforeseeable evil if she did not learn how to control her raven's powers.

"How did Rhan abuse these powers?"

The king gazed at the candle and recounted, "Trystan, then a Regni boy of fourteen under my ward, overheard Rhan conspire with other nobles. She promised to give them riches if they would assassinate me and transfer my sovereignty over to her. She bragged about being able to change moments in everyone's life. If they aided her, she would change their destiny for the better." Amren sniggered. "What hubris she had. A boy instead changed her fate."

"What happened?"

Amren waved his hand through the candle flame as if the burning pain eased the discomfort of what he was about to reveal. "When Trystan told me about Rhan's treachery, I had to make my most difficult decision as a ruler—mete out punishment on those I counted as friends and on someone I loved. I beheaded every noble who conspired against me. Their spiked heads were displayed along a pathway which led to my trial by fire. When my feet did not burn after walking barefooted on hot stones, I knew the gods concurred with the punishment I would exact on Rhan for treason. Before I removed her head, I mercifully allowed her to speak, a decision I will regret until my dying day."

Amren stared at Catrin. She struggled to remain stone-faced, hiding her revulsion of the king's acts of mercilessly striking down his friends and queen. How could she reconcile the brutal actions with the love and admiration she had for him?

The king's gaze shifted to the burning candle, as if looking for some kind of succor as he continued his grim tale. "I remember every word of Rhan's curse as if she said it today. 'The gods demand the scales be balanced for the life you take. If you deny my soul's journey to the Otherworld by beheading me, I curse you to the same fate as mine. I prophesy your future queen will beget a daughter who will rise as a raven and join your son, Blood Wolf, and a mighty empire to overtake your kingdom and to execute my curse.'"

He sighed ruefully. "The raven is you."

9

KING'S CHARGE

"I didn't understand what this meant until you told me about the inscription on the dagger that foretold Marrock would ally with Rome."

Catrin gasped, pushed her chair back and rose from the table. Rapidly breathing, she rasped, "No, no, Father, you are wrong! I would never betray you. I love you." Blood rushed from her face and the room whirled around her. Unsteady, she staggered and bumped against the table.

Amren rushed to her side, cradled her in his arms, and reassured her saying, "Don't fret, daughter. It's all right. Sit back down. I need to show you something."

Catrin gingerly lowered herself in the chair and gazed at the candlelight before shifting her eyes to the back corner where her father picked up a wooden box from a shelf. When he set it on the table before her, she studied the handcrafted oak case, the size of a jewelry box. The panels were inlayed with black and white ravens. A brass-winged deadbolt clasped the lid to the front panel. She assumed it was where her father kept his prized gold torcs and gemstone rings.

The king took out a key from a drawstring pouch attached to his belt and inserted it into the deadbolt. He raised the lid, revealing a lapin-crested dagger on gold brocade fabric. He reverently lifted the dagger with both hands and kissed the blade. After he set the weapon on the tabletop, he sat across from Catrin and pointed to the inscription on the blade. "I had Rhan's curse recorded on the blade to deflect all misfortune from me. By the time you were born, the etching of the inscription began to blur, giving me hope the curse could be reversed. On the night Marrock abandoned you in the woods and you were found alone with the raven, the inscription transformed."

Amren's forefinger skimmed over the etched Latin lettering as he read the words aloud. "The gods demand the scales be balanced for the life you take. At the time your daughter rises out of Apollo's flames as a raven with the powers of Ancient Druids ... Blood Wolf will ally with the Roman Empire."

Catrin rubbed the rough edging of what appeared to be missing words. "Some of the words are blurred. What does this signify?"

Amren shrugged. "I'm not sure. It's as if the curse is still re-writing itself. What I know for certain is that something happened on that day you were with Marrock that altered the inscription. As you can see, some words disappeared while others were added. That is why I believe the gods have a divine plan for you."

Catrin tried to grasp what her father just said. "What plan?"

"I don't know yet." The king set the dagger back in the box. "Mortals don't always understand the ways of the gods and goddesses. Our lives are fated by their whims. When I showed this to Agrona, she told me that she could teach you how to control these divine forces to reverse Rhan's curse."

A foreboding chill in the chamber made Catrin tremble. "Agrona's black magic frightens me."

The king set the dagger case on the tabletop nearer Catrin. "Forces can be used for either good or evil. Only Agrona can show you how to balance these forces."

Catrin rubbed the raven inlay on the front panel of the dagger's case, contemplating what her father just said. How could she possibly reverse a curse cast by a powerful Druidess? She muttered, "I ... I don't have that kind of power."

Amren leaned on his elbows. "You must have these powers, or will soon have them. The altered curse says you fly out as a raven with the powers of the Ancient Druids. It no longer says you will join with Marrock and overthrow me. This gives me hope."

"I'm not sure if it was me who altered the curse or someone else," Catrin said. "My mind is like a blank slate on what happened that day with Marrock. It troubles me that the curse now identifies the empire as Rome."

The king exhaled a heavy breath. "The Roman visit is a bad sign. Never before has the Roman emperor sent a senator to convey his demands. Every muscle in my body twitches with mistrust. After fighting in the Roman auxiliary in Germania, I know of their tactics to divide foes for their advantage. The senator has forced my hand to re-negotiate another contract to wed Mor and Adminius. The only way I can discover why Cunobelin betrayed me and befriended Marrock is to meet him face-to-face."

Amren held his hand over the candle flame and pulled it away. He inspected his reddened palm as he continued. "I have every reason to war with Cunobelin for his betrayal, yet as king, I must first consider my people's well-being." His gaze shifted to Catrin. "You will learn as you mature, a rival has no qualms about stabbing you with one hand while extending the other in friendship. I don't trust Cunobelin. He is a coward going behind my back to plead Marrock's case to the Roman emperor. I know he wants more of my jurisdiction transferred to Adminius as part of the marital pact. I must swallow my pride and yield to his demands to maintain peace. Cunobelin must, in return, drop his support of Marrock's claims. If Marrock ever becomes king, he would surely slaughter everyone in our family and mistreat my people. I can't let this happen. This is a matter I must address, but there are other ways you can help me during this difficult time."

"What can I do?" Catrin asked, emboldened by her father's confidence in her.

"Try to remember how you may have altered the curse. You have been blessed with the gift of foresight. If you can see the future, you can change the future. You could help me counter our enemies by knowing their next moves."

"What about Vala and Mor, don't they have this ability?"

"They don't." Amren frowned. "There is a reason for this, but it is best I tell you at another time when you are older and wiser about human frailties."

Catrin knew she should not broach the topic of her sisters further, yet she needed to understand more about the unwieldy forces she struggled to control. "Sometimes ... I am afraid of what is happening to me. I feel as though ... I am going mad. At one moment, I'm in my body; the next instant, I am in the raven's head. I first connected with the raven after Marrock left me alone in the forest. It still frightens me that I cannot remember what he did."

Amren growled, "That monster will pay a heavy price for all the vile deeds he has done."

Incited, Catrin's anger boiled to the surface. "I have seen ravens attack Marrock in my nightmares. My hate for him burns like a flame."

The crease on Amren's forehead deepened. "I have seen how this hate has made you withdraw into a cocoon. It hurts me when I no longer see you smile or talk with others like you once did. The only time your face brightens is when you are talking to your raven. Although I suspected, I did not realize until today how much mystical ability you have."

Amren shut the lid on the dagger's case and stepped around the table to pull Catrin into his arms. "Do not let this *cathos* control you. You must find the strength to balance your rage with love, loyalty, and sacrifice to become a great queen. Soon you may need to confront the monster from your past, and be called upon to fight Marrock."

Catrin nestled into the comfort of her father's arms. "I am afraid of what Marrock might do. Though it has been almost seven years since he was banished, I recognized him with his moon-pitted face. I pray to the goddesses of war everyday that the ravens peck out his hideous eyeballs!"

"That is why Agrona must teach you how to direct your raven's forces against Marrock. Rage will eat away at you like a maggot, unless you can direct it into action."

Still uneasy about working with Agrona, Catrin pulled out of her father's embrace. "I sometimes fear using the raven's magic. I remember your warning. After being in its mind, I am dizzy when I return to my world. I sometimes lose consciousness and am weak for hours."

Amren regarded Catrin. "Rhan also spoke of ill effects by doing these feats. She learned how to overcome these difficulties. She explained that she was a soul traveler who journeyed into the past, the present, and the future at the same time. Her soul could enter other humans and beasts, the first step to shape-shifting. Perhaps Agrona can help you do the same."

Catrin sat down at the table and stared at her wavering reflection in the candle flame. "What worries me most is my soul might not return to my human form. I fear the raven pecks away my soul every time I enter its mind. I don't know why I feel this way, but sometimes I am afraid it will possess me." A sob caught in her throat, and she wiped away a tear with the back of her hand. "I am confused on what happened to me at the ritual today. I had a vision of fire-breathing eagles, red shield walls, corpses, and skulls swirling over the Romans. I didn't understand what this meant until you told me about the inscription on the dagger that foretold Marrock would ally with Rome. What good is it for me to have these visions if I cannot interpret what they mean? How could I possibly change the future … the curse?"

Amren stepped behind Catrin and placed a heavy hand on her shoulder. "Hopefully with Agrona's help, you will learn how. It must be like being a baby learning to walk. How many times does a small child fall before he or she gets back up and tries again? A child must learn to put one foot in front of the other. It has to be as simple as that. And before long, you will be as fleet as a deer in the forest, buoyant as a raven in flight, and quick as a fish in water. Now that we know the curse can shift, we must use every weapon in our arsenal to break the curse, to stop Marrock."

He gripped her shoulder and lowered his voice. "I need you to do one more thing for me."

Catrin tensed. "What is that?"

"I can see the young Roman nobleman has taken a liking to you."

Taken aback, Catrin's voice quavered. "How do you know that?" She flinched when her father stroked her neck with the palm of his hand.

"I saw how his eyes lingered on you," he said. "I also gazed at your mother the same way when we first met. And you blushed from his gaze."

Catrin looked down, her face uncomfortably hot. "I didn't blush. I was warm ... from the hearth's fire."

Amren lightly squeezed the nape of her neck. "Nonetheless, you need to be wary of Marcellus. He is a predator that Rome left behind to gather information."

Catrin stiffened. "I don't sense any ill from him. Besides, you said he was our guest." She felt her father's hand brush her shoulder as he stepped away. Turning her head sideways toward the sound of his footsteps, she watched him walk to the weapons wall and rub a sword's hilt for a moment. He turned and his eyes flashed in the torchlight.

"Marcellus is not one of us. Do not delude yourself into thinking that this Roman is a friend. Still, you must find out the truth about why Emperor Tiberius dispatched his envoys here."

Catrin gave a perplexed look. "He already told you. He wants you to take Marrock back."

Amren shook his head. "No. There is more. That viper Marrock has promised the Romans something. Cunobelin and Rome would not demand I take him back without substantial recompense. You must use your charms on Marcellus to find out what they really want."

Catrin was stunned. Her father had never asked her to deceive another person. "How can I do that? I've never even kissed a man, and have no interest in doing so with a Roman."

Amren gave a wry smile. "Show him some interest. Ask questions. Flatter him. Romans think of themselves as conquerors. The moment he thinks he has captured your affection, be evasive! The chase will keep him intrigued."

When a frigid breeze crept into the dank room and a spider's web shimmered in the corner, Catrin's stomach knotted. "I can't do that."

Amren walked over to Catrin, pulled her up, and traced a fingertip over her cheekbone. "I know my enemy better than my friends. When I was retained as a hostage in a Roman noble's household, I learned how to think like him. You, too, must learn this. Show friendship to Marcellus and discover his secrets. Perhaps then, we will know how to counter Rome. Change the future. Change the curse."

Catrin reluctantly nodded. "You taught me to fight my foes head-on as a warrior, not hide like a snake in the shadows."

"True. These are honorable traits the Cantiaci embrace. Even so, Romans do not have this quality. You have already confronted the face of evil—your half-brother who I am ashamed to have sired. Only my daughters bring me pride. Again I ask. Will you save our family and our kingdom from our enemies?"

Catrin finally relented and gave him a big hug. "Yes. I will."

With a glint in his eye, Amren said, "I knew you would accept the challenge. Now give me a kiss."

Catrin pecked her father's cheek. His arms wrapped around her, almost squeezing the breath out of her lungs.

"Now I will go see your mother," he said. "After I talk with her, she will give you a new dress to wear tonight at the feast. Put it to good use. Remember to think with your head, and not with your heart."

10

PAST LOVER

... but his earthy eyes unsettled her, awakening a desire she had long buried. "I forbid you to look at me that way."

Queen Rhiannon's heels clicked on the wooden floor as she paced back and forth in the reception hall, waiting for Amren to finish with Catrin. Her heavy garments restricted her movements and the gold torc pinched her neck. Trystan's defiant actions and her husband's decisions broiled in her mind. Why would Amren agree to meet with the treacherous Cunobelin and Marrock in Catuvellauni territory? Amren not only put himself in danger, he also jeopardized the life of their eldest daughter, Vala, who would be held as a Roman hostage.

She stopped and rubbed her throbbing temple, her thoughts diverting to Trystan. Of all days, why would he draw his dagger to defend her honor after the senator's insult? The consequences of his insolence could result in his banishment. If Trystan ever left, she would wither like a flower at first frost. She sighed, memories of when she was fifteen floating into her mind.

Then, Rhiannon believed each day with Trystan would last forever. His smile seemed to light up the golden specks in his hazel eyes. She loved his wild, lime-washed hair that flew back like a horse's mane in the wind. With Trystan, she was carefree. During the day, they raced horses, hunted boars, and held each other tight when they kissed. At night, when he made love to her, they were like birds in an aerial dance. She grasped the wings of his eagle-tattooed arms as his hips pressed into hers. He then maneuvered her on top of him and their ecstasy soared to the heavens.

The summer of bloom turned into the autumn of blood. Her father, the king of the Regni, made a costly decision to ambush Amren's southern territory to seize fertile farmlands, even though he knew of Amren's reputation as a battle-hardened ruler. Amren's legacy held true in his decisive victory over the Regni people that decimated her father's army. To stop the carnage, her father had to break his promise that she could choose her own husband. She was instead awarded as a prize to Amren in a truce. Though she was secretly pregnant with Trystan's child, she wed Amren, a man more than twice her age, and fulfilled her duty to forge their marriage into a strong political alliance that established peace between their kingdoms.

But she could never stop loving Trystan.

A tap on the shoulder startled Rhiannon out of her reminiscence. She turned to find Trystan within inches of her lips, his sultry gaze reminding her of the intimacy they once had. Taken aback, she looked all around the beamed chamber for any onlookers. Near the chamber's entrance stood a guard who cocked an eyebrow at her.

She glowered at Trystan. "What do you want?"

Trystan did not answer, but his earthy eyes unsettled her, awakening a desire she had long buried. "I forbid you to look at me that way."

He leaned over, brushing her ear with his warm lip as he whispered, "If only I had the strength."

Rhiannon jerked away. From the corner of her eye, she glimpsed Mor and Belinus peeking around the thrones. Heart quickening, she wondered if they had noticed Trystan's intimate touch. When she narrowed her eyes at the couple, they shuffled back and disappeared into the shadows. Their behavior struck her as odd. Considering it further, she suspected they were hiding a budding relationship—the last thing Amren needed during his negotiation with Cunobelin. She turned to Trystan and said in a hushed tone, "Join me in the meeting chamber at the back. First, I must speak with Mor."

Trystan nodded and strode to the back.

Approaching the couple, Rhiannon arched a stern eyebrow. Mor's eyes darted down, her face a blossom of red. Belinus gave a thin-lipped smile.

"What are you two doing?" Rhiannon asked sharply. "Were you not clear about your duties, Belinus? You need to direct the servants on converting Catrin's bedchamber to the guest quarters for the Roman hostage. Fit the door with a bolt to prevent him from escaping."

"I'm on my way there now," Belinus said, then turned on his heels to leave.

Alone with Mor, Rhiannon said, "For the last couple months, Belinus has leashed on to you like a puppy."

Mor bit down hard on her lips. "We were discussing our tactics from weapons training today."

"And what did you practice with?"

"Spear and sword."

"Formidable weapons," Rhiannon said, a tinge of sarcasm ringing in her voice. "I want you to spend less time with him. Don't do anything stupid that could jeopardize your father's negotiations."

Mor raised her head in anger. "Even though Father promised I could marry whomever I wanted?"

"Exactly," Rhiannon snapped. "Don't argue with me about this. We will have words later! Go back to your room and get ready for the feast tonight."

Mor stomped out of the chamber.

Rhiannon vowed to put an end to the relationship as she made her way to the chamber to speak with Trystan. She drew back the room's curtain and found Trystan standing next to the table. A burning candle cast their shadows up the stone wall as she stepped toward him.

"What were you thinking out there?" she asked brusquely. "Somebody could have seen what you did."

Trystan lowered his eyes, his silence disquieting.

"Answer me," Rhiannon demanded. "You raised the king's hackles when you defied him earlier. What made you foolishly brandish your dagger, not once, but twice while he was talking with the Romans?"

Trystan grabbed her wrist hard. "Amren did not defend your honor from that Roman pig's insult. I did."

Rhiannon squirmed to escape Trystan's tight grip. Seeing the fire in his eyes, she knew any display of anger would inflame him further. With a steady voice, she said, "As king, Amren must show restraint. Your actions, on the other hand, could have started a war."

Trystan pulled her up to his chest, his lips almost touching hers. "Perhaps the king does not love the queen as much as I do."

Rhiannon's heart seized. He had not said that to her in years. She had believed the flames of their love affair had been snuffed out. No matter, she could not rekindle that fire with him. She gave him a frosty glare, pulled away, and straightened her skirt.

"You cannot say those things!" Rhiannon scolded. "With the threat of Marrock inciting Cunobelin and the Romans to war against us, you must respect and obey Amren in all things. It is only through his mercy and love for me that you stand here as his commander."

Trystan retorted, "It was his mercy that kept me from loving you again."

Rhiannon backed away, her eyes pierced at him. "Why are you professing your love after so many years? I swore to remain faithful to Amren. You must also keep that oath to him."

Trystan fisted his hands. "The only reason I swore my fealty to Amren was to stay close to you, to protect you and our daughters. Now, I fear you will pay the price for his past deeds. Remember, I was there when Amren executed Rhan."

Shaken, Rhiannon asked, "Why bring this up now?"

Trystan's jaw tightened. "Because of what happened today, when the raven flew out of the fire at the ritual, I recalled Rhan's curse. She proclaimed Amren would sire a daughter with his future queen who would rise as a raven and ally with Marrock. I warned you not to sleep with Amren. He knew the risks of you bearing that cursed child. Up to that point, he tolerated our affair and agreed to accept both our daughters as his own. Yet, when he returned from Germania, after fighting in the Roman auxiliary, he tricked you into his bed and hardened his stance about us. And now we must deal with Catrin."

Infuriated that Trystan would proclaim Catrin as the cursed daughter, Rhiannon slapped him. "You forget yourself, warrior!"

Trystan grabbed her arm before she could hit him again. "I want you to hear me out! Ever since Marrock left Catrin for dead in the woods, she has never been the same. Rumors abound that she is a sorceress who casts evil spells through her raven."

Pushing her elbows against him, Rhiannon flared, "Those rumors are false!"

Trystan's eyes blazed. "Today, when the raven landed at Catrin's feet, I knew those rumors were true. She is a sorceress. Something else bothers me, that slimy Roman—the way his eyes feasted all over Catrin as if she were a common whore. She has never shown any interest in a man, that is, not until today with that Roman. It is no coincidence he is our hostage!"

Trystan's accusation of Catrin's possible collaboration with the young Roman sliced at Rhiannon's heart. She pounded her fists on his chest, but he met her outburst with an embrace. Struggling like a wild animal caught in a trap, she stomped on his feet and fought against his unyielding arms, twisting, wriggling, and contorting her body to escape. His bull-like strength was too much for her to overcome. He held her tighter and demanded, "Stop it! Stop it! Calm down."

"Let me go!" she ordered.

He snapped back, "Keep your voice down or the entire village will hear!"

Knowing he was right, she shot a seething glare at him—a silent weapon more formidable than any other in her arsenal.

Trystan stepped back and clutched himself as if shot by an arrow. "Why do you always have to fight me like that?"

"So you remember that I am your queen, not your lover."

"I never thought otherwise," Trystan said, shuffling backward, his boots scuffing the wooden floor. He bumped against the table and crumbled into an armchair. His eyes languished on the candle flame as he said in a cracked voice, "Can't you see, I am afraid for your life; I only want to protect you."

Seeing the anguish on Trystan's face, Rhiannon leaned over the table. He looked up and his face turned pallid. He said, "I believe Rhan has arisen from the dead. Not only will she avenge Amren for what he did to her, she will destroy you. You need to escape. Get away from Amren, get away from here!"

Rhiannon lowered herself into the chair across from him. "You know I can't do that. I swore my loyalty to Amren to be his wife and queen. He has only shown me love and respect. I cannot turn my back on him when he needs me most, and neither can you."

"If you stay with him, it will be your death," Trystan said with fear-struck eyes. "Escape with me to Gaul. I know you still love me. We could live as husband and wife."

Conflicting emotions grappled at Rhiannon's heart. Of course, she would always love Trystan. As a young woman, she foolishly believed nothing could ever stand in the way of their dream of being together. Older and wiser, she knew the survival of her family and her people depended on her. She finally proclaimed without a blink, "My flame for you burned out long ago. Amren demonstrated his mercy by declaring Vala and Mor as his own daughters. They must never know you are their true father."

Trystan rose from his seat and stared at Rhiannon. "You ask the impossible from me. Every day I must hide my strong feelings for my daughters. Amren gave no second thought about Vala being held as a hostage by the Romans. He thinks so little of Mor, he barters her off to Cunobelin. It is just like he forced your father to hand you over to him like a prized filly." He pulled Rhiannon into his arms. Her resistance melted when he lifted her face and said, "Look into my eyes and tell me you cannot ignite that fire again."

Struggling to resist his smoldering stare, she said firmly, "I will not jeopardize my daughters' status by reigniting our cold ashes to the flames we once had."

Trystan pulled her hand against his chest where she could feel the strong beat of his heart. "I can never love another woman. If all I can have are cinders of your love, I will accept them as long as I can stay near you."

Dumbstruck, Rhiannon froze when he lowered his lips to hers. A sudden movement of the curtain caught her eyes. Hearing footsteps, she gasped.

The king appeared at the opening.

Rhiannon recoiled. Trystan's eyes and mouth flew open as if a serpent had struck him.

Amren glowered. "Trystan, leave now!"

II

KING'S CURSE

She regarded the stubbornness etched on Amren's face and told him, "As your queen and wife, I fall to your command. Yet, I sense Agrona will be our doom."

When Trystan's face turned crimson, Rhiannon knew he was ready to unfurl his rage and pummel the king. She quickly grabbed Trystan by the arm and said sternly, "Do as your king commands! Go!"

Trystan stood firm, his eyes darting from Rhiannon, to Amren, and back to her again. He must have seen the horror in her face because he finally backed down and lowered his head to Amren. He said with a bitter tone, "I fall to your command."

With a blistering scowl on his face, Trystan removed himself from the room.

Amren closed the curtain, his deadly stare making Rhiannon flinch. He turned his back on her and said bitterly, "After all these years."

His silence thundered accusation.

Shaking, Rhiannon touched his shoulder. "It is not what you think."

Amren turned and glared. "Did my eyes lie? Were you not in Trystan's arms?"

She stammered, "He … he was troubled by the events today … and what you might do to him. I tried to reassure him."

"Events he made worse by openly defying me—not once, but twice." Amren gripped Rhiannon's wrist, the pressure so tight she feared the bones would break. "Is this a sign you have again cuckolded me after all these years?"

Rhiannon felt her stomach drop like an executioner's axe, and she dropped to her knees. "No, my king! My loyalty remains steadfast, even more so after today's unfortunate events."

Amren's blue eyes hardened into steel. "If only I could be moved to believe you!"

Rhiannon kissed the back of her husband's hand, so he would soften his grasp. "You must believe me. As your queen, I stand united with you against our enemies. If we cannot trust each other, then divided we fall."

Amren loosened his grip, giving some relief to the throbbing pain in Rhiannon's wrists. He looked down on her with a clenched jaw. "That is what I am trying to do—hold my kingdom together; maintain a tenuous peace with Cunobelin. Yet, when I heard of Cunobelin's betrayal, I wanted to rip out his bloodsucking heart! Trystan's reckless actions only made it worse."

Throwing away caution, Rhiannon said, "I warned you. So did Trystan. Do not trust Cunobelin. You can't barter Mor away like a whore. Don't capitulate to Cunobelin's demands and proffer your sovereignty to his son."

Clenching Rhiannon's shoulders, Amren pulled her to his chest. She cringed when his hot breath assaulted her nostrils with the pungent odor of the washed-rind cheese he had eaten earlier.

"What would you have me do?" Amren growled. "Go to war? Spill more blood? I've had my fill of so-called glory. You know where my ambition led me—a dark journey into my soul's depths from where I might not have returned. If it weren't for you, I would still be warring to satiate my hunger for more lands and plunder."

"No one knows more than I how much you have sacrificed," Rhiannon said, squirming, again trying to soften his grip by appealing to his pride. "You are an honorable king. I knew of your resentment to fight in the Roman auxiliary to fulfill your father's obligation, to maintain peace with the Roman Empire."

Amren tightened his hold as if aware of her ploy to pander to his ego for advantage. "I discovered the limits of your sacrifice when I caught you in Trystan's arms. Even so, I forgave you. Yet today, you showed me your true face at the time I most need your loyalty."

Rhiannon yanked out of his strong embrace and leveled her eyes at him. "You accuse me of being disloyal, but you dismissed my counsel when you summoned Agrona back. You know how I despise her."

"I did not summon her to spite you," Amren quickly replied. "She came back to help me counter Marrock. There is something else I needed to tell you before I walked in on you and was rudely greeted by Trystan." He grew quiet, his chest caving in as if the weight of what he was about to reveal would crush him.

"Tell me," Rhiannon said. "What is it?"

"Today's omens tell me Rhan's curse has begun," Amren said, his voice shaky. "Catrin just confirmed what I had already suspected. She can enter the raven's mind."

"You mean that she can shape-shift?"

Amren shook his head. "No, not yet, but she is on the verge. She has learned how to channel the raven's powers. That is why I believe the curse rewrote itself on my dagger. The gods must have chosen Catrin to be a conduit for their supernatural powers. I believe Agrona can teach Catrin to control these forces and can change the curse."

"I don't trust Agrona," Rhiannon said sharply. "Everyone in the village knows of her black magic. You have other Druids who can advise you. Use them instead."

Amren sat at the table and waved his hand over the burning candle. "Agrona was there when I beheaded Rhan. Mute since birth, she spoke for the first time at the execution. I took this as a sign the gods had chosen to speak through her. She knows things about me only Rhan could have known. No matter what you think of her, I need to use her sorcery against Marrock."

Rhiannon sat across the table from Amren. She moved the melting candle aside to study his face as she spoke. "Remember, Agrona begged you to spare Marrock after your guards found him with the headless bodies of the children from the nearby village. You should have executed him. Instead you kept his dark secret from everyone."

Amren shifted back in his seat. "I didn't have enough proof."

Rhiannon flared. "Enough proof! Due to your inaction, he did something vile to Catrin that day he abandoned her in the forest."

Amren snuffed out the candle, and the room darkened. Only the torch light filtering through the thin curtain dimly lit the room. "Don't forget, I forsook him as my son and banished him. Exile is worse than death."

Her face prickling with heat, Rhiannon leaned forward and said, "Is that so? Explain how Marrock can return with two powerful forces backing him. He never suffered for what he did to Catrin. She isolates herself with the raven. Sometimes, I wonder if she is in her right mind."

"I'm also haunted everyday that Catrin can't remember what happened that day," Amren said, grimacing. "I fear she does not understand the dangers of summoning the mystical powers from her raven."

A foreboding chill iced down Rhiannon's spine. "What dangers?"

"Powerful forces such as these can overwhelm a person and cause ill effects. Agrona warned Catrin could go raving mad."

"Amren, you promised me these forces would never be summoned again. You said the powers of the Ancient Druids died with Rhan."

"I did not invite these forces back," Amren said. "These powers came to Catrin only after Marrock abandoned her. Only the gods know what that monster did. My head runs rampant with fears that he might have cast a spell on Catrin and controls her."

Rhiannon reached for his hand. "You're right. His mind is twisted. Catrin was an innocent lamb until that day with Marrock. Every muscle in my body twinges with dread that he raped and cast an evil spell on her."

"That is the reason I summoned Agrona," Amren said. "I truly believe she can help Catrin counter any of his spells." He paused and furrowed his eyebrows together. "There is something more I need to tell you. I have charged Catrin to use her charms on the Roman hostage, to trick him into revealing Rome's intent for our kingdom."

Rhiannon's mouth dropped. "Have you lost all senses? First, you risk your life by agreeing to meet with Cunobelin and Marrock in their territory. Next you allow Vala to offer herself as a hostage. And now this! You offer Catrin as a whore to a foreigner."

"I did not ask Catrin to lie with him," Amren quickly replied. "I told her to entice him, get his hopes up. She can then pull the anchor up after he unloads all the information we need. Marcellus is a political piece that we should play to our advantage."

Appalled that Amren would proffer Catrin to Marcellus, Rhiannon said, "Catrin is inexperienced with men. What makes you think that she will not falter under the Roman's charm? She overstepped your authority to save him. Would she not do that again?"

Amren rose from the table. "My mind is set. Catrin will do whatever is necessary to get information that may help us counter the Romans. Although Julius Caesar never completed his conquest of our lands almost seventy years ago, we are still held under Rome's yoke with the hope its legions will not crush us. After having served in their army, I know how they spin webs to divide rival rulers. Rome is looking for an excuse to attack us. The only leverage we hold is Marcellus. While I negotiate with Cunobelin and the Romans, you will rule the village on my behalf and safeguard the dagger with the inscription of Rhan's curse. Keep a close eye on the blade and warn me of any changes to the wording. If I am taken prisoner, hold

Marcellus for ransom and threaten to kill him, if I am not released. If you must lead our army into battle to defend our kingdom, have Agrona oversee the village."

Rhiannon angrily pushed her chair back to stand. "What? Leave Agrona in charge? You cannot do that! Someone from our family like Mor should rule instead."

Amren drew Rhiannon into his arms and softly kissed her lips. "My love, you asked me to trust you when you said there is nothing between you and Trystan. I, in return, ask you to give me that trust. Agrona foresees shadows lurking in my future, but she cannot yet discern what these specters are. In the meanwhile, both you and I must heed what she advises."

Rhiannon sighed with resignation, knowing that once her husband's mind was made up, he was as immovable as a mountain. She regarded the stubbornness etched on Amren's face and told him, "As your queen and wife, I fall to your command. Yet, I sense Agrona will be our doom."

12

ROMAN SPY

"Don't get caught," Lucius said with a smirk. "You volunteered to be a hostage. Make the most of it. Find out what you can."

A Roman guard pulled away the flap to the massive tent, allowing Marcellus to join his father and Decimus inside. The spacious headquarters welcomed them with a central brass brazier radiating heat. The main chamber was sparsely furnished with a long wooden table, fold-out chairs, and multiple standing shelves. Behind the table was an embroidered gold eagle tapestry that divided the larger room from the living quarters.

Marcellus thought it a mixed blessing that he would be exchanging his father's ire and living quarters for the hospitality of painted barbarians. Soaked from the rain, Marcellus removed his cape and laid it on a bench near the doorway. He hesitated joining his father and Decimus, who were both warming their hands over hot coals in the brazier. The chilly ride back to the encampment had been quiet. Too quiet. His father had refused to look at him and remained silent as they traveled on the sodden path.

Apprehensive his father would castigate him for not keeping his mouth muzzled and obeying him like a trained dog, Marcellus's throat tightened. Would his father lash out at him in the presence of the tribune? Shivering, he stepped next to Decimus to warm his numbed hands and looked down, averting his father's burning stare.

Decimus asked Lucius, "Do you want me to stay?"

Lucius's voice grated. "By all means stay. I want you to hear what I am about to tell him." Lucius grabbed Marcellus by his tunic with one hand while lifting the other to strike. "Never, let me repeat, never overstep me again in front of my enemies. I am the paterfamilias! You are my son; it is your duty to obey me!"

Marcellus recoiled from his father's fist that was waving in front of his face. He could overpower his father, but that would only inflame him further. Fighting for composure, he apologized. "Father, I'm sorry; I misunderstood. I thought we agreed I would stay as a hostage if negotiations broke down. I didn't know you wanted the last word."

Chest heaving with anger, Lucius growled. "That was exactly my plan, only if we were in danger of losing our heads. Our talks had not reached that point."

Decimus stepped in and intervened. "May I speak?"

Lucius glanced at the tribune and loosened his grip on Marcellus. "Go ahead. Speak."

"With due respect, I beg to differ with your assessment," Decimus said, lowering his head, but keeping his eyes fixed on Lucius.

"Tell me why."

"King Amren may have negotiated a little longer," Decimus continued, "but his commander had a knife hidden at his side. He stared at us as if he was ready to spike our heads alongside the other skulls in the king's receiving chamber. The cut to your son's neck is proof King Amren was losing control of his warriors."

"Did you think I was not aware of this?" Lucius said gruffly. "That is why I didn't want to leave Marcellus with these savages."

"We had no other choice," Decimus said. "As a result of Marcellus volunteering to stay, Amren finally conceded to your demands. He, like you, wants a peaceful solution. He has a lot to lose if his eldest daughter is harmed while held hostage. The deed is done. Let us move on and discuss our next steps."

Marcellus blew a breath of relief when his father released him and turned to Decimus.

"Tell me your thoughts," Lucius said.

"I will have my best men hide near the Cantiaci village and keep an eye on Marcellus," Decimus said. "The meeting with Cunobelin should give us time to get more troops and supplies from Gaul just in case conflict breaks out."

"Where do we house the king's giant daughter?" Lucius asked with disdain. "The men will grumble about a female in camp, especially one that ugly."

"Why not set up a separate tent outside the encampment," Decimus suggested. "I will order my most experienced soldiers to guard her, making sure that she does not escape. Meanwhile, you can arbitrate between Amren and Cunobelin."

Marcellus studied his father's face. Throughout their journey to Britannia, his father had never clearly explained the emperor's directive and what role Marcellus would play in the negotiations. He asked, "What is my mandate as hostage?"

"Socialize," Lucius mocked. "Is that not your special talent?"

Decimus interjected. "Amren's family should allow you freedom to move around the village. See how well-armed the Cantiaci are—" The tribune's words cut off when he began coughing.

Lucius slapped him on the back. "Are you all right?"

Still hacking, Decimus nodded and waved Lucius away. After a moment, he spat and cleared his throat. "Sorry. The damp weather and mold makes me wheezy," Decimus rasped. "As I was saying, Marcellus should count how many warriors are in the village and find out what neighboring rulers have sworn their allegiance to King Amren."

"How can I find this out?" Marcellus asked. "I don't speak their awful-sounding language."

"Perhaps,"—Lucius snickered and winked—"the youngest daughter can teach you how to use your tongue on her."

Marcellus did not know how to take his father's comment. At one moment, his father could be as eloquent as any Roman orator, but at the next, he was as crude as any battle-hardened soldier. Not wanting an argument, Marcellus bit back his snide comment.

Perhaps, you should bite off your own tongue.

Lucius sat down at the table and stroked his chin, as if churning over some clever plan. His eyes glinted when he looked at Marcellus. "The youngest, what's her name?"

"Catrin," Marcellus answered.

"Catrin," Lucius repeated. "For some reason, she spoke up to save your pretty head. She gazed at you with starry eyes."

Decimus grimaced. "I didn't like the way she looked at Marcellus. She looked as if she was casting a spell on him. Why would King Amren proclaim Catrin as an escort to Marcellus if she didn't serve some kind of purpose? The raven flying through the blast of smoke at the ritual and landing at her feet is a sign she is a sibyl or a sorceress."

"That is superstitious nonsense," Marcellus said. "More likely, I can bewitch Catrin with my magical fingers."

Lucius gave Marcellus a twisted smile. "That's not a bad idea. You could charm the wench to find out more information about her family. Does the queen have additional loyalties we should know about? Find out why Amren banished Marrock. If need be, take the wench to bed. That way, you could thrust out any secrets about Marrock. It might help us understand the best way to handle him."

The suggestion by his father unnerved Marcellus. Though he'd enjoy a lively frolic with Catrin, he had not anticipated his noble father sanctioning a tryst with a foreigner. Senator Lucius Antonius had just crawled out of the mire of his forefathers' debauchery.

Welcome back to the family cesspool, Marcellus! Ah, tradition!

He frowned at his father. "I'm surprised that you have me take this risk."

"You do what you must, boy," Lucius said, slapping the table to emphasize the point.

Marcellus flinched. "Didn't you see those skulls on the walls when we were in the king's receiving hall? Mine could join the others."

"Don't get caught," Lucius said with a smirk. "You volunteered to be a hostage. Make the most of it. Find out what you can."

Decimus almost wagged his head off. "I don't like this. Marcellus shouldn't be seducing the king's daughter. By the looks of her, she may still be a prepubescent girl."

"She's older than that," Marcellus said. "But I agree with you. I don't feel right about taking her for political reasons."

"At least you can have some pleasure," Lucius sneered. "Think of it this way, you are doing your duty for Rome by finding out why Amren and Marrock are at each other's throats."

Decimus stepped to the table across from Lucius and leaned forward. "Catrin is not a whore. She may be a priestess like one of Rome's vestal virgins. She must possess some mystical power for her to assist in the ritual. It was she who proclaimed that Apollo would favor all decisions made at our meeting today. The raven—"

Lucius interrupted. "Get to your point."

Decimus swallowed hard. "The raven may give her god-like powers from Apollo."

Marcellus blurted, "That is utter nonsense!"

Lucius pressed his lips together, as if repressing a chuckle. "The trouble with you, Decimus, is that you're ruled by superstitions despite your brilliant command of seasoned soldiers."

The tribune's face colored bright red. "I sacrifice to the gods, the same as my ancestors. I make offerings to them to retain their favor. Do not bring the wrath of Apollo down on us for defiling his priestess. The gods—Mars, Apollo, Jupiter—fated Rome to rule the world and crush its enemies. It is no accident that the Druidess declared Catrin as Apollo's oracle."

The chamber quieted like a temple. Lucius regarded Decimus for a moment, then stood, stepped heavily around the table and placed a hand on the tribune's shoulder.

"Forgive me, Decimus. I did not mean to insult you. I, too, honor the gods and pay homage to Apollo. I believe the king ordered the Druidess to proclaim his daughter as Apollo's oracle, so he could assuage his people who were ready to riot. Nonetheless, I agree with you. Marcellus should be cautious when dealing with Amren's daughter. There are perhaps other ways he can get the information."

His father's concession to Decimus surprised Marcellus. Their friendship must be deeper and more abiding than what he had thought.

"Enough said." Decimus pulled away. "What are our next steps for speaking with Cunobelin and Marrock?"

"Arrange separate meetings with Cunobelin and Marrock where I can speak with each privately," Lucius said. "I want to know where each of them stands with Rome. Are they willing to pledge their fealty as client kings, to supply our legions with their warriors, and to sell their captives as slaves to us? Would they go as far as giving no armed resistance to a Roman invasion in exchange for filling their coffers with coins and offering them political influence as client kings to the empire? I have dealt with Cunobelin before, but Marrock is a mystery. Tell me what he is like."

Decimus rubbed the crescent scar below his eye. "Well, he does have more facial scars than me, but not from battle. It is as if chucks of his tissue were gouged out of his face. I was told he was attacked by wild beasts and left to die."

Marcellus turned to his father. "Why is Rome so adamant about recognizing Marrock's claims, if Amren refuses to take him back?"

"Marrock might be more willing to cooperate with us to invade Britannia if we help him overthrow his father," Lucius said.

Marcellus considered what his father said for a moment. "What I don't understand is why Tiberius supports your plan to invade Britannia. He has proclaimed that he will not expand the empire."

"This is a highly guarded secret," Lucius said, emphasizing each word. "I must prove to Tiberius that it is in the empire's best interests to conquer Britannia. There is wealth to be mined here—gold, silver, tin. If I can convince the emperor, this would elevate my political standing. I could be appointed as governor of Britannia or another province. This is my time to rewrite the legacy of the Antonius family name. If Mark Antony had been emperor of Rome and not Augustus, our family legacy would have been different. My father, Iullus, would not have been forced to fall on his sword for having an affair with the daughter of Augustus. I wouldn't have been banished to Gaul for more than fifteen years for what my father did. I have been given the opportunity to reclaim my great heritage." Lucius shifted his eyes to Marcellus. "This could also be your legacy, my son."

A soldier's voice from outside yelled, "We are here to escort Marcellus!"

Decimus pulled a dagger from his belt and handed it to Marcellus. "Keep this hidden in your tunic. Take votives to give as offerings to Apollo, so he will protect you. Remember, Celtic warriors are mad for war and do not fear death. To gain their respect, you must not show them any weakness."

Morbid images whirled into Marcellus's head of what could happen to him: torture, execution, beheading, or hanging. What had he gotten himself into?

Decimus clicked his boot heels together and saluted. "Senator, I believe we are in agreement that some of my soldiers will hide near the village, so they can keep an eye on Marcellus. If you would excuse me, I will assign these men and give them further instructions."

Lucius nodded. "Go ahead."

After Decimus left the tent, Lucius surprised Marcellus with a warm embrace. "Pay no attention to what Decimus said. As I said earlier, do whatever you must to pry out information from Catrin."

Marcellus gave his father a befuddled look, thinking the issue had been settled that he would not seduce Catrin. "What exactly are you asking me to do?"

The corner of Lucius's mouth twitched into a sly smile. "I think you understand my meaning."

Marcellus shook his head. "What about Decimus's warning that I should not defile Catrin?"

"We both know that Decimus can sometimes be irrational with his beliefs. I respect him for his military intelligence, but the only reason I tolerate his superstitions is to keep his loyalty. I am secretly asking you to get information from Catrin by any means. If that means bedding her, do it!"

Marcellus shook his head with disbelief. "How can I do this after you bemoaned what happened to you when your father committed adultery."

"There is a big difference here. Julia was the emperor's married daughter. Catrin is a barbarian whore who you can use as you please."

Marcellus retorted, "She is the king's daughter!"

Lucius shot a piercing scowl. "Enough of your belligerence! If you won't obey me on this, I will banish you to the Roman Legion as a common soldier. Then you'll learn how to obey! Do I make myself clear?"

Marcellus glared. "Understood."

Lucius placed a hand on Marcellus's shoulder. "You have always had the wild nature of Mark Antony. Think … Don't get caught in bed with the king's daughter. Your mother would never forgive me if you didn't return home."

Marcellus stepped to within inches of his father's face. "Don't worry, I won't get caught."

13

FIRST ENCOUNTER

She realized then, the raven had for the first time entered her mind and changed how she perceived the world.

After washing for the evening's festivities, Catrin dressed in a pine green gown that dragged behind her like a pheasant tail. The front-lace leather bodice was as tight as a sausage skin over her bust. Awkward in the garment, she almost fell on her face because of tripping over her skirt. She looked around her windowless, musty bedchamber now converted to a makeshift cell with a bolted door.

Marcellus would soon arrive and sleep in her quarters.

Heart aflutter, she dusted the oak table and set a glass jar of lavender-scented oil down to refresh the stale air. Her father's instructions to beguile the young Roman weighed heavily on her. She was a warrior. What did she know about plucking a man's strings to gain more information?

Most of all, she dreaded sharing a cramped bed with Mor, who was now yelling from the next room.

"What's taking you so long? Get in here, so I can comb your hair."

Lifting the heavy skirt, Catrin bustled into her sister's bedchamber where she was sitting on the edge of the bed and plaiting her hair. Mor turned and arched her eyebrows. "Why are you in such a dour mood?"

Seating herself on the bed's edge, Catrin said, "I was thinking about what happened today and the upcoming parley between Father, the Romans and Cunobelin."

"Me, too," Mor said, pinning the braid on top of her head. "What did Father say to you after today's meeting with the Romans?"

"He confronted me about overstepping his authority." Catrin hesitated, not sure how much more to confide to Mor who had a reputation for spreading gossip. "I told Father that I saw an omen that something bad would happen to our kingdom. Then I confessed that I had learned how to use the raven's magic. He told me that Agrona needed to train me on how to control its mystical powers."

"I'm surprised he agreed," Mor said with a bite to her voice. "Nobody else in our family is allowed to use these forces. I don't understand why he wants Agrona to train you. Mother detests her. There are other more agreeable Druids he could use instead."

Catrin frowned. "Did you tell Father about my raven casting evil spells on me?"

"I didn't say that." Mor nervously cleared her throat. "I said that you were acting oddly around that bird."

"Why did you have to say anything?"

Mor twisted some loose strands of hair around her forehead into curls. "Then explain what happened earlier when your raven flew into the chamber like a ghoul and scared everyone. Why would Agrona declare you some kind of prophetess who can speak directly to the sun god? I heard you ate a ram's eyeball after the raven had its share. Is that not ominous, don't you think?"

Catrin knew Mor was right. Melding with the raven's mind had become more bewildering, even frightening. She did not want to admit this to Mor. "Agrona used that as a trick to appease the people who were ready to revolt over the Roman demands."

Mor coughed into her hand and pointed to the shelf where she stored her personal belongings. "Get me something over there to comb your hair."

Catrin retrieved a bone-toothed comb and handed it to Mor, who then mercilessly raked a tangle the size of a bird's nest out of her hair.

"Ouch!"

"Don't whine," Mor scolded. "What do you expect with such thick hair?"

"Not this abuse. Are you angry at me?"

"Not in the least," Mor snapped.

After another handful of hair ripped from her scalp, Catrin grabbed Mor's hand. "Stop it! You must be mad at me."

Mor's eyes blazed. "Why did Father take you into the meeting with the Romans and assign you guard duty over the senator's son? He usually asks Belinus or me to do that."

Taken aback, Catrin said, "I don't always understand his decisions."

"Did he ask you about Belinus and me?"

"No. Not a word."

"I think he suspects we are lovers."

Catrin regarded Mor for a moment. "I don't think so. Besides, if you were honest about your relationship with Belinus, he might grant your wish to marry him. I doubt Father would force you to wed Cunobelin's son, especially after what happened today."

"I think Father would do anything to reach a truce with Cunobelin," Mor said bitterly. "And that includes marrying me off to Adminius in exchange for Marrock's head."

Catrin pursed her lips. "Father has also asked me to do something I do not feel right about."

Mor raised her brow in curiosity. "What is that?"

"He wants me to charm the Roman hostage into revealing Rome's true intent for our kingdom. There is no honor in extending a hand in friendship and then turning around and taking it away."

"Silly girl," Mor mocked. "That young foreigner is from an empire that crushes weaker kingdoms under their legions."

"I'm not stupid," Catrin snapped. "I understand all that."

"Well, at least you don't look like a scruffy boy tonight." Mor chuckled. "I see breasts peeking out of your dress."

Catrin looked down at her bodice and blushed as she adjusted it. "Is that better?"

Mor smirked.

Catrin picked up a polished bronze mirror and brightened at seeing her noble transformation. Thin braids tied with leather straps were now blended into her loose hair. The open square front of her dress revealed the upper curvature of her small breasts. Her belly tingled as she imagined Marcellus touching her there.

Why would I think about that?

She set the mirror aside, trying to calm her unsettled stomach.

I should sweep these thoughts out of my head.

Catrin turned her attention to Mor, who was squeezing herself into a low-cut dress. As Mor dabbed lavender scented oil on her wrists, she smiled sweetly at Catrin.

"Would you do me a favor?"

Catrin eyed her suspiciously. "What is that?"

Mor beamed. "I'm going to spend the night with Belinus, but you can't say a word to Mother."

"And what is in it for me?"

Mor hugged Catrin tightly. "I am your sister. Please…please… do this for me."

Once again the lifetime sibling scheme reared its head. So what other choice did Catrin have? Belinus and Mor always dragged her into their little arrangements. *Oh, the joys of sisterhood*, she thought, and reluctantly agreed. "I will do it. Besides, Mother seems more distant after I met with Father earlier."

Mor flicked her wrist. "Don't be a ruffled goose. She treats everyone the same. Oh, by the way, I overheard her argue with Father about his plans for you."

"What plans?"

"Mother does not want Agrona training you. She doesn't trust the Druidess or her black magic. Further, she doesn't want you guarding that handsome Roman."

Annoyed, Catrin frowned at Mor. "Why didn't you tell me this before?"

"Your foul mood bothered me."

"You are —" Catrin's words were cut off by a shrieking *meeoooowww* and a loud thump. Men speaking Latin could be heard outside their chamber. The door from the next room opened then slammed shut. A man's voice groaned, "Not even a candle to light up this forsaken place." Then a metal clank rang through the thin wooden wall.

Catrin nervously glanced at Mor. "Who do you think is in my bedchamber?"

Mor whispered, "I'm not sure, but I hear Belinus from the corridor."

A loud clap startled them. Mor walked to the door and peeked outside. She grinned when Belinus stumbled in. The two lovers embraced. Belinus pushed Mor against the wall and nibbled his way down her neck. Taking her clue, Catrin scurried into the corridor where she was greeted by a rat scampering over her feet. Nearby, she saw a one-eyed cat stalking its vermin dinner and in a dark corner was her raven, its amber eyes aglow. A frosty breeze swirled around her, and she followed the raven to a barred windowsill where a long-legged spider had trapped a moth in its web.

A light flashed in Catrin's mind, and she was surprised to see herself as a bird-shaped mist in the corridor's gloom. From another darkened corner, a sun flare shaped like a horse flamed forth into the image of Marcellus. It was as if the raven had entered her mind and transported her to another dimension. She heard Marcellus clear his throat loudly. Frozen and locked in the raven's mind, she couldn't answer.

Then, a very real Marcellus moved closer and whispered, "Catrin."

A tingle burned through Catrin's belly as she came back to herself. Head spinning, she felt her knees buckle and she collapsed on the wooden floor.

Marcellus leaned over her and offered his hand. She grasped his hand as he helped her up. Unsteady, she wrapped her arms around him. When he held her closer, her knees began quivering. He said softly, "Sorry. I didn't mean to scare you."

For a moment, she savored his warmth, but her father's mandate to find out more information from him leapt into her mind. She pushed him away.

"Are you all right?" he asked. "You seemed to be in a trance."

Catrin nodded. In truth, her arms were still tingling and her mouth ached from the hard fall. She realized then, the raven had for the first time entered her mind and changed how she perceived the world. This creature's tricks on her mind were frightening, as more and more of her reality crumbled under the new sensations from the raven's realm.

The touch of Marcellus's hand on her arm swept her out of the grim reflection she was losing her mind to the raven. He asked, "You speak Latin, correct?"

She nodded demurely.

"Good. I know I should not ask you, a noble princess, but I couldn't find any servants to help me," Marcellus stammered, appearing uneasy. "Would you help me find a candle … a lamp, a torch … anything to light my room?"

Still woozy, Catrin asked him to repeat his question.

Marcellus spoke slowly. "Please help me … find candle … light my room." He flapped his hands around his eyes like a moth.

Catrin grinned at his funny hand gestures. "Oh, light."

"Yes, that is right." Marcellus's blue eyes brightened to almost a violet color. "I need a candle. A lamp or torch would work."

Just then, the raven poked its head through a window, flopped down on the wood-plank floor, and shrieked. Marcellus slammed back against the stone wall and cursed. His reaction to the raven amused Catrin. She impulsively grasped his hand and led him down the hallway, the raven waddling behind them.

Marcellus gaped at the raven. "What is with that thing?"

"It is my animal guide that protects me," Catrin said, opening the outside door for the raven to fly through.

Marcellus gave Catrin a puzzled look, then walked through the doorway and looked all around. "Is there a candle out here?"

Trying to contain a nervous giggle, Catrin motioned him toward an alley that looked upon open horse stalls at the side of the royal residence. A black stallion poked its head over a rail and snickered at Marcellus. He chuckled and patted its neck. "This looks like one of the Spanish horses that my family breeds for chariot racing."

"You drive chariots?" Catrin asked excitedly, surmising Marcellus was a warrior trained for combat.

Marcellus smiled. "No, we have drivers for that. I did help train horses when I lived my boyhood at our villa in Gaul. It has almost been six years since I lived there. I still ride, though."

Catrin's cheeks warmed as he stepped closer. Grinning, she said, "Perhaps we could ride together tomorrow. You can teach me some of your words and tell me why you are here."

"I would like that." Marcellus glanced down the narrow pathway between the stalls and the dwelling. "Are the king's guards quartered here?"

"Only the stablemen sleep here."

Marcellus drew even closer to Catrin and lifted one of the thin braids out of her loose hair. Heart racing, she felt hot blood rush into her face when he carefully placed the braid on her shoulder. His touch made her stomach skitter, and so did his piercing stare.

"You look different tonight," he said, feasting his eyes on her face. "You are beautiful with your hair down. Tomorrow on our ride, I would like to learn more about you."

"Uhh...." Catrin panicked when Marcellus leaned closer, the heat of his lips descending on hers. *Oh sweet Mother Goddess, think!* She jerked her head toward the sound of approaching footsteps. At the alley's entrance, she saw two men carrying a spitted and roasted boar with an apple crammed in its mouth. Her face felt on fire when she looked at Marcellus and announced, "Time to eat!"

He gave her a mischievous grin and reached for her hand. "I can hardly wait—"

A door slam startled both of them out of the moment.

Belinus was striding toward them with a knife in hand and yelling in Celtic, "Catrin, what are you doing with that Roman?"

Placing hands on hips, Catrin roared back, "Who are you to question me after your reckless antics with my sister? Put that weapon away!"

"I bolted the door to that Roman's room. You must have let him out."

"No, he let himself out."

"Not likely. When I checked on him, he was gone and so were you. Then the gods piss on me. I bumped into the king in the hallway. He almost tore my head off!"

Catrin smirked. "Did he catch you with Mor?"

Belinus tilted his head to look at the sky. "No … thank the gods. The king would have me flogged and dismissed for leaving my guard." He looked at Catrin again. "Your father demanded to know where the Roman was. Then he ordered me to find you. He wants you in his private chambers now!"

The unexpected chuckle from Marcellus distracted Catrin. He seemed entertained by their boisterous Celtic ranting. Now infuriated at Belinus for ordering her around like a naughty child in front of this engaging foreigner, she said, "Tell my father that I will join him shortly."

"No, you are coming with me," Belinus demanded, taking a hold of her arm. "Let someone else show this pompous cock where to roost."

At that moment, Catrin only wanted to stay with Marcellus. Besides, she reasoned, it was more important to gain his trust, so he would more willingly answer her questions. She ordered Belinus, "Deliver this message to the king. I am making our Roman guest comfortable. I'll speak to him after I am done."

Belinus blocked Catrin. "His wrath will fall on me for not controlling his defiant daughter."

Catrin softened her voice, trying another tactic. "Please do what I say. I will make sure my father understands your predicament of watching me."

Belinus rolled his eyes and scrunched his face in exasperation. Catrin smiled; she knew he would acquiesce. Shaking his head, he turned and strode toward the back of the dwelling.

Catrin smiled sweetly at Marcellus. "Now, I take you to feast."

He returned her smile with a broad grin. "I would enjoy that, thank you."

Taking Catrin's hand, Marcellus interlaced his fingers with hers, a magical moment as if their hands became one. Drawn to his deep-set eyes, she felt giddy every time he smiled at her as they ambled down the alley.

Then, at the sound of loud hammering from a weapons forger, she felt his hand flinch. His eyes shifted to armed warriors at the end of the alley. When they walked to the entrance of the reception hall, she noticed Marcellus warily watching two warriors wearing hostile glares. She touched his hand reassuringly. "Let us go inside and eat. We can talk awhile in there. Then I must speak with Father."

Inside the stone-walled Great Hall, tables were set with platters of roasted boar, bread, and boiled leeks. Most of the guests were the king's champions, some of them maidens who had delayed marriage to train and fight as soldiers. A group of warriors sitting at one table scowled at Marcellus as they gnawed on their supper and drank dark ale. She wisely led Marcellus to another table where they sat on a wood bench. Across from them were Cynwrig, a skilled axe man, and his red-haired wife. In the past, the bare-chested warrior with spiked, lime-bleached hair had been celebrated for hacking off an enemy's head with one swipe of his battle-ax. He then was celebrated as the Red Executioner. His bride tamed him, though. He always gave her a bouquet of wild flowers before the morning meal. Even so, no man in the village would challenge Cynwrig who relished being a husband and farmer. At feasts, he always seated himself at the center of the high table—a dare for any warrior to challenge him.

In Celtic, Catrin introduced Cynwrig to Marcellus. "This is our Roman guest, Marcellus."

Cynwrig grunted, "Does he know our tongue?"

"No."

"So what do you want me to do? I cannot speak his."

"Just give him a friendly smile," Catrin suggested.

Cynwrig gave Marcellus a haughty smile and turned to Catrin. "I can do that, but some warriors here want me to contest his manhood."

"Contest?"

"Yes. With axes."

Catrin questioned leaving Marcellus alone. Competitive games sometimes turned deadly in the drunken revelry. She said, "Don't do anything until I return."

Cynwrig nodded. Noticing his wicked-looking smirk, Catrin nervously poured some wine from an amphora into a goblet for Marcellus. His fingers touched her hand as he took the stem. Seeing a kindred soul hiding behind his eyes, she felt herself floating into him until, suddenly, the goblet slipped out of their hands. Wine splashed all over him.

Flustered, she swiped at the red liquid. "Sorry, sorry…clumsy hands."

He clasped her hand. "I can do that."

When Catrin heard a man clear his throat from behind her, she pulled her hand away. Then a strong grip on her shoulder shook her.

"Maiden, your father wants you to join him in his chamber now!" Belinus said sharply. "He ordered me to watch the Roman. I warn you. Do not defy the king again."

Rising quickly, Catrin glanced at Marcellus. "I will be back. Eat. Drink. Enjoy."

Marcellus gave her a worried frown. "How long will you be gone?"

"Not long," Catrin quickly replied. "Belinus will stay with you. He can translate what Cynwrig and his wife says."

Marcellus gawked at Belinus as Catrin mouthed to Cynwrig. *Give Marcellus some meat.*

As instructed, Cynwrig plopped some boar meat on a terra cotta platter, shoved it in front of Marcellus, and grunted, "Eat."

Marcellus stared at the platter for a moment "What does that Cynrectum want me to do with this?"

"Cynwrig," Catrin corrected. "Eat. If you drink with him, you become good friends."

Marcellus looked at Cynwrig. "Does he know that?"

"Of course, he does," Catrin reassured.

Marcellus gave an uneasy smile.

Somewhat assured that Marcellus was in safe hands with Belinus and Cynwrig, she said good-bye and left to join her father.

14

DEADLY WARRIOR GAMES

Belinus stared at Marcellus like a crazed boar and snorted, "I accept your challenge. We will then see who the better warrior is."

Marcellus tensely watched the Celtic barbarians feast on roasted boar, the juices dripping down their chins. The boisterous men readily helped themselves to wine and ale, the aroma so thick he could get drunk off the fumes. He would make a toast to these savages, if only he knew how to speak their guttural language. He wondered what was taking Catrin so long. At least, he could have an amiable chat with her. Now he questioned his sanity for volunteering to be a hostage, imprisoned in the musty royal suites guarded by a one-eyed cat and a foreboding raven.

The warrior called Cynwrig said very little and spoke only Celtic, but his tattooed lightning bolts and demeanor thundered his ferocity. Not wanting to appear unfriendly, Marcellus raised his wine-filled goblet to him. "*Gaudete omnes.*"

Cynwrig grunted and raised his brass goblet in salute. Marcellus acknowledged him with a nervous smile. Then his eyes turned to a group of warriors moving to his table. Each one greeted him with a snarl, their bodies covered with a menagerie of tattooed monsters and animals. Looking more closely, he noticed several of the men had shaved their chests. He had to admit that was, at least, one admirable Roman trait. That was where the similarity ended between Britons and Romans.

Except for the king and his commander, the men had long lime-bleached hair and unruly mustaches shaped like tusks. If it were not for the king's fair skin and straw-colored hair, he would pass as a Roman. Marcellus was surprised to learn that his father had known King Amren as a young man being educated in the Roman culture. Though the king did not appear to accept the Roman patriarchal view toward females, Marcellus could not understand why the Roman emperor and the Senate were so disgruntled with their client king.

Looking around the table at the drunken warriors teetering on their seats, guffawing, Marcellus resigned himself to indulge in their barbarian celebration. The tribune's words "show no fear" emboldened him as he fingered the raven figurines curiously gawking at him from the cup's handles. He gulped down his wine and poured some more from a flagon with a bronze duck on the spout that appeared to be paddling in the red liquid.

"*Nunc est bibendum*," he cried out. "To Bacchus."

Cynwrig and the other warriors grunted and raised their goblets for another toast.

After awhile, Marcellus began losing track of how many "sloblets" of wine and flasks of ale he had washed down since Catrin had left. The sweet scent of honey mead would have intoxicated his nostrils if it were not for the stench of sweat clinging on the men's bare chests pressing against him. The sunny warrior, Belinus, now next to him, refused to speak Latin. Instead, he set a bone-handled dagger on the table and garbled some fierce-sounding Celtic words. Eyeing the weapon, Marcellus rubbed his throat that still throbbed from the thin cut that Belinus graced him with at their first encounter. Every time the wild savage pounded his goblet on the table after each swig, he snorted maliciously, making Marcellus flinch. He again recalled the tribune's advice that to gain these warriors' respect, you must not show them any weakness. Hence, the best way he could demonstrate this was to join in their drunkenness and games. That should not be any problem, he figured, except the Britons drank their wine straight, unlike Romans who diluted it. There had to be something more in the mead and wine that made him feel as if he was Mars. Praise Bacchus for whatever that was. The foreign revelers almost seemed like old friends at one of his drink fests in Rome, except for the weapons' glints winking at him.

Across the table, Cynwrig was hungrily nibbling at the neck of his red-headed wench. She moaned with delight as she drank in Marcellus with her chestnut-brown eyes. Another table slam from Belinus made Marcellus jump off his seat.

At last Belinus spoke familiarly. "Cynwrig challenges you to an axe fight."

Marcellus gawked at Belinus. "Cynwrig? You mean the warrior across the table?"

Belinus answered with a sneer. "We call him the Red Executioner."

"What about you?" Marcellus asked brashly. "Are you man enough to face me when I have a weapon in hand—unlike today, when you put a blade to my throat like a coward when I was unarmed?"

Belinus stared at Marcellus like a crazed boar and snorted, "I accept your challenge. We will then see who the better warrior is."

Marcellus inwardly groaned. *The gods curse me! Now what?* He knew the ways of a gladius, that short sword used for slashing; he had even used a pilum, the heavy javelin preferred by many soldiers, but a battle-ax? A crude weapon used by savages?

Why not? Let me show these painted men what Roman men are made of.

Marcellus raised his goblet. "Let's do it!"

Then he paused, reconsidering. *Is this to the death? Am I a fool for their sport?*

Belinus slapped Marcellus on the back. "An enemy's skull waits outside for your pleasure."

Steadying himself by gripping the table's edge, Marcellus staggered to his feet. He recklessly shouted, "See if you are man enough to take my skull."

With Belinus leading the way, Marcellus stumbled through the doorway into the biting mist. A Bacchanals' mob had gathered around a domed, thatched-roof house. Against the reed façade was a spiked skull, its jaws locked in horror. The frenzied warriors cheered Cynwrig as he swaggered through their midst like a monolithic rock parting them as waves.

In Latin, Belinus blustered contemptuously, "Before Cynwrig competes with this Roman dog, I want a piece of him to hang on my wall!"

Marcellus looked around and muttered, "That must be me." Staggering, he tried to focus on the long-handled blade of the axe, figuring he could copy Belinus's moves. He watched the sun-tattooed warrior plant a leg, swing the axe, and snap his wrist. The blade flew into the skull, shattering an eye socket.

Several boisterous men shoved up against Marcellus, taunting him savagely. He tried to reassure himself, *They must be cheering me on.* Looking all around, he soon thought otherwise.

The sun-tattooed Belinus bellowed a war cry and handed Marcellus another axe suitable for the hands of a child. Realizing his toga was inappropriate attire for axe-throwing, Marcellus unraveled the unwieldy fabric and handed it to Belinus.

"Here, make yourself useful."

Marcellus then wiped the warm sweat off his face with his arm. He spun the heavy handle, leaned back, and swung it forward. The axe handle crashed into an assisting warrior's groin, sending the other warriors into spasms of laughter.

Raising a finger in drunken glee, Marcellus shouted, "Score one for Marcellus!"

Cynwrig pounded Marcellus so hard on the back that his feet slipped on the muddy ground, releasing a faint smell of dung. The Red Executioner offered him a horn-full of mead. Gulping it down, Marcellus ignored the sickening rumble in his belly and finished the brew off. He belched and moaned, "Ahhh, sweet nectar of Bacchus."

Cynwrig, a full head taller than Marcellus, glowed fiercely in the firelight. Marcellus recoiled from the specter of tattooed bolts flashing down the warrior's chest. He knew by the size of Cynwrig's battle-axe, the blade could slice him in half. Puzzled that Cynwrig was offering him a skull, Marcellus turned to Belinus.

A grin flashed across Belinus's face. He pointed to a nearby open stall. "The Red Executioner wants to knock the skull off your head."

Marcellus said with a brash bravado, "If I do this, then I challenge you to do the same. This time, it will be a weapon of my choice to bash that skull out of your head."

Belinus glowered. "Do you think me stupid?"

"No, I believe you a coward."

Belinus's face scrunched and contorted like an angry boar. Marcellus smiled, then staggered to an open stall and balanced the skull's jaw bone on his forehead. The flaming torches whirled around him as the blurred axe flew at his head. In an eye's blink, the blade smashed the skull into the thatched structure. With the weight lifted, Marcellus patted the top of his head and looked at his hand for any sign of blood.

Laughing hard, Cynwrig swaggered to Marcellus and lifted his arm as if they were both victors. The Red Executioner shouted, "*Argom!*"

The wasted warriors raised their brew-filled horns in toast. "*Argom!*"

Taking another horn filled with foaming ale from another warrior's hand, Marcellus forced the gut-wrenching ale down and yelled, "*Argom!*" He could have been calling himself an idiot for all he knew, but with the strong alcohol stomping with delight in his brain, he no longer cared.

The rest of the night became a blur of flaming torches as he stumbled through the boisterous celebrants, determined to find Belinus for one last bout. All around him, warriors were competing in an assortment of contests: sword-thrashing combats, bone-crunching fist fights, and spear-thrusting matches. Finally finding Belinus, Marcellus balled his hand into an iron fist. He screamed, "You cock-sucking barbarian," then punched Belinus in the jaw with such force, the warrior crashed on the ground, his legs spread-eagle.

Before Marcellus could land another punch, Cynwrig cranked both his arms back and restrained him as King Amren, mounted on a chestnut gelding, approached them. On foot behind the king were Queen Rhiannon and their three daughters.

With Cynwrig's tight grip, Marcellus settled down and observed the king handing the sword's jewel-studded hilt to the queen. She raised it up for her people to see, a clear demonstration that she was now in command.

Eyes ablaze from the bonfires, King Amren reined his horse near Marcellus and told him in a commanding voice, "Marcellus Antonius, you are my guest. As a demonstration of my good faith, I have asked my people to treat you well. While I am gone, Queen Rhiannon will rule in my stead and see to your reasonable requests. My youngest, Catrin, will escort you wherever you go. Make no mistake! Make no attempt to escape. Don't even think about overpowering my daughter. She is one of our best warriors."

Marcellus nodded and warily stared at Catrin. She was donned in leather chest armor with plaid breeches, and a sword hung down her back. Her mien was steel-edged, her hair fiery red from the flames of the torches. Earlier, she displayed the sweetness of an innocent girl in her tight-fitting dress and golden hair cascading over her shoulders. He had even caught her biting her lips a couple of times. Yet now, she held her head with confidence and did not look at him. The only person who had shown him kindness was now distant.

Being among these strangely painted people suddenly overwhelmed him. The mixture of wine, ale, and who knows what else sloshing in his stomach, was rendering memories of his puking on the sea voyage. With a moment of lucidity, he questioned himself for getting so drunk and almost losing his head. If he was to carry out his father's mandate, he couldn't make such idiotic moves as challenging these warriors. He resolved to be more cautious during his stay as hostage.

Belinus then gripped Marcellus's arm and said with contempt, "Roman, I have been ordered to take you to your quarters."

The warrior's acrid disposition added to Marcellus's nauseated misery as they walked to the back of the royal residence. When they entered the torch lit corridor, the one-eyed striped cat, cowering in a dark corner, greeted them with a bone-chilling hiss.

Belinus then shoved Marcellus into the chamber and bolted the door, leaving him in total darkness. Trying to orient himself to the set-up of the room, Marcellus crawled on the cold, splintered floor. He bumped his head into a stone wall a couple times before touching a soft pelt on a bed. As he lay down, his head felt as if it were ready to spin off his neck.

Finally settling into the softness of the straw-mattress bed, he snuggled under the pelt to get warm. From the other room, he heard Belinus speaking to two women, one he recognized as Catrin. Soon after, the door opened and shut, and footsteps faded down the outside corridor.

With the night's silence finally sinking in, Marcellus groaned from the wine clashing with the ale in his stomach.

15

NIGHT TIME ANTICS

"Take off your clothes," she demanded, trying to pull herself together. "You will sleep here until daybreak. Tomorrow morning, I will fetch you some clean clothes."

Alone in Mor's candlelit bedchamber, Catrin shifted restlessly under her blankets. Not having to share the bed with her sister, she thought slumber would come easy with Mor gone most of the night with Belinus. Yet an ominous fire lingered inside her and foreboding thoughts crackled through her mind about what her father had said at the family meeting during the festivities. When he announced that Mor must be prepared to wed Cunobelin's son after he renegotiated a matrimonial agreement, she wilted like a flower denied water. The burden of keeping Mor's secret about Belinus weighed heavily on Catrin's conscious. If Cunobelin found out, it could unravel the tenuous negotiations for peace between the powerful tribal kingdoms.

More troubling, her father instructed her on ways she could beguile Marcellus into revealing Roman's schemes for their kingdom. Her stomach tossed with conflicting emotions about the striking Roman. How could she carry out her father's directive when this young man made her heart race every time he gazed at her?

A loud moan from the next room disrupted Catrin's thoughts. Retching noises were followed by a loud bang on the wall and a thud. Alarmed, she lurched out of bed and hurriedly wrapped a shawl around her shoulders. She peeked out the door and confirmed the corridor was empty, the only movement from wavering torch flames. Then she heard loud gagging. A frosty breeze swirled around her, and she knew Marcellus was reaching out to her for help. She glanced up and down the hall again for guards. Seeing none, she scurried out of her room and found the door to the other chamber bolted.

An agonized moan from the room struck panic into Catrin's racing heart that Marcellus was deathly ill. She struggled to draw the bolt back, her fingers stiff like ice as they slipped around the metal rod. She tightened her grip and yanked it harder and harder until the bolt clicked and the door opened. The rancid odor of vinegary wine assailed her nostrils when she looked into the chamber's darkness. To see more clearly, she grabbed a torch from the corridor's sconce to illuminate the room. She found Marcellus leaning over his knees on the floor, his white tunic besmeared with purplish-brown mush. A tinge of panic waved through her as she knelt beside him and wiped cold beads of sweat from his pallid forehead.

She said urgently, "Let me get you out of here and clean you in the next room."

Marcellus nodded weakly.

She wrapped his arm over her shoulders and they lumbered into Mor's bedchamber where she helped him lie down on the bed. The sickly odor permeating the room reinforced her need to clean him. She rinsed a cloth in the ceramic washbowl, but the thought of removing his clothes and seeing him naked gave her pause. What if Mor and Belinus returned early and caught them together? Would they tell the queen?

Catrin shook off the uneasiness; she could use Mor's liaison with Belinus as an inducement to keep her sister's mouth sealed. Besides, the queen was well aware of her role to glean information from Marcellus. With wet cloth in hand, she stepped over to Marcellus and grunted as she struggled to pull the tunic up his torso. The sudden grip of his hand startled her.

"What are you doing?" he asked sharply.

Warm blood rushed into her face and her voice shook when she answered, "Taking off your clothes."

Marcellus's eyes widened with dismay. "To do what?"

Catrin bit her lower lip. "Wash you."

"I can do it," he said, his fingers intertwining hers to coax the washcloth out of her hand.

Not letting go of the wet cloth, she stared at the reflection of the candle flame in his blue eyes. He finally yanked the wet cloth from her grasp, then staggered over to a bowl to rinse his face. Beaded water glistened on his olive skin as he dried himself with a towel. When he turned and his lips parted slightly, Catrin's heart almost stopped when she imagined him holding her face between his hands as he pressed his luscious, thick lips on hers—the kiss so hard, it engulfed her body and soul. Feathery tingles fluttered in her stomach as he slowly approached her. She shyly looked down, her face in hot bloom. When she felt his hand on hers, she swallowed hard, anticipating her first kiss. Heart racing, she lifted her eyes and met his piercing gaze.

He smiled and said softly, "Is it possible to get some clean clothes?"

The unrequited moment sunk into Catrin's belly like a glob of tar in water. Abashed, she muttered, "What? Tonight?"

Marcellus sniffed at his underarms. "I don't know how much longer I can bear to wear these stinking garments."

Rattled by her dashed expectations, Catrin muddled over her options. She could offer Marcellus her trousers, but they were too small. Her mother's fury would surely ignite if she asked for the king's breeches. The best choice was for him to sleep off his stupor. She bit her lower lip, hard.

"Take off your clothes," she demanded, trying to pull herself together. "You will sleep here until daybreak. Tomorrow morning, I will fetch you some clean clothes."

"Are you sure … about this?" Marcellus asked with a surprised look. "I could go back to my room."

"The stench in the other room is not even fit for pigs to sleep in," Catrin snorted. "It is easier I tend you here."

Then to Catrin's dismay, Marcellus unabashedly bared himself, first taking off his wine-stained tunic and undoing his loincloth. The room suddenly sweltered and Catrin could hardly breathe as she beheld the young Roman in all his glorious nakedness. He seemed unaware of her as he staggered to the bed and sat on the edge, lowering his head into folded arms.

Becoming flustered, breathing harder, she turned her back on him and rubbed her temple, trying to regain her wits. *Think. Think. Think. Don't let your emotions rule your head. He is built just like any other man.*

Catrin shifted her eyes to the soiled garments on the floor and gingerly picked them up. She dashed into the other bedchamber that still reeked of sour wine. Pinching her nose with one hand, she dropped the stinking clothes on the floor with the others. When she returned to Mor's bedchamber, she found Marcellus sprawled on the bed, openly displaying his manly attributes. He appeared asleep, his chest slowly rising and lowering. With his eyes closed, he appeared as harmless as a little boy. The temptation to give him a closer look overrode her father's warning to beware of him.

Marcellus was more slender than most warriors from her village, but he nonetheless had broad shoulders and a muscular torso that tapered into an abdomen with a slight pouch. She quietly giggled. A line of dark hair wisped from his belly to his groin. Slowly moving her eyes over him, she noticed his legs were toned and bowed like hers. When she looked at his neck, she noticed what appeared to be an amulet around his neck. Curious, she lifted the marble figurine of a nude man armed with bow and arrow. She wondered if this was the sun god the Romans called Apollo. She recalled a Greek merchant's tale about Apollo asking the northern people to hide his arrow in a winged temple. As a little girl, she had traveled east to what she believed was Apollo's temple. The circular structure was built of massive stone columns supported with flat-rocked beams. Perhaps, the Apollo amulet protected Marcellus from evil spirits. Setting the figurine on his chest, she caught a waft of sour odor and noticed some residual wine stains on him.

She retrieved a linen cloth and poured some lavender-scented oil on it. Sitting on the bed's edge, she gently wiped his forehead with the sweetly-fragranced cloth, but the sudden movement of his eyelids opening startled her.

She gasped and jerked up.

He gazed blankly at the ceiling and did not blink when she waved a hand over him. Presuming he was still in a wine-induced stupor, she resumed cleaning his neck, chest, and abdomen. When she reached his groin, her hand shook as she rubbed the remaining residue away. The only remaining task was to fragrance his skin with more lavender oil.

She covered his hips and legs with a fox-tail pelt to warm his cold skin, then dripped some oil on his torso and massaged the viscous fluid into his skin. The repetitive motion of her fingers moving over his chest mesmerized her. She could feel his strong heartbeats drum into her hands. In her mind's eye, she was again dancing around him and capturing his heat, hot sweat beading on her forehead as she felt herself floating over his sexual fire.

Then a strong grip on her wrist pulled Catrin out of her muse, and she found Marcellus gaping at her with bewilderment.

"What are you doing?"

"I ... I was ... putting oil on you," she stammered.

"It felt much more than that," he said, narrowing an eye. "Are you planning to sleep with me tonight?"

Catrin could almost feel his eyes caressing her breasts. Though she ached with desire, the gigantic leap into a sexual encounter was not where she was ready to venture. "Th ... that is not a good idea."

"Then where will you sleep?"

Catrin jumped to her feet. "On the floor."

Marcellus chuckled and sat up. "That does not seem fair that I take your bed while you sleep on the hard floor."

"This is not my bed."

"Whose bed is this?"

"My sister, Mor, but she and Belinus will not return until morning."

Marcellus cocked an eyebrow. "Why is she with him? I thought she was betrothed to Cunobelin's son."

Catrin bit her lip, chastising herself for letting the secret out. She said sharply, "We should not talk about this."

"All right. Let us then … discuss sleeping arrangements." Marcellus curled his lips into a mischievous smile. "Why don't you take half the bed while I sleep on the other half?"

Catrin wrestled with the suggestion. "Um … um … I should not sleep with you."

"And if Mor were here, you would be sleeping with her, right?"

Catrin shrugged. "I suppose so."

"Think of it this way," Marcellus said, patting the straw mattress with an eager hand, "we must share this bed because no others are available."

Catrin considered his argument for a moment. It did seem reasonable. The morning chill made her shiver. Still, she could not quite convince herself to be in bed with the young Roman who moments earlier she had wanted to kiss. She tore her eyes away.

After what seemed like an interminable period of awkward silence, Marcellus said, "Feel my arms. I have flesh bumps. Unless I get warm, I won't be able to sleep."

Catrin peeked at him. His skin did look bluer. "I can put a blanket on you."

Marcellus shot her a playful grin. "That will help. But, I have a better idea, you can lie on top of the blanket if that would ease your mind about sleeping with me. Then you can snuggle up to me and get me warm. I promise not to do anything, except sleep."

Catrin stared at the bleak, uninviting dark oak floor. Why should she sleep there? The night's events had been out of her control. How could she have known that strong drink would make Marcellus so sick? She tried to reassure herself.

Commoners always invite overnight guests into their family beds.

Pursing her lips, she nodded reluctantly. "Agreed, only if I sleep on top of the covers and you face the other way."

The color on Marcellus's high-boned cheeks turned annoyingly rosier. "Agreed, hop right on."

Catrin retrieved a woolen blanket from a corner shelf and covered Marcellus from neck to toe. The sight of his mouth breaking into an eager grin unnerved her. She waved him to turn over. He wrapped the blanket around his shoulders and rolled over. She draped a shawl around her shoulders, crawled into bed, and turned her back against his.

For several moments, Marcellus bumped against Catrin as he shifted restlessly. After awhile, he tapped her on the shoulders. "I'm still cold. Would you get a little closer?"

Catrin turned over and gave him an icy scowl. "How can that help?"

Marcellus gave an impish grin. "There is something special about a woman's warmth. It is like a mother tucking a child into bed at night."

"I am not your mother," Catrin snapped.

"No, but I still long for your womanly touch."

Exasperated, Catrin sighed. "All right, turn over."

After Marcellus rolled to his side, she pressed her chest against his back. Reticent about the intimacy, she stiffened her arms. "Is that better?"

"Yes, much better," Marcellus said. "Thank you for showing me so much kindness tonight."

Swelling emotion lumped in Catrin's throat. His genuine gratitude warmed her heart. As his breathing slowed, she felt more at ease and resituated herself, wrapping an arm around his waist and molding herself into the curve of his back. Pillowing her head against his shoulders, she had never felt this close to another human as she did with him. She inhaled the lavender scent and lightly stroked his soft hair. Relaxing, she drifted into a deep sleep and dreamt they were lovers in a past life.

A hard shake on her shoulders jarred Catrin out of her slumber. Opening her eyes, she was shocked to find her mother's eyes soaring above her.

"What is going on here?"

Catrin quickly pushed herself up. "We are sleeping. Marcellus is sick. I brought him here … to tend him."

Her mother shot a scathing frown. "Tending him in bed? Where is Mor?"

Catrin hopped from the bed to her feet. "I don't know."

The queen's eyes hardened. "Is she off with Belinus?"

"Oh …" Catrin could feel her heartbeats pounding in her neck. Her eyes flitted to Marcellus, who was staggering to his feet. He mumbled, "Sorry for the trouble. Catrin was only trying to help. Just show me where I can sleep off the wine."

The queen regarded Marcellus for a moment, then turned to the gray-haired servant beside her. "Take our guest to the room next to mine. The cold floor will make a nice companion for him. Tell Belinus to get over here now! As for Mor, she can sleep in my chambers."

The servant humbly asked, "Where is Mor?"

The queen roared, "She is with Belinus! And keep your mouth shut at what you find."

The servant bowed. "Yes, Your Highness."

Catrin's stomach twisted so tight, she felt nauseated when she watched Marcellus clumsily wrap the blanket around his waist, drag himself out of bed, and follow the servant down the hall. After all his efforts to get her into bed, he would now be the one sleeping on the floor. Turning to her mother, Catrin began shivering under the queen's cold stare.

"As for you, young maiden, we will speak at breakfast!"

16

BREAKFAST INTERROGATION

The conversation's turn made Marcellus gag. Was the queen's intent to glean more information about his family's political connections to Tiberius?

Without a stitch of clothing on, Marcellus could not keep warm on the hard cold floor no matter how tightly he wrapped the wool blanket around him. On the other side of the thin wall that divided the royal bedchamber from his locked quarters was Queen Rhiannon. He heard her speak harshly in Celtic to a man and woman he believed were Belinus and Mor. From the tone of her voice, he surmised she was scolding them for their reckless affair. He knew this could jeopardize the nuptial pact being negotiated for Mor to wed Cunobelin's son. Perhaps his father could use this information as leverage against Amren to demand more tribute in exchange for keeping the affair secret from Cunobelin. No wonder the queen's attention had been diverted from him after she caught him in bed with Catrin. Although she had not said a word to him after finding them together, her eyes burned with fury.

With the pitched fervor of the queen's voice, Marcellus's head felt as if a mallet was hammering his brain. Becoming nauseated again, he curled into a ball and moaned, regretting the copious amount of ale and wine he had drunk. The queen must be delighting in his misery by forcing him to wait before she confronted him about sleeping with Catrin. Perhaps he could use the secret tidbit about Mor's affair to his advantage if the queen's hostility spilled over to him.

The voices on the other side of the curtain suddenly quieted when someone left the room. Nonetheless, powerful men continued arguing in Marcellus's head about his next move with Catrin. On one side was his father asserting his authority as the paterfamilias. *Get whatever information you can. If that means bedding Catrin, do it! But don't get caught.*

On the other side was King Amren, astride a steed and extending his sword. *Make no mistake! Don't even think about overpowering Catrin. She is one of our best warriors.*

Even Tribune Decimus Flavius joined in the lively argument. *Apollo will bring his wrath down on you for defiling Catrin.*

The loud arguments finally subsided when Marcellus inhaled a waft of sweet lavender. In his mind's eye, the image of Catrin massaging scented oil into his skin aroused him. The curves underneath her thin undergarments brought a prurient smile to his face. With his sexual experience, he knew by the way she blushed every time he gazed at her that he could have easily taken advantage of the situation. Yet, after she wrapped her arm around him as they fell asleep, he felt a special connection to this kind woman who had only showed him friendship. It was as if they had known each other in another lifetime, as she had said, and rediscovered each other.

The sexual drought on this trip must have finally gotten to him. Rubbing his eyes to ease his headache, he muttered, "How did I get myself into this predicament? Apollo, get Catrin out of my mind and let me sleep."

Fatigue and wine finally conquered him and he floated into deep slumber.

The next morning, Marcellus was roughly awakened by Belinus. His tavern opponent's face had been sorrowfully ravaged by the storms of alcohol from the feast and the queen's late night rebuke. The red veins spidering around the warrior's puffed green eyes seemed a reflection of Marcellus in his recent battle with the grape. Marcellus's spirits lifted when Belinus tossed him fresh garments. As Belinus watched, Marcellus inspected the plaid trousers and gray tunic for any defects. Seeing none, he pulled on the oversized garments. The breeches hung low on his hips and the shirt stretched to his knees.

"Follow me," Belinus grunted. "The queen wants to see you in her chambers, now!"

Armed with the knowledge of this warrior's affair with Mor, Marcellus asked with an undertone of sarcasm, "Did you have a pleasant romp with Mor?"

Belinus instantly slammed Marcellus against the jagged stone wall. "Shut your mouth, Roman, if you want to keep your head!"

With pain shooting through his back, Marcellus thought it wise to contain his tongue, at least for the moment. He apprehensively followed Belinus through a corridor to the chamber where Queen Rhiannon and Catrin were eating porridge at a wooden table. Rhiannon motioned for Marcellus to sit by Catrin, who was dressed in brown leather breeches and a burgundy-and-rose plaid shirt. She looked tired and lifeless. Her eyes seemed pasty as she stared at her bowl of porridge. It was no wonder after last night.

Marcellus noticed the queen's icy stare at Belinus as he left the chamber. Sitting down, Marcellus jabbed at the unappetizing glob of porridge with a crude spoon as he anticipated hard questioning.

Rhiannon politely asked, "Did you sleep well?"

Glancing up, Marcellus was surprised to see the queen smiling. He twitched a half smile in return. "At first, I found it difficult to sleep with the loud voices from the other room. It sounded as if you were scolding Mor and Belinus. What could they have done to raise your ire?"

Other than arching an eyebrow, the queen's face remained emotionless. "It was a slight misunderstanding of expectations that has now been resolved." She handed Marcellus a plate of berries. "You must be famished. Eat. Gather your strength."

Unlike Catrin, the queen spoke Latin eloquently without a trace of accent. Wary of her pleasantries, Marcellus swallowed a few bites of porridge and blackberries. His stomach still queasy, he pushed the bowl aside and glanced at Catrin. He wondered what the queen had told her before he joined them for breakfast. As he sipped some mint water from a brass goblet, the queen apprised him of the day's activities.

"At all times, Catrin will escort and interpret for you. She will serve as your guide, showing you our village and lands. You may want to wash off last night's festivities in our nearby river. My daughter can show you the place."

Marcellus gave a bewildered look. After last night's adventures, why would she suggest having her daughter watch him while he bathed? He turned to Catrin for her reaction. Her cheeks were a sunburst of red as the spoon dropped out of her hand.

Rhiannon cleared her throat, regaining Marcellus's attention. "Catrin told me you train chariot horses."

"No, we have special slaves for that," he replied.

"Interesting," Rhiannon tapped the corner of her mouth. "I train my own horses for battle."

"You fight?"

"In my younger days, I did." As the queen sipped some water, Marcellus could feel her eyes probing him. She continued, "Catrin told me my husband's black stallion took a liking to you when she showed you the stables last night."

Marcellus glanced at Catrin and caught her with a sheepish grin. He wondered what else she had told her mother. Turning to the queen again, Marcellus said, "The stallion looks like the Spanish breeds we raise for chariot racing in Gaul."

Rhiannon appeared confused. "But I thought your home was in Rome."

"Now it is," he clarified. "As a boy, I lived in Lugdunum."

"But now you reside in Rome?"

"Yes."

"Do you know the emperor?"

The conversation's turn made Marcellus gag. Was the queen's intent to glean more information about his family's political connections to Tiberius? He again glanced at Catrin who quickly averted her eyes. He wondered if the queen had instructed her to dredge more information out of him when they were alone.

The queen repeated, "Do you know the emperor?"

Marcellus hesitated. "I met him once."

"And your father?"

"As you know, he is the emperor's envoy."

"Does your father speak often with Emperor Tiberius?"

"Not that I am aware."

The queen leaned back in her wooden chair. "In Germania, my husband fought for Tiberius when he was in the Roman auxiliary. Tiberius often told Amren how much he valued the Cantiaci warriors in his army. As reward for fighting with him, he recognized my husband as a client king of Rome."

The queen's revelation disconcerted Marcellus. His father never spoke of Amren's close ties with the emperor, but he knew the tribune had previously met the Cantiaci king when they both fought in Germania.

Marcellus added, "The tribune, Decimus, also fought for Tiberius. He, too, speaks highly of your people's skill with weapons and horses."

Rhiannon reached over and patted Catrin's hand. "You will see we are a peaceful people, loyal to your emperor. I hope you convey this to your father."

Marcellus shifted uncomfortably in his chair. Yesterday, these wild barbarians openly challenged him with their bravado and raucous games with weapons. Yet today, the queen was proffering a softer image. His gut told him not to trust her, to end the conversation. Perhaps later, he could gain more insight from Catrin, who seemed more genuine, about the political rivalry between the tribal kings. He scooted his chair back, stood, and stretched his arms above his head. "If you don't mind, I would like to ride that black stallion."

Rhiannon smiled slyly at her daughter. "Escort Marcellus to the stream where he can bathe. Take a couple of spears for hunting and, of course, for your protection."

"Yes, Mother."

Marcellus gawked at Catrin. *What did your mother mean by that?* He then turned to the queen. "Is there a way I can send a message to my father?"

Rhiannon considered Marcellus for a moment. "That will be quite impossible. The location of his meeting has been kept from me."

"How will I know how the negotiations are proceeding?"

"Hmmm ... good question. The king will likely send word after the meeting ends." Rhiannon abruptly stood and waved her fingers. "Enjoy the ride. I have a council to attend."

17

SEDUCTION

Breathing harder, he pulled her closer and deftly unsheathed the sword at her side and dropped it on the ground.

Uneasy that he could not get a message to his father, Marcellus followed Catrin to the great hall where the tables from the previous night's feast had been replaced with women weaving at looms with long strands of yarn weighed down with flat stones. Their fingers interlaced brightly colored threads at right angles to form the plaid cloth. Walking alongside Catrin between the rows of looms, he asked, "Do you weave?"

"Widows weave for our family. In turn, we protect and feed them," Catrin answered. "I've tried weaving, though, but the threads often unravel on me. It is a skill I have yet to master."

"Oh …" Marcellus opened the heavy front door for Catrin and followed her outside where he continued. "My mother sometimes weaves with other noblewomen, but we primarily use slaves for that."

Catrin stopped and turned to Marcellus. "The gods have a different purpose for me."

The confidence in her voice intrigued Marcellus. He still struggled to understand his role as the youngest in his family while she boldly exclaimed her divine destiny. He asked, "What is that purpose … to be a queen?"

"Something more," Catrin said, squaring her shoulders. "The gods have yet to reveal this to me. I am like a spirit warrior who travels to other worlds. No, not that ..." Catrin lifted her eyes as if searching for another word. "Otherworld."

"Otherworld? You mean the Underworld where the dead go?"

"No, it is a place where souls await to be placed into another body. I was born with a raven spirit. It is possible we met in a previous life when our souls were in different bodies."

Marcellus puzzled over what Catrin meant by meeting in a previous life. He then recalled the tribune's warning that the raven at the sacrificial ritual was a sign that Catrin was a sorceress. Though Marcellus had seldom sought advice from oracles, Decimus often spoke of consulting various priests, particularly those serving Apollo, before making any major decision. He said, "I would like to learn more about this world."

Catrin glanced sideways. "We need to go."

Marcellus became cognizant of two other elderly women gawking at them. He trailed Catrin down the alley beside the royal residence. At the stables, a dirt-smeared stableman in torn trousers greeted them with a broad grin that displayed rotting teeth. As Marcellus took the reins of the black stallion, the steed reared its head, but he quickly calmed it and jumped onto its back.

The stableman helped Catrin fasten a sheathed sword to a leather baldric on her back, then boosted her onto a bay horse and handed her two spears. He said something in Celtic, but she waved him away.

Eyeing Catrin's bone-hilted sword, Marcellus wondered how skilled she was with the weapon. He asked "What did that servant say to you?"

"He asked about your trousers."

"My trousers?"

"What you are wearing. They are his."

"Oh ..." Marcellus looked down at his loose trousers, then kneed the steed and followed Catrin out of the alley.

They threaded through several domed structures to the entrance gate where metalworkers were forging iron. He yelled above the clanking hammers. "Are these your father's weapons makers?"

"Some are," Catrin answered.

Marcellus stopped his horse in front of a roundhouse where he studied a blacksmith hammering away the jagged edge of a red-hot sword blade as a warrior awaited nearby. Another nearby metalworker was pushing on bellows, feeding air into a blast furnace where iron was being smelted. Several swords and spears were leaning against the thatched façade, giving the appearance that additional armaments were being forged in preparation for battle—something of note he should tell his father.

Catrin shouted, "Come on!"

He caught up with her near the entrance gate. They rode through the rampart and descended the hilltop to the farmlands where laborers worked the dark soil. A group of warriors were practicing nearby. He recognized one of the warriors as Cynwrig, the hatchet-thrower from the contest. The Red Executioner's eyes bore into Marcellus, spiking a chill down his spine. Uneasy, Marcellus trailed Catrin onto a patchwork pathway of grass and gravel. Beyond the fields was a meandering river along the forest's edge.

Marcellus shifted his gaze to Catrin's backside. Her multi-braided golden hair bounced off her broad shoulders with each sway of the horse. He could tell she had small hips in her tight-skinned breeches which were more typical of an athlete. In Rome, women with rounded hips that accentuated a small waist had always aroused him, but the prospect of exploring between Catrin's legs excited him even more. He knew it would be reckless to seduce her, particularly after the long night when the queen had caught them in bed together. Even so, Venus must be turning his sound reasoning into unadulterated desire for the exotic princess.

He reined his horse next to Catrin and flashed a big grin. "You look beautiful today. Are you taking me to a special place where you show all young men?"

Catrin smiled demurely and brushed a strand of hair from her eyes. "You might say that. I am taking you to a place my ancestors worship. Here, in early summer, young warriors celebrate Bel's fire ritual to assure fertility and good harvests. You did say you wanted to learn more about my world."

Imagining how lovers might celebrate the fire ritual, Marcellus smiled lewdly. "And who is this Bel?"

"The sun god you call Apollo." Catrin tilted her head sideways, appearing reticent about what she was going to say, but then her eyes lit up. "I dreamt of you last night."

Curiosity piqued, Marcellus asked, "And what did we do in this dream?"

"I saw you as a boy on a majestic black stallion. You galloped down a pathway in a forest where two rivers joined. You looked so happy. The special place I am taking you looks just like the woods in my dream. Is this close to Rome?"

Marcellus stared at Catrin in amazement. "You dreamt of the countryside near my family's villa in Gaul. So is it true. You talk to the gods in your dreams."

"Maybe …" Catrin's voice trailed off as she reined her horse around. She pointed to a towering oak and challenged him to a race.

Marcellus smirked. "Now let us see which one of us is the better rider."

Catrin shot him an arrogant smile.

Marcellus kicked his steed into a gallop. Misty air whipped at his face as he sped toward the woods. Behind him, he could hear the pounding of hoofs. Then suddenly, Catrin bounded past him. He kicked his stallion to run faster. He again caught up with her. They raced head-to-head for a while, but then she surged ahead, reaching breakneck speed. She released a spear that bore into a gigantic oak at the forest's edge.

Astonished by the force of her throw, Marcellus slowed his mount toward the quivering spear while she veered to the left. He dismounted and yanked the weapon's shaft out of the gnarled bark. Few Roman men were as skilled with horses and javelin as Marcellus, but today he had met his match. The lively horse race with Catrin invigorated him and the cloudless sky promised a bright day. He turned and watched Catrin confidently ride toward him. He looked all around to make sure no guards had followed them. The thick woods would obscure his next move with her. He handed the spear to Catrin.

"I've never seen a woman, much less a man, hurl a spear like that. Did you intend this as a warning?"

She chuckled. "My father did order that I guard you."

Marcellus laughed. "Indeed, you have proven your point. I rather you watch me than that brute warrior with the sun tattoo. What is his name, the one with your sister last night?"

"Belinus."

"Ahh … Belinus. I thought for sure he would have slashed my throat if it had not been for your bold action."

Catrin beamed. "Not me, it was Father who stopped him."

"But you made your father pause. And for that, I am grateful." Marcellus held the reins as Catrin dismounted. "Why did you save me—a foreigner?"

Not answering, Catrin tethered her horse's reins to a low-lying oak branch. She appeared an enigmatic goddess standing under the sunrays filtering through the treetops. He drew closer and gazed into her bright turquoise eyes. He said, "You didn't answer me. Why did you save me?"

Catrin averted his gaze. "No one should attack a guest. I would have done that for anyone."

Marcellus clasped Catrin's wrist. "Is that how you view me now—a guest?"

Catrin pulled away. "I meant hostage. I do not understand why you support the Catuvellauni instead of my father. He is ally to Rome.

My father served in the Roman legion and is more Roman than Cunobelin."

Marcellus contained his smirk, now thinking back to the interrogation at breakfast. He was now sure the queen had instructed Catrin to garner more insight about Roman politics from him. He decided to play her game. "Your father is no more Roman than I am a Briton."

Catrin seemed puzzled. "What is Briton? My father is Cantiaci, my mother Regni."

"Do you not think of yourself as Britons, a united people?"

Catrin regarded Marcellus for a moment. "No, we belong to different tribes."

"Is that how you view me, like them?"

"Them?"

"The Catuvellauni ... Cunobelin, Marrock."

Catrin grimaced. "No, you are from a great empire across the sea."

"Yet, you saved me as if I were one of your people."

Appearing flustered, Catrin shook her head. "I saved you because we honor our truces with enemies. My only purpose was to stop a conflict."

"I am not the enemy here," Marcellus said emphatically. "The only reason I am here is to accompany my father to address the emperor's concerns about your brother's claim to the throne."

Catrin's eyes grew big. "Marrock is not my brother! We have the same father, but different mothers."

The venomous hate in her voice spiked Marcellus's interest. He decided to dig deeper. "What did Marrock do to make your father banish him?"

Catrin's jaw tensed. "I do not want to talk about this!"

Now that Marcellus had lifted the lid off Pandora's box—Catrin's family secrets—he probed harder. "Did Marrock challenge your father?"

Not answering, Catrin turned away, but he grabbed her arm to halt her. "Did he harm someone in your family?"

Catrin struggled against his restraint, but he held on tighter.

"Let me go!" she demanded.

He pressed further. "Did Marrock do something to you?"

Catrin froze, her face becoming pallid with horror.

"Did he hurt you?" Marcellus asked more bluntly than he intended. When her eyes began glistening with swelling tears, Marcellus felt like a scoundrel. The vulnerability in her beautiful eyes reached out to him for solace. He raised her chin and said softly, "You never answered me. Is there more you feel about me?"

Catrin's gaze met his. "More?"

Breathing harder, he pulled her closer and deftly unsheathed the sword at her side and dropped it on the ground. When he traced the curvature of her mouth with a forefinger, she closed her eyes and parted lips, inviting him for a taste. He held her face firmly between his hands and whispered, "Sweet Venus, you are so beautiful."

No longer able to resist this radiant goddess, Marcellus pressed his lips on hers. Desire consuming him, he embraced Catrin and lifted her slightly off the ground. With lips locked on hers, he leaned her against a giant oak, holding her arms up against the trunk. For a mere second of mercy, he let go of the kiss, but when she gasped for air, he saw the rapture on her face, further heightening his arousal. He again devoured her with a kiss, nibbling at her lips and coaxing them open for his tongue to thrust through. The wetness of his tongue sliding over hers was driving him crazy, the swaying of her hips in a slow moving dance against him driving him to the precipice. An overpowering delirium took control of him. His heart pounding harder, he was ready to possess Catrin—body and soul.

Or so he thought.

18

JOINING OF SOULS

Conflicting emotions began to whirl inside Catrin—passion, anger, and fear. Her hand shook and she lowered the blade.

Catrin still reeled from the first kiss as Marcellus nibbled at her earlobe. Though she had dreamt of his kiss the previous night, she could never have imagined the throbbing delight of his lips pressed against hers, eliciting pleasurable tingles. Instinctively, she swayed her hips into him and tilted her head sideways, so he could leave a trail of light kisses down her neck.

He then pulled her to the ground with him and pinned her arms down on the grassy tufts. A breath clutched in her throat when she strangely felt herself floating into him. It was as if she was losing control to his thoughts, his sexual desire steering hers. Raw, carnal sensations danced over her body as his fingers and mouth performed their epicurean delight. Yet, the emotions she felt bewildered and frightened her. It was as though she had intruded in his mind—his thoughts, memories, and emotions intermixed with hers.

Then suddenly in her mind's eye, the image of a Roman noblewoman projected on what looked like rippling black fluid. Standing in front of this woman was Marcellus at a younger age. He was naked, posed like a statue with one arm extended forward with the other stiff at his side. The woman, attired in fiery-colored garments, looked like a voyeur as she circled him, her ringed fingers crawling like spider legs over his shoulders, down his chest, and to his groin. She stroked his erection with one hand and the long nails of the other left thin lines of blood on his chest.

Repulsed, Catrin then saw her image appear next to him. She scolded, "Marcellus, what are you doing with that woman?"

He had a shocked look on his face. "How did you get in here?"

A light flashed in Catrin's mind, and she again found herself hot and sweaty in the real world underneath Marcellus. She felt his body tense, and then his heavy weight lifted off her.

A panicked breath hitched in her throat. *What just happened to me?*

Even though she had never kissed a man before, her desire had matched his. Instinctively, she knew how to arouse him. More unsettling, she had dredged out a dark secret from the recesses of his memory, warning her not to take the next step with him.

When her dizziness settling, she focused on Marcellus, sitting next to her. He gazed vacantly in the distance, rejection etched over his face. He sighed and somberly said, "When you slept with me last night, it took all my strength not to touch you. Yet today, I was so taken by you, that…that…" His eyes dropped and he said with a cracked voice, "Something happened I can't explain. It was like… you were in my mind."

Catrin abruptly sat up. "What did you see?"

Marcellus's eyes widened. "You said something … and I knew then, it was not right for us … for me to take your innocence."

Catrin knew then, she had caught a glimpse of his past with an older Roman lover who had deeply affected him. At first she hesitated talking about it, uneasy that she had ventured into his dark memory of a tryst with an older woman. When Marcellus stared at her with anguished confusion, she felt the same confusion for him. How could she withhold that she had merged her thoughts with him?

She couldn't.

Taking a deep breath, she knelt before Marcellus and clasped his hands. "I need to tell you something. You asked if the gods talk to me ..." She swallowed to release the constriction in her throat. "I sometimes have visions of the past ... other lifetimes, the future. But this is the first time that somebody else saw exactly what I did when I had a vision."

Marcellus hardened his stare. "What exactly did you see?"

"An older woman awaits your return back in Rome."

"How do you know this?"

"I could see her image inside your mind."

Marcellus recoiled and bounced to his feet. "Dark gods beneath me! What are you? A sorceress? Did you bewitch me? Cast a spell to make me reveal this?"

Taken aback by his accusation, Catrin said, "Please do not be angry with me. Give me a chance to explain."

Marcellus shot a burning glare. "Explain what, that your father knew exactly what he was doing when he chose you, his ultimate weapon, to pry out my seedy past. I knew, by the way you kissed me, that you weren't a virgin. Tell me, Catrin, am I not right?"

The cruel comment stabbed at Catrin's heart. She tore her eyes away and chastised herself for being a fool for placing so much trust in an enemy and showing her vulnerability. Marcellus was nothing more than a hostage and that was how she should have treated him. His only worth was the information she could pry out of him, as her father mandated. She would not show any weakness to him. She scowled at Marcellus. *Make no mistake, I am in command here.* Her eyes then shifted to the sword on the ground.

She quickly pushed herself up, scooped the weapon into her hand, and extended the blade toward his chest. She growled, "Careful, Roman, what you say or do to me."

Marcellus's mouth flung open. "Gods! Easy, Catrin! You're not planning to use that weapon on me, are you?"

"If need be," she said, pressing the sword tip harder into his chest.

Eyes fixed on Catrin, Marcellus said, "You confuse me. Are you a warrior or a sorceress?"

She gave a bewildered look and momentarily released the tension on the sword. "What?"

"You wield that weapon like a warrior, but you captured my heart with your magic," Marcellus said without any inflection of fear in his voice. "What are you?"

"Neither!"

"Then what?"

Conflicting emotions began to whirl inside Catrin—passion, anger, and fear. Her hand shook and she lowered the blade. The words gushed from her soul. "I am a woman, and what I feel for you is real, not magic. I can sense what you feel, but I cannot control your emotions. What I feel ... is consuming me—"

Sunlight suddenly broke through the overhanging branches and showered Marcellus in golden light. His crystal-blue eyes beckoned her to pierce through his veil of hidden secrets to find the truth. Catrin recalled her mother's words. *You can judge a person through the eyes. If you look deeply enough, you can see into his soul.* She felt a powerful connection to him she could not understand. She perceived he was loyal and trustworthy to those he loved, and could trust him. A passing cloud cloaked the sun and the forest darkened.

Marcellus's eyes filled with wonderment. "Did you see that, too? Did you cast another spell on me?"

A warm glow suffused Catrin's face. "Not a spell ... something spiritual. Last night, I felt safe with you and wanted to know more about you than anyone in my kingdom—your desires, your secrets. Just now, your soul joined mine. I have only experienced this with my raven."

Marcellus chuckled. "Mmm ... I have never heard of love described that way. Quite profound. Yet, I'm not sure if I like competing with a raven for your affection."

Flushed with embarrassment, Catrin said, "No, it is different ... yet similar. It is hard for me to explain how souls join."

Marcellus walked slowly toward her and lowered his hands in a conciliatory gesture. "Would you please give me that sword before we go any further. It is making me nervous."

When he reached for the sword, she relinquished the weapon to him. He sheathed the sword into the scabbard at her side and exhaled an exaggerated sigh of relief. "That is better, though I have to admit it was quite thrilling to have a beautiful warrior pull a sword on me."

Catrin didn't know how to take his comment. "Are you making fun of me?"

"No ... well, yes," Marcellus said with a glint in his eyes and mischievous smile. "I never thought you would draw a sword on me like that. You had me worried, I must admit. You said that you wanted to know me better. Let us start over again and talk. You need to trust me, though, and keep that sword sheathed."

"Yes, I do trust you." She quirked a smile. "I should not, but I do."

Marcellus burst out in a grin. "Good ... now that I know about your abilities as an oracle, I am curious to know what else you know about me by looking into my eyes."

More at ease, Catrin described the images she observed on the surface of his blue eyes. "I see a wild stallion that wants to run free. You must have been born with a horse spirit. That is why working with horses brings you so much joy, and why my father's stallion took a liking to you, yet I sense someone is trying to rein you in and break your spirit."

A lump formed in Marcellus's throat. "That is my father. What did you see in your vision about the noblewoman?"

Catrin pictured the scene in her mind as she described it, "I saw you standing naked in front of a woman dressed in fabric that swirled around her like a flame. You stood like a statue, very stiff and hard. She then slid her hand down you." A warm blush spread across her face when she looked at his groin.

Marcellus winced. "What did this woman look like?"

"She had hooded dark eyes with black hair coiled on her head," Catrin said with disdain. "Her long fingers crawled all over you like a spider spinning its web."

"What meaning did you take from this vision?"

"This woman has a special hold on you. What is her name?"

"Eliana."

A twinge of jealousy struck at Catrin, and she asked bluntly, "Do you love her?"

Marcellus paused. "She is married to a shriveled old man. I give her company—that is all."

"But do you love her?"

"I do not want to talk about her," Marcellus snapped.

"I want to talk about her," Catrin said sharply. "I sense she might harm you. Her husband is powerful. If he finds out about your affair, he could destroy you and your family."

Marcellus's jaw tightened. "What are you planning to do with this information?"

"What will you do with your knowledge about my sister and Belinus?"

"I thought we agreed to trust each other," Marcellus said.

Catrin stepped up to Marcellus and looked him in the eye. "If you trust me, you would tell me about your … woman. I promise not to tell anyone."

Marcellus regarded her for a moment. "Fair enough. If you keep my secret, I promise to keep yours. Still, I don't want to talk about Eliana."

Catrin stubbornly asked again, "Do you love her?"

"Why does it matter to you?"

"I am not sure if I should let you kiss me if you love that woman."

Marcellus grinned. "Are you jealous?"

Catrin stammered. "No … maybe. Yes. I did not like the way she looked at you in the vision. She clawed you like a cat. And …

and …" The fiery glimmer in his eyes distracted her when he leaned closer.

"You have nothing to worry about," he reassured her.

"You must love Eliana if you are still with her," Catrin said, throat constricted with conflicted emotions.

"I would not call it love," Marcellus asserted. "She makes no difference about how I feel about you."

"Yet you fear you will destroy my innocence as Eliana destroyed yours. I want to know why."

Marcellus quieted for a moment, then said in a subdued voice, "I swear you can see into my very soul. Indeed, you must be an oracle. Nothing gets past you. All right, I will tell you. When I moved from Gaul to Rome, I was a lonely gangling boy in the midst of refinery and snobbery of the upper echelon. I felt isolated until my mother introduced me to Eliana when I was fifteen, about your age. Eliana showered me with compliments and invited me to her villa with the promise of companionship. It turned into something much darker …"

He swallowed hard and gazed at Catrin. "Why do you pull at me so? When I am with you, I am fifteen again and rediscovering the joy of being with a woman for the first time. You are so kind, genuine, yet fearless—a true companion I never had. I don't want you to lose any of those qualities because of me. I'm older and know how to please a woman. That is what Eliana taught me, but she did not teach me about—" Marcellus looked away, swallowing hard. "I've said too much."

Catrin did not understand Eliana's hold on Marcellus, but sensed he had been damaged by the relationship. "Be careful, Marcellus," she warned. "This woman is a venomous snake who could strike you if you ever left her."

Marcellus looked at her with languished eyes. "Please, let us not talk about this anymore. You have forced me to run a gauntlet by sharing my dark secret. It is something that I never want to speak of again."

Catrin impulsively grabbed his hand. "What about us?"

"Us?"

"Can there be more between us than what you had with Eliana," Catrin said, searching his eyes.

"I suppose … that is possible." Marcellus smiled. "We can get to know each other better. You enjoy riding horses, the same as me. Perhaps, we can find some other activities we both like. Do you like to hunt?"

"Yes, I like to hunt." Catrin beamed. "We can be friends, can't we?"

"Yes, when I shared my secret, you showed me how to find my way back."

Though Catrin didn't understand what Marcellus meant, unbridled emotion overcame her and she kissed him.

He pulled back, surprised. "I thought you didn't want to kiss me again."

She tilted her head sideways and smiled. "I want you to kiss me like you did before."

Marcellus pulled her into his arms and gently covered her lips with his. Unlike before, the kiss was gentle and undemanding, but too short. He released the kiss and reached for her hand.

"Let us go find this special place that you wanted to show me."

19

GATEWAY OF SKULLS

At eye level, he found his most precious skull wrapped in white linen. He carefully pulled it out, and unraveled the fabric from the cranial bone.

The meeting to be held with the Roman envoys in two days weighed heavily in Marrock's mind. After his initial meeting with Senator Lucius Antonius, he had been excluded from all mediations among Cunobelin, the Roman envoy, and his father, King Amren. Marrock seethed that his father-in-law, Cunobelin, might concede to Amren's demands that he be denied the Cantiaci kingdom. The throbbing pain from his scar-pitted face robbed him of sleep. The odor of turnips and beets, now boiling in the cauldron over the hearth, made him gag.

Marrock walked to the curtained-off bedchamber at the back of the dome-shaped home. Towering over six feet, he stooped to avoid hitting his head on the low ceiling and quietly admired his wife, Ariene, nursing their youngest one-year-old son. With her back turned, she was the epitome of beauty, her hips shaped like a daffodil bulb. He could wrap his hands around her tiny waist. The shimmer of her silver-blonde hair reminded him of lustrous wolf fur. He bent over to nibble her neck, but when she turned and winced, he knew his grotesque face repulsed her. Though some had said the same about his wife, he found the purplish birthmark on her forehead and eyelid as part of her allure. He gave Ariene a faint smile and crawled around his older sleeping son, barely two, to watch his youngest suckle her breast. Thank the gods both of his sons had fair smooth skin, ruddy cheeks, and hair as red as the rising sun.

When Ariene was pregnant with each, she beseeched the Mother Goddess to bless her children with comely looks absent any marks. She was granted her wish. Some people from the village said the boys had the faces of gods.

Marrock felt a twinge of regret that he once had similar features as his sons. That was until seven years ago when Catrin summoned the ravens to peck out chunks of his face. Every day since, he had to live with relentless pain that at times became unbearable on cold wintry days. The only way he could escape the suffering was to shape-shift into a wolf. Just then, he sensed his wolf pack calling out to him for a hunt.

Only blood and raw flesh could assuage his hunger pangs now.

First, he had to tell his wife that he would be away that evening.

An ear-racking wail jerked Marrock from his predatory craving. He looked down to find his older son hanging onto his leg. Not only did Marrock's face throb, but his ears rung from his little warrior's shrieks. He lifted the boy and shook him. "Enough!"

The boy's face scrunched and he screamed his lungs out until his skin turned ice blue, and he went limp.

Marrock glanced at Ariene. "That boy of yours needs to control his temper and take a breath."

Ariene rolled her eyes. "Set him down. He will be quieter when he wakes."

Laying the boy next to Ariene, Marrock said, "I need to go to the forest and join my wolf pack."

"Will you be gone long?"

"As long as it takes for my wolf's essence to give me a sign about what to do in the meeting with the Roman senator." Marrock sat next to Ariene. "Did you speak to your father about including me in the council? I fear he wavers on his promise to place us as rulers over the Cantiaci kingdom."

Ariene picked up the waking toddler while juggling the younger at her breast. "I have told Father that he needs to speak with you on all matters, but my pleas fall on deaf ears. He insists a political marriage between my brother, Adminius, and one of Amren's daughters might give him what he needs to wield control over the Cantiaci."

"Bahhh!" Marrock spat. "I swear to the gods of the Otherworld that I will never let this happen! Nothing can stand in my way of taking what is rightfully mine. And you, my beloved, will share in the glory as my queen."

Ariene reached for Marrock's hand. "I also desire this. I want my people to look at us with respect and not avert their eyes as if we are monsters."

"That still happens to you?" Marrock asked, grimacing. "I had hoped those minions had accepted the marks on our faces as signs from the gods that we are their divine messengers."

"Well ... I do not see it that way." Ariene paused. "Some of the people believe I was born with the mark of an evil spirit."

The sadness in his wife's face reflected what Marrock felt every time a person cringed at his hideous face. He reassured her, "I promise this will all change."

Ariene asked with pleading eyes, "Why not stay here with me when you connect with your wolf?"

Marrock stiffened. "I need the forest's temple stillness." He staggered to his feet, trying to avoid hitting his massive shoulders against the wall. "I need to go. Walk me to the door."

Ariene pushed herself up, the baby's mouth still clutching her nipple and the toddler clinging to her skirt. Shifting the youngest boy to her hip, she walked with Marrock to the entryway where he leaned over, dodging his son's punch, to kiss his diminutive wife on the cheek.

Now ready to join his wolf pack, he pushed the door open.

Outside, Marrock walked around the house nestled in a clearing. A half-morning ride from the Catuvellauni capital, his domain provided him the isolation he needed to conjure spells and perform sacrifices. Beside his thatched-roof house was a small plot of land where his wife grew awful-tasting turnips that made his stomach cramp. Toward the back of the home were corrals for white cattle, sheep, and a couple of pigs—their meat more agreeable to his predatory stomach.

He continued his journey into the forest where a canopy of trees, thickets, and vines snaking from branches obscured the sunlight, making it difficult for him to find the patchwork footpath of gravel and grass. The path meandered around a majestic beech, to a scrubby hazelnut, and between some white willows—trees that provided natural ingredients for his concoctions. He finally spotted the towering oak that rose above the verdure landscape. Near the oak, he yanked some creeping plants away to reveal skulls lodged in carved-out cavities in a wooden gateway. At the bottom were children's skulls, some of which had been stillborn babies. Higher up were the cracked skulls of unfortunate travelers who Marrock had sacrificed. At eye level, he found his most precious skull wrapped in white linen. He carefully pulled it out, and unraveled the fabric from the cranial bone. He lovingly gazed at its empty eye sockets.

"Hello, Mother."

The clenched jaw did not respond. For Marrock, there was something pure and spiritual about the silent skull. It was the temple that encased his mother's soul before she was brutally beheaded by his father, King Amren.

Marrock recalled the day, almost twenty years past, when his father forced him to watch his mother's execution. Since then, he recited his mother's curse word-for-word every morning to emblazon him to pursue his ambition of overthrowing his father. To do so, he knew he had to ally first with the mighty Roman Empire. With Cunobelin and the Romans now wavering on their support for his claims, he was no longer sure if he could fulfill his mother's curse.

Rubbing the skull's eye sockets, Marrock again relived the horror when he was an eight-year-old boy watching his beloved mother's head fly off her body. He should have caught the head, not the dim-witted Agrona who let it slip through her hands and thump on the ground. When Marrock knelt to touch his mother's head, rivulets of blood stained his hands.

Emptiness rotted away Marrock's soul. Two weeks after the execution, he dug his mother's head out of the refuse heap. The sight of maggots slithering in and out of the nasal cavities, eye sockets, and teeth made his stomach roil with disgust. The putrid rotten-egg odor made him retch.

Then a compulsion to remove the filth from his mother's head took control of him. He polished her skull as brilliant as the full moon at its zenith. Using vinegar-soaked cloth, he wiped the greenish-black slime away from his mother's face and rinsed her head in healing pond water. For a week, he soaked the head in a vat of urine to remove any residual filth away from the bone, then meticulously scraped off all the hair with a knife and polished the bone with a whetstone. This was the first head he enshrined in the Gateway of Skulls.

Until he was a young man, Marrock believed his mother's soul resided in the skull, but Agrona informed him otherwise. "Queen Rhan's soul possessed me the instant her severed head slipped through my hands. I am your mother, Rhan."

Marrock at first refused to believe Agrona, but he slowly accepted the Druidess, the same age as him, was indeed the essence of Rhan. Although Marrock knew the skull was an empty vessel, rubbing its smooth surface soothed him before joining the wolf pack. He sat down on thick grass, crossed his long legs, and placed the skull on his lap. Eyes fixed on the setting sun's crimson light filtering through the trees, he chanted:

Red Wolf, join my soul.
Forge my thoughts and body into wolf form.
Take me forward to the sunset of my father's demise
And to the dawn of my rising.
Reveal the portal from which I will reap new powers.

A light flashed in Marrock's mind, a sign he had connected with his red wolf's essence, his eyesight sharpening and ears hearing the crunch of faraway twigs. The next step was to shape-shift. His jaw tensed in anticipation of the ordeal when he began the transformation. He howled from the horrific pain racking his body. His head spun in a vortex of white light. It felt as if glass shards were blasting into his brain.

An instant later, he felt a cold breeze whisk past his face and below him, he found wolf paws bouncing off the ground. His heart beat faster, keeping pace with his stride. Around him were three she-wolves and a juvenile male forging as a unified pack with him. The wolf companions understood his true essence—a predator born to cull weaker creatures from his kingdom. The pack followed him without question and worshipped him as the horned god who blessed them with bountiful prey.

Born under the blood moon, Marrock believed he was destined to reap the dark powers of the Ancient Druids. With god-like abilities to summon nature's forces and to shape-shift, he would strike fear into his enemies like lightning bolts. Then he would overthrow his father and conquer all tribal kingdoms on the isle. Ultimately, he would clamp the people under the power of his jaws.

The musky odor of a deer suddenly tantalized Marrock's nose. He moved toward a meadow where he saw an eight-point stag, a doe, and their fawn grazing. With so few wolves in his pack, he knew they could not overtake all the deer in an outright chase. He changed his strategy: move upwind, surround the prey, and maneuver them into a weakened vantage.

Marrock slowed his pace to a crawl. He growled at the nearby slate-black wolf and directed her to the other side of the glade. The other wolves hid in the thickets and quietly waited for his signal. For the plan to work, the Black needed to chase the deer toward the other wolves. She must bring the fawn down, forcing the stag and doe to defend their young. He sensed the black she-wolf's excitement when he finally gave the command.

The Black leapt between two hedges and three strides later locked her fangs around the fawn's hind legs while the stag and doe dashed toward the woods. As Marrock anticipated, the stag slowed, veered, and lowered its antlers in full charge at the Black that was pulling the struggling fawn down to the ground. Just as the stag lowered its head to thrust the antlers into the Black's side, Marrock and the silver-furred wolf lunged at the stag's flanks. His fangs sheared through the thick hide and into tissue. The stag's powerful body jolted and twisted, shaking Marrock off. The next instant, he felt sharp antlers thrust into his side, knocking the air out of him. His head then spun from the motion of tumbling and rolling on the ground until he smacked against a tree trunk. Slightly dazed, he watched the stag disappear into a grove of hawthorn trees.

His attention then turned to other wolves surrounding the Black as she tore the hide away from the fawn's belly to expose the guts. The pompous glint in the Black's stare caught Marrock's eye. The bitch reminded him of his step-mother, Rhiannon—the Regni slut who stole his birthright and feasted on what was rightfully his. The bitch's insolence of solely devouring the meat before him, the alpha male, made his blood boil. Infuriated, he sprang to his paws and charged the Black. Snarling and baring his fangs, he forced the Black away from the carcass.

The she-wolf cowered and pressed her head on front paws in a bow. From deep in his throat, Marrock growled and snapped his jaws, reinforcing he was alpha male. The Black scooted back and crept to the nearby brambles. The other wolves took their rightful place at the blood-soaked feast and heartily gorged on the baby deer's tissue, sinew, and blood.

Marrock's powerful jaws crunched the fawn's head and cracked the skull open. Through the cracks in the bone, he sucked out the brain and fed on the fawn's essence. With his hunger sated, another physiological need took hold of him.

The aroma of the silver wolf in heat excited him. The Silver bit at his neck and yelped. He playfully tossed his head and pounced at her. She jumped back and teased him with her musky scent. He sniffed and licked the sumptuous tissue under her tail, the taste driving him mad with lust. Only the Silver could appease his libido. He mounted the she-wolf and wrapped his front legs around her girth to thrust into her, his head dizzy with euphoria.

The ecstatic delirium was disrupted when he heard shrieks that ran a shiver down his spine. Ravens, circling overhead, swooped one-by-one down on the fawn's body. The other wolves made faint attempts to ward off these unwelcome scavengers. The ravens dodged the wolves' jaws while scooping bloody tissue into their elongated beaks.

Cunning creatures, Marrock fumed. *Foragers always stealing my meal.*

Agrona told him that ravens carried souls to the Otherworld. The raven's ability to fly readily between the spiritual and mortal worlds was a power a wolf did not have. Only Catrin, born with the raven spirit, had this ability.

The sun's gold light suddenly pierced through the trees and projected a vision before Marrock. The antlers of the stag were entangled in the branches of a hawthorn. Nearby was a rosewood staff capped with a gold globe. On the globe's polished surface was etched the image of the sun god driving a two-horse chariot. When he touched the staff, electrical charges webbed from the surface of the globe into him and then flashed through the air into the antlers.

When Marrock drew out of his vision, he found himself in his human form sitting near the oak under streams of twinkling stars. Head pounding, he sat there for awhile orienting himself to the human world, his breathing labored.

When his mind finally settled, he flinched from the stabbing pain in his side where the stag had butted him. He staggered to his feet and stumbled blindly through the pitch-black forest, stretching out his hands to detect any obstacles. Lumbering between the trees, he mulled over the vision's meaning and then words mystically tumbled out of his mouth. "The power lies in the head. The gateway of skulls connects to the portal."

By the time Marrock reached home, he realized that for him to summon the dark powers of the Ancient Druids from the Otherworld, he must place his father's skull with the others in the archway. Considering it further, he must also harvest the skulls of the bitch queen, Rhiannon, and her daughters, to serve as a conduit to the forces from the Otherworld. He could then summon the mystical energy to meld with his enemies' minds to subdue them while the forces of nature destroyed them.

Though the meaning of the sun god's emblem on the staff's globe confounded Marrock, he knew the staff was symbolic of the Ancient Druids' ability to draw magic from the Otherworld. With the potential that Cunobelin might concede to King Amren and withdraw his support, Marrock recognized that he had to win Rome's alliance, so their legion could help him overthrow his father. He could no longer rely only on Ariene to influence her father for support.

Somehow, someway, he must retrieve the Apollo staff's authority to assure his legacy as the King of all Britons.

20

OUT OF ASHES

*Give me a glorious victory in Britannia, so I can
rise out of the ashes of my fallen forefathers—
Mark Antony and Iullus Antonius.*

In the tented Roman headquarters near the Catuvellauni capital, Senator Lucius Antonius again read the letter from Emperor Tiberius and groaned. After all the meticulous planning he and his compatriot, Praetor Marcus Licinius Crassus Frugi, had done to prepare for the invasion of Britannia, everything was starting to fall apart. Ever since the mysterious death of the emperor's son, Tiberius was losing heart for invading. There had to be a way he could convince the emperor of the necessity of conquering the isle rich in farmlands and metals that would add substantial wealth to the imperial coffers. If Lucius demonstrated his political prowess by spearheading the invasion, he would assure his ultimate ambition of being elected as consul. Perhaps, he could persuade the emperor's most influential confidant, Praetorian Prefect Sejanus, to speak in favor of the expedition. He would write his oldest son, Brutius, to gain Sejanus's ear about the benefits of the invasion.

Lucius sighed. If only Marcellus was more malleable to his will like his older brother. With comely features resembling Mark Antony, Marcellus would be a perfect match for Praetor Frugi's daughter. The nuptial agreement between the families would be another step for Lucius's elevation to consul.

Lucius mumbled, "What on earth happened to Marcellus that changed him so much the last two years?"

Up to the age of sixteen, Marcellus had demonstrated the qualities of becoming a successful politician—a top student in oratory, rhetoric, and military strategy. But, earlier in the year, Lucius had to quell ugly rumors that his youngest son had been hauled drunk to the family villa after bedding a harlot. His greatest fear was Marcellus would repeat the curse of the Antonius men who drew women like ravens to carrion.

Lucius grimaced, recalling his humiliation after being banished to Gaul when his father, Iullus, was accused of adultery with Augustus's daughter and forced to fall on his sword. It was only after the death of Augustus that Tiberius allowed him to return to Rome. Lucius clawed to give Marcellus every advantage for success that he never had. Still, his son recklessly squandered all that away. Perhaps, the barbaric Cantiaci could enlighten Marcellus on the errors of his ways while he was held as their hostage.

The sound of loud footsteps entering the tent drew Lucius out of his contemplation. Looking up, he found Tribune Decimus Flavius saluting on the other side of the table piled with scrolls, wax tablets, ink bottles, and styluses.

"I was told you wanted to see me," Decimus said.

"Yes. Sit down. Help yourself to wine while I seal this message for delivery to the emperor."

Lucius dripped melted wax on the edges of the parchment and pressed his signet ring into the soft wax, imprinting the family seal of Apollo in a horse-driven chariot. He handed the scroll to his slave, a balding Greek with only a few tufts of gray hair left in his head.

"Give this to my courier for immediate delivery to the emperor," Lucius ordered. "Tell the guard not to allow anyone entry until I have spoken with Decimus."

The slave meekly bowed and left.

Lucius took a glass of wine offered by Decimus. He swirled the full-bodied Pompeian wine and took a sip, savoring the taste. It was one of the few luxuries he had brought to the inhospitable isle. After taking a few more sips, he said, "Before we meet with Marrock, I'd like to know more about Cunobelin. How strong of an armed resistance would he mount if we invade Britannia?"

Decimus traced the rim of the goblet and licked the wine off his finger. "Cunobelin is formidable. He was educated in the imperial palace of Augustus and was trained in Roman military strategy. He is a shrewd politician and always bows to Rome's demands to avoid conflict. Yet Verica, the king of the Atrebates, told me Cunobelin begrudges Julius Caesar for forcing treaties on the Catuvellauni almost seventy years ago."

"What about Amren?" Lucius asked.

"I would not underestimate Amren and his queen," Decimus said, furrowing his brow." Through their marriage, they have forged a powerful alliance between the Regni and Cantiaci tribes. They also have strong ties to Verica of the Atrebates. Together, these rulers control the southeast coast of Britannia. Another consideration is Amren served in the Roman auxiliary at the same time as the Germanian prince Arminius. He thus knows our military tactics. Cunobelin told me in confidence that Amren secretly supplied warriors to Arminius, who then destroyed three of our legions at Teutoburg Forest."

Lucius tapped his fingers on the table. "What about Marrock? Would he be amenable to helping us invade Britannia, if we help him overthrow his father?"

Decimus rubbed his chin. "He reminds me of a monster with an insatiable appetite for power."

"Even more reason for him to lap up the scraps from our hands. That monstrous barbarian appears willing to do anything we ask."

"Senator, may I speak freely?"

"Of course, I consider you my most loyal patron and friend."

"Marrock can't be trusted," Decimus said firmly. "Although he speaks with a honeyed tongue, his hideous face reflects who he truly is. I cannot put my fingers on it, but the words "grotesque" and "twisted" come to mind. Even Cunobelin now wavers on his support for him."

"No doubt Marrock appears a freak," Lucius concurred. "I also cringe every time I look at him. Have you uncovered the true reason Amren banished him?"

"Not yet," Decimus said, shifting on his chair. "I did confirm that Amren executed Marrock's mother. This is a grisly act that would send a son over a precipice into madness. Nobody that I have talked with has refuted Amren's reason for banishing Marrock. He was caught holding the severed heads of two children from a nearby villa."

With the wine's taste suddenly souring, Lucius set the brass goblet on the table with a clang. "If that is true, why would Cunobelin marry his eldest daughter to a deranged man and present his claims to the emperor?"

Decimus leaned forward on his elbows. "I am also baffled by this. From what I've seen, Cunobelin speaks from both sides of his face to gain a vantage. He supports Marrock's claims, but still negotiated a marital pact with Amren to marry his daughter to Adminius. My gut tells me that Cunobelin is using Rome's support to pressure Amren into sharing some of his sovereignty with Adminius. Their mutual rule would offer Cunobelin immediate power over the Cantiaci rather than waiting for Amren's death when Marrock is proclaimed king."

Lucius mulled over what Decimus said. "With Cunobelin's shifting alliance toward Amren, we could easily control Marrock by playing to his ambitions. What would we need for a successful invasion?"

"Roman ships must land near the white cliffs where our legions could disembark with minimal resistance. Cunobelin and Amren would fiercely attack us, no matter what we promised them." The tribune paused, then had a glint in his eye. "Now I understand where you are going with Marrock. He would be indebted to us if we helped him overthrow his father."

Lucius slapped the table with exuberance. "Politicians must sometimes deal with monsters for the greater cause. Marrock's loyalty could be sealed by promising him additional power and freedom to rule the Cantiaci as our client king. Before we invade, we will mandate that he build a fortressed lighthouse on the cliffs to aid our ships in the landing. Could this task be completed in one to two years?"

"That is possible," Decimus said, rubbing his chin. "I could leave one or two of my engineers to help with the design and construction. But, sir … I do not trust Marrock!"

"And neither do I, but that is why, once we have conquered Britannia, our legions will stomp that grotesque savage under our heels."

Decimus nodded. "Put that way, it might be advantageous to explore Marrock's willingness to work with us when we meet tomorrow. We must keep utmost secrecy. I fear if Amren catches wind we are secretly dealing with Marrock, he may break his truce and harm Marcellus."

Lucius glowered. "I am still vexed at myself for allowing Marcellus to stay as a hostage."

Decimus lowered his head. "Regrettably we were left with no other choice but to meet the king's demands. Our heads would have joined the other skulls in his reception hall."

"What is done is done," Lucius said, still agitated that Amren had gained first advantage by retaining Marcellus. "How can we move forward with Marrock without jeopardizing my son's life?"

Decimus rubbed his lower lip with a forefinger. "We should secretly barter separate agreements with each of the potential rulers and determine who will concede to our demands. For now, we should not publicly insist that Amren recognize Marrock as the legitimate heir to the throne until we can get this sorted out."

Lucius chose to finish his wine and then said, "It is settled. Arrange for Cunobelin to speak with Praetor Frugi while we talk with Marrock tomorrow."

"I will do that right away," Decimus said, scooting his chair back to stand, but Lucius, remembering the sticky situation with Tiberius, motioned the tribune to stay. "There is something else I need to tell you. The emperor has lost heart for invading Britannia since losing his only son. He is now in Campania and difficult to reach."

Decimus's mouth dropped. "Has something happened that I am not aware? I am, after all, duty-bound to obey the emperor."

Lucius waved the concern away. "No, no, a small snag. Tiberius directed me to communicate directly with Prefect Sejanus on what we find here. I will convince Sejanus that it is in his best interest to invade Britannia. As you know, Praetor Frugi is already a staunch supporter of our plan. We are negotiating a marital agreement for Marcellus to wed his daughter. This marriage will forge our political alliance into steel. Praetor Frugi will then support my political climb to consul. If I spearhead the glorious conquest of Britannia, that would seal my election as consul. Let me remind you, your promotion to Legate is tied with my political rise. For this to happen, no harm can come to Marcellus. Is there any way you could send some of your soldiers to secretly watch him at the Cantiaci village and rescue him, gods forbid, if anything goes wrong?"

"Amren's village is well-fortressed," Decimus said grimly. "It would be difficult for my men to pass through the gate without notice. Our best course of action is to uphold the truce with Amren and maintain secrecy whenever we meet privately with any of the

Briton rulers. We need to make sure Amren's eldest daughter is safely returned, so Marcellus is released. Then we can carry out with our invasion plans."

"My boy holds the key for sealing an alliance with Praetor Frugi through this marriage," Lucius said fervently. "Yet I fear, even if Marcellus is freed, I will still need to squash ugly gossip about him flexing his manhood with a married woman. This could unravel the marital agreement."

"He is impetuous like his great-grandfather and needs to be reined in as Julius Caesar did with Mark Antony. He is a young man who needs action and given command of soldiers. He will quickly fade in the shadows of the Senate." Decimus rose from his chair and leaned his hands on the table. "I could give Marcellus that training and discipline. His military service to Rome would be a tribute to you."

Lucius said, "You may be right, but you will never have that chance if my son is not safely returned."

Decimus squared his shoulders. "Sir, what would you have me do?"

"Dispatch your best soldiers to watch the Cantiaci village from a distance. Tell them to be ready to rescue Marcellus if they sniff any danger to him." Lucius shot a piercing stare. "Remember, I will never forgive you if anything happens to my son."

Decimus said, "I will not let that happen," then saluted, and pivoted on his heels to leave.

Left with a foreboding tremor in his heart that he might not see Marcellus again, Lucius lifted his eyes and quietly prayed, "Apollo, almighty god of the sun who lights each day, I beseech you to keep Marcellus from harm. Give me a glorious victory in Britannia, so I can rise out of the ashes of my fallen forefathers—Mark Antony and Iullus Antonius. In return for your favor, I will offer you ten white bulls at my triumph."

21

MASKED INTENTIONS

*Suspecting his father may have told the senator
all the sordid details, Marrock would need
to counter the tale with his own.*

The rooster's crow awoke Marrock, reminding him of his eventful meeting that day with Senator Lucius Antonius. He rolled over to see Ariene scraping cut vegetables into the cauldron that hung over the hearth. His oldest son hung onto his mother's dress while the youngest crawled on the floor. He again pondered his vision from the other night. The stag had been debilitated by what, at first, had not appeared a threat—the low branches of a hawthorn tree. As he thought more about how the ravens feasted on the wolves' kill, his hatred for Catrin broiled inside him. How could a small raven garner so much power from the Otherworld and not the wolf? If she can access the magic of the Ancient Druids as Agrona proclaimed—blaming him for altering the curse when he abandoned Catrin in the woods—could not his half-sister use them against him? On the day he first met Senator Antonius near the white cliffs, he sensed Catrin in the raven flying overhead, but he failed to bring the feathered creature down with his death stare, an ability he had yet to master.

I will make sure that does not happen again!

Marrock rose from his bed, pulled his trousers on and picked up a striped Roman toga. He walked to the cauldron and leaned over to see what was in it. His stomach recoiled from the stench of boiling turnips.

"Do you have anything else to eat?" Marrock grumbled. "You know how I hate these roots!"

Ariene pointed to the table near him. "Over there, you can find some cheese and pork strips."

Marrock picked up the moldy cheese and took a bite, the flavor tantalizing his palate. He looked at his wife. "Did you see any omens on how today's meeting will go?"

"I dreamt you were a red wolf watching a couple of eagles feast on what looked like a horse's corpse. I am not sure what that means."

"Possibly the horse represents my father," Marrock said. "He was born with a horse spirit. Who do you think the eagles represent?"

"My father has an eagle spiritual guide. But why would there be two eagles feasting on the horse and not you?"

"Good question. I will think on it."

Marrock finished eating the cheese and picked up his shield and long sword. He pushed the heavy door open and walked to the open front stables where he bridled and mounted a small horse. He kneed the compact steed into a trot on a gravel road and weaved between plots of farmlands until he reached the Roman encampment, a half-mile from the Catuvellauni capital of Camulodunon. The fortress was fortified with a rampart and wooden palisade that lined its perimeter. He dismounted and smoothed the toga's fabric over his breeches. He walked to the grizzly sentry by the watchtower and announced, "I am Marrock, advisor to Cunobelin, here to see Senator Lucius Antonius."

When the burley sentry eyed Marrock, he winced. Marrock smiled faintly and handed the scrolled credentials to him. Reading the parchment, the guard said, "Everything looks in order." He motioned to another infantryman standing at his side. "Take this man back to the praetorium."

Following the soldier, Marrock looked all around, studying the camp's set-up. Lined along the pathway on both sides were tents that housed soldiers who were milling around and performing various tasks. He guessed six hundred men, an unusually high number to guard so few diplomats. When he reached the massive red-striped tent at the camp's center, he noticed banners emblazoned with a gold image of the sun god in a horse-driven chariot.

Cunobelin had told Marrock that Apollo was the senator's patron god. Marrock again pondered the meaning of his vision when the stag was entrapped by the tree branches. Perhaps, the emblem of Apollo on the staff's gold globe was symbolic of the senator's authority. He had to find a way to trick the senator into using his Roman forces against his father.

A Roman guard drew back the tent flaps to allow Marrock entry into the senator's palatial headquarters. Seated at a long wooden table was the graying senator and across from him was Marrock's richly garbed father-in-law, Cunobelin. The Catuvellauni king was garishly clothed to display his status as king: fox pelt cape over his shoulders, gold torc coiled around his thick neck, and gemstones ringed his fingers. Cunobelin's tusked mustache curved over his jaw whereas the senator was clean shaven. Standing behind the senator was a commander armed with a red-crested helmet and bronze chest armor that had the same imprint as the banners outside. Marrock then noted the gold embroidered eagle on the scarlet tapestry that partitioned the main chamber from another area.

Cunobelin motioned Marrock forward for introductions. "Senator Antonius, let me present my Master Druid, Marrock. He is married to my eldest daughter who has borne me two healthy grandsons."

The senator's mouth scrunched in repulsion. The fissured-face tribune stared back without a flinch. Cunobelin gestured toward the senator. "Marrock, it is again my honor to introduce Senator Lucius Antonius—the grandson of Mark Antony and descendent of Apollo. The senator represents the "might and will" of Emperor Gaius Tiberius.

He is here to adjudicate your claims to the Cantiaci throne. As you know, the senator's son will be held hostage until Amren and I reach a settlement. Senator Antonius has asked to speak with you privately about this matter."

Marrock bowed deeply at the waist. "Greetings. How shall I address you?"

"You can call me Lucius," the senator said amicably. "To my side is Tribune Decimus Flavius. He will stay and write down our conversations as a record for the emperor."

Though the senator's tone seemed friendly, Marrock thought it odd the diplomat would ask to be called by his first name. Speaking fluent Latin, Marrock embellished his words with arm gestures. "Lucius, I am indebted to the emperor for considering my claims. I have been told you were educated in Massilia as a young man. I, too, lived there with a Roman nobleman who was charged with my education until I was thirteen. I pride myself in speaking your language and embracing your culture. When I returned to my homeland, I adopted many of your customs as my own."

Lucius arched his eyebrow at Decimus. "Escort Cunobelin to Senator Frugi's tent, so he is not late for their meeting."

Decimus saluted and escorted Cunobelin outside.

Marrock sat across from the senator who kept looking down at the table. He knew the best strategy for dealing with Lucius's repulsion to his disfigured face would be to openly talk about it.

"Before we begin, I sense your discomfort with my appearance. It is a face that reminds me every day of my good fortune to be alive, as I was savagely attacked by wolves that left me unconscious. When I awoke, I wandered the woods, my mind gone from the loss of blood. A forester found me and took me to his cottage to treat my wounds. Alas, my face healed into this monstrous mask, but I can assure you that underneath I am a Roman at heart."

Lucius regarded Marrock for a moment. "I appreciate your candor. I would like to wait for the tribune's return before we start."

As they waited, Marrock watched the senator shuffle through some scrolls strewn on the table. He then noticed the wax seal imprint of Apollo in a horse-driven chariot on one of the scrolls—the same emblem on the globe in his vision. Darting his eyes around, he scanned the shelves packed with scrolls, bottled inks, and quills, but could not locate the stamp that had sealed the parchment.

When the tribune returned, he sat at the far end of the table and smoothed out a parchment. Dipping a quill pen into a bottle of black ink, he asked the senator, "Are we ready to begin?"

"Yes." Lucius turned to Marrock. "Let me be clear. What we say here today does not leave this tent. You will soon understand our need for secrecy."

Marrock noted the senator's eyes which appeared black in the dim lamplight. To study Lucius's reaction when they spoke, Marrock requested another candle. He then said, "You must realize Cunobelin will ask me about what we say today."

"I am aware of this," Lucius said, as the tribune lit a candle that clearly illuminated the senator's chestnut-brown eyes. The senator poured some wine into goblets and offered one to Marrock. Taking a sip, Marrock waited for the senator to start.

Lucius cleared his throat. "King Amren refuses to recognize you as his son. Why is that?"

Marrock gave a thin smile. "Did he not tell you?"

"Yes, but I would like to hear your side."

"Did my father say anything about what happened on the day I was banished?"

"He did."

Suspecting his father may have told the senator all the sordid details, Marrock would need to counter the tale with his own. "Shortly after the wolf attack, Father accused me of casting a curse on his kingdom. In truth, my presence was a constant reminder to him of his heinous deed of beheading my mother, the rightful queen.

You should know that he forced me to watch as he lopped off her head."

Decimus leaned forward and narrowed his eyes. "Interesting, but that is not what your father told me."

Marrock twitched a smile. "Exactly what did he say?"

"He said you cut the throats of two children, then tried to do the same with his youngest daughter."

Marrock did not flinch as he considered how to deflect his father's accusation. "That is a blatant lie. I came across the gruesome act on my walk home. The boy and the girl were already dead. It is no coincidence that some of the king's warriors were conveniently there as I cradled the heads and wept for the children's souls that had been entrapped in the skulls."

Lucius's voice quavered, "What do you mean by 'entrapped'?"

"It is our belief that the skull is the temple of a person's soul. When the head is removed from the body, the soul—the essence of the person—cannot escape the skull and travel to the Otherworld."

Lucius jerked his head back. "Oh, gods above! If that is so, why does your father line his receiving chamber with skulls?"

"Power!" Marrock spewed with disdain. "He believes he can use the strength of his enemies' skulls to protect his kingdom. I believe as the Romans do; it is barbaric … a desecration."

"That we can both agree on." Lucius took another sip of wine and regarded Marrock for a moment. "What if I were to tell you that I support your cause?"

Finally, progress on my claims. Smiling slyly, Marrock said, "That conclusion would confirm the accolades I have heard about you being a wise man."

"What if I were to tell you that Cunobelin is considering withdrawing his support of your rights as heir to the Cantiaci throne? And that he favors a political marriage between his oldest son, Adminius, and Amren's daughter. Amren has already made several concessions, promising Cunobelin that he will transfer some of his authority to Adminius after the wedding. In exchange, you will be handed over to Amren for his pleasure."

At that instant, Marrock's temple began to throb with the image of his fangs tearing away his traitorous father-in-law's throat. He said sharply, "I would say my father has led Cunobelin astray. My father-in-law has been my most ardent supporter for ruling the Cantiaci kingdom on his behalf."

The senator leaned back in his chair and tapped a corner of his mouth. "Sadly, people's true motives are sometimes masked. I must admit that what your father and Cunobelin are considering is not in Rome's best interest."

Marrock stared at the reflection of the wavering candle flame on the senator's eyes. He knew Lucius had some other insidious plan in mind. Now was the time for him to pounce on the opportunity and to maneuver the senator to his cause. "I understand your meaning. Quite possibly, I could offer something more to your liking. If Rome were to proclaim me as the Cantiaci king, I would gladly give my fealty to the emperor and open the harbors for Roman ships and trading, but my loyalty does not need to stop there."

Lucius furrowed his brow at Decimus who then set his quill down. The senator looked at Marrock. "I would like to further explore where your loyalty might go."

"How far would you like it to go?"

Lucius extended his left hand on the table. "This is my signet ring with the imprint of my patron god, Apollo. What would you offer this god?"

Marrock smiled wryly. "I also worship Apollo and would offer gifts deserving of his favor: tin, silver, grains, cattle, and slaves. Cantiaci warriors are renowned for their ferocity and skill with weapons. As gladiators, they would draw crowds to your arenas."

"I would like to move forward with your claims, but there is the sticky issue if Cunobelin agrees to the nuptial agreement proposed by Amren." The senator sipped some wine, his eyes fixed on Marrock.

"I fear what your father might do to my son, Marcellus, if I proclaim my support for you. At the first meeting with Amren, his maggot put a blade to my son's throat—an act I will never forgive."

"A despicable act!" Marrock snarled, meeting the senator's hard stare.

"Will your father and his queen keep their truce and not harm Marcellus, if I pronounce my support of you as the rightful heir, regardless of whether the marriage pact is finalized?"

Marrock rubbed the corner of his mouth to hide his smirk. "Based on my own experience, neither my father nor his queen can be trusted to keep their treaty. It is well-known that Father will extend one hand in friendship while thrusting a sword into your heart with the other. The queen and their youngest daughter, Catrin, are sorceresses. If either of them suspects treachery from you, they will gladly sacrifice Marcellus to their war goddesses."

The senator's mouth gaped open. "Sacrifice! A human sacrifice?"

"An abomination!" Marrock exclaimed, matching the senator's fervor. "To prevent this, I strongly advise you take my father prisoner now and demand Marcellus be released. After your son is freed, you can do whatever you please."

Decimus interjected, "Senator, we need to talk before you go further with this discussion."

Lucius paused, then pushed his chair back to get up. "Agreed. I will give this further consideration before I make a decision." He acknowledged Marrock with a nod. "If you will excuse me, I must join Cunobelin and my fellow envoy. Later, we can again discuss your generous offering."

Marrock rose and bowed, the toga almost slipping off his arm. "I am here to serve you as your client king."

When Marrock left, his mind twisted around the inroads he had made with the hubris senator. He was now ready to shed his Roman attire for the comfort of his wolf skin as he planned his next steps to ensnare the stag, the symbol of his father in his vision. For that, he needed Agrona to set up the next phase of their scheme. He sneered, knowing the senator's seal of Apollo would give him the authority he needed to ignite the political firestorm between his father and the Romans.

Soon enough, Blood Wolf will outsmart the eagles and feast on the Cantiaci kingdom.

22

WAR CHARIOT

With reckless glee, he again cracked the leather straps. The chariot lurched when the horses accelerated into a full gallop.

A month had passed since Marcellus first kissed Catrin. Since that day, he had relished every moment he spent with her. Today, he felt invigorated from the morning sun and the scent of freshly cut hay from a nearby pasture. With excited anticipation, he watched Catrin instruct two stablemen on how to harness the bay mare and the black stallion to the queen's war chariot.

He chuckled.

She definitely likes to take control.

Waiting for them to finish, he reminisced about his outings with Catrin, a constant companion who shared his love for racing horses, hunting, and hiking in the pine-scented woods and sweet-flowered pastures. The island was so unlike Rome where he had to duck excrement thrown out of upper flats on his walk to the pubic baths. He had grown apathetic about exercise, preferring the dull tales of his friends as they leisurely soaked. At night, even his sexual adventures with Eliana no longer excited him as it had at the start.

Marcellus sighed wistfully. Catrin, this "Celtic Diana" had opened his eyes to the joy of sharing the bounty from their hunting trips with her people. Unlike Roman nobles, who hoarded wealth for their own extravagances, the Cantiaci royal family shared food and wine in exchange for the people's fealty. The previous week, Catrin donated two boars she had killed on a hunt for the people to feast on. The raucous celebration, he discovered, was a public way for a warrior to elevate himself by challenging others to single combat. Out of what seemed a chaotic contest was how a warrior acquired and maintained his status.

The last couple of weeks had given Marcellus a different perspective of why he had grown to hate Rome and resent his father for forcing him into politics. With the Cantiaci, he could meet his opponent face-to-face in combat to settle differences. The political fighting among Roman patricians was done in the shadows of the Senate, where alliances formed in clandestine meetings. Sometimes, patricians hired hooligans to resolve any quarrels by dumping the bodies of their adversaries in sewers that flushed into the Tiber.

Although he had at first viewed the Cantiaci as ignorant barbarians, his opinion had changed, particularly after Catrin explained their religious beliefs. No one died, but all lived in a cycle of destruction and rebirth. Souls could reincarnate into a human being or animal form. With each new incarnation, the living being lost memory of a prior life, but was influenced by past deeds.

Catrin proclaimed she was born with a raven spirit which allowed her to travel to other spiritual realms. The bards sung of ancestral warrior queens born with the raven spirit that bestowed them with the ability to foretell the deaths of their enemies. Though Catrin never professed she had been a warrior queen from a previous life, Marcellus assumed so. She matched his physical intensity and skill with weapons, and had a rebellious nature like him, though at times she seemed vulnerable.

In Rome, Marcellus considered women as empty vessels whose only purpose was for sexual pleasure and child-bearing. However, Catrin was more like a reflection of his soul. The mystical way they began their relationship, joining their thoughts and sharing deep secrets, intrigued him. With his growing love for Catrin, the urgency of fulfilling his father's mandate to find out more information from her was waning. His father's lofty aspirations of invading Britannia now sank ingloriously in his chest. A war would destroy Catrin. He would never forgive himself if he didn't at least try to persuade his father to ally with Amren and leave in peace.

The loud snorts of the chariot horses pulled Marcellus out of his reverie. He shifted his gaze toward the queen's chariot to study its distinct differences from the quadrigae his family sponsored in races at the Circus Maximus. The rectangular, flat-bedded vehicle was unlike the Roman cylindrical chariot. Built for speed, Roman chariots had front panels that arched to tapered sides. In contrast, the queen's chariot had two low-lying, ribbed sideboards on each side, the front and back open for a warrior to jump off and on during battle while another drove. Another factor to consider was the circuitous race track in Rome was smooth and sandy whereas here he had to drive the chariot over grasslands, rolling hills, and gullies. He was anxious to meet Catrin's expectations, particularly after his bold claim of being a skilled charioteer. She had somehow persuaded the queen to allow him to drive her war chariot. Now presented with the challenge, he was determined to prove his boast true.

Marcellus flashed a prurient grin when Catrin ambled toward him. Gods above, she looked stunning in her leather chest armor that provocatively laced at the front. With no visible shirt underneath, her alabaster skin glistened in the sunlight. Tight multi-plaid breeches accentuated the curvature of her small hips. His perception of what construed a woman's beauty had completely changed. With a spear in hand, Catrin had the pale lunar radiance of the goddess Diane. Though her close communication with the raven had at first unnerved him, he now accepted this as part of her mystique. She seemed more a goddess than a mortal.

And his sexual self-restraint was melting away.

Sweet Venus! How did you get past your mother dressed like that?

More baffling, why did the queen trust her daughter to be alone with him during the day without any additional guards? Had he imagined the shadows lurking in the forest a few days back, when he was alone with Catrin. If they were ever caught in an intimate moment, the queen would undoubtedly rip out his heart. Though he should be cautious with Catrin, his loins told him otherwise when his eyes wandered down to her sweet spot. He glanced around to make sure no one was watching. He playfully patted her hind side. She jumped and wheeled around, her lustrous blue-green eyes warning him not to do it again.

Marcellus curled his lips into an impish smile. *Just try to stop me.*

When Catrin glowered, he frowned and asked in a matter-of-fact manner, "Do you still plan to ride with me?"

"Yes, of course," Catrin said sharply. "I have brought spears for hunting. Can you drive this chariot, so you do not scare the game away?"

Though Marcellus inwardly prayed to Apollo that he would not crash the chariot into a tree, he haughtily proclaimed, "Hah ... I'm lightning fast. No prey will ever hear me coming."

In truth, he most wanted to capture the affection of Catrin. He hopped into the back of the chariot and waved his arms over his head, signaling the great champion was ready to go. Then he extended a hand to assist Catrin into the chariot. A stableman gave her a couple of spears that she leaned across the side rail. She gave Marcellus a dubious look.

"Have you driven this kind of chariot before?"

"I've only driven Roman chariots," he admitted, "but I assume they all work about the same."

"You will need to squat, so I can throw the spear over your head."

"Squat?"

"Yes. Squat. Can you do that?"

Of course, he could do whatever the goddess asked and much more. He bent down and balanced his weight on his right foot as the two stablemen finished adjusting the harness. After a few moments, his legs began cramping in the crunched-up position.

Shit! I must be crazy!

He took the reins from one of the stablemen. Raring to go, he cracked the leather straps on the horses' backs. The chariot squealed into motion on a grassy pasture populated with rocks and boulders.

Whoa! Not a good idea!

Immediately one wooden wheel hit a rock.

Marcellus bounced up, nearly losing his balance and spilling him out the front. He contracted his thigh muscles to stabilize himself as the chariot sped across the open terrain. Behind him, he felt the rocking motion of Catrin shifting her weight back and forth as he negotiated the vehicle onto a dirt road, toward the forest. Relying on his experience with Roman chariots in Gaul, he pulled one rein, directing the horses to the left, while tightening the other to whip the vehicle around a tree. Exhilaration surged through his veins at every sharp turn. At the top of his lungs, he cried out, "Aaaah hooah!" Catrin mimicked his war cry.

After awhile, Marcellus was skillfully maneuvering the chariot back and forth across a gully. His legs screamed bloody pain as he fought to control the reins, looking for any obstacles through the open gap between the horses, their manes swooshing back. With reckless glee, he again cracked the leather straps. The chariot lurched when the horses accelerated into a full gallop.

Up ahead, he glimpsed a white stone jutting from the grass. He yanked hard on the reins barely missing it, but the other wheel crunched over a boulder. The chariot flipped up and catapulted Marcellus across the field where he landed face down in the grass.

The wind knocked out of him, he struggled to his hands and knees. Afraid Catrin had met a similar fate, he glanced up to find her. To his shock, she was unscathed as she drove the chariot toward him. The embarrassment of being hurled from the chariot wounded his pride. He rolled on his back and slowly inhaled to ease the pain anchored in his ribs. The clacking of the approaching chariot's wheels silenced, and he heard footsteps rushing toward him.

Catrin knelt and stroked his forehead. "Are you all right?"

"Everything is fine," he rasped.

She showed him the crimson tinge on her fingertips. "Your head is bleeding."

"It is only a scratch," he groaned, playing to her sympathy.

When Catrin interlocked her arms under his back to lift him, he sputtered, "Let me ... rest ... a moment."

She set Marcellus back down and checked his arms for broken bones. Seizing the moment to capture his prize, he wrapped his arms around her and pinned her flat on the ground. Even with her strength, she could never escape this hold if he had full weight on her.

Catrin protested. "Marcellus, you had me scared! Let go of me!"

He knew how to disarm her with a whimsical smile followed with a breathless kiss. Ready to kiss her, he noticed a glint in her eyes signaling she desired more. He stroked her cheekbone with the back of his hand and traced his thumb over her bottom lip. She gently clamped it between her teeth, the tightness reminding him of what he would feel inside her. A breath hitched in his throat when he gazed at her lustrous lips. She had an intoxicating scent that was driving him crazy. He recalled his Roman lover's mantra. *Every woman wants to be taken like a goddess. Touch her in the right places and she will soar to the heavens.* Though his heart raced with excitement, he hesitated, glancing around for any unwelcome visitors. Perhaps he should wait until they found a more secluded spot, where he could slowly build her arousal to match his.

His caution melted away when she placed his hand on her armored breast cup.

Aroused, he interlaced his fingers into hers, the movement of their palms in an ethereal dance connecting their hearts. An overpowering desire to press against her hips burned away all his caution. He kissed her passionately, but could not fill his hunger for her. Wanting more, he said, "I want you to join my soul like when we first kissed."

Catrin gave him a puzzled look. "You said that sharing our thoughts and feelings were unsettling."

Gazing at her blue-green eyes, Marcellus stroked Catrin's hair that sparkled like gold under the sunlight. He nibbled at her lips. "I want to touch you in other ways, to taste the depths of your love. For this to happen …"

He pressed his lips against her and pulled her closer. She wrapped her arms around his neck as he savored the sweetness of her mouth. He deftly pulled the bindings on her chest armor. As they loosened, he spread the lacing apart and slid the palm of his hand over a soft breast. As he fondled the supple tissue, he moaned when her mouth floated open in delight. He knew then he could take her.

Yet, an ominous chill that somebody was watching clawed at his neck. Glancing sideways, he saw two bare-chested warriors riding on horses. His heart thwacked against his ribs. He hurriedly staggered to his feet and helped Catrin up. Her face blushed as red as a shiny apple as she turned to tighten the bindings of her chest armor.

When Belinus and Cynwrig reined their horses to a halt, they looked down on Marcellus and Catrin with the all-seeing eyes of judges ready to pass sentence.

23

MISDEEDS OF ANCESTORS

She felt like a ship sailing aimlessly on a vast ocean toward hurricane forces. Like Marcellus, she wondered how much of her fate was controlled by her father ... the curse.

Catrin could see the distrustful glints in the warriors' eyes as they approached. Tightening her fists, she turned to Marcellus. "Let me talk with them."

"Do you think they saw what we were doing?" Marcellus said quietly.

"I'm not sure," Catrin whispered. She turned, raised a hand and greeted the warriors. "Good day. What brings you here?"

Belinus looked down on them from his mount. "The queen ordered us to keep an eye on him."

"Father charged me to guard the Roman hostage, not you." Catrin said emphatically. "Why would Mother give you such an order?"

Belinus spat. "She does not trust the Roman."

"Is that so?" Catrin said, her eyes pierced at Belinus. "How long have you been watching us?"

"Since the first day he was put under your charge." Belinus kneed his horse next to Marcellus. "And I've seen everything this Roman has done to you."

Catrin could feel heartbeats throbbing in her neck as she fought for composure. "What have you reported to my mother?"

"The Roman's every move. Whenever he kisses, touches you—"

"I can't believe you spied on me!" Catrin lashed out. "I was doing what my father ordered: find out more information. Mother is well aware of this."

"We do what the queen commands," Belinus said with a scowl. "You need to bring this up with her."

"I will," Catrin barked, then stomped over to Belinus and pulled the reins of his horse. "You can leave now. I have the hostage well in hand. You can tell my mother that."

Belinus pointed to the chariot. "What happened there?"

"We were thrown," Catrin quickly replied. "Marcellus was helping me get up."

Belinus cocked an eyebrow. "When did you last fall out of a war chariot? From what I saw from the hilltop, this pompous rooster drove the queen's chariot over a rock and was thrown. When I rode up, he was ready to flaunt his manhood."

"I resent your insinuation!" Catrin hissed. "Remember, I know about your secret with Mor."

Before Belinus could reply, Cynwrig burst into laughter. Belinus's face flamed as red as burning embers. Catrin darted her eyes back and forth between the warriors as they began to spar verbally with each other.

Belinus snarled, "What's so funny?"

Cynwrig jested, "Everyone seems to know about your little secret."

"What do you mean 'everyone knows'?" Belinus paused, eyeing Catrin. "We'll have words about this later. Go see how much damage the chariot has sustained."

Snickering, Cynwrig rode to the chariot. After circling it, he looked at Belinus. "The wheels and axle look fine. Catrin can drive, so that idiot does not crash again. We'll escort them back. You can tell the queen about what you saw between the two at your own risk."

"She can account for her own actions," Belinus grunted.

Cynwrig winked at Catrin. She turned to Marcellus and gave him a sweet smile. "Everything is fine now."

Marcellus's jaw tightened as he leaned closer and murmured, "What did they say? They sounded vexed."

"Oh … Mother summoned me. That is all," Catrin said calmly, trying to ease his concerns.

"What was that horse-haired warrior laughing about?"

"Something that Belinus said."

"And what was that?"

"He thought it odd that we had fallen out of the chariot."

"What's so funny about that?" Marcellus said, creasing his forehead. "Did he see what we were doing?"

"Oh … I told him what happened to the chariot," Catrin said, lightly touching his arm. "I said it flipped and threw us out."

Marcellus motioned his eyes toward Belinus, making Catrin aware the warrior was trying to listen to their conversation. He whispered, "What if your mother questions me? I want to make sure our stories match."

"I can handle Mother," Catrin said firmly. "We need to go now. I will drive the chariot. Do not say anything along the way. Belinus has big ears and will be escorting us."

Marcellus nodded.

Catrin walked to the chariot where Marcellus hoisted himself up and offered his hand to assist her. She moved to the front of the platform, took the reins, and crouched. She cracked the leather straps on the horses' backs and the chariot jerked into motion.

On the journey to the village, Catrin mulled over what she would say to her mother. She first thought about confronting her mother about not trusting her with Marcellus. She admitted to herself that she had become amiss carrying out her father's mandate, gleaning little information from Marcellus about Rome's intent for her kingdom. Instead, she became increasingly absorbed with Marcellus, learning about his interests, his beliefs, and his family. She should consider him an enemy, but they had more in common than not. Each of them was overshadowed by older siblings, their fates seemed more determined by the misdeeds of their ancestors than by their own actions.

Catrin recalled her unsettling conversation with Marcellus when he revealed his greatest fear was to die young like his namesake—the nephew of Augustus—who was considered the presumptive monarchic heir to the emperor. The charismatic noble married at the age of seventeen to the emperor's daughter, Julia. Two years later, his life was cut short by typhoid before he could fulfill his destiny.

Marcellus disclosed that he wanted to emulate his great-grandfather. As a boy, he imagined himself leading his army into battle against Celtic hordes in Gaul, like the legendary General Mark Antony. Marcellus even asked Lucius, his father, to change his first name to Marcus in tribute to his great-grandfather, but Lucius declared, "As your paterfamilias, I not only decide your name but also your fate."

After Marcellus told Catrin this, he gazed at the setting sun as though longing for it to rise again. The lines around his eyes deepened when he divulged that he no longer believed plundering other homelands for personal gain was honorable and that he would make sure his father knew this. It was as if he was warning her that Rome intended to attack the Cantiaci kingdom.

In retrospect, Catrin could have dredged more information out of him. Yet, at the time, she felt like a ship sailing aimlessly on a vast ocean toward hurricane forces. Like Marcellus, she wondered how much of her fate was controlled by her father … the curse.

She recalled the altered curse etched on the dagger and struggled to understand its meaning. *At the time your daughter flies out of Apollo's flames with the powers of the Ancient Druids ... Blood Wolf will ally with the Roman Empire ...*

The curse no longer foretold that Marrock would destroy their father. Rather, the curse gave her a different path to use the ancient powers to save her father and their people. She wondered how Marcellus would weave into all of this. As the empire's agent, he was empowered with the authority of his family's patron god—Apollo. Perhaps, she could convince Marcellus to plea with his father not to ally with Marrock.

A man's shout and animal squeals jolted Catrin back to her reality that she needed to halt the horses before they stomped on piglets romping away from a beleaguered herder struggling to direct them through the fortress entry into her village.

"Get back inside, you stupid swine," a gruff voice shouted above the pig snorts.

The chaos compounded when other villagers jumped on the piglets and scooped them into their arms. A strapping farmer clamped a sow's mouth with an elbow while lifting the forelegs to pull the animal through the entryway to a pigpen.

When the entrance finally cleared, Catrin drove the chariot down the sodden pathway to the royal stables where Trystan met them. He first ordered Belinus to report his findings to the queen, then stared at Marcellus. "What happened to the Roman? It looks like he got the worst of a cock fight."

Before Cynwrig could answer, Catrin blurted, "He was hurt in a chariot accident."

Catrin nervously watched Trystan walk around the chariot, stopping at times to scrutinize the scrapes and gouges caused by the accident. After making a complete circle, he grumbled, "The queen will not be pleased to see this damage." He flicked his eyes toward

Cynwrig. "Take the Roman back to his quarters where a servant can tend to him. Catrin, you come with me."

Marcellus gave Catrin a puzzled look. She said, "You must go with Cynwrig. I will see you later at the evening meal."

Marcellus stitched his eyebrows together with concern. "What about your mother?"

"I will speak to her. Do not worry," Catrin said smiling, though her stomach knotted from the dread of what her mother might do.

Marcellus seemed to relax and touched her hand. Though she had only known him for about a month, it felt as if she had built a lifetime of trust with him. He jumped down from the chariot and proffered his hand to assist her down.

Catrin watched Marcellus trail Cynwrig to the rear of the structure. Before entering, Marcellus glanced back and grinned. She returned a whimsical smile, but she pressed her lips into a firm line when she heard Trystan clear his throat and order, "Follow me, Catrin. The queen wants to see you right away."

Apprehensive about what her mother would say, Catrin walked beside Trystan to the back door and they both entered. About halfway down the torch lit corridor, he halted and said, "The queen awaits you in her private chambers. I will stay here for any further instructions. Be forewarned, your mother watches your every move."

Taken aback by Trystan's warning, Catrin asked, "Why are you telling me this?"

He didn't answer, but gestured for her to continue. Leaving Trystan, Catrin passed her bedchamber that had been converted into a makeshift cell for Marcellus. She peeked through the open doorway and found an elderly female servant swabbing lavender ointment on his chest. Reassured that Marcellus's wounds from the chariot mishap were being properly tended, she turned her full focus on her mother's bedchamber down two rooms. Squaring her shoulders and breathing deeply to steady her shakiness, the fear of how her mother might punish her indiscretion with Marcellus prickled the hairs on her arm. Was Belinus in there now revealing all the sordid details?

Reaching the chamber's door, Catrin hesitated. She looked down at her chest armor and tightened the lacing to seal the leather panels together. Swallowing hard to ease the tightness in her throat, she brushed some loose strands of hair from her face. Finally ready, she lightly tapped the door, her hand feeling as heavy as a mallet. "Mother," she said quietly, hoping her mother would not hear.

Queen Rhiannon's voice blasted, "Come in here now!"

Opening the door, Catrin observed a lady-in-waiting adorning her mother's neck with a gold torc. Sitting on a stool, the queen was looking at herself in a mirror, fingering her braided hair coiled on top of her head. The queen snapped her fingers for the attendant to leave, and she twisted her torso, still with mirror in hand, and arched a discerning eyebrow at Catrin. "That is quite an outfit you have on. Where is the undershirt?"

With hot sweat beading between her breasts, Catrin tugged at her chest armor to loosen so she could breathe. "I thought it was too warm to wear today."

"You thought leather armor would be cooler?" Rhiannon said, a tinge of sarcasm in her voice. "Your bare midriff is making quite an announcement."

The sweat now streaming over her abdomen, Catrin feigned ignorance of her mother's insinuation. "Announcement of what?"

Rhiannon shook her head with obvious chagrin. "Do not think me a fool? I know of your shenanigans with the Roman."

Catrin stiffened. "Is that not what Father instructed me to do? Find out more information from him."

"And ... what did you find out today?" Rhiannon asked, setting the mirror on the nightstand. "Did he reveal anything new about Rome's true intent for sending his envoys here?"

Catrin scrambled for any new tidbits that might satisfy her mother. "I learned Marcellus has a half-brother just like me. He rides horses and drives chariots as well as any Cantiaci warrior. Marcellus is only here because his father is teaching him to be a diplomat. Now that he better understands our situation, I'm sure he will support us over Marrock's claims."

"You actually believe that?" Rhiannon said, sternly lifting an eyebrow.

"Yes, I do."

"That is what you said yesterday … and the day before that. It hardly seems worth the effort to glean so little information."

Uneasy that her mother was ready to deliver her ultimatum of not escorting Marcellus, Catrin snapped, "Why did you summon me?"

Rhiannon picked up a scroll from the table and held it in the air. "This is a message from your father. He says negotiations are going well with Cunobelin … almost too well. To the point, your father anticipates negotiations will end soon. There is no need for you to escort Marcellus. After today, I have ordered Belinus to guard Marcellus until his release."

Shaken by her mother's order, Catrin argued, "You can't do this. Father charged me to guard Marcellus. Besides, Belinus detests Marcellus. And … and Marcellus likes my company."

Rhiannon frowned. "Oh, I see. Now the truth comes out."

"Mother, let me escort Marcellus until he leaves. I have learned so much about Rome from him. I can uncover more information if you give me more time. Besides, it is the first time a man has shown interest—" Catrin almost bit her tongue off to stop the words "in me" from escaping her mouth.

Rhiannon gaped at Catrin. "Oh! In the name of the gods, why would you say that? There are lots of young men interested in you."

"Tell me who," Catrin demanded.

"There is Ferrex—a warrior, Cynwrig's close friend," Rhiannon said. "And there are others, but you wave them away like flies pretending they do not exist, ever since that day…"

"What day?"

"That day with Marrock," Rhiannon said with hesitation. "Since that day, we have tried to shield you from any young man until you were ready."

Catrin felt as if her eyes were ready to burst. "Until I was ready for what?"

"Affection with a man that is blessed by Mother Goddess." Rhiannon then tripped over her words as she continued, "But ... because ... of what happened—well ... let me be blunt. I do not believe you are ready for a man's touch."

Catrin could not believe what her mother had just said. "Not ready?"

Rhiannon rose, walked over to Catrin, and gave her a pat on the hand as if soothing a young child. "Sweet girl, you isolate yourself and have spent entire days with only your raven. That is why we ordered Belinus to train you as a warrior, to empower you. That way, you can protect yourself from any man who does not treat you with honor."

Insulted, Catrin stepped away from her mother. "I thought you trained me to defend our kingdom, to be a warrior like Vala."

"That, too," Rhiannon quickly replied, "but I had not anticipated how strong your infatuation for the Roman would be and—"

"Mother! He has a name ... Marcellus," Catrin blasted. "I have more in common with him than any man from our village."

"Marcellus is a foreigner as smooth and sweet as honey," Rhiannon cautioned, keeping a steady voice. "He is, at least, four years older than you and most likely sexually experienced. I can see by the glint in his eyes that he has special plans for you and that is not to be your friend, nor to help us!"

Catrin felt hot blood surge into her face. "Mother, I cannot believe we are having this conversation! Father placed his trust in me to guard Marcellus. Now that I know him, I can assure you he is not who you think he is. Our friendship has developed into much more. I truly believe he will help us."

Rhiannon's mouth flung open. "After a couple of weeks with him, you can declare this! You owe your loyalty to your family, not to an enemy who charades as a friend. You have wavered on your father's mandate to find out what Rome wants from us."

"I've been—"

"Don't say anything until I'm done," Rhiannon said, raising her voice. "Are you blind? That Roman rogue is beguiling you. Remember, the Roman emperor supports Marrock's claims to the throne. If that monster overthrows your father, he will kill everyone in our family. Face it, the feelings you hold for Marcellus ring true because you are young and stupid. You have no future with him."

"What do you know of such things?" Catrin charged in. "You hardly touch Father and when you do, it is to maneuver him. You show more affection for Trystan."

Rhiannon recoiled, as if struck by a venomous serpent. She raised a clenched hand, "Careful, Catrin, what you say. I serve the king with more loyalty and love than you realize. I know how strong young love can be. In life, choices are often taken out of our hands. We decide your fate!"

Catrin became reticent, regarding the nasty scowl on her mother's face. She knew it was fruitless to continue the heated argument and thus resorted to a softer approach. "Please allow me to spend the few remaining days with Marcellus. I promise to gather more information that we can use. What harm would this be?"

Rhiannon slowly inhaled and blew out an exasperated breath. "All right, then. I only do this, so Marcellus doesn't become suspicious of your sudden absence. Yet, for me to agree, you must keep that promise to find out more from him and a guard who speaks Latin must be with you at all times. And that guard is Belinus."

Catrin burst out, "Not Belinus!"

"Those are my conditions!" Rhiannon met Catrin's eyes with an icy stare. "Accept them or be confined to your bedchamber."

Catrin's heart trembled with the prospect she would never see Marcellus again. Though the conditions sunk like tar in the pit of her stomach, she reluctantly agreed, "I will do it. Still, you have made a big mistake in changing Father's mandate for me to escort Marcellus."

"Enough!" Rhiannon roared. "You brought this on yourself!"

Brimming with rage, Catrin fought for composure. "I would like to leave now and change for dinner."

Rhiannon waved her off like a dog. "Suit yourself, go!"

Catrin wheeled around on her heels and stomped out.

24

AGRONA'S SPELL

A waft of sweet fragrance drew Catrin's curiosity. She walked over to where Agrona was stroking the wolf-headed pelt and sat to rub the soft fur.

That night at dinner, Catrin noted everyone's silence at the table, except for Cynwrig smacking his lips, the juices dripping from the corners of his mouth, as he heartily ate roasted boar ribs. Mor and Marcellus, both sullen, sat at the opposite end of the table near the queen while Catrin was seated between Belinus and Trystan and across from her was Agrona.

Catrin was unnerved by the way Agrona's wolf eyes appeared to smile, turning green to amber in the candlelight. Sensing another entity hiding behind Agrona's dilated pupils, Catrin visualized her with a tail wagging in predatory delight. She closed her eyes to erase the grotesque image, but opening them again, she found Agrona's amber eyes glowing at her. Fearing the Druidess was conjuring some black magic, Catrin tore her eyes away and squeezed her shaking hands. She then concentrated on eating the roasted boar meat, turnips, and round bread set before her.

When everyone finished the meal, Rhiannon pushed her chair back and stood to explain the night's arrangement in Celtic. "Mor's bedchamber has been prepared for Mor and Catrin to sleep there. Although I have immensely enjoyed Mor's companionship in my bedchamber the last couple of weeks, I would like to be alone now."

Catrin noticed Trystan was rubbing the corner of his mouth, as if restraining a grin when her mother gazed at him.

Rhiannon continued, "Cynwrig has agreed to guard Marcellus tonight to give Belinus a break from his nightly duties. Beginning tomorrow, Belinus will be escorting Catrin and Marcellus at all times."

Catrin noticed poor Marcellus frowning in confusion as he looked around the table trying to understand what was being said. Rhiannon gave him a smug smile and said in Latin, "Marcellus, we have enjoyed your company tonight. After Agrona presents her gifts to our family, Cynwrig will escort you back to your sleeping quarters."

Catrin wondered why the Druidess would present gifts without the king's presence. She warily watched Agrona step to the back corner where various animal pelts were rolled up and stacked. Agrona took the top one and unrolled it over the wooden floor. She knelt, stroking the lustrous silver fur and saying in a sultry voice, "Soft and warm."

When Catrin gazed at the wolf-headed pelt, the image of Marcellus lying beside her on the pelt planted in her mind. When she noticed Mor and Belinus mooning over each other, an idea seeded in her mind on a way she could be alone with Marcellus. For almost a fortnight, the queen had strictly forbidden Mor to be alone with Belinus. The separation had put Mor in a sour mood. Perchance, she could lift Mor's spirits by suggesting a way that Belinus could rendezvous with her.

A waft of sweet fragrance drew Catrin's curiosity. She walked over to where Agrona was stroking the wolf-headed pelt and sat to rub the soft fur. A heady aroma of sweet lavender and musk released from the wool and the image of Marcellus caressing her nude hips wandered into her mind. Unsettled about the tingling sensation below, Catrin pulled her hand away and looked at Agrona who twisted her lips into a crooked smile and stood up.

The aroma continued to intoxicate Catrin and she obsessively rubbed the fur back and forth as she gazed at Marcellus. When he met her eyes, she had an overpowering impulse to keep the pelt. She rose and asked Agrona, "Can I keep this?"

The Druidess bared her teeth with a broad grin. "Of course, my love. The fox pelt is for Mor, the marten for the queen ... and the black wolf for the king upon his return."

Suddenly light-headed from the heavy aroma, Catrin felt herself floating into Agrona's amber eyes. Panicked the Druidess was casting a spell on her, Catrin dropped her eyes. When she rose, her eyes alighted on Marcellus standing next to her. When he leaned closer to whisper, his words were drowned out by her mother's blustery order in Latin, "Cynwrig, take Marcellus back to his room. Belinus, you are dismissed!"

Appearing frustrated, Marcellus mouthed, "See you tomorrow," and then pivoted on his heels to follow Cynwrig out of the chamber.

A shiver shot down Catrin's spine when she caught Agrona gawking at her like a hawk ready to swoop on its prey. Catrin hastily picked up and cradled the rolled pelt under her arm and walked out of the chamber with Mor.

25

MOR'S SECRET

Every time I am in his arms ... it is like I am flying," Mor said with wistful rise in her voice. "Something has happened that could destroy us both ..."

When the sisters entered Mor's bedchamber, Catrin noticed the bouquet of flowers on the table: lavender, roses, and heather. The room had been freshly dusted and the bed covered with blankets. The strong aroma from the wolf pelt she was carrying suffused into the room. The sensual smell elicited an erotic image of Marcellus kissing her neck and below. Heart beating faster, she impulsively rubbed the splintered wall that divided Mor's room from the makeshift cell where Marcellus had been taken.

Warm electrical pulses discharging through her fingertips lulled her into a trance.

Moments later, Mor's shrill voice jerked Catrin out of her altered state. "What is wrong with you? Are you going to rub that wall all night?"

Catrin flicked her hands on her trousers and wiped the sweat off with her fingers. When she turned, Mor appeared as a shadow sitting on the bed.

Mor asked with a slight crack in her voice, "Did Mother summon you earlier to her chambers?"

Catrin stepped closer to see Mor's face. "Yes, why do you ask?"

"Mother also summoned me earlier. She told me Father's negotiations were going well ... with Cunobelin ... and ... " Mor paused and sniffled. "She told me that Father would soon announce the conditions of the marital pact with Cunobelin's son."

"Adminius?"

"Yes, Adminius," Mor gasped. "He was pleasant enough when he stayed with us two summers ago as a ward of Father. He is handsome, but I don't love him. And I don't want to leave my family."

As Catrin's eyes adjusted to the dim light, Mor's teary eyes came into focus. Her sister's distress tugged at Catrin's heart and she asked with concern, "Does Belinus know?"

"I think he does," Mor whimpered, "but Mother has made sure we are never alone with each other."

"Do you love him?" Catrin immediately chastised herself for asking such a stupid question.

"You know I do. Every time I am in his arms ... it is like I am flying," Mor said with a wistful rise in her voice. "Something has happened that could destroy us both ..." She almost choked on her words. "I ... am ... pregnant!"

Catrin's mouth flung open. "Pregnant! How do you know?"

Mor's face contorted with anguish. "It has been six weeks since my bleeding."

"Maybe you are just late."

"No, I am sure. I have been sick the last couple of mornings."

"Have you told anyone besides me?" Catrin asked, her stomach still lurching from Mor's disclosure.

"I haven't even told Belinus." Mor's voice became unsteady, tripping and stammering at times. "If I tell Mother ... I do not know what ... what she will do. Earlier this month, I told her I refused to marry Adminius. It is my right as a free woman to choose ... my own husband. Mother lashed out, saying 'Father makes the final decision.'"

Mor paused, wiping some tears from her reddened cheeks. "Why would Father place all the burden of brokering a peace pact with

Cunobelin on me? Why must I be the one to sacrifice my life to forge a political alliance through my marriage with a man I hardly know? The gods curse me! If Father's negotiations fail … because of me, because I am with child, everyone will blame me. Who knows what Father and Mother might do … to me, to Belinus. Father could disown me … flog Belinus, flog me … banish us …" Mor's voice faded as she sank her head into her hands, her chest heaving from loud sobs.

Sitting down, Catrin wrapped an arm around her sister. She pulled Mor closer to stroke her thick dark hair and to reassure her. "Our parents would never do that to you. Be patient. In their hearts, they know you have the right to say no to any marriage they arrange. Besides, in the eyes of Mother Goddess, you and Belinus were married the moment you first made love."

Mor pulled away and shook her head. "Why would Father jeopardize our kingdom for my happiness? Mother never had a say about marrying him either."

Catrin was lost for an answer. The brunt reality that Mor had no choice in the arranged marriage hit Catrin like a fist. Conflicting emotions about taking the next step with Marcellus now anguished her. If negotiations broke down with the Romans, common sense told her to forget Marcellus, but she was drawn to his flame, the light so bright she could not resist.

Mor's chestnut-brown eyes grew big. "What if I am forced to marry Adminius? I don't know what he would do if he finds out the child was not seeded by him. He might beat me. Cunobelin might do something worse … kill the baby! And then there is Marrock. He would stop at nothing to undermine my marriage if he felt his power threatened. He might even kill me! Chop off my head like he did those children right before he was banished. What did I do to enrage the gods?"

Catrin clasped Mor's shaky hands between hers. "You need to tell Mother right away. It only makes sense you should marry Belinus.

Nothing could be crueler than to separate him from you and his baby. Maybe Vala would be willing to marry Adminius. She is the eldest."

Mor looked at Catrin with hopeful eyes. "Do you think so?"

"It only makes sense." Catrin said, knowing Vala preferred the company of other women. "You need to talk with Mother now. She told me negotiations will end soon. Father needs to know about your condition before he seals the nuptial pact in blood."

"You're right," Mor sighed. "I must also tell Belinus that I am carrying his child, but I need to be alone with him."

"Maybe, I could ..." Catrin hesitated.

"Say it. Do what?"

"Belinus has been charged to escort Marcellus and me on all of our rides from now on. On one of our jaunts, we could stop at the cave by the river where warriors hide during time of war. You could meet us there."

"You would do that for me?" Mor paused and stared at Catrin. "You can't tell anyone about Belinus and me until everything is settled, you must promise."

Catrin pressed a forefinger to her lips. "My lips are sealed."

Mor raised an eyebrow. "What about Marcellus?"

"Oh ..." Catrin muttered, wondering how much she should disclose to Marcellus. "He will be happy just to be with me."

Mor squeezed Catrin's hand. "Be careful what you tell him ... understood?"

"Yes, I promise," Catrin agreed. "Everything will work out, I am sure."

Mor smiled. "I feel better now that we have a plan. Tell Belinus that I need to meet with him the day after tomorrow. That will give me a chance to speak with Mother tomorrow and to see her reaction."

Catrin nodded, knowing this would be her last opportunity to be alone with Marcellus.

26

BETROTHAL

The hairs on Catrin's neck prickled. Something was amiss.

Next morning at breakfast, Catrin wondered why Mor had mysteriously left at dawn's first light without leaving a message on when she would return. Had last night's meeting between Mor and their mother turned bitter, which might explain why neither of them joined the morning meal?

Normally, Catrin would devour her favorite berries, but her stomach felt unsettled. Across the table, Belinus heartily scooped porridge into his mouth and gulped down some water from a brass cup. She could tell his sandy-brown hair, neatly combed into a tail at the back of his head, was freshly washed. The tattooed sun on his bicep appeared to flare whenever he moved. He had been in a jubilant mood since Catrin told him of Mor's plan to rendezvous with him that morning. The promise she would watch over Marcellus while he met Mor at the cave seemed to melt his hesitancy about disobeying the queen's order to guard them. She surmised, once Mor told him that she carried his child, he would no longer pay any mind to what Marcellus and she were doing.

Catrin nervously looked at Marcellus sitting next to her. A grin flashed across his face which made her smile back. He looked so handsome in his half-open gold shirt that revealed the Apollo amulet around his neck. She glanced down at his manly bulge in the tight, dark-leathered pants that she had made for him. When he gripped her hand below the table, she yelped. With a mischievous grin, he played with her fingertips, pulling them apart. A warm blush prickled her face. Breathing rapidly, she pulled her hand away, slamming the knuckles on the table.

"Ouch!"

Her face must have blossomed to a cherry red because Marcellus gave her an amused smile. In no mood for his games, again thinking of Mor, Catrin frowned. She hoped Mor would show up, so they could proceed with their plan.

A gray-haired, double-chinned woman holding a platter of fruit waddled into the chamber. She set the platter on the table and leaned next to Catrin to whisper, "The queen wants to see you now in her meeting chamber."

Surprised by the unexpected summons, Catrin asked, "What is this about?"

The servant shrugged. "She only said it would not take long."

With a sense of foreboding that something had gone terribly wrong between Mor and her mother, Catrin asked, "Did Mor leave a message for me before she left this morning?"

"She only told me that she was making an offering to the Mother Goddess," the servant said.

This was not quite the response that Catrin expected, but she assumed the scheme for Mor to meet secretly with Belinus was still on. If Mor wasn't at the cave, she would surely be at the Ancestral Oak praying to Mother Goddess.

Catrin rose and looked at Marcellus. "Please excuse me. My mother has summoned me. I will be back shortly."

He gave her a disconcerted look, but she gave him a reassuring smile and left. When she walked behind the thrones on her way to the corridor leading to the queen's chamber, Trystan intercepted and said, "I have been asked to escort you to the queen's chamber."

His escort usually meant the queen had an important announcement to make, which Catrin assumed was Mor's pregnancy. She walked alongside Trystan down the dimly lit corridor where torch flames stretched up the arched stone walls in line on both sides. At the end of the hallway, Trystan opened the door and followed her into the queen's dank chamber.

Rhiannon stepped into the candlelight's illumination and gestured for both of them to sit at a round table. Seating herself, Catrin noticed the webbed veins in the corner of the queen's reddened eyes that strangely lingered on Trystan before shifting to her.

"Let me get straight to the point," the queen began. "Mor just told me she is pregnant and that you already know this."

Catrin squirmed in her chair. "I just found out. Mor wanted to tell you."

Rhiannon sighed, the wrinkles deepening around her eyes. "I was up all night with Mor discussing the difficult decisions she must make. I advised her to seek advice from Mother Goddess on what she should do with the child."

The first idea that came to Catrin's mind was Mor had been given the choice to ingest pennyroyal to abort the baby, an act frowned upon in her village where children were cherished and often mentored by other villagers after they reached a certain age. Perhaps her mother would grant Belinus custody of the child, leaving Mor unencumbered to marry Adminius. That seemed the most viable choice, the more she considered it. At least Belinus would be given the child to care for. Catrin hesitated saying anything until she knew more about her mother's feelings on the matter.

Rhiannon pulled a scroll out of her sleeve and set it on the table. She tightly folded her hands on the dingy tabletop and said, her voice sometimes grating, "Last night, I agonized on what I should do with Mor. Then, this morning, I received a message from your father elaborating the final terms of the marital pact with Cunobelin.

When I read it, I thanked Mother Goddess for showing me the way out."

The hairs on Catrin's neck prickled. Something was amiss. Why would her mother talk to her before speaking with Mor about the agreement? Studying Trystan's face, she could tell he already knew what her mother was about to say.

Rhiannon sipped some water from a cup and cleared her throat. "Cunobelin told Amren that his son, Adminius, refused to marry Mor. You can imagine the discord this caused the negotiations."

Beaming with hope, Catrin blurted, "Does that mean Mor can marry Belinus instead?"

"Yes, she is released from any obligations. But …" Rhiannon inhaled and released a long heavy sigh. "Adminius wants to marry you, instead. Cunobelin and your father agreed."

Shocked, Catrin could feel the blood rush from her face and her heart sinking like the sun into a night sky. Numb, she stared vacantly at her shaking hands. Her thoughts muddied. *How can this be? Why does Adminius get the choice? Not me? How could I ever live with a man I hardly know? Oh, gods, no … Marrock! What will he do to me, so near, so deathly close? Is this Rhan's curse? Is it rewriting itself? Am I now cursed? This can't be. This can't be. I cannot let this happen!*

In stunned silence, Catrin lifted her head and regarded the queen's face that reminded her of a death mask. Why would her mother treat her with such brutal decorum usually reserved for treacherous nobles? She shifted her eyes to Trystan. He dropped his dampened eyes. Why was he sad, but not her mother? The floor seemed to collapse underneath her feet, and she felt herself adrift on a vast ocean watching images stream like clouds across the sky. From above, Marcellus reached for her from a horse-driven chariot. When she grasped for his hand, she gripped her own fist.

Marcellus disappeared into a fog. In his place, her mother's stern face appeared.

Catrin blinked hard, but she couldn't obliterate her bleak future. Her mother was waiting for a response. Choking back sobs, she rasped, "I ... I cannot do this."

Rhiannon lightly touched Catrin's arm. "I know this is hard not to choose your own husband. I assure you it is for the best. Mor cannot fulfill this obligation. You can. No one binds you."

Tears swelled in Catrin's eyes. "The sacrifice you ask of me will be my doom!"

"Cunobelin is ready to withdraw his support for Marrock, only if you do this," Rhiannon said with urgency in her voice. "Don't you see? Mother Goddess has shown us the way. You can bring peace to our kingdoms."

At the moment, Catrin was drowning in lost moments she had hoped to share with Marcellus. She asked bitterly, "How long have you known Father was bartering me instead of Mor?"

Rhiannon stammered, "The final agreement ... well, it takes time ... to hammer out, to forge, that is. It may not have worked. So we waited until it was done."

Catrin could feel her jaw quivering with anger. "You did not answer me. Did you do this when you caught Marcellus in bed with me?"

The queen's steely silence answered what Catrin suspected in her heart. Her mother would do anything to thwart her blooming relationship with Marcellus. She slowly rose, pressed her hands on the tabletop, and defiantly glared. "I will not do this!"

"It is already done." Rhiannon reached over the table and clawed sharp fingernails around Catrin's wrist to reinforce the finality of the decision.

Catrin recoiled from the pain and yanked her arm away. The room spun around her as she moved toward the doorway.

"Where are you going?" Rhiannon shouted.

Catrin halted, turned, and glared at her mother. "I promised Marcellus that I would ride with him today. Belinus is also waiting."

Rhiannon bolted up from the chair. "You cannot pretend this is not happening. I ask you but once, do you accept your duty?"

Catrin reeled herself out of drowning emotions, and she anchored a fist into her other hand. "You have given me no choice. At least, for today, allow me to bid farewell to Marcellus. Is that too much to ask before I am sacrificed?"

Rhiannon regarded Catrin for a moment, then blew out an exasperated breath. "This is it, the last time. At all times, stay with Belinus. Do not say a word to either man about what has happened. I will speak privately with Mor and Belinus later. After today, you will be confined to your room until the wedding ceremony. Do not buck me on this!"

Sizzling with rage, Catrin left without a further word.

Reaching the isolation of the corridor, she collapsed against the hard rock wall, her head pounding as if she was being stoned to death. *I have no choice, no choice. I am nothing, nothing but a farm animal to be auctioned off. A commoner has more rights. How can the gods be so cruel? This is Father's curse, not mine. Why must I suffer for his sins?*

A slight nudge on the shoulder startled Catrin, and she bumped into Trystan. He steadied her by gripping her arm and said, "Please don't be angry at your mother. She loves you more than you realize. She may not show it, but she is anguished to see you in so much pain."

"Then why doesn't she tell me this herself?" Catrin said bitterly. "You, above all others, should know how much she resents marrying my father, but yet, she forces me to do the same."

"She selflessly did her duty," Trystan said firmly. "In doing so, she stopped a war and saved her people from slaughter. She helped forge an alliance between two tribes. You can do the same."

Though Trystan's words rung with truth, Catrin could see in his downcast eyes that his heart must have also been ripped out of his chest as hers was now. What else could explain why he never took a wife? She asked bluntly, "What about you? Do you agree with my mother's decision?"

Trystan stared at Catrin for a moment before answering, "I believe in the king and the queen. I do what they command."

The deep groove of anguish on Trystan's brow told Catrin otherwise. She turned her back on him and stomped down the dark corridor. This would be her last ride with Marcellus and she would make the most of it.

27

APOLLO'S AMULET

Marcellus regarded Catrin for a moment, then pulled off an amulet around his neck and put it around hers.

Later that morning, Catrin silently rode alongside Marcellus and Belinus on the dismal riverside pathway, her heart wrenched from the resentment digging at her core. She feared Rhan's curse had forced her father to negotiate with Cunobelin from a weakened vantage. The curse was now her doom. She would pay the ultimate price of sacrificing her happiness to ensure Cunobelin withdrew his support of Marrock.

As they approached the cave, Catrin sensed Marcellus's eyes on her. More than ever, she needed to feel his warm arms around her, but doing so would only make it harder for her to accept the upcoming marriage. She avoided his eyes and shifted her weight on the horse to look around for Mor. Catrin's chest tightened when she could not find her.

Oh, gods. She is not coming.

Overcome with crushing emotion, Catrin gasped. Any fleeting moments with Marcellus would forever be lost. Everything blurred through the tears forming in her eyes.

Look away. Don't let Marcellus see me like this!

Then in a corner of her eye, Catrin glimpsed Mor emerging from the woods. The heavy weight lifted from her chest when she saw

Belinus dismount, a grin bursting across his face. He ran and embraced Mor, lifting her off the verdant ground.

Catrin felt momentary joy watching Belinus take Mor's hand and lead her into the cave. Then bitterness that her parents had been so cruel began eating at her. She bit her lower lip hard until she tasted blood. If the king had not mandated she use her charms to mine information from Marcellus, she would not now be plunging head-first into his flame. She decided then to burn in the moment rather than live the rest of her life in cold ashes.

She turned her gaze to Marcellus, whose eyes sparkled like violet gemstones in the bright sun. He struck her as a god astride his majestic black steed. A warm flush spread across her face when he asked, "Are you ready to finish our ride?"

"Can you keep up with me?" she jested.

Marcellus smirked. "I have yet to be left behind. Has anyone followed us?"

With the danger that someone might catch them, Catrin darted her eyes all around and confirmed they were alone. She said, "I don't see anyone. Only Belinus was charged to watch us."

"Where do we go from here?" asked Marcellus, his eyes firmly fixed on her.

"To the Ancient Oak near the river."

He grinned. "The same place you showed me last week?"

"Yes, not far from here."

Catrin kneed her horse onto the pathway and Marcellus joined her. As they rode, she cupped her ear with a hand, listening intently for any change in the birds' chatter that would signal any unwelcome visitors. A flock of wrens in some bushes vibrantly chirped with no care in the world. On a high branch of a beech tree was a sleeping brown-faced, horned owl.

From overhead, the mocking cackle from a raven disrupted the sweet melodies of the forest.

Marcellus looked up. "Is that your raven?"

Catrin tilted her head back to watch her raven fly to another tree. "Yes, it follows me everywhere I go. It is like my eyes."

"How is that?"

"It warns me of danger."

He cocked an eyebrow. "Is that how you view me now? You've hardly said a word since we left the village. I find it strange that Belinus would risk the queen's ire by leaving us alone."

Cautious about not revealing Mor's secret, Catrin replied, "Mor needs to speak with him in private."

Marcellus reined his horse closer to her. "You must realize your sister is playing a dangerous game with Belinus. And you are playing fire with me."

Catrin's throat clutched. "I wanted to speak to you about our future."

Marcellus stared at Catrin for a moment, then dismounted and grabbed the reins of her horse. "Why don't you tell me what is on your mind? You've been close to tears ever since we left the village."

Annoyed with herself for showing her angst, Catrin bristled. "I am fine!"

"Your face tells me otherwise." Marcellus moved to the side of her horse and placed a hand below her foot to help her down.

Clamping her legs tight against the horse, she blurted, "Why should I trust you?"

He stepped back with a stunned look. "Did I say something to offend you?"

Inexplicably enraged, Catrin glowered. "Mother warned me about you, that you would seduce me for information. I told you about Marrock, yet you refuse to tell me why Rome supports this monster over my father."

Marcellus stared into her eyes. "And what do you offer in exchange for this information?"

"I do not understand."

"You accuse me of trying to seduce you to get information. Is that not your game also?"

Catrin huffed. "No!"

Marcellus shifted his feet. "All right, I'll freely give you the information you seek. Rome's support for Marrock is not set in stone. When I see my father again, I will speak against supporting your half-brother. There, does that make you feel better?"

Catrin jumped off her horse and pushed against Marcellus. She blurted, "What else have you not told me?"

He gripped her by the shoulders. "I should ask the same of you. What did your mother say this morning to put you in such a foul mood?"

All caution tossed aside, she said, "That you are sexually experienced. And … and you want more from me …" She froze when he tightened his hold and leaned closer, almost touching her face.

"You already know that about me," Marcellus said. "I never hid my desire for you."

Catrin pursed her lips. "Is that what you are doing now? Seducing me for information?"

Marcellus took a step back, his eyes ablaze. "Gods, woman! After all the time we have spent together, is that what you believe? What is this really about? You said you wanted to talk about our future."

Catrin fought back the tears swelling in her eyes. "How can we have a future together if we are duty-bound to serve our fathers?"

He pulled her flush against him. "That is why we cannot let this moment escape. Right now, I want you more than life itself. I thought you felt the same, but something is standing in the way. I need to know what."

"What if I told you my father has agreed to marry me to Cunobelin's son, instead of Mor?"

Marcellus stepped back, his mouth flung open. "Is that what your mother told you?"

"Yes, my father bartered me off like one of his prized cows!" Catrin raged. "I'm a princess and deserve better than this. I choose my own husband. I'm sure Mother told Father to force me to marry Adminius. She wants to punish me because of my feelings for you, an enemy."

Marcellus again pulled Catrin into his arms. "I am not your enemy. The thought of another man touching you makes my heart wrench. I'm also put in the same position. My father has complete authority to arrange my marriage as it will serve his ambitions."

"Is that supposed to make me feel better?" Catrin asked, pushing him back. "If that is the case, why don't you confront your father about forcing you to marry someone you do not love? Tell me, have you played with my emotions only to bed me, as Mother accuses?"

Marcellus slowly shook his head, his eyes reaching for hers. Catrin, unable to stop the tears, spun around and clutched herself to ease the stab in her heart. Then she felt his strong hands turn her around into his embrace, and he hungrily searched for her mouth—the kiss so ravenous that she could hardly breathe. Her need for him could no longer be denied. She wrapped her arms tightly around his neck pulling him closer, her body molding into his.

After what seemed like a lifetime, he released the kiss and proclaimed, "I choose you, Catrin."

The blue flames of his eyes burned away all her doubt about her next step. She glanced around for a place where they could lie down together. Seeing a cluster of violets, she pointed. "Over there, I can roll out a pelt."

Marcellus nodded and gave her another lingering kiss. They reluctantly parted, so he could tether their horses while she smoothed out the wolf pelt, the fur's sensual scent permeating the air.

After taking care of the horses, Marcellus held Catrin as she caressed his face, her hand pale against his rich olive skin. In turn, he traced her cheekbone with a forefinger and rubbed her lower lip. "So what did you want to show me?"

She interlaced her fingers with his. "Before you return to Rome, I want to show you this sacred site where we pray and make wishes. Look on the ground and tell me what you find."

Marcellus knelt beside the Ancient Oak, picked up a wooden votive and handed it to Catrin. She fingered the carved woman flanked by two horses and said, "This is Epona, the goddess of fertility. Couples come here to make offerings, so she will bless them."

Marcellus lifted his brow. "Epona. Cavalrymen pray for her to protect their horses. I'm not sure what this has to do with us."

From her pouch, Catrin pulled out a gold torc with bulbous horse heads on both ends, and she placed it around his neck. "This is my gift to show you my love. Before Mother Goddess, I pledge myself as wife to you."

At first, Marcellus appeared baffled, but then his eyes lit up. He smiled. "My sweet love. Are you sure you want to do this? Our families will never recognize our consummation as marriage."

Catrin tilted her head back to stare into his sparkling eyes. "I am not a child. I pledge myself to you, so Mother Goddess will forever bind our souls and no one can break that bond."

Marcellus lifted her chin and said what she most wanted to hear, "I also pledge my love to you. I want this moment to be special for both of us."

For several seconds, he quietly gazed at her face and finally said, "I want to explore all our feelings in this sacred place. To begin our journey together, we must join our bodies. Let me release you of your clothes."

An excited breath caught in Catrin's throat as he unbuckled her sheathed sword and dropped it on the ground. Her desire heightened when he unclasped the gold broach from her cloak and brushed his fingers over her bare shoulder as he took the garment off. He pulled her against his chest and whispered, "Close your eyes."

Trying to contain a nervous giggle, Catrin squeezed her eyelids shut. As he fumbled at the bindings of her leather bodice, she trembled from his touch. He told her in a honeyed voice, "Relax, my love."

Catrin swallowed hard with excited anticipation as he pulled the lacing out of the notches of her chest armor and parted the leather flaps. The palm of his hand slid over each breast like a warm gentle wave. She thought her heart would soar into her throat when he kissed a nipple.

Oh, sweet Mother Goddess, she wanted to look at his face. Opening her eyes, she found Marcellus smiling at her. He tapped her on the nose. "No, Catrin, keep those pretty eyes closed."

She did as instructed and stood still as his fingers peeled off her bodice, exposing her. He captured a breast in the heat of his hand and moaned, "Sweet Venus," his finger and thumb slowly rubbing the nipple. The circling motion mesmerized her as he moved his hand over to her other breast.

He suddenly pulled away.

Bewildered, Catrin opened her eyes and saw him pulling off his gold shirt to reveal his bare chest. The dark hair that wisped from his navel to below his long-hung trousers drew her eyes. She loosened the straps to his breeches and slowly moved her hand beneath the waistband.

He flinched. "What are you doing?"

"Touching you like you are touching me," she cooed.

"Mmmm … I like that," he said, a soft growl deep in his throat.

Slowly moving her hands lower, she hesitated when she saw his feral eyes lingering on her. Suddenly cognizant of his lusty hunger for her, she pulled away and covered herself with crossed arms. He leaned forward and pulled her arms away.

"Don't, I want to see you."

Unsettled by his aggressive behavior, she felt like a little girl again—vulnerable and innocent. The sun faded behind a cloud and the misty air rapidly cooled. Goose bumps erupted all over her skin and she began to shiver.

Marcellus stepped back with regret on his face. "I'm so sorry. I didn't mean to frighten you. It is just … when I thought you would touch me that way … oh gods, Catrin. I want you so badly, but before we go on, I need to be sure you still want this."

For the last few nights, Catrin had only dreamt of him. The desire was there, but something was holding her back. She averted her eyes from his piercing stare. Her voice quavered when she confessed, "I am in a cocoon. And I don't know how to emerge. It is just … I need more time … more patience."

Marcellus regarded Catrin for a moment, then pulled off an amulet around his neck and put it around hers. He placed her hand on his chest where she could feel the strong beat of his heart. "This is my offering to you, my love," he said. "Keep Apollo close to your heart. Whenever you look at his face, remember it is I who loves you and protects you."

Catrin lifted the statuette off her breasts to study its marble features. She stroked the hard marbled surface and exclaimed, "He looks just like you."

Marcellus chuckled. "My father had an artisan sculpt Apollo to my likeness. Hubris, I know, to fashion the sun god after oneself."

"This is how I see you in my dreams," Catrin said, overcome with powerful feelings. "You descend as Apollo in a chariot and take me back to the heavens with you."

Marcellus stepped closer and gently lifted her face. "A dream is a journey to your soul; listen to your inner desires."

Catrin embraced him. "I do desire you, I want us to be together forever."

He held her tighter and whispered, "I want this, too, but you need to trust me. Relax. Let your emotions take over on our journey together."

She closed her eyes. "I do trust you."

Without another word, he pressed his lips hard on her mouth. This time, her unbridled passion matched his, their tongues swirling around each other in a sensual dance. He emitted a heady, musky scent that made her swoon. She went limp, savoring his wet kisses down her neck. His teeth clamped the skin on her shoulder and sharpened into a bite. She moaned, the pain exquisite as he lightly stroked her back.

He then captured her backside, pressing her down on the plush wolf pelt. Musky lavender fragrance released, intoxicating them both with desire. His fingertips touched her as though he was an artist brushing new sensations all over her body. When he drew a nipple into his mouth, her inner core fired with dull electrical pulses, pleasing yet unnerving. It was as if the raven was trying to connect with her.

She tensed for a moment and then relaxed. This must be the sensation of lovemaking, she reassured herself. As she nestled into the softness of the fur, she reached out for the touch of his warm hands and wet mouth exploring every curve of her body. When he slid a hand beneath her breeches, she winced from the unfamiliar thrust of his fingers probing inside. He must have sensed her discomfort, because he immediately pulled his hand away and lifted off her.

With his gaze still on her, he knelt at her feet, untying and removing her sandaled shoes, first the right then the left. He kissed the insole of each foot that shot feathery tingles to her toes. While massaging her ankle, his mouth parted—lips thick, luscious. She wondered if he had made love to his Roman noblewoman the same way. No Cantiaci warrior would take so much time to arouse a woman like he was doing.

After several glorious moments, he leaned over and pulled her trousers down over her hips. She nervously giggled as he wrestled the plaid fabric away from her feet. Now fully naked, she had nothing left to hide, no more dark secrets. She openly displayed herself and delighted at the glint in his eyes.

Marcellus lowered himself beside her and passionately kissed her as his fingertips explored her inner thighs up to the pinnacle of her bundled tingles. When his forefinger rubbed over a most sensitized spot, she arched her hips from the unexpected arousal. He strummed the tissue like a harp until she cried out.

He then rose above her like a god and released his remaining garments. His skin glowed in the sun's brilliance. She closed her eyes from the blinding glare and parted her legs. When he pulled her into his sexual fire, she gripped his muscular arms to embrace his power. They were two stars merging into a brilliant glow—forever changed, forever connected.

28

WHITE RAVEN

Catrin's eyes lowered and her lips began to quiver. "Marrock also set me on a wolf pelt before he abandoned me in the woods."

As Marcellus pinned Catrin's arms against the wolf pelt, he beheld her ivory-crème face that reminded him of the roses at his family's villa. She was a tight bud opening to his heat. Seeing the rapture on her face, he knew she wanted him as much as he wanted her. His needs urgent, he roughly broke through her initial resistance and plunged into watery depths. The rhythm of his body on hers was like a wave crashing on a beach. He was no longer Roman, she no longer Cantiaci. They were as one.

When her fingernails clawed into his back, he soared into climatic ecstasy and cried out, "Oh, sweet Venus," then fell limp and immersed in her heat.

A few moments later, he gazed into her bright turquoise eyes and swept a strand of golden hair from her face. Finally catching his breath, he kissed her gently. Not until then had he understood how Mark Antony could have been so bewitched by the Egyptian queen. Now this exotic Celtic princess possessed him—heart, body and soul.

She gave him a sweet smile and sighed, "We are now forever bound in marriage."

Marcellus tensed.

Marriage!

Reason returning, he questioned himself for boldly claiming Catrin as his wife in the throes of passion. For matters as important as marriage, nuptial vows were chiseled in the hard negotiations of their fathers. Saying this to her seemed cold-hearted and he instead said, "I love you." Yet the timbre of his words did not sound convincing. Feeling a pang of guilt, he rationalized that he at least gave Catrin a moment of joy before she was forced to wed. Marriage was not about love; it was about assuring the family line. The hard reality was he could not keep his vow, but it still pained him to see the sadness on her face.

"I love you, too," Catrin said somberly, "but where do we go from here?"

"The memory of our time alone will forever be etched in my mind," Marcellus quickly replied, but the next words caught in his throat: *but we can never have each other.*

Catrin froze in his arms, as if she had heard his thoughts. He tried to ease her tension by stroking her hair, but she pushed hard against his chest. "That is not enough! Get off of me. I'm burning inside."

The sharp tone of her voice and the pained grimace on her face yanked at his heart. He untangled himself out of her legs, so she could get up. When she sat up, her mouth suddenly gaped in horror.

Marcellus also bolted to a sitting position and looked in the direction of her eyes. To his dismay, a dark crimson stain besmeared the silver pelt. Although he knew taking her innocence might cause some bleeding, the excess worried him. He chastised himself for being too rough on their first sexual encounter. Concerned, he fingered a tiny braid in her mussed hair. "I didn't hurt you, did I?"

Catrin's lips quivered as she continued gawking at the pelt. Marcellus turned her face toward him, so she would look into his eyes. "Please answer me. I want this to be special, this being your first time."

Catrin answered him with teary eyes.

Regret now weighed heavily in Marcellus's chest that he had hurt her physically and emotionally. He poured out his heart. "I'm so sorry. I just wanted to feel close to you. It was as you described—our bodies and souls bound as one."

Catrin's eyes lowered and her lips began to quiver. "Marrock also set me on a wolf pelt before he abandoned me in the woods."

Taken aback, Marcellus flinched. *What did I do to prompt such a memory?* He cupped her face between his hands to reassure her, to reassure himself. "For the love of gods, Catrin, why do you say that?" His voice cracked when he said, "At this moment, I have never been happier."

Misty-eyed, Catrin said ruefully, "I also wanted this. I don't know why … it wasn't what I had expected."

Marcellus embraced her. "It was special for me. It still is. Don't let the memory of Marrock steal this time from us."

"Did I please you?" she asked, voice shaky.

He tightened his arms around her. "Beyond all my expectations. Beyond what Venus could have conjured. I have never known such joy. I thought you felt this also."

Catrin pulled back and regarded him with doe eyes, then collapsed her head into her folded arms and wept. Each sob stabbed at Marcellus's heart. Trying to find that bond with her again, he wove his fingers through hers. "Please tell me why you are so upset."

"I saw the white raven in your eyes," she said, voice fading.

Marcellus wasn't sure if he heard her correctly. "White raven? I don't understand your meaning."

Catrin wiped the tears away from her face with the back of her hand. "I also saw the white raven's reflection on Marrock's eyes … the day he set me on the wolf pelt … my sun disappeared. I can't remember what he did, but in my heart I know he did something vile … something so terrible it will forever change me. The memory hides like a festering wound in my mind. The truth of what he did boils to the surface whenever I feel—" She fell into sullen silence.

A dread crawled over Marcellus, recalling the raven bursting through the billowing smoke at the ritual. Decimus had warned him that this was a sign that Catrin was a sorceress. He asked her, "Do you take this as an omen?"

"I am not sure," she said, her eyes languished on him. "But I'm afraid our love could curse us ... destroy us, destroy my family and kingdom."

Marcellus pressed her head against his chest, and he ran his fingers through her hair. "You can't think this."

She pulled away and her eyes lowered to the pelt. "Do you smell that?"

Marcellus whiffed a strange mix of sweet body odors. "Lavender. A hint of musk."

"When Agrona gave me the pelt, my desire for you grew stronger whenever I inhaled its scent."

"What are you trying to tell me?"

Catrin's eyes widened. "I fear Agrona cast a spell on us. I don't know why she would do that."

A slight panic surged into Marcellus's rapidly beating heart. He gripped her arms. "What are you saying? That I am bewitched, that what I feel for you is not real?"

"I don't know what to believe anymore." She looked vacantly in the distance. "When I saw the white raven disappear from your eyes, it made me tremble. It made me think of Marrock, and what my father said."

"What is that?"

"He told me about Rhan's curse."

Marcellus jerked his head back. "Who is Rhan?"

"Marrock's mother, the former queen. She cursed my father at her execution, before I was born. Rhan foretold he would sire a daughter with another queen." Catrin pointed to herself. "That daughter is me. The curse says, 'When I fly out of Apollo's flames as a raven, Marrock will ally with the Roman Empire.'" She lifted the

Apollo's amulet off her breasts with a trembling hand, as if the marble stone was too heavy. "Did I release Rhan's curse by wearing this?"

Flabbergasted, Marcellus fumbled for words. "For the love of gods, Catrin, you have done nothing wrong! You gave me your love. Nothing is more precious to me than that. This is not about Rhan's curse."

When Catrin began weeping, he lifted her in his arms like a small child. "It is tearing my heart out that all I can give you is this moment. I thought you understood."

"I do," she whispered. "You are right. I cannot ask any more."

Marcellus kissed her gently on the cheek. "Perhaps, if we bathe in the river, you'll feel better. We can leave the pelt here as an offering to Epona. Let us enjoy the remaining time we have together."

Catrin nodded slightly and relaxed in his arms.

29

RAVEN'S ATTACK

The raven suddenly dived at Marcellus in an all-out assault.

Marcellus carried Catrin to midstream where he set her down. He scooped water into his hands and rinsed her body as if he was performing a healing ritual before they began their separate journeys. A deep sense of remorse washed over him that he would leave her when she needed him most. Not only did she carry the burden of not knowing what Marrock did to her, she also faced an uncertain future with a foreign husband she did not love. Her nakedness against him did not evoke a lustful desire, but something stronger—a deepening bond. Now that he had pledged his love to her, would his promise torment him after he left Britannia? How could he ever leave now, not knowing if she was all right? The heartache of losing her pierced into his soul.

Marcellus tenderly massaged Catrin's shoulders. A serene smile floated across her face and he again fell under her spell. He pressed her back against his chest and cupped her rounded breasts. Feeling her heart beat in synchrony with his, he whispered, "I love you."

Suddenly, to his dismay, she leaned over, clutched her stomach, and groaned as if she was ready to vomit. Trembling, she waved him back. "Something is wrong. I feel sick. My head is spinning. It is as if …" She touched her temple. "I need to be alone."

He reached for her hand. "What do you mean 'be alone'?"

She slipped into the water's current and waded downstream. "I need to make an offering to Epona and ask for her blessing. I must do this alone. Go ahead, finish bathing. I will be ready soon."

A cold breeze over the water made Marcellus shiver as he watched Catrin swim to the riverbank. On shore, she hurriedly dressed and armed herself with a sword. His heart began pounding with trepidation when he observed her wandering aimlessly near the trees, staggering as if she were drunk. Worried that she was deathly ill, he rushed to shore to check on her.

As he stepped on the embankment, a raven suddenly darted over Catrin's head like an arrow shot straight at him. He dropped to the ground like a rock, but the creature's sharp talons sliced his head as it swept over him. Keeping low on the ground, he listened for flapping wings. The only sound he could hear was his rapid heartbeats in his ears.

A moment later, the raven shrieked, chilling him to his bones. He glanced sideways. A few feet from his face, the creature was perched on a moss-covered log. The raven bobbed its head and blasted another teeth-shattering screech.

Marcellus scooted away from the ruffled bird and cried out, "Is this raven warning me of something?"

Catrin yelled, "Yes, get away now!"

The raven cocked its head sideways and peered at Marcellus with its glowing amber eyes.

He bounced to his feet and shuffled backward, shouting, "That raven looks like it is ready to make a feast of me!"

Not answering, Catrin pointed her sword at the sky, toward the woods and finally to the raven. In turn, the raven hopped sideways, first to the right then to the left, as if its dance was directed by her.

"What are you doing?" Marcellus asked, confounded by her bizarre behavior.

The raven suddenly dived at Marcellus in an all-out assault. He instinctively crossed his arms to shield his face from razor-sharp talons and screamed, "Get your cursed bird off me!"

Peeking through a crack between his arms, he glimpsed Catrin dashing toward him and flapping her arms like a bird. "Stop it! Stop it! Get away!"

The raven swooped over Catrin, and she quickly whirled around to chase after it. When she disappeared into the thick woods, an eerie silence pervaded the landscape. No birds chirped. No bees buzzed. No squawking ravens, either. A shiver ran down Marcellus's back as he recalled the tribune's warning that Apollo's wrath could fall on him if he defiled Catrin. He looked at the sun now abandoning him behind billowing clouds.

Apollo, did you send that cursed raven to be my scourge?

A flurry of wrens suddenly flapped at his head, startling him. He shrunk from a sensation of evil crawling all over his skin. He glimpsed a shadow lurking between dense pines.

"Catrin, where are you?" he cried out.

The shadow stretched through the trees, and Catrin appeared under a beam of sunlight with sword in hand and the raven perched on her shoulder. She looked at Marcellus for a moment and strode back into the trees.

Catrin's bizarre behavior unnerved Marcellus. Was he a fool to love a cursed woman entranced by a raven? Conflicting emotions whirled inside him that their love was cursed, but he couldn't just leave her. Not like that. He scanned the woods for her.

All doubts about his love for Catrin swept away when he heard her scream, "Get away! Get away from me!"

Terrified that she was being attacked, he scrambled through bushes, ignoring the pain of thorns stabbing his bare feet, and dashed into the woods where he found Catrin frozen in a defensive position, sword extended.

He followed her fear-struck eyes toward the treetops.

No movement.

He darted his eyes around the forest.

No predator or attacker.

Finally he asked her, "What attacked you?"

She didn't answer, her eyes as listless as what he had previously seen when she was in a trance. He reached for her sword, but the raven on her shoulder arched its wings and shrieked. Avoiding the bird's jabs, he took the weapon away. The creature then hooked its claws into her cloak. She never flinched when he fumbled to unclasp the fabric. Frustrated, scared, he ripped the cloak away and threw it on the ground, along with the raven entangled in the fabric.

The creature went limp.

When Marcellus looked at Catrin, the overhead cloud cast a shadow that seemed to switch her blue eyes to the color of brilliant amber gems. Unnerved by the phenomenon, he touched her pallid face.

A burning spark jolted into his hand.

Shocked, he recoiled and gaped at the two black pinpoints that looked like a snake bite in his hand. Shaking his head in disbelief, he muttered, "What in Hades?"

Though he did not detect any movement in Catrin's lips, he heard her voice saying, *Help me! Help me to escape!*

Seeing the terror in her eyes, he asked, "Escape from what?"

Catrin touched his arm and emitted another painful shock.

Startled, he jumped back and stumbled over what felt like a stone. He looked down. The raven's head was turned upside down and its black eyes turned blue-green.

Fearing the raven was casting a spell, he lunged at the creature to smack it away. His fist barely missed the bird as it flew away.

Then to Marcellus's horror, Catrin collapsed on the ground, her hands curved like talons. A shrill erupted from her throat and milky foam bubbled from her mouth. Her arms flailed, legs jerked. He helplessly watched her convulse from what he guessed to be the falling sickness—an affliction great men like Julius Caesar had suffered. Although he heard tales about the ailment, he had never witnessed the violent, gut-wrenching muscle contractions. He turned Catrin on her side to ease her breathing. Her mouth continued frothing like a rabid dog's, her teeth clicking.

After several agonizing moments, her convulsions finally eased and she went limp. He examined her eyes and was relieved they were blue again. When he touched her clammy forehead, she groaned and looked at him in bewilderment. He gently stroked her face. "Relax. You have awakened from a nightmare."

She tried to speak, but he couldn't understand the garbled words.

"Do you know who I am?" he asked.

She nodded weakly.

Marcellus knew that he had to get her back to the village. How could he explain what happened to any native who could not speak Latin? He must find the queen or Belinus.

Hearing twigs snap, Marcellus spun on his heels to find three bare-chested warriors, one he recognized as Cynwrig with the battle-ax. He didn't know the others. One was holding the reins of the black stallion and the bay. The third man, brandishing a spear, had a broad nose and upturned eyes. Disheveled coppery hair and heavy beard crowned his face like a lion's mane. The warrior's feral eyes scoured over Marcellus's chest down to his groin.

Marsellus shuddered, realizing in his haste to protect Catrin, he had not put a stitch of clothing on. A frigid breeze swept over him as he looked at the storm clouds rumbling over the treetops.

How do I explain this?

He stretched out his hands toward the disgruntled men as if he was calming skittish colts. "Let us not get too excited. It is not what you think."

The men shifted their eyes from Catrin to Marcellus and back to her. It was obvious they were not jubilant to see him in natural armor. He forced a thin smile, wondering if they would view him more favorably if he had been a Celtic Gaesatae at the Battle of Telamon. Undoubtedly, he would suffer the same fate as the Gaesatae—who fought naked and were slaughtered by the Romans—if the painted warriors suspected him of any disrespectable behavior toward their beloved princess.

Fighting to keep his wits, he pointed to Catrin. "She is hurt. I need your help. Do you understand? Hurt."

The barbarians looked blankly at each other.

Cynwrig knelt beside Catrin and pressed two fingers on her neck.

As Marcellus focused on Catrin, he was ambushed with a hammer fist into his gut, knocking him to the ground. Gasping for air, he curled his legs to his chest in agony. The sadistic, lion-face warrior added humiliation by rubbing trousers in his face.

Finally catching his breath, Marcellus staggered to his feet, hurriedly dressed, and warily watched the coppery-haired warrior lift Catrin into the arms of Cynwrig, astride the black stallion. Cynwrig cradled her in his arms and kneed the steed onto the river pathway.

With a sword pressed against his back, Marcellus followed Cynwrig on foot. Glancing back at the Ancient Oak, a sense of doom quaked through him when he saw the lion-faced warrior crouching and inspecting the wolf pelt.

30

SCORCHED RAVEN

"Every decision you make from now on can change how the life-threads will weave into the tapestry. Be forewarned ..."

Catrin hovered between consciousness and disturbing visions on her ride with Cynwrig to the village. At times, she could feel the sway of the horse beneath her and Cynwrig holding her tight. Though she had initially resisted the raven from entering her mind, the bird ultimately forced itself in.

She no longer knew if she was human or raven.

With the unbearable pain of sharing the raven's essence in her skull, her human soul escaped in the form of a raven to the sanctuary of the Ancient Oak. As she floated around its welcoming branches, she wondered if she was yet alive. Perhaps, her soul had wandered to the Otherworld and was unable to find its way back to the mortal world.

The Ancient Oak's gigantic boughs sheltered other creatures in the forest—chattering birds, humming bees, and nipping foxes. At first glance, every living entity seemed disjointed, but she knew they were all bound to each other. Streams and rivers flowed into the sea, connecting water and land; birds flew into the sky, connecting heaven and earth. What happened to one happened to all.

Suddenly, a bright light broke through the forest canopy. Looking up, she saw the sun slowly descending upon her, its molten tongues bursting out from the red globe. The sun morphed into a horse-driven chariot driven by Marcellus, his body naked and hair as golden as a sunrise. He landed the chariot on an upper branch of the Ancient Oak and summoned her. "Take a journey with me into your soul."

Catrin then recalled her father's words: *Dreams are glimpses into your soul. Time stands still and destiny flies over life's currents.* She hesitated to join Marcellus. Her dream might transform into a nightmare that could threaten her soul.

Finally finding the courage to accept Marcellus's invitation, she swooped through the quivering leaves and landed on his extended arm. When he raised his forearm, she saw the reflection of the enigmatic white raven on his crystalline blue eyes. The words "pure, loyal, brave" resonated in her ears.

Marcellus clasped her pristine-feathered body and set it on a wooden pyre. He spread out his fingers and emitted sparks onto the kindling, igniting it. A powerful force burned through Catrin like a firestorm. New strength surged into her muscles as the flames devoured her tissue and the blood boiled beneath her skin. Smoke released soot that she breathed into her lungs. Her skull felt as if it were ready to explode with hot gases. Smoke blasted into her nostrils as the inferno burned hotter and hotter. A bone-crackling shriek escaped her throat as her eyes shot from the sockets. Raw pain screamed all over her charred skin as she beseeched the raven, "Help me! Help me escape Apollo's fire!"

A charge bolted up her spine and clamped her jaw shut. Cackles echoed in her ears as she was then transported through a crevice and into a tunnel of light. She had experienced this before in the raven's mind, but had always leapt out before entering the dark portal inside the rainbow arch. This time, the force was so strong, she could not escape.

Bracing herself to burst through the dark gateway, she was surprised finding herself bouncing off its flexible surface and somersaulting several times. After stabilizing herself, she floated up the multicolored arch and studied the flashing life-threads on the fluid surface. Each thread connected, then disconnected with others.

The raven explained in a man's baritone voice, "This is the transitional barrier between the mortal world and Otherworld. It is called the Wall of Lives. It is here where nature's forces coalesce and time stands still—past, present, and future merging into one."

As Catrin drew closer to the wall, she could see moments of everyone's life project on each respective life-thread. She asked the raven, "What is this?"

"In the spiritual realm, you can harvest universal truths from past, present, and future," the raven explained. "You are like an Ancient Oak that anchors its roots into the earth's womb to nourish the leaves that capture truth's light. Each living thing is a life-thread that weaves in and out a fluid tapestry from birth to death. As you can see, every person has a unique colored thread that joins others to conjoin everyone's fates."

A brilliant light flashed before Catrin's eyes. Full of wonderment, she asked. "What was that?"

The raven cawed with delight. "At each birth, a bright light flashes on the wall whenever a soul reincarnates into its next form—fish, bird, animal, human. It is here Ancient Druids could see the future. Only a few humans are chosen by the gods and goddesses to have this gift. You are one of them. Born with the raven spirit, you can hover between the white spiritual realm and black earthly existence."

Awestruck, Catrin asked, "Have I always had this ability?"

"Yes," the raven answered. "But you were too afraid to acknowledge it. Forces such as these often manifest when you are besieged with hate, rage, and fear."

Catrin now realized her dreams and foreboding visions were flashes of moments that she had seen on the Wall of Lives. Many of these images were surreal and she did not know how to interpret them. She asked, "What good is it to prophesy if I cannot change the future?"

The raven lifted its beak and cawed, "Study the past and tell me what you see."

Catrin studied the life-threads of a coppery haired woman and a dark haired girl, their lustrous life-threads weaving and joining each other. She concentrated on the life-thread of the woman whose features were similar to Marrock's. At one point, a white-robed man was tying the wrist of King Amren as a young man to the woman, a radiant adolescent, at a wedding ceremony. At the next twist in the life-thread, the woman was giving birth to a baby boy.

But the last image on the life-thread struck horror into Catrin.

Before a towering bonfire, the stately woman fell on her knees and raised her arms to the blood moon—the image Catrin had seen before the Romans landed. The woman never flinched when the king chopped off her head with a longsword.

Repulsed, Catrin looked away, a taste of bile in her mouth.

The raven shrieked, "You cannot escape the past! Look again and tell me what you see."

Turning her eyes to the Wall of Lives again, Catrin observed something odd. The woman's life-thread did not end at the portal leading into the Otherworld, but whipped back and entangled with the gray thread of the diminutive, dark haired girl. Their images then blurred on the adjoining thread that slithered back and forth like a striped serpent over a black sea. It was heading toward Catrin's life-thread at the point where she saw herself on the fiery pyre where Marcellus had placed her. She struggled to understand why she flew out of the flames as a scorched, black raven. A foreboding chill feathered down her back.

She asked the raven, "What does this mean?"

The bird's silence screamed to her soul. The white raven that Marcellus had placed on the pyre had scorched black in the fire. She quavered. "What have I become?"

The raven crooned, "Look backward and you will understand as you fly forward."

Puzzled, Catrin again examined the thread-lines of the woman and girl. The truth finally dawned on her like a rising sun.

Rhan never died. She and Agrona are one and the same. The eidolon hiding behind Agrona's eyes is Rhan. If Rhan can possess Agrona, she can also take control of me!

Catrin shuddered. "What does Agrona want from me?"

"She wants to reset Rhan's curse by having you burn in Apollo's flames," the raven said with grated voice.

Catrin gasped. "Do you mean Marcellus is Apollo?"

"Yes," the raven resoundingly replied. "Every decision you make from now on can change how the life-threads will weave into the tapestry. Be forewarned, the time a person dies can only be determined by the gods."

"Rhan defied death when she possessed Agrona," Catrin retorted.

The raven replied in a thundering voice. "At what cost?"

Everything then silenced and the Wall of Lives tumbled into a waterfall that transformed into flames.

Waking from her vision, Catrin found herself astride a horse near a farm field, her head leaned against Cynwrig.

He touched her forehead and gasped, "She is on fire."

31

RHAN'S SECRET

For almost twenty years, she had patiently waited for this moment, finally spinning her web of deception for Amren's downfall.

Standing near the fortress gate, Agrona looked down the hilltop and watched the group begin their climb. Catrin appeared ill leaning against Cynwrig, both of them astride the black steed. Marcellus was afoot with a guard holding a sword to his back. Ferrex was farther back, riding Catrin's bay horse. Belinus was not with them. Agrona suspected he was with Mor, confirming local rumors of their affair. That could only mean that Catrin and Marcellus had consummated their love, despite the queen's command that they be escorted by Belinus.

Agrona smirked.

For almost twenty years, she had patiently waited for this moment, finally spinning her web of deception for Amren's downfall. She wiped a bead of sweat from her forehead. The afternoon sun was unusually hot, reminding her of the heat from the bonfire during Rhan's execution. Agrona clutched her throat, reliving the excruciating pain of tendons snapping away from her spine as Amren sliced the sword blade through her neck. When her head flew off, she stubbornly clung to life with only an infinitesimal time to possess another being. If her soul was entrapped in the severed skull, she could not finish the journey to the Otherworld and complete the circle of death into life.

Miraculously, her head slipped through the dainty fingers of the feeble-minded girl before falling on the hard ground. That was when Rhan entered Agrona's mind.

At first, Marrock refused to believe Agrona was Rhan and that his mother's soul no longer lived in the skull that he had enshrined. Later, when he was a young man, he reluctantly accepted Agrona as Rhan's embodiment. Like any mother fighting for her son's birthright, Agrona unveiled an exquisite plan for Marrock to embrace his legacy that she had foretold in her curse.

Agrona chuckled at her own cleverness.

For years, she had deceived Amren into believing she was a powerful Druidess selected by the gods to be his spiritual advisor. After gaining the king's confidence, she amazed him with her ability to describe intimate details that only Rhan could have known. Everything went perfectly to plan, almost too perfectly. Catrin changed all of that.

Agrona was at first overjoyed that Catrin had been born with a raven spirit. She knew when Catrin joined forces with Marrock, they would be an unstoppable force, overthrowing Amren and conquering all tribal regions on the isle—a mighty nation to rival the Roman Empire.

But she had not predicted the raven's fervor to protect Catrin.

The tightly woven scheme unraveled after Marrock abandoned Catrin in the woods. A week later, Amren banished Marrock without a public hearing. Although Agrona had been the king's closest confidante, he refused to reveal the reason for his judgment. He instead showed her the dagger on which he had transcribed Rhan's curse. To Agrona's dismay, the inscription had transformed from the original curse. That was also the day her mystical powers began to fade.

Infuriated that Marrock had somehow altered the curse, she questioned him about what he had done to Catrin, hoping to discover what altered the curse. He refused to cooperate, instead mocking her,

"Perhaps you are not the most powerful Druidess of all times as you claim. If you were, the curse would be steadfast."

Agrona lashed out, "You ungrateful numbskull!" She pushed against his chest. "I laid the groundwork for you to bring down your father. Without me, you are nothing."

Marrock shot a seething glare that burned into Agrona's inner core. "You forget yourself, Mother. Do not test my patience."

Nonetheless, she stood her ground. "You idiot! How did you goad the ravens to peck out chunks of tissue from your skull? You are now nothing but a monster with a moon-cratered face!"

Before Agrona could run away, seeing the fire in Marrock's eyes, he yanked her up with a hand and shook her like a rabbit within inches of his ghostly, pitted face. "Don't forget, Mother, I have the powers you once had! I can shape-shift into a wolf. And soon, I will be the mightiest Druid of all time."

What could Agrona do but meekly acquiesce? If her son ever found out the true extent of her diminishing powers, he would spit her out like rotten meat. With every gain in his supernatural abilities, his hubris swelled. How could she trust such a self-serving son to carry out her curse?

She couldn't—not now, not ever! She had to outmaneuver him, a well-known secret for bringing down pompous rulers. First, she had to find a way to reset the curse and to regenerate her mystical capabilities. The only option was to use Catrin as an agent to mine the forces from the Otherworld. Though the princess appeared a clumsy toddler trying to control her raven's magic, Agrona knew that she needed to proceed cautiously until she could fully determine Catrin's strengths.

When Agrona noticed Cynwrig and Catrin approaching the fortress gate, she drew out of her ruminations and held up a hand.

"What do we have here?"

Cynwrig halted his horse and shifted Catrin's head against his shoulders. "Princess Catrin. She burns with fever."

"I can treat the princess in her bedchamber," Agrona said. "Why is Marcellus on foot with a sword to his back?"

Cynwrig darted his eyes at the gathering spectators gawking at them with wide eyes. "I should first speak with the queen about what I found."

Noticing the apprehensive grimace on Cynwrig's face, Agrona surmised he had found Marcellus in a provocative position with Catrin. The aphrodisiacs of lavender and stag musk oil she had sprinkled on the wolf pelt must have done their magic. She pressed her lips together to hide her smirk.

"Where is Belinus?"

"Only the gods know," Cynwrig said, lifting his eyes to the sky. "I couldn't ask that idiot Roman about Belinus's whereabouts. He is too stupid to understand our tongue. Thus, I brought him here for the queen to question."

Agrona stepped closer and examined Catrin. The princess was limp, her eyes glazed and face ashen. She looked at Cynwrig. "I will follow you and calm the people's fears about what has happened to the princess." She glanced around at the growing number of villagers pressing on them. She smirked, thinking of ways to incite them further.

Following Cynwrig on foot, Agrona squeezed through the crushing throng anxiously asking what happened to the princess. She said with a fervid pitch, "Get back! Let us through. We must appease the gods! A curse has befallen our beloved princess."

Most of the agitated villagers swarmed around Agrona and Cynwrig like mad bees at the royal courtyard where Trystan was waiting. By then, Catrin had regained consciousness and appeared shaken as Trystan helped her down. He placed an arm around Catrin and assisted her to the entrance where Queen Rhiannon and a servant greeted them.

With the clamor growing louder, Agrona turned around and saw some enraged men shoving Marcellus.

A soot-faced blacksmith bellowed, "What did you do to our princess?" He whacked a hammer into Marcellus's back, making him scrunch over.

Angry voices of other men rumbled, "Roman scum! Dog! Swine!" Their fists pelted Marcellus in the front and back, finally knocking him to his knees.

As Agrona watched the increasingly hostile mob, she could not contain her sly smile. The rabble would certainly rip the Roman's limbs off, if the queen's guards did not put a stop to it.

Trystan slammed into Agrona's shoulder as he shoved the mass back trying to reach Cynwrig still astride his horse. He shouted, "Stop anyone attempting to harm Marcellus."

As directed, Cynwrig circled his horse around Marcellus and threatened the amassing crowd with a sword. Trystan threw fist-wielding men out of his way like empty sacks and ordered, "Get back! Get back to your tasks! We will handle this."

When Trystan finally reached Marcellus, he gripped the Roman by the arm while extending the other to push anyone aside who dared challenged him. Agrona trailed Trystan and Marcellus through the crushing crowd, now fearing the out-of-control mob might harm her. She forced herself through the pressing mass and finally reached the Great Hall's entrance where assembled guards with extended spears helped her through the doorway, then marched toward the crazed mob to stop them.

Inside, the queen met Agrona and Trystan, who had a grip on Marcellus's arm. She snapped her eyes at Trystan.

"What is the commotion outside?"

"The villagers want to tear the Roman hostage apart for raping Catrin," Trystan snarled.

"Raping Catrin?" Rhiannon repeated, eyebrows scrunching together. "Where is Belinus? I want a full report on what has happened."

Trystan grunted, "Belinus was not with them."

Rhiannon bristled. "What do you mean 'not with them?' Go find Belinus now!"

Trystan clicked his heels together. "I will get to the bottom of this."

Rhiannon turned to Agrona. "Come with me. You need to treat Catrin."

As Agrona strode alongside the queen down the corridor to the bedchambers, she inwardly chuckled from the people's nasty reaction toward Marcellus. When she entered Mor's bedchamber, Catrin was lying on the bed with a pillow beneath her head. Agrona flinched when she noted the burning glint in Catrin's glare directed at her. She quietly observed the queen examine her daughter.

Rhiannon smiled thinly as she placed a hand over Catrin's forehead. She asked, "What happened?"

Catrin garbled, "Vis … sion … fire … storm …"

Rhiannon lifted Catrin up and gave her some water. Some color returned to Catrin's face after she took some sips. She then mumbled, "Fire-breathing eagles."

The queen looked at her with bewilderment. "Did Marcellus do anything to you?"

"He helped me," Catrin rasped.

"Do you know where Belinus is?"

Catrin's eyes lifted as if she knew, but she said, "I don't know."

A loud rap on the door captured everyone's attention and they turned to find Cynwrig poking his head in. The queen waved him in. His belted sword banged against the doorjamb when he entered. He asked, "How is Catrin?"

Rhiannon gestured toward Catrin. "See for yourself."

Cynwrig stepped to the bed and cracked a smile. "Look at you—a fierce warrior. Nothing keeps you down."

The queen nudged Cynwrig's arm. "Speak with me outside about what is happening." She turned to Agrona. "Watch over Catrin while I handle my people outside. Later, we can discuss the healing rituals you will need to perform."

Agrona bowed. "Yes, your grace."

After the queen left with Cynwrig, Agrona leaned over the bed and observed that Catrin's pupils were dilated and that her forehead was hot to the touch. When she noticed the amulet around the princess's neck, Agrona lifted the statuette to inspect, but was stopped by a strong grip around her wrist that emitted a burning charge. She recoiled and was shocked to hear the rage in Catrin's voice.

"I forbid you to touch that!"

Agrona stood and rubbed her sore wrist. She warily looked at Catrin. "Where did you get that amulet? It looks Roman."

"Marcellus gave it to me as a gift," Catrin replied.

Agrona sneered, "Did he give it to you so you would lay with him?"

Catrin abruptly sat up and pointed her to the door. "Get out of my sight. Now!"

Detecting the amber sheen in Catrin's eyes, a sign of a clairvoyant possessed by a divine force, Agrona surmised the raven had already conveyed some of the mystical powers of the Ancient Druids to her, as foretold in the altered curse.

"Who are you?" Catrin asked sharply. "And why are you here?"

Agrona winced. *Odd question.* She kept her eyes fixed on Catrin and said, "You know who I am. I am Agrona, your father's Druidess and spiritual advisor."

Catrin's forehead furrowed. "No. There is someone else behind your eyes."

Unsettled by Catrin's comment, Agrona nonetheless maintained a stone-cold demeanor. "You are hallucinating, my love. The Roman's talisman has cast a spell on you. Let me have it so I can remove the curse."

Catrin clasped the amulet. "I forbid you to take it. And, I plan to tell my mother who you truly are."

Agrona knew then that the princess had somehow found out she was Rhan. Perturbed, she nonetheless maintained a steely facade.

"My love, you are not yourself. That must be a demon talking inside you. Don't worry. We will fix that."

Catrin raised a fist. "I will strike you down, if you touch me."

Apprehensive of Catrin's unexpected hostility, Agrona backed away. She had to act quickly to shut the bitch up. Hearing footsteps at the door, she opened it to find the red haired warrior, Ferrex, with something in his hand.

"Is the queen in here?" he inquired. "I want to show her the pelt I found at the Ancient Oak where we found Catrin and the Roman."

Agrona gnarled her lips into a smile. "The queen will be here shortly. Set the pelt down, so you can help me strap Catrin down. I must give her a potion to expunge all her evil spirits."

32

EXPOSED

Marcellus lifted his shoulders and said resoundingly, "She gave her consent. We pledged our love for one another before Mother Goddess."

With his wrists tightly bound with leather straps, Marcellus waited on a straw bale in the horse stables. Trembling, he clenched his swollen hands to settle himself after the barrage of fists. Based on the pounding pain in his face and shoulders, bruising had already set in. The fury in the villagers' eyes still shot shivers down his spine. They were out for blood, undoubtedly believing he had defiled their beloved princess.

Even now, he felt as if his conflicting emotions about Catrin were running a gauntlet. He thought he had accepted her mystical aura, but her strange behavior after they made love caught him off balance. Her ramblings of the white raven and Rhan's curse disconcerted him. The bizarre interaction between Catrin and her raven completely unhinged him. The tribune's warning that she was a sorceress tormented him.

Did our souls join, as she said, or did she bewitch me?

He looked at his shaky hands and muttered, "What is wrong with me? Why can't I get Catrin out of my heart?" With the sun setting, the darkening stall shrouded him in gloom. Not only was his life endangered, but Catrin had appeared deathly ill.

The sudden movement of a shadow startled Marcellus. He glanced up and glimpsed the blue lightning bolt on Cynwrig's arm. The warrior grunted and gestured for him to get up.

Marcellus anticipated an inimical meeting with the queen. Putting on a fierce facade, he gave Cynwrig a ferocious scowl, which he immediately regretted when the barbarian, having the strength of Hercules, threw him against the wall like a spear.

Shaken, ears ringing, Marcellus found himself face down with a mouthful of straw seasoned with savory dung. He gagged on the stench, then wrenched his head up, and spat and spat until he ejected the foul-tasting grit. A strong hand smashed his face into the brownish muck again and yanked his head back by the hair to the point his neck cracked.

Cynwrig then put Marcellus into a headlock and squeezed his throat. Marcellus gasped and pounded his fists against the warrior's metal-hard arm, but the pressure against his windpipe tightened. Fighting for breath, Marcellus kicked his legs out and twisted his body with all his might. Every muscle cramped as he pounded on Cynwrig's arms to break the choke, but he weakened and darkness overtook him.

Marcellus awoke with the splash of cold water. Opening his eyes, Trystan and Cynwrig came into focus. The warriors gripped Marcellus's shoulders and forced him to his feet. Foul-smelling water dripped into his eyes and he flinched from the burning sting. He felt his feet lift as one of the men body-slammed him on the hard dirt floor. Rough hands then gripped Marcellus by the shoulders and dragged him like an animal for butchering down the alleyway.

Fed up with his rough treatment, he dug his heels into the ground and demanded, "Let go of me! I can walk on my own."

Trystan snarled, "Then stop resisting, dog!"

Marcellus nodded and clenched his jaw.

The warriors yanked him up and plopped him on his feet, so he could walk. With both men close behind, Marcellus staggered to the back of the structure and lumbered down the dimly-lit corridor past the bedchambers. Near the end of the hall, he confronted the one-eyed cat with a rat the size of a small dog in its mouth. He cautiously stepped around the hissing creature and entered the reception area where the queen was seated on her elevated throne. She asked brusquely, "What happened to my daughter?"

From the fiery glow on her face, Marcellus suspected she already knew about his delicate predicament with Catrin. He drew in a deep breath, slowly exhaled, and answered with a steady voice, "She was stricken with the falling sickness."

"Falling sickness," Rhiannon repeated. "Explain."

"Catrin had convulsions. Foam spewed from her mouth. When your guards discovered us, I was caring for her. Is she better?"

Rhiannon frowned. "As we speak, she burns with fever. Tell me exactly what happened before she was stricken."

Marcellus rolled his neck to loosen the tension in his shoulders. "I was bathing in the river. Catrin was on shore, guarding me. For some reason, she was drawn into the forest. The next instant, she screamed. I was afraid she was caught unawares by a charging boar or some kind of predator. When I found her, a raven was on her shoulder. It looked as if it was casting a spell on her, so I pushed the thing off. Then she collapsed."

"Why was Belinus not with you?" Rhiannon asked, raising a stern brow.

Marcellus hesitated, wondering how much she knew about Mor's affair. "He left us earlier in the morning."

"Why would he do that?"

"Why don't you ask him?"

"Was it because he met Mor there?"

"Perhaps. I'm not sure."

Rhiannon turned her head and swore under her breath. She again looked at Marcellus. "Did Catrin prearrange this meeting between Mor and Belinus?"

Strange that I did not think of that. Marcellus answered, "I don't know."

Rhiannon narrowed her eyes to the point of an arrow. "Did Catrin say anything to you about the marriage agreement with Cunobelin?"

Marcellus hesitated and regarded the queen's hostile glare. "Yes, she said that the king has betrothed her to Adminius."

"What was Catrin's mood when she told you?"

"Angry."

"How did you feel when she told you?"

Marcellus tensed. "To be frank, I felt sorry for her. Why don't you get straight to the point and tell me what you plan to do with me."

The queen called out, "Agrona, present yourself."

Hearing footsteps to his back, Marcellus pivoted and saw Agrona walk out of the shadows and into the illumination of the torch light. Her wolf eyes appeared to glow under the wavering flame as she moved toward him. His heart shuddered when he saw the silvery wolf pelt in her arms, the brownish-red stain clearly visible.

Agrona slowly circled him and sniffed. "I smell Catrin on you," she growled, then pressed the pelt against her nose. "I also smell your body fluids on the fur."

Throat constricting, Marcellus rasped, "What are you implying?"

Agrona turned to the queen. "The warrior called Ferrex found this pelt. Remember, this is what I gave Catrin a few days ago at the family dinner. The blood on the fur is proof this Roman brutally ravaged Catrin."

Enraged at the accusation, Marcellus lurched at Agrona, but Cynwrig gripped him by the arms to stop him. Fighting against

Cynwrig's restraints, Marcellus roared, "I would never do anything to hurt Catrin! That blood could have been left from any injured animal."

Agrona again circled Marcellus like a wolf stalking its prey. "This is Catrin's blood after you tore her maidenhood away like a wild beast."

Rhiannon interjected. "Isn't that why Cynwrig caught you naked with Catrin?"

Marcellus leveled his eyes at the queen. "As I said, I was bathing. In my haste to protect Catrin, I didn't think to put my breeches on. Ask Cynwrig. She was fully dressed when he found us. If Catrin was here, she would corroborate my story."

Agrona dropped the pelt at Marcellus's feet. "Unfortunate for you, Catrin is out of her mind with fever." A nasty smirk twisted on Agrona's face as she opened her hand, revealing the leather-stringed Apollo amulet. "I found this around Catrin's neck. Is this yours?"

Marcellus stared at the amulet, wondering how Agrona got hold of it. "Yes, I gave it to Catrin as a gift of thanks for her hospitality."

"I have been told your god Apollo can curse mortals with the falling sickness." Agrona smiled grimly and rubbed the statuette's marble surface. "Did you use this to bewitch Catrin and rape her like a crazed beast?"

Marcellus raged, "You mad woman! I gave this to Catrin to protect her!"

"Protect her from what? You?"

"Everything I have done with Catrin has been done out of love —" Marcellus cut off his words when the queen's eyes blazed. His chest tightened as he watched Agrona slowly walk to the queen.

The Druidess turned and pointed an accusatory finger at him. "Beware, the Roman's patron god has put a spell on Catrin!"

"How can you be sure?" Rhiannon asked.

"The gods deliver their messages through me," Agrona proclaimed. "They tell me Catrin will again be stricken. The words spewing from her mouth are from demonic forces insider her. I have strapped her down, chanted, and given her potions to expel these evil forces. Nothing has yet worked."

Marcellus's mind flashed back to what Catrin had told him about Rhan's curse. He thundered, "This is not Apollo's curse. Catrin is in danger from Rhan's curse."

In parallel, both women turned toward each other and said, "How do you know this?"

"Catrin told me," Marcellus said. "She said there is a curse looming over your kingdom. I am being falsely blamed for this!"

Agrona stomped next to Marcellus. "You are lying! Apollo told you to say this, to cover up for what you did." She then turned to Rhiannon and pointed to herself. "Let me take Catrin away from here. At my lair, I can cast her demons out. Then I can train her to use the raven's powers as the king ordered."

Rhiannon's stare burned at Marcellus. "Did your god Apollo put a curse on my daughter?"

Marcellus bristled. "No!"

"Did you join my daughter?"

Marcellus gave the queen a confused look.

"Did you seduce my daughter?" Rhiannon asked bluntly.

"No matter what I say, you will not believe me. I swear on the honor of my ancestors that I never tricked her."

"Yes or no! Did you take Catrin by force?" the queen said with a deep growl to her voice.

Marcellus lifted his shoulders and said resoundingly, "She gave her consent. We pledged our love for one another before Mother Goddess."

For several seconds, Rhiannon gripped the throne's armrest and stared at Marcellus with deadly silence. Then she slowly rose from her throne and barked something in Celtic.

Cynwrig and Trystan immediately restrained Marcellus by the arms and escorted him back to his sleeping quarters. There, they unbound his wrists and clicked the door's bolt to lock him in.

Perplexed, Marcellus did not know whether to take this as a good sign that the queen was reconsidering her judgment. Rubbing his swollen wrists, he wondered what more he could do to find out what happened to Catrin. With the Red Executioner ready with battle-ax outside his room, he plopped on the bed, frustrated that he could do nothing.

The word "rape" ripped in his mind. He ruminated over what the queen would do to him if she reached this conclusion. Would she make sport of him and make him run through a gauntlet of savages, eager to bludgeon him to death? Most likely, they would chop off his head, spike it, and hang it as a decoration on the Great Hall's wall. Hands shaking, he fumbled to remove his shirt, so he could inspect the swollen bruises left by the villagers.

Suddenly a woman's wail from the next room made his heart tremble. Catrin must be in the room next to his. When he heard her scream again, he jumped up and wildly paced back and forth, rage building that he could not help her.

When he again heard her agonized wails, he slammed his fists on the door and shouted, "What is happening to you, Catrin?"

The door clicked open and Marcellus backed away from the battle-ax in Cynwrig's hand. Realizing that one blow would smash his skull in, he held out his hands in a conciliatory manner. "All right, Cynwrig, I see your point. I will stop shouting, but for the love of the gods, can't you tell me what is happening to Catrin?"

Cynwrig muttered something in Celtic and pointed to the bed. As directed, Marcellus sat on the bed and uttered, "Why can't I talk with someone who can speak my tongue?"

Cynwrig rotated the axe handle a couple times, then left and slammed the door shut. Marcellus felt as if his guts were ripping out of him when he again heard Catrin's anguished cries. Then her screams stopped and footsteps could be heard leaving the other room.

He pressed an ear against the wall and held his breath, trying to capture any sound from the other room.

Nothing.

He tapped on the wall and said in a hushed voice, "Catrin, are you there?"

She answered in his mind. *Don't let Agrona take control of me.*

Marcellus pressed his palms against the wall to feel her essence. *How can I do that?*

Catrin's voice whispered into his ears. *Keep me in your thoughts.*

The wall suddenly warmed, and Marcellus envisioned Catrin as a goddess with golden orbs circling her head. Her hair swept back as if she were flying. Then the wooden wall suddenly chilled when he heard shuffling feet and Catrin's moans fading in the corridor outside his chamber.

33

DAGGER'S TWISTING FATE

Taking a closer look, she knew her eyes were not lying. The inscription on the blade had been obliterated. It took a moment for her to comprehend what that could possibly mean.

The events from the last two days and nights weighed heavily in Rhiannon's mind. Droopy-eyed, she glanced around the king's gloomy bedchamber where Catrin had been placed. She placed a hand on her daughter's forehead. The skin felt clammy and cold—a sign her daughter's fever had broken. Catrin now seemed at peace, her breathing even.

But how long would it last?

The agony of seeing her daughter wail and thrash as if an evil spirit was controlling her movements still racked Rhiannon's heart. Fatigued from the sleepless nights, she could no longer think clearly or remember hour to hour. When her stomach grumbled from hunger, she could not recall the last time she had eaten.

She snagged a finger in her tangled hair and muttered, "When did I last brush my hair?"

The candle on the table cast a shadow of her up the wall. She sighed, her eyes filling with tears. She gazed at Catrin again and was filled with terror that her daughter might lose her soul. Regret bubbled to the surface that she may have made her gravest mistake by not abandoning Catrin as a baby in the forest and allowing her to die.

Rhiannon recalled Agrona's proclamation that Catrin was the daughter foretold in Rhan's curse. The weaker of identical twins, Catrin was ghostly-white as a baby and on the verge of death, unlike her sister Seren, a ruddy newborn wailing vigorously for the breast. Rhiannon had considered sacrificing her sickly child, so Mother Goddess could suckle her in the Otherworld and Rhan's curse could not be fulfilled. However, she reconsidered when the inscription of the curse began blurring on the dagger blade which gave Amren hope that the spell could be reversed. When Agrona said Catrin had been born with the raven spirit and was destined for the same greatness as ancestral warrior queens, Rhiannon agreed with Amren that the gods should decide Catrin's fate. As a mother, she could not deny her baby girl the milk she needed for sustenance.

Paradoxically, Catrin survived whereas Seren died tragically at the age of twelve of a fever after Agrona ceremonially branded her with Amren's family totem animal—the horse.

Wrestling with her grim recollections, Rhiannon mulled over what she should do next with her daughter. Agrona warned that Catrin's short periods of tranquility would be shattered with further outbursts.

Rhiannon could only trust her one loyal and true champion to advise her. She stepped to the doorway and motioned her servant. "Summon Trystan. Tell him to meet me in the king's council chamber. After that, tell Agrona to watch over my daughter."

The servant bowed and scurried away.

Rhiannon kissed Catrin on the forehead with deep remorse of what she might have to do. She stepped out of the room and wearily shuffled down the corridor to Amren's private council chamber. In the room, she sat at a round table and gazed at the burning candle while she waited for Trystan. She flinched when the image of a fire-breathing eagle appeared on the orange flame. During one of her crazed states, Catrin had cried out that these creatures would raze the village to the ground. *This is an omen*, Rhiannon concluded, leaving no doubt in her mind that her daughter was cursed. But who cast the spell? Was it Apollo, as Agrona insisted, or was this the next step in Rhan's prophecy that Catrin would rise out of the fire as a raven?

Or gods forbid, is this Marrock's sorcery pulling the threads of Catrin's fate?

In desperation, Rhiannon silently prayed, *Divine Mother Goddess, shine your light on the pathway I must take.*

When brilliant light illuminated the chamber, the hairs on Rhiannon's neck prickled. She glanced over her shoulder and saw light glowing through the woolen shawl that covered the dagger case. She slowly pushed herself up from the table, stepped to the back shelf, and pulled the blue-and-green fabric off the wooden box. The chamber dimmed as she touched the front panel of the case. The wooden surface felt strangely cold, even though the last two mid-summer days had been unusually warm. With both hands, she carefully picked up the box and set it near a three-wick candle on the table. The dark oak surface suddenly radiated to an amber color.

Rhiannon trembled. "Blessed gods!"

For several seconds, she stared at the glowing case, thoughts churning in her head about what supernatural forces she was dealing with. Was this a sign from the *Dea Matres*? Or was this an omen from Rhan's curse? Were evil spirits playing tricks on her?

Despite the foreboding jitteriness in her stomach, she needed to see if the inscription on the dagger had altered again. She sat at the table and inserted the pin into the brass lock. When she tried to open the lid, her fingers singed from the hot surface, and she jerked back against the chair's splat.

"Cursed *scaxsion*!"

Looking at the wooden box again, she swore that it was breathing like a living thing. She questioned if her mind was frazzled from the lack of sleep. Struggling to regain mental clarity, she took several calming breaths, then wrapped her fingers with a piece of her cape and gripped the upper edge of the case. The top snapped from her grasp like a crunching jaw.

She squealed and recoiled like a snake ready to strike at whatever might crawl out.

For several seconds, she gaped at the box glowing red. Apprehensive that Rhan's curse was transforming, she kept telling herself: *Open the box ... open the box ... open the box.* Curiosity finally overtaking her, she clasped the top edge of the case with her cloth-covered fingers and slowly lifted the cover. She could feel the heat rise out of the box as she pulled the hinged top back.

To her amazement, the dagger blade was aglow. The brilliant red surface appeared as if it had just been pulled out of a smelting furnace. *Perhaps*, she thought, *the candle flames were causing the illusion.* Taking a closer look, she knew her eyes were not lying. The inscription on the blade had been obliterated. It took a moment for her to comprehend what that could possibly mean. Her first reaction was joy that Catrin had lifted the spell during one of her fits. Maybe Amren was right after all. Catrin had been divined by the gods to reverse Rhan's curse.

Then Catrin's wails that sounded like a wounded animal burst through the cracks in the wall. A chill iced down Rhiannon's back. She slammed the lid shut and sprang to her feet. The inlaid ravens on the wooden panels began flapping their wings against the golden background. Frozen with terror, she gaped at the case as it slowly dimmed to its original dark color.

A panicked thought cut through her mind that she had inadvertently reset Rhan's curse when she opened the box.

The sound of a man's cough caught Rhiannon's attention. She turned toward the doorway and found her gallant champion standing there. Trystan was attired in military uniform—a chain mail shirt, a belted longsword at his side, and trousers with the tartan blue-and-green tribal colors of the Regni. A gold torc adorned his neck, each of its ends crafted in the shape of a stag's antlers to ward off predators. He bowed slightly.

"Did you summon me?"

At that moment, Rhiannon wanted to rush into the comfort of his arms, but she couldn't move, the anguished words caught in her throat.

Trystan must have sensed her distress, as he rushed in and enveloped her in his arms. "What is wrong, Rhiannon?"

Chest heaving from sobs, she stuttered, "I need … a friend, someone I can trust."

Trystan hugged her. "You know I am always here for you. What is this about?"

Rhiannon nuzzled her head into the comfort of his shoulder. "I've seen a horrible omen and don't know what to do."

Her head began spinning and the floor seemed to collapse beneath her feet. She went limp, but Trystan held on tight and helped her into the chair. He sat across the table and told her, "You look worn out. You need to get off your feet."

She noticed his eyes shift toward the raven-inlaid dagger case on the table.

"Is this new?" he asked.

She shook her head. "This case is old, but it holds a dark secret that is yet to be revealed."

Trystan leaned over. "What is in it?"

"A jewel-crusted dagger," she answered. "I swore to Amren that I would safeguard it while he was gone. If I tell you the dagger's dark secret, you must swear not to tell anyone."

Trystan reached across the table to clasp Rhiannon's hand. "I swear on the graves of my ancestors that I will keep your secret. Now tell me what it is."

Rhiannon hesitated. Amren had told her not to reveal the dagger to anyone while he was gone. Yet the situation had become dire and she finally said, "On the blade is the inscription of Rhan's curse that Amren had engraved after her execution. The words on the dagger's blade began blurring at the time of Catrin's birth. It was as if the curse was rewriting itself and yet to be revealed. Amren took this as a sign that Catrin might be able to alter the spell, but when I inspected it today, the inscription had disappeared. I thought perchance the curse had been lifted, but then the inlaid ravens on the panel began flapping. Then I heard Catrin wail." Rhiannon placed her trembling, folded hands on the table. "Now I fear the curse has transformed again. Open the case and tell me what you see."

Trystan rubbed the upper edge of the case with a forefinger. "That is odd. It feels like ice."

Rhiannon quavered. "Open it."

Trystan nodded and slowly lifted the lid. A foreboding shiver prickled across Rhiannon's shoulders and she turned her head away, afraid to look. "What do you see?"

"A jewel-studded dagger as you said," Trystan replied.

"Is the inscription gone?"

"I don't see anything. It looks like some scratches on the blade." Trystan paused. "Wait, I can't believe this. Letters are forming on the blade!"

Shaken, Rhiannon looked at the blade. Her heart leapt into her throat when she saw the words etching on the steel blade: *The gods demand the scales be balanced for the life you take. If you deny my soul's journey to the Otherworld by beheading me, I curse you to the same fate as mine. At ... the time ... daughter rises ... out ... Apollo's flames ... the ... curse—"*

She screamed at Trystan. "Shut the lid! Shut the lid!"

Trystan slammed the cover down.

"Rhan's curse is resetting itself," Rhiannon exclaimed, hurriedly locking the case with the key. She continued rambling from one thought to another like ripples in a stream. "The dagger is shedding its skin, a snake revealing something more venomous. I thought Mother Goddess had answered my prayers. Adminius wants to marry Catrin, not Mor. It made sense. Mor is with child. I told Catrin she was betrothed. She took it badly. And now—"

Rhiannon pressed her hands on her face and wept. Trystan stepped around the table and wiped the tears from her face with his fingertips. The heartfelt gesture only made it harder for her to contain her anguish.

"Please don't do that."

He held her face between his hands. "I'm worried about you. You are not your usual self."

Rhiannon could not stop sobbing. "I know. It's just … I don't know … what to do … what to believe … who to trust."

"That is why I am here," Trystan reassured and smiled. "Now take hold of yourself and dry your tears. Tell me what is really troubling you."

She clenched her trembling hand to steady herself and said, "There is something else that I've tried to hide. Maybe it is because I cannot accept it."

Trystan raised his brow. "What is that?"

"When Cynwrig brought Catrin to the village two days ago, he confided that he found her in the arms of Marcellus." Rhiannon noticed the red streaks spreading across Trystan's face.

"I already got wind of this from Cynwrig," Trystan said, voice grating with anger. "He suspects our Roman guest may have raped her."

"No, no … I don't think so," Rhiannon quickly replied. "Marcellus denies this. I've tried to quell these rumors. The last thing I need is an uprising from my people demanding his head."

Trystan slapped the table, making the candle flames flicker. "If that Roman raped her, I'll do the pleasure of taking his head."

Rhiannon stared at Trystan. "Don't do anything brash. Catrin admitted she loves him, and Marcellus confessed that he had pledged his love for her at the Ancient Oak. That can only mean one thing." She paused, her throat clutching. "They consummated their vows. I blame myself for this happening. I knew how strong Catrin's feelings were for Marcellus. Yet, I foolishly allowed her to ride with him that day."

"Rhiannon, you are too hard on yourself. It does not make sense that she would recklessly lie with a foreigner. The Roman lecher must have taken advantage of her."

"Whatever the truth, I fear the ramifications of what they have done. Until such time when Amren returns, I must treat Marcellus as a guest, but locked under heavy guard," Rhiannon said sardonically. "With the unraveling situation here, I need your help."

Trystan placed a firm hand on Rhiannon's shoulder. "How can I help?"

"I need you to deliver a message to Amren about what has happened before he finalizes the marital agreement with Cunobelin. I can't risk having such a sensitive message intercepted."

"For you, I will do anything," Trystan said, smiling "The Catuvellauni capital is a hard two-day ride from here. While I am there, I'll also assess the Roman fortifications. Give me a week to return. I will take Cynwrig with me. That way, if anything goes wrong, he can ride back and warn you."

"I am so grateful, Trystan, for your loyalty and devotion. You are truly my best friend." Rhiannon clasped Trystan's hand. "Before you go, I ask one more thing."

"What is that?"

"I need your advice about Agrona."

"Agrona?"

Rhiannon frowned. "Agrona says the Roman god Apollo cursed Catrin. That is why she was afflicted with the falling sickness and has gone stark mad. Agrona insists that she must cast out Apollo's evil spirits for her to recover. To do so, she must isolate Catrin in her lair where her strongest potions are stored. I've never trusted Agrona, but I fear my daughter might not recover unless I agree. Last night, Catrin ranted the raven was trying to steal her soul. Agrona warned me her raven could unleash its dark forces on her if she did not learn how to control its powers. I am at wit's end on what I should do."

"In spiritual matters, you should follow the advice of the king's most trusted spiritual advisor," Trystan said firmly.

Rhiannon tapped her lips with a forefinger. "Should I wait for Amren's concurrence on what I should do with Catrin?"

"With the grave situation here, you cannot wait," Trystan cautioned. "You must decide now. I'll explain this to Amren. I am sure he will support whatever decision you make."

"Thank you, Trystan," Rhiannon said, more relieved. "Those were my exact thoughts. If you would excuse me, I must speak with Agrona and decide whether to proceed with the healing ritual for Catrin."

34

MOTHER'S BETRAYAL

*"There, she can remove demons that are infesting your mind.
Be assured, my dear, she will help you recover and train
you how to control your raven's powers."*

With her mind clearing, Catrin first focused on the overhanging wooden beam, then glanced around the room. She wondered why she had been placed in her father's bedchamber. Images of what had happened to her the last few days jumped through her mind like a pebble skipping over water. At one point Marcellus was holding her in his arms, the next she was blocking Agrona's attempts to enter her mind, and finally she envisioned eagles blowing flames out of their beaks and igniting a firestorm on her village. Between these nightmares, she traveled to other realms in the raven's mind—or maybe they were other worlds she imagined. Days and nights merged together. At times, she could not distinguish between the physical world and the land of dreams.

She now realized that she was in the real world. A foreboding cold swept through the room, making her shiver. She lifted her eyes and found Agrona hovering above her. The gray aura surrounding the Druidess was as terrifying as the monstrous eagles she had seen in her visions. When Agrona bared her teeth into a wolf grin, the hairs on Catrin's neck stiffened like icicles. She twisted and squirmed to escape, but something was holding her down. Lifting her head, she observed leather straps around her legs and arms. She fiercely wiggled back and forth to loosen the restraints, but a strong hand squeezed the back of her neck, making her stop. She couldn't see who was behind her as Agrona held a cup to her mouth. "Drink this, my love. Soon the ritual will begin."

When the edge of the cup pressed against her lips, Catrin clamped her mouth shut.

"Stubborn girl," Agrona snarled. "You can't resist me forever. It is only a matter of time before you weaken and you are mine."

The words "are mine" blasted into Catrin's mind. She hurled her head back, fighting against the hand clawing her neck. When pincer-like fingers squeezed her nose, she gasped. A warrior she recognized as Ferrex clamped her chin between his fingers and pushed the cup's rim hard against her gritted teeth. Metallic-tasting slime filled her mouth. Feeling as if she was drowning in blood, she sprayed the greenish solution all over Ferrex's face.

He still held steadfast and clenched her jaw to force her mouth open. The gritty solution flooded her mouth, and she had no choice but to swallow or choke to death. When he took the goblet away, she gulped for air like a fish out of water and coughed violently. After hacking spasmodically for several moments, she finally caught her breath and spat out what was left in her mouth.

"Too late, my sweet," Agrona sniggered. "I will drop feathers. Soon you will become a raven."

Panic clutched Catrin's throat when she realized the elixir was again heightening her senses and making her hallucinate. The dark-wooded walls began twirling like dancing colored balls. The creaks of a door thundered into her ears. She glanced at the doorway and winced when her mother entered, her skin multicolored.

The queen's voice rang in Catrin's ears. "Are you feeling better?"

Catrin wanted to run away from the loud noises attacking her ears, but she couldn't move her legs. She opened her mouth to speak. The words stuck in her throat like scratchy wool.

Agrona's reply to the queen blared like a battle carnyx. "There is no change. You must let me perform the cleaning ritual."

The queen's words echoed in Catrin's ears. "Do what ... what you must ... must."

The first obsidian-colored plume floated down in slow motion, swooping back and forth, and jabbed into Catrin's forearm. The quill pierced a maggot into her skin. When the slimy creature began crawling into her tissue, she screamed in terror. The horrific creature then slithered into her blood vein.

Another feather dived at Catrin, and she whipped her head back and forth to avoid its assault. This time, the shaft thrust into her nose and transformed into a beak. As more feathers volleyed at her like arrows, she cried out from the pain of razor-edged plumes slicing her skin open.

Adding to Catrin's horror was Agrona wailing, "I beseech Bel and his consort Belisama to cleanse this cursed woman of all evil things. I command all demons to leave her body."

When Catrin gaped at her arm, she envisioned them shape-shifting into black wings. Losing grip of all reality, she shrieked with terror, "The raven is stealing my soul!" She then vaulted over a crevasse into a vortex of light to escape, but plunged deeper into the dark essence of her raven spirit.

Loud footsteps startled Catrin out of her horrific nightmare of ravens pecking away at her body, transforming her into one of them. When she opened her eyes, she turned her head toward the direction of splashing water and found her mother rinsing a cloth in a ceramic bowl. Glancing around, she recognized the king's bedchamber, but was no longer restrained. Fuzzy-headed, she rolled on her side and asked, "What has happened to me?"

Rhiannon stepped over to the bed and kissed Catrin lightly on the forehead. "You have been in and out of a fever."

Suddenly chilled from the rivulets of cold sweat on her chest, Catrin began shivering and her teeth clacked. "How ... how long have I been in here?"

"Three days," Rhiannon said, wiping Catrin's forehead with the wet cloth. "You had us worried. You were hallucinating. Can you remember anything from the last few days?"

Catrin tried to remember. "I just dreamt that I changed into a raven."

"What about before you had the fever?"

Catrin didn't think her mother needed to know about her sexual encounter with Marcellus. Then the images of Rhan and Agrona from the Wall of Lives flashed in her mind and her chest seized with panic.

"Agrona! Where is she? You need to keep her away from me!"

Rhiannon gripped Catrin's arm. "Why do you say that?"

Catrin stared at her mother. "Agrona is not who you think she is. She wants to control me."

Rhiannon smiled grimly and set the washcloth aside. Disconcerted by her mother's muted reaction, Catrin raised her voice. "Did you hear what I said? Agrona is evil. Rhan lives inside her."

"Oh, sweet child ..." Rhiannon's eyes lingered on Catrin for a few uneasy moments. "I now understand Agrona's fears about what is happening to you. Your mind is no longer right."

Catrin jolted to a sitting position, her mouth flying open. "What do you mean my mind is 'not right'? You can't trust what she says. She is a wolf ready to pounce on us."

Rhiannon's jaw tensed. "Although I've never taken Agrona into my confidence, it is with a heavy heart I must do what she advises. She will help you overcome Apollo's affliction."

Catrin gave her mother a bewildered look. "Apollo's affliction? You are not making sense. What has happened?"

"You were stricken with the falling sickness when the guards found you with Marcellus. When they returned you to the village, Agrona discovered the Apollo amulet around your neck."

Catrin grabbed at her bare neck. "It's gone. Did you take it from me? It was a gift from Marcellus."

"Agrona said that Marcellus used the amulet to curse you with the falling sickness."

"That is utter nonsense," Catrin said. "The amulet protects me and I want it back."

Rhiannon's eyes glistened with swelling tears. "Why are you fighting me? For the last three days, I have watched you writhe in pain and rant about fire-breathing eagles burning our village and ravens pecking out your eyes. What am I supposed to believe?"

The taste of the bloody potion spewed into Catrin's memory. She pushed herself off the bed to stand. The walls began to spin around her, and she staggered and bumped into a chamber pot on the floor. Images of Agrona forcing slimy solutions down her throat flushed in her mind. She looked at her mother. "Can't you see what Agrona is doing? She drugged me. She tried to poison me. I am still dizzy from the awful tasting elixirs she forced on me."

"That is what she did to calm you," Rhiannon said, her voice clutched with emotion. "I can see our conversation is going nowhere. As such, I have decided to grant Agrona permission to isolate you at her lair. There, she can remove demons that are infesting your mind. Be assured, my dear, she will help you recover and train you how to control your raven's powers."

Catrin's chest constricted to the point that she could hardly breathe. "No! No! You can't make me do this. Agrona wants to control me! Why don't you believe me? Agrona and Rhan are one and the same. She will destroy us if you don't stop her!"

Rhiannon said with a firm voice, "It was only after Marcellus gave you the Apollo talisman that bad things began to happen. Marcellus is the enemy here."

"You are wrong about him," Catrin said fervently. "He did nothing wrong. He tried to help me. Agrona is the enemy. Are you so stupid that you cannot figure out she tricked you? I am perfectly sane!"

Catrin felt her mother's sharp fingernails stab when she gripped her arm. "Marcellus blinded you to what he is. He gave you that amulet, so he could charm and seduce you. I am now speaking to you as your queen. My first priority is to protect our kingdom from any treachery you pose because of your blind loyalty to him. You have no say in my final decision. Agrona will take you away tonight."

Incensed, Catrin shot a seething glower at her mother. "You believe me a traitor!" Feeling betrayed, Catrin yanked her arm away from her mother's grip and stumbled against the wall. Her rage let loose and she ranted, "You can't do this! I must stay here. You must obey Father's charge that I guard Marcellus."

Rhiannon's brow creased into a deep cleft. "Not any longer. Ferrex is now charged with that duty."

Catrin felt her chest seize. "What will you do with Marcellus?"

"The same as always. He will be our guest until your father returns."

Breathing becoming ragged, Catrin rasped, "Will I get to see him again?"

"No. You are not to see anyone except Agrona."

Fury flamed into Catrin and without thought, she shouted, "I refuse to go," and slammed her mother into the stone wall.

Her mother crumpled to the floor and went limp.

Catrin froze in shock. *What have I done?*

When her mother did not move, she hurriedly checked her wrist. No pulse!

She then placed two fingers on her mother's neck.

No heart beat!

She pressed harder on her neck. A faint throb. A momentary relief. Her mother's eyelids flicked open, her brown eyes ablaze.

Catrin jerked back. She had crossed the line of no return. There was nothing she could do to stop her mother's iron first.

The queen staggered to her feet and pushed Catrin's shoulders against the wall. "If you do that again, I will strap you until your back welts. If you refuse to go willingly with Agrona, I will have Ferrex tie your wrists with leather straps and cart you off like the beast you are."

Catrin felt as if her heart was speeding toward a precipice. There was nowhere to go but jump over the cliff. She refused to acquiesce. "I will not go. You will regret putting your trust in Agrona instead of me."

Rhiannon snapped her head back. "I think not." She called out, "Agrona and Ferrex! Come in here now and take Catrin!"

Ferrex walked through the doorway, rapping the end of a rope on his hand, followed by Agrona, twisting a black cloth around her hand.

The Druidess sneered, "Ready, my love."

35

WEB OF DECEPTION

*Catrin warily stepped around the wolf and sat at the table.
She asked, "How do enemies think—hide in the shadows
and lure the prey into their traps?"*

Isolated and locked in Agrona's musty hovel, Catrin waited for the Druidess to return. It had now been over a week since she had been tied-up, blindfolded, and carted to the ramshackle lair. Bitterness ate away at her like a maggot feeding on rotting tissue. She glared at the dead birds strung together and hanging from the ceiling's log beams. On the wattle and daub walls were spiders spinning their lattice traps. Shield bugs scurried across the earthen floor only to be eaten by her raven. The only raw emotion she could feel was *cathos*—a fiery rage burning away to her core. Her father had sold her in marriage to the enemy. Her mother refused to believe the threat that Agrona posed.

Now she feared for her life. Exposed to the Druidess's skullduggery, she had no possible way to escape with a guard always stationed outside. She had been forced to drink awful-tasting concoctions that racked her brain with hallucinations of fire-breathing eagles. The only respite she had from these nightmares was the dream of Marcellus descending as Apollo from the heavens to rescue her from the firestorm. She felt closer to this foreigner than her own family and also sensed imminent danger to him. She prayed to Epona that he not be harmed.

The door's click jolted Catrin out of her foreboding thoughts. As she anticipated, Agrona walked through the doorway. When a red wolf with glowing amber eyes bounded behind the Druidess, Catrin's stomach knotted. She had seen the mammoth creature in her nightmares.

The wolf trailed Agrona to the table near the entrance, sat on its hind legs, and intently watched as she set a copper bowl, several linen pouches, and a beeswax candle on the splintered, wood table. When Agrona turned to Catrin, her green eyes switched to the same amber color as the wolf. Catrin's heart raced. She knew the Druidess was preparing a potion that would make her hallucinate, but what role did the wolf play in Agrona's schemes to manipulate her?

Agrona's lips twitched a wry smile. "Do not let my wolf concern you. Today, we must gain insight from our animal guides. What did you learn from your raven today?"

Catrin, instantly on guard that Agrona was spinning a deceptive web, answered with a cynical bite to her voice, "Nothing of worth, except the raven has a lovely appetite for bugs crawling on the floor. I did enjoy, though, the spiders spinning their webs and eating their victims."

Agrona snickered and waved Catrin over to the table. "Even the smallest of creatures can teach you something. Today, they taught you how your enemies think."

Catrin warily stepped around the wolf and sat at the table. She asked, "How do enemies think—hide in the shadows and lure the prey into their traps?"

Agrona lit the candle on the table and the flame illuminated woad-painted wolves loping across her forehead. "That is right. The enemy will entice you … flattery, money, power, whatever you desire. At the moment you least expect, they will snatch you up and devour you. To survive, you must think like them. That is the raven's lesson today."

"I disagree," Catrin said with eyes fixed on the wolf for any untoward movement. "You can deal with enemies without losing your honor."

Agrona mocked, "Silly girl, is that what you think? You believe you can trust Marcellus. You think of him as a lover and a friend. He blinded you to what he is—a predator."

Catrin raised her head in ire. "He is nothing like that. He is loyal and trustworthy— not at all like the evil eidolon hiding behind your eyes."

"Trustworthy!" Agrona spewed with contempt. "You forget who is enemy and who is friend. Marcellus volunteered to remain as a hostage to reap information out of you. He has used every charm in his bag of tricks to win you over. He lured you to his web, so he could seduce you. I, on the other hand, am your father's most trusted advisor. You must not delude yourself into believing that I am someone I am not."

"How can I trust you after you tricked my mother into forcing me to stay with you?"

"That is the point!" Agrona slammed her fist on the tabletop, making Catrin flinch and the wolf's ears pick up. "You cannot trust anyone. Can't you see it was your mother who betrayed you, not me? That is why your father asked me to train you because he knew that only through me could you gain full powers from your raven."

What is your game today? Catrin wondered, studying Agrona's stone-face. "Why would Mother betray me?"

Agrona waved a hand over the burning candle. "Do you see your mother's reflection in the flame?"

Catrin gazed at the wavering flame. "I only see mine."

"Have you ever wondered why your sisters have such divergent features from yours?"

The shift in conversation disquieted Catrin. "My sisters look like Mother. I take after my father."

"You must surely realize Mor and Vala take after Trystan rather than your father. Now think. Why is that?"

Without answering, Catrin stared at her reflection in the candle's flame. Her blue-green eyes and pale features did closely resemble her father's. She nervously looked at the Druidess, whose lips curled into a smug smile.

"You know, don't you love?" Agrona said. "How could your father possibly seed offspring when he was in Germania fighting for the Romans? Could it be, I wonder, your mother was unfaithful?"

Though Catrin already suspected the truth, she lashed out, "You are lying! Father loves Mother —"

"With all his heart," Agrona interjected. "And that is why your father adopted your bastard sisters. The ugly truth is your mother deeply wounded your father. He wanted a child with her. I fulfilled his desire by giving your mother a love potion, so she would accept your father's advances. That is why she despises me so. She believes you are a curse that will join Marrock in his quest to overthrow the king. The only daughters she can embrace are those fathered by Trystan—the only man she ever loved. She never loved your father."

Agrona's words discomfited Catrin. "Why are you saying these things?"

"So you understand love is an illusion. You gave little thought to endangering our kingdom by placing your trust in the Roman." Agrona again waved her hand over the candle. "Whose reflection do you now see in the flame?"

When the raven's reflection suddenly appeared, Catrin blinked hard, but she could not obliterate the image.

Agrona walked behind Catrin and leaned next to her face. "Yes ... I see it, too. You and the raven are one and the same. A raven's true nature is to feed on hate, war, and carnage. That, my love, is your true essence. Do you truly believe Marrock took your innocence?"

The wolf raised its head and snarled, making Catrin jump. Rapid breaths grated in her throat as the creature's feral eyes consumed her. Catrin shifted her eyes toward Agrona. "I have good reason to hate Marrock for what he did to me!"

"What do you think he did?"

"He tried to rape me … kill me!"

Ominously lowering her voice, Agrona asked, "Did he? Or is this in your mind? Can you distinguish between reality and fantasy?"

Though Catrin was beginning to question her own sanity, she said, "Yes, I know the difference."

Agrona uncapped a jar in her hand and smelled. "Do you recognize the odor?"

Catrin whiffed the pungent odors of clover, rotting meat, and blood. "It smells like what Marrock gave me to drink on that day we searched for the white raven in the forest."

"I thought so." Agrona lowered the jar for the wolf to smell, then set the container on the table and sprinkled some green powders into the bowl. "This magical herb can merge two souls together into one." She sliced her palm with the knife tip and allowed the blood to drip into the mixture. "Did Marrock cut his hand before he gave you the potion?"

Catrin shuddered. "No … I can't remember."

Agrona pinched some dried lavender into the concoction. "Your father's favorite aphrodisiac. He gave this to your mother before he seeded you in her belly."

Catrin recognized the fragrance as one of the scents from the wolf pelt on which she and Marcellus had made love. Doubts began to gnaw at her that her love for Marcellus was real.

The Druidess added other dark powders into the bowl and stirred the mixture with a feathered quill. "Ahh! Now I must put in the most important ingredient—a beating heart." She pulled out a limp chickadee from a bag, sliced the bird's breast with a knife and pulled its ribs apart to cut the arteries away from the heart. She marbled the greenish mixture with the blood pulsating from the still-beating heart.

Repulsed, Catrin asked with a shaky voice, "What are you planning to do with that?"

Agrona fingered the bowl's edge. "My love, you already know. You must take this, so I can also travel with you to the inner depths of your raven's mind. Together, we will discover the powerful forces from the Otherworld."

You mean powers that you can use! Catrin puckered her lips. "I will not drink that!"

Agrona's eyes seemed to dance with delight. "I thought you might say that. You still defy me, even though your father ordered you to train with me. Tell me, Catrin, what were you doing with Marcellus before Apollo cursed you with the falling sickness?"

Catrin wiped her clammy hands on her woolen breeches. "I don't remember."

The raven hopped onto the table, flapped its wings, and knocked the candle off the table, extinguishing the hissing flame on the earthen floor.

"Look at what you made your raven do!" Agrona scolded. "It knows the truth. You are a sexual creature that no man can get enough of."

Catrin gripped the table's edge. "You are wrong!"

The Druidess gave a wry smile and mixed the solution with a quill. "Of course, you were not always like that. You were once as pure as the white raven—unblemished, innocent. Your father treasured you as such, believing he could hide you from all predators. He was mistaken." Agrona stopped stirring the solution and stared at Catrin. "Do you know why a white raven cannot survive in the wild?"

Catrin watched her raven cock its head and gawk at the bowl. Not wanting to hear the answer to the riddle, she shook her head.

Agrona twisted her upper lip into a half-smile. "A white raven cannot hide from predators in the forest. When Marrock lured you into the woods, your raven spirit had to be scorched black, so you could fight back. I wonder …" Agrona squinted. "Was it your raven that attacked Marrock? Or was it you who slashed and sculpted his hideous face?"

The raven's flapping wings startled Catrin as the bird darted over her head and flew to an upper ceiling beam. Looking up, she watched the bird bounce back and forth. She lowered her eyes to Agrona and proclaimed, "The ravens attacked Marrock!"

Agrona dipped a finger in the mixture and lowered it to the wolf's muzzle. The creature sniffed and licked her finger, then staggered to a back corner and curled into a ball. The gigantic animal appeared to sleep, its chest steadily rising and lowering.

"See, no harm came to the wolf," Agrona said, which gave Catrin scant reassurance. "The elixir will help you sleep and dredge out dark memories from the recesses of your mind." The Druidess paused. "You are faced with a conundrum. You can blindly follow Marcellus to your destruction, or you can heed your raven's omens. What visions has the raven shown you? You must tell me the truth, or your raven will punish you."

Catrin glanced at the raven overhead, wondering if Agrona had taken control of it. Quivering, she finally revealed, "A fire-breathing eagle will destroy our village. Marcellus will descend in a horse-driven chariot from the heavens and save me from the firestorm."

Agrona smiled. "What meaning did you take from this?"

Catrin blurted, "I am destined to be with him."

Rising from the table, Agrona fixed her eyes on Catrin. "Listen to yourself. You foresee our kingdom being destroyed, yet you conjure up an image of Marcellus as a god who will save you."

Catrin hesitated. "You are trying to trick me."

Agrona slowly walked around the table. "You have joined your thoughts with Marcellus, haven't you? You pulled him into your mind. Is that how he gained secrets about our kingdom?"

Catrin could feel Agrona's dark aura spinning around her like a web, entrapping her as the Druidess spoke in a hypnotic, monotone voice. "Ahh ... your silence answers my question. You are a soul traveler who can enter minds of other living beings. Your body is solid, your soul fluid. Only a few are chosen by the gods to be soul travelers. Are you one of them? Did your soul enter the Roman's head, so you could escape my thoughts?"

Agrona pressed both hands down on Catrin's head. "You have more mystical abilities than I first realized. Not only can you see the past from the raven's perspective, but you can also see the future— the destruction of our village. That is why you must allow me to enter your mind, so we can travel to the Wall of Lives. Together, we can uncover hidden mysteries from the past, present, and future."

Catrin swallowed hard. "At what cost to me?"

Agrona pulled her hands away, leaned over and poured some of the mixture from the bowl into a brass goblet. "If you drink this, the truth of what Marrock did to you that day will be revealed. Then you will no longer be afraid of the wolf in your nightmares."

Catrin hesitated.

I could lose my soul and humanity.

Yet, if she continued resisting, Agrona would again call upon the guard outside to force the potion down her throat. The previous day, Catrin passed out when the slimy mixture went down her windpipe, denying her lungs of air. When she awoke, she was facedown in vomit, her throat raw. This could happen again. With no chance to escape, she only wanted relief from nightmares and hallucinations driving her mad. She finally capitulated. "If I take you into my mind, you must stop tormenting me with these potions."

Grinning, Agrona offered the large goblet to Catrin. "Enlightenment only comes after you confront the past to face the future."

Taking the goblet, Catrin gagged from the pungent smell. She tilted her head back and drank the metallic-tasting potion, forcing it down. Her stomach revolted and ejected some of the acrid contents, but she forced it back down with a hard swallow.

Agrona chanted, pressing her hands harder on Catrin's head:

Let our souls join,
Raven and wolf together.
Searching for dark portals,
To shine truth's bright light.

The force from Agrona's fingertips made Catrin dizzy as the fluidic energy flowed into her head. A light flashed in her mind and she could sense Agrona's soul entering. Together, they plunged into the light tunnel that led to the Wall of Lives. As they approached the transitional barrier, they decelerated and floated up the watery surface until they found the red life-thread to Marrock's past.

36

MARROCK'S LIFE-THREAD

At the instant she was losing consciousness, she visualized moving Marrock's life-thread aside with her forefinger. She inwardly beseeched her raven to help her.

Agrona told Catrin to study Marrock's life-thread's crinkled juncture where he had led her as a girl into a forest glade. Catrin observed stacked rocks that encircled smoldering ashes. Based on the circumference of the stone barrier, a large fire had recently burnt there. Three altars, each covered with a different colored wolf pelt, formed the point of a triangle outside the perimeter of the rock containment.

Catrin, then a nine-year-old girl, was waiting at one of the altars covered with a pristine white wolf pelt. Repressed memories began surfacing and piecing together as she studied Marrock's life-thread. A chill ran down Catrin's spine when Marrock appeared through some oak trees. His coppery hair was spiked into the horns of a ram. He told her to sit on the altar, so he could coax the white raven from the treetops. She trustingly climbed onto the altar top, and he handed her a gem-crusted goblet filled with what looked like blood. She took a couple of sips, but refused to take any more of the awful-tasting mixture. After a while, her eyelids became droopy, and she snuggled into the soft fur and fell into a twilight sleep.

As the next moments unfolded on Marrock's life-thread, Catrin realized she had slept through the original horror of what happened next. He placed a listless, freckled-face boy with wild chestnut hair on one altar and set a silver haired girl, about four years of age, on another alter. With a serrated knife, he sliced the girl's neck. Her eyes were opened in sheer terror as he brutally cut away at her throat like a butchered animal.

Catrin suddenly recalled the gut-wrenching gurgles of blood spurting out of the girl's severed windpipe when she was in twilight sleep while this happened. Continuing to watch the events project on the life-thread, she felt nausea hit her like a fist when she saw Marrock yank the girl's blood-soaked head off. He then desecrated the boy's body like his female victim.

But that was not the worst of it. The horror of what happened next numbed Catrin to her core.

Marrock undressed himself and stretched his arms toward the setting sun. On his back were tattoos of interconnecting human skulls and wolves that encircled three flames. He ran and leapt into the air, his shadowy figure shape-shifting into the black outline of a wolf. When he pounced on the altar where the body of his young female victim lay, he had become a monstrous red wolf. He lustily lapped the blood from the girl's severed head. With one crunch of his massive fangs, he cracked the skull open and gobbled the brain matter. As the girl's headless body dissolved into the silvery fur, the wolf pelt jerked and the paws jutted out of it. Then Marrock's fangs gripped the long nose of the pelted wolf's head as though he was breathing new life into it. The pelt puffed out and transformed into a normal-sized wolf.

Marrock licked the silver wolf's face and let her up. The she-wolf jumped off and pressed her paws forward in a bow. Likewise, he transformed the boy into a coppery male wolf. Both of the resurrected wolves then scurried into the woods.

When Marrock shape-shifted back to his human form, a foreboding dread crawled over Catrin's skin as she watched herself as a little girl lie helplessly on the altar and relived the horror of the next moments as images projected on the life-thread. He raised the jagged-edge blade above her head with one hand while pinning her shoulder down with the other. "Be a good girl. Keep still," he snarled. "Soon you will be my wolf queen."

The instinct to survive and the sheer terror that she could transform into one of Marrock's wolves galvanized Catrin—or perhaps it was some unknown force that unlocked her muscles into action. She rapidly kneed Marrock in the jaw. His head jerked back and he released her shoulder. She curled her left arm under his elbow and snapped his wrist joint with her fist—a maneuver she had learned from her father.

The knife dropped from Marrock's fingers, his face flamed as red-hot embers. He slammed his shoulder into Catrin's chest, knocking the air out of her lungs. The next instant, he towered over her like a bear and bared his teeth.

"You bitch!" he roared. "I will fuck you until you bleed to death."

With a wildcat's fury, Catrin lunged at him and bit off the tip of his nose. She spat the bloody tissue at his face, then clawed at his face with sharp fingernails.

Marrock bellowed, raising his hand, "You ugly witch!" He backhanded her across the face so hard, she was knocked off the altar, slamming her chin on the stone base.

Momentarily dazed, she felt Marrock's strong hands raise her naked hips to his wet tongue. Rage struck Catrin like a lightning bolt. She rammed her pelvic bone into his bleeding nose.

Marrock howled, "Ahhooooooo," and flipped her over, reaching for her throat.

She pounded her fists on his hands, but to no avail. The choke-hold closed off her windpipe; her eyes felt ready to burst. Her chest seized struggling for air. At the instant she was losing consciousness, she visualized moving Marrock's life-thread aside with her forefinger. She inwardly beseeched her raven to help her.

Hundreds of ravens streamed out of a dark portal into a black waterfall of rippling wings falling onto Marrock's face. His grip loosened around Catrin's neck as demonic ravens dived into him, their black wings furiously flapping around his face and sword-beaks thrusting again and again. He flung himself back, screaming in agony.

The forest echoed with the war cries of shrieking ravens.

Panic-stricken, Catrin crawled away from the black wings batting his head, sharp beaks boring into his face, and curved talons shredding his skin. At the moment he writhed on the ground, trying to shield his face with bloody hands, she knew that was her chance to escape. She scooted herself out of his reach and staggered to her bare feet.

Catrin's eyes then turned to her life-thread that disconnected from Marrock's. She saw that with renewed strength in her legs, she could dash like a doe through the dense trees. Thorny brambles tore at her shins as she sprinted deeper, deeper, and deeper into the darkening woods. Not able to find the pathway back home, she was lost, but nonetheless ran and ran under serpentine branches that hissed in the gale winds. She remembered her lungs burning as she continued scrambling aimlessly through the labyrinth of trees throughout the afternoon.

By nightfall, an owl's yellow eyes blinked at her, and she collapsed on the ground. Weary, she glanced all around for any sign of Marrock. With no clothes to cover her body, she hid underneath a fallen tree's hollow. The long night felt like weeks as she shivered against the knotty bark, the hairs erecting from goose bumps on her arm. She wrapped knees to chest like a newborn, struggling to get warm. Losing hope, she again prayed to the raven to show her the path to safety.

Her raven protector appeared as a black ship sailing across the full moon. Silver beams magically streamed down and illuminated a pathway. Though her body ached from the horrible ordeal, she left the shelter of the fallen tree and walked a short time on the path. She stopped, noticing a skull embedded in red-hot stone. A woman's voice emanating from the skull's locked jaw said, "Only through *cathos* can you rise out of Apollo's flames with the forbidden powers of the Ancient Druids."

    Catrin could no longer bear to witness the past events unroll on the life-threads. She looked away, contemplating what the raven had shown her. Finally, it dawned on her why Marrock had appeared as a wolf in her nightmares. Not only could he shape-shift, but he could also transform children into wolves for his pack. When death almost claimed her, she had somehow unleashed the forces of ravens from the Otherworld. By doing so, she blocked her half-brother's attempts to transform her into one of his wolves. She had indeed altered Rhan's prophecy that she would join Marrock's wolf pack and overthrow their father.

    Drifting into darkness, Catrin sensed Agrona's rage toward Marrock. Realizing that Agrona was still in her mind, she expunged the Druidess from her mind and fell into oblivion.

37

INTERCEPTED MESSAGE

At first glance, he did not recognize the handwriting. Silently reading further, he could feel his jaw drop. The directive was not meant for the queen's eyes. It was intended for Decimus.

Marcellus rummaged through the shelves for an object he could use as a weapon. After being locked up for almost two weeks in the bolted bedchamber, he had to find a way to escape during one of his twice-daily excursions to the latrines. He knew the countryside well along the public pathways, but could he find his way to his father's encampment about one hundred miles north?

At the back of one shelf, he felt something metallic and slid it forward with his fingertips. It was a polished bronze mirror. On its backside was the etching of a triskele that looked like animal heads interconnected with tendrils, the same pattern he had observed on King Amren's high-back throne and shields. The fine craftsmanship seemed inconsistent with the bellicose nature of the Britons. It was dream-like, the tendrils wrapping around what looked like a horse's head, but from a different perspective shape-shifted into a boar's head.

Political schemes, he darkly chuckled, *twisting on each other, not what they appear at first glance.*

Holding the mirror up to his face, he grimaced at his reflection. He had not thought of himself as vain, but his disheveled appearance disturbed him. Dark bristles shadowed his gaunt face. The puffy eyelids and deep wrinkles around the corners of his eyes aged him ten years. With only a daily bowl of water to rinse himself, his hair felt oily and his scalp itched. He fingered the matted strands of his dark hair for telltale signs of lice nits. Seeing none, he set the mirror down on the shelf and sighed ruefully. The stark reality, that he was a prisoner with little chance of escape using the mirror as his weapon, swirled him into a vortex of gloom.

Glancing around the bleak chamber, he felt like a caged animal. It was eight steps from the bolted door to the straw bed against the back wall and five steps across. In one corner was a globe-bellied brown spider that reared its front legs whenever he retrieved a glass jar containing fragranced oil. If he wasn't careful, he bumped into the round-top table or stool crammed in the middle of the room. An occasional rat would crawl through a crack in the side wall to visit him as he feasted on burnt meat and moldy cheese.

Lovely stuff!

The vermin were friendlier than the villagers whose icy stares chilled him every time the guards escorted him to the latrines. With no other human company, Marcellus reflected on his life like never before. He spent most of his boyhood in Gaul with his banished father. His embittered father blamed sorceresses for the downfall of Mark Antony and Iullus Antonius, both considered traitors by Rome. With such a family history, Marcellus feared his indiscretion with Catrin would doom him like his forefathers.

The dread he would die young like his namesake loomed over him. With his precarious situation, he might journey headless to the Underworld while his skull remained in King Amren's receiving chamber. He grimly chuckled.

If I had used my right head to begin with, I wouldn't be in this predicament.

Although he could rationalize this, he still couldn't get Catrin out of his thoughts. He picked-up a jar of lavender oil from the table to whiff. The sweet fragrance evoked the memory of their making love—a bittersweet moment, considering her bizarre behavior afterward that seemed to be directed by a demonic force. Nonetheless, he could strangely sense her presence whenever he had to wrestle with his angst about what the queen might do next. His throat clutched with the prospect he might never see Catrin again. Struggling for composure, he slapped his forehead and muttered, "Idiot. Forget her. Focus on getting out of here alive."

With the unexpected click of the door, Marcellus was jarred from his grim thoughts. He tensely stared at the doorway.

Belinus and a warrior with a wild mane of red hair stomped into his chamber. Based on their grimaces, his bleak situation would not soon improve. He asked curtly, "Why are you here?"

Belinus snarled, "The queen wants to see you. Now!"

"Oh! I finally get to see the queen—a welcome change from the two of you."

Belinus grabbed Marcellus by the shirt and slammed him against a wooden post. "I've had enough of your mouth, Roman!"

The lion-maned warrior ground his fingers into Marcellus's shoulder blade and shoved him through the doorway.

The warriors, one on each side, yanked Marcellus through the corridor into the receiving chamber, where they skirted the elevated thrones to the queen's chambers.

Entering the room, Marcellus first saw the queen's shadow stretched up the wall like an avenging fury. He then shifted his eyes to Rhiannon who sat at a candlelit table. She acknowledged him with a scowl, which he returned with a glower. She motioned for Belinus and the other guard to wait outside.

Marcellus warily sat across the table from the queen. She scrunched her nose, rose, and stepped to a dark corner where she picked up a stiff rat by the tail. She flung it through the doorway. A hissing meow, which Marcellus presumed was from the one-eyed cat, rolled through the room. The queen returned to the table and shot a seething glare at Marcellus. "I wonder if there are any other vermin hiding behind these walls."

He nervously scratched the bumps on his neck as he watched the queen pour some water into two brass cups and then hand one to him. "Do you find your quarters agreeable?" Rhiannon asked.

From the sharp tone in her voice, Marcellus surmised she would soon throw hard questions at him about Catrin. He responded, "I would find my quarters more agreeable if allowed a bit more freedom."

Rhiannon's eyebrow arched. "Have my guards mistreated you?"

Marcellus suspiciously eyed the queen. *What games are you playing today?* He said, "No, but I am locked up at all times. The room reeks of mold and rat dung."

"Better that, than sleeping with our pigs," Rhiannon snorted.

"That may be so," Marcellus said, struggling to steady his shaky voice, "but the king assured me I could roam freely as your guest."

Rhiannon tilted her head back, gulped some water, and slammed the goblet on the table. "Unfortunately, there are ugly rumors flying in the village that you raped Catrin. It is in your best interest that we provide you with armed escorts."

Aggravated at her accusations again, Marcellus exhaled a blast of hot air. "I already told you. I never raped her. I always treated her with respect. If she was here, she would corroborate my story. Where is she?"

Rhiannon slapped a scroll on the splintered tabletop. "As far away as possible from you!"

Frowning, Marcellus looked at the scroll. It appeared to be made of the same ivory parchment that his father used. The broken wax seal of Apollo's chariot was his family's insignia. He rubbed the rolled-up parchment with a forefinger and wondered if his father had been informed of his delicate situation with Catrin. He looked at the queen. "What is this?"

"You know what it is. A message from your father!"

Marcellus leaned back in the chair, trying to conceal his growing discomfort. "What did he write?"

The queen's nostrils flared. "Read it!"

Great Jupiter above! Aren't you the Medusa! Marcellus grumbled to himself. He spread the parchment on the table. At first glance, he did not recognize the handwriting. Silently reading further, he could feel his jaw drop. The directive was not meant for the queen's eyes. It was intended for Decimus. Bewildered, he lifted his head and regarded the queen's eyes narrowing like a wolf ready to attack.

"Read it to me!" she snapped.

Marcellus took a sip of water to quench his parched throat. When he read the mandate aloud, his voice rasped.

Greetings, Tribune Decimus Flavius.

I hope this message finds you in good health. The time for executing the emperor's directive has been advanced. Tiberius ordered me to imprison both King Amren and his eldest daughter. As a loyal senator and Roman citizen, I am duty-bound to obey the imperial order. Both of them are now prisoners in my encampment as I write this.

I have formed an alliance with Marrock and have promised him the emperor will recognize him as his client king. As such, I have ordered all ships to land at a bay near the white cliffs in preparation for an attack on the Cantiaci capital of Durovernum.

As you probably surmise, these actions endanger my son's life if word ever reaches the queen. Make due haste and free Marcellus before she finds out.

Do not fail me!

Senator Lucius Antonius

Quietly reading the directive one more time, Marcellus suspected it was a forgery. The mandate was not written in his father's usual windy and grandiloquent style. His father usually ended his letters with the words "with greatest respect, your loyal patron and friend." Marcellus could not fathom his father issuing such drastic orders without first assuring his release. He considered the possibility that the queen had written it to pressure him into confessing that he had dishonored Catrin. He regarded the queen, but could not detect any outward expression of trickery.

He asked, "How can you be sure that this is from my father?"

The queen creased her brow with obvious irritation. "Is that not your family insignia on the seal?"

"Yes, but this is not my father's handwriting."

"This could have been written by one of his scribes." She glowered. "Let me be clear. I take this threat seriously."

Marcellus swallowed hard. "What do you plan to do with me?"

"I had planned to keep the truce and not harm you regardless of what you did to Catrin," the queen said. "Of course, that has all now changed. Your father broke his oath to keep my husband safe. Tell me, was that always his intent?"

"What if I told you that it was not, would you believe me?"

"This message tells me otherwise," the queen retorted. "Did you know he would do this when you volunteered to remain a hostage?"

Marcellus didn't answer, reconsidering his initial suspicion that the queen had written the message, but she was highly agitated, unlike her usual stone-cold demeanor of being in control. If she didn't write the message, who did? Was it Cunobelin? Marrock?

Rhiannon leaned over the table. "Answer me!"

"My father did not write this," Marcellus said adamantly. "It is a fake. Until such time we find out who did write this, let me remind you of your pledge not to harm me."

The queen rapped her fingers on the table. "I have kept that promise. I forbade my guards from gelding you in retaliation for raping my daughter."

Marcellus felt his stomach sink as the image of his dangling testicles crept into his mind. He said, "Let me repeat, I never raped

Catrin! You underestimate your daughter. She could have speared me for any such attempt."

Rhiannon's stare hardened. "That may be so. Still, I have no doubt you took advantage of her. It was only after you gave her the Apollo's amulet that she went mad." She rose and pressed her hands flat on the table. "My daughter is not the main issue here. I want my husband and Vala freed."

A twinge of panic made Marcellus's heart pound harder. He took a couple of deep breaths to ease his jitteriness. "I already told you that my father did not write this. Someone else did. If you don't believe me, send a trusted messenger to my father's encampment to verify."

Rhiannon reached for another scroll on a shelf behind her and set it next to the ink bottle and quill on the table. Sitting down again, she ordered Marcellus, "Write the following message to your father."

Somewhat relieved that the queen was following his advice, Marcellus picked the quill up and dipped it into the black ink. "Do you want me to confirm your husband has been taken prisoner?"

"No. Start out ..." The queen stroked her chin, as if considering her next words. "I have treated your son well, but your sinister plan to attack our kingdom puts him in grave danger."

Taken aback, Marcellus set the quill aside and stared at the queen. "Don't you want first to verify that my father actually wrote the directive?"

Rhiannon's forehead creased into a firm line. "The five Roman soldiers we captured yesterday trying to gain entrance inside our walls are proof enough. They are being tortured, as we speak."

The queen's revelation made Marcellus's heart shudder. Of course, his father would have sent soldiers to rescue him if there were any signs he was in danger. Did someone warn his father that he had been imprisoned? Thinking further, he felt something was amiss. He needed more pieces of information to get a clearer picture. He was sure his father's directive was a fake, but he again asked himself, *Who wrote it and why? How can I convince the queen to work with me to uncover the truth?*

Masking his trepidation, he leveled his eyes at the queen. "You must realize that torturing my father's soldiers will not help your cause. Threatening me could start a war and jeopardize your husband's life."

Rhiannon slapped the table. "Do you think me a half-wit?"

"No, but I am asking you to pause and reconsider. We both have a lot to lose here. Let us work together to make sure we reach a peaceful settlement."

The queen furiously tapped a forefinger on the blank parchment. "All right. Let's start again. Write exactly what I say in large letters: 'If you do not return King Amren alive, I will rip your son's ribs apart and tear out his beating heart as a sacrifice to the war goddesses. The captured Roman soldiers will be thrown on the pyre alongside your son and burned alive!'" The queen gave an evil smile. "Do you think my message is clear enough?"

Horrified, Marcellus felt a nasty pain rip through his chest. His hands paralyzed as if a knife had impaled them to the table. "Are you mad? This will only infuriate my father!"

Rhiannon roared, "Write it!"

He fumbled to clasp the quill. When he dipped the tip into the ink, he almost knocked the bottle over. He considered thrusting the quill into the queen's throat and overpowering her, but how could he get past the guards? The blood-thirsty savages would most likely send him ignobly to the Underworld. First, they would take great delight in torturing him: cut off his balls, spill his guts, and flay him alive. Breathing becoming ragged, he clasped the quill tighter.

You idiot! Keep your wits. Find out how she got the message.

Regaining composure, he scribbled on the parchment, then stopped and glanced at the queen. "How did you get hold of my father's message? Did you intercept the courier charged with delivering these orders?"

Rhiannon hesitated, the lines around her eyes wrinkling into crow's feet. "It was found on a dead Catuvellauni warrior. His throat was slit."

Marcellus inhaled deeply, suspecting the warrior's murder had been staged. "Why would my father entrust a Catuvellauni to deliver his message? Don't you find it odd the courier's throat had already been slashed?"

Rhiannon grimaced. "Are you playing games with me?"

Marcellus set the pen aside and proclaimed, "Only a Roman courier would deliver a message this important. As I told you, the letter is a fake. You are being played for a fool. Forcing me to write this threat will not help your cause. Trust me, I know my father. He will slaughter everyone in your family for this affront. If you release me, I promise to speak to him on your behalf."

The queen's eyes probed him as if searching for the truth. She finally said with disdain, "Why should I trust you? A Roman … a rogue. There is no doubt in my mind you took advantage of Catrin and cursed her with Apollo's affliction. Do you think me a fool to believe you would actually help me now?" She stood up and turned toward the doorway. "Guards! Get in here now! Take the prisoner away!"

Two warriors crashed the door open and trampled into the chamber. Belinus yanked Marcellus to his feet as the other elbowed him in the mouth, the pain shooting from his jaw to the back of his head.

Infuriated, Marcellus spat out blood and shouted, "You piss-sucking pigs." He butted his head into Belinus, knocking him to the ground, followed swiftly by a hammer punch into the other guard's jaw.

The blow hardly fazed the lion-maned warrior. He roared and hurled Marcellus against the jagged stone wall, smacking air out of his lungs. Dazed, Marcellus crumbled, banging his chin hard on the floor. The pain spiked to his teeth. He gasped for air through blood-clogged nostrils, his ears ringing from the queen's shrieks.

"Get him out of my sight! Lock him up with the other pigs!"

Finally catching his wind, Marcellus yelled, "The Romans did not do this! Look for a traitor in your ranks. Look for someone who wants to bring the king down."

The queen snarled, "The only traitor I see is you!" She turned to the guards. "Teach this animal how the Cantiaci deal with Roman scum!"

The next instant, the lion-maned warrior punched Marcellus in the upper jaw. The walls spun around him, colored dots jiggling before his eyes. Struggling to stay on his feet, he teetered until a blunt blow to his temple finally brought him black peace.

38

CO-CONSPIRATORS

*"Marvelously done, my king—to trick that imposter queen
into believing the senator had written the message,
never suspecting it was you."*

At the sacrificial site deep in the forest, Agrona looked for any movement between the gnarled oak boughs. Seeing none, she mumbled, "Where is Marrock?"

She grabbed two adders out of a linen bag that she had carried from the lair and whipped them around a nearby tree branch. With a quick flick of her knife, she sliced off their heads. The headless vipers coiled wildly around the branch, their blood spattering on the verdant ground. She pulled the headless bodies from the tree limb and peeled off their skins with the blade. Glancing around again, she ruminated about what could have caused her son's delay.

A mishap? Perhaps, the Romans detained him?

Darker thoughts then crept into Agrona's mind. What if Marrock spurned her request to discuss the next steps in their scheme? He was, after all, a shape-shifter with worrisome powers. It was not until she had travelled to the Wall of Lives in Catrin's mind that she learned of his ability to transform children into wolves for his pack. His failure to transform Catrin was surely the reason the curse had been altered. She altered the future by summoning her raven warriors from the Otherworld to attack him.

More disturbing, Marrock had more magical abilities than he disclosed to her. Even though Agrona sacrificed everything for him, a chasm was widening between them, particularly after he married Ariene, a preeminent Druidess in her own right.

Now that Agrona's powers were fading, she further considered how to draw more from Catrin. The raven had only chosen a handful of women before Catrin who could easily travel between the earthly world and the Otherworld. They were warrior queens who fought off Greek invaders. Their spirits were immortalized in the stars as raven goddesses. Their light shone on mortal warriors who died gloriously in battle. Untested, Catrin still needed to complete a series of trials before the gods would deem her worthy to join her ancestral raven goddesses in the heavens.

Perhaps, Agrona thought, *I could instead rise as a raven goddess instead of Catrin.* But first, she had to find ways to counter Marrock, if he ever turned on her. He was, after all, the son of Amren and inherited some of his displeasing traits.

Thus far, Agrona had failed to channel Catrin's powers to her vantage. When she was on the verge of controlling Catrin's mind, the princess somehow blocked her. Even the hallucinogens, monkshood, and hazelnuts no longer seemed to break the princess down. There had to be a way to lure Catrin into her web of deception.

Mind spinning around contingency plans, Agrona dropped the snakes' cross-barred skins into a cauldron hanging from a metal tripod. The snake skins sizzled and the smoke rising from the ashes reeked of burning skin. Crinkling her nose, she waved her palms over the brass metal pot, chanting, "Let my soul capture the viper's essence. Strike once. Strike quick. Strike deadly."

Hearing crackling twigs from the nearby woods, she turned. Marrock appeared in his shape-shifted wolf form under the archway of oak branches. Twice the size of a timber wolf, he viciously snarled and bared his teeth, but she would not abide her son's truculent behavior. From deep within her throat, she ferociously growled. At the next inhale, she captured Marrock's bark and gritted her teeth to snuff the sound. She picked up a stick and whacked her son's canine muzzle.

"Down beast! Or you will regret threatening Rhan."

The wolf yelped, cowered, and bowed his head on front paws. She waved him off to the woods. "Come back as a man!"

The wolf scooted backward, then slinked past her and retreated to the forest.

Marrock then reappeared as an elongated shadowy man beneath the branched archway. When he swaggered into the crimson light of the rising sun, his monstrous face appeared as a fractured rock with lips petrified in a grotesque smile, his hair spiked into rusty stalagmites. He raised a hand to acknowledge her.

Studying his pitted face, Agrona recalled the time when he was a strapping man of twenty years, his pale skin as unblemished as a newborn lamb. His eyes were a brilliant sea blue-green, the same color as Catrin's. He towered above all others like a god. That was until his curse-altering sojourn with Catrin in the woods. Thankfully, today promised to be a warm summer day. On cold nights, his moon-cratered scars tormented him with relentless pain that put him into an uglier mood.

"What took you so long?" Agrona asked with a scowl. "I expected you at midnight."

Not answering, Marrock stepped over to the cauldron and looked inside, sniffing. "What is this awful smell?"

"Snake skins," Agrona hissed. "Now answer my question."

Marrock lurched toward her. "I will not parry your flickering tongue."

Regarding the snarl on his face, Agrona thought it wise to back down and appeal to his arrogance. Only then could she spin a web around him, so he would do her bidding. She bowed humbly. "Accept my apologies. I spoke in haste, anxious to learn of Senator Antonius's reaction to Rhiannon's threat to sacrifice Marcellus to the war goddesses."

Marrock curled his upper lip into a sneer. "My father's face flamed like a fire when he read the bitch queen's message aloud to the senator."

Agrona chuckled with sordid delight. "How does Amren now fare?"

"Not nearly as well after the senator confronted him with his queen's threat to cut Marcellus's heart out. The timing of the queen's letter was most fortunate. Cunobelin and Father were jointly announcing, at a gathering of Catuvellauni nobles, that they had negotiated a marital contract for Adminius to wed Catrin. To my dismay, Cunobelin shamed me by proclaiming that he had withdrawn his support for my claims to the Cantiaci throne."

Agrona winced when Marrock spat into the hot cauldron. The sputum burst into droplets that hissed and skittered over the metal. He stared vacantly at the eastern horizon, the morning light making his face glow like a blood moon. He said with a bitter bite to his voice, "Most insulting, my worm of a father-in-law proclaimed, 'the great King Amren graciously agrees to share his sovereignty with Adminius as part of this pact.'"

Agrona gently touched a deep scar on Marrock's face. "Both kings are spineless and slimy maggots that feed off each other."

"Of course," Marrock said, one side of his lips contorting into a half-smile, "that all changed when the senator and his contingency of soldiers stormed into the receiving chamber and accosted my father. The senator read the bitch queen's message to everyone and slapped the rolled parchment across Father's nose, as though he was a little boy. The Senator demanded to know why Father could not control his queen. He then went on a rampage of words so vile that I dare not say them aloud. Lucius concluded by saying that he had generously housed the king in the Roman encampment while arbitrating a just settlement between the Celtic rulers. Of course, Father's mouth was open in shock, as if lightning struck him. Cunobelin and his dogs ran out of the chamber like the cowards they are. Only I and Ariene had the courage to remain."

Agrona arched an eyebrow, suspecting her son was embellishing the story. Her dubious expression must have caught his eye because he bristled and said sharply, "Everything I have said is true."

"Of course," she quickly replied, knowing how easily his temper could flare. "I never thought otherwise. Go ahead, finish your tale."

Marrock stared at Agrona for a moment and then relaxed into his story. "Despite my father's protests, the senator ordered his guards to shackle him like a common criminal that he is. King Amren was brought to his knees, where he belonged. He groveled and begged to be released, so he could look into the matter. The senator's guards dragged him away like the beast he is."

Marrock chuckled with evil delight. "Later that night, I overheard some soldiers say the king was hung upside down with a rope and carved away like a piece of butchered meat. I thought to myself, 'Good. Nothing gives me greater joy than for the almighty king to meet his death by torture.' A little later, I learned from Cunobelin that the senator decided to spare Father. The senator feared the final act would doom his son, Marcellus. I thought at first the gods had played a cruel trick on me. But upon further reflection, I accepted my fate to fulfill your curse and behead my father instead."

Agrona's stomach tickled with wicked mirth. "Marvelously done, my king—to trick that imposter queen into believing the senator had written the message, never suspecting it was you. How were you able to borrow the senator's signet ring to seal the message without him noticing?"

Marrock drew a small knife from his belt to dig out black muck underneath his curled fingernails. "I am a sorcerer of deception. The senator placed his confidence in me like a son. He told me to call him by his first name, Lucius. I told him that I worshipped his patron god, Apollo, and requested to see the insignia on his family ring. He took it off and proudly showed it to me. When another Roman diplomat entered the headquarters, the king set the ring on the table and rose to speak with the other dignitary. With the diversion, I stole the ring."

"How did you know the envoy would enter at that time?" Agrona asked.

Marrock wiped the knife's blade on his tunic and picked at a bleeding hangnail. "Romans are like trained dogs. They need a daily routine. Eat at dawn, shit after breakfast, and bark at each other throughout the morning. Every time Lucius gaped at my raven-sculptured face during one of our amiable chats, another Roman always appeared. He would then excuse himself. If it weren't for my face, I believe he would have genuinely enjoyed my company. I can converse in Latin as eloquently as any Roman."

Agrona could no longer contain her smirk that any Roman could abide her son's company.

Marrock glared. "Do you find me amusing? Do not make the mistake of mocking me."

Agrona humbly lowered her eyes. "I would never do that. I think of you as a sly wolf that dines on hapless sheep."

Marrock smiled. "I did win the senator's complete confidence. I told him that I was educated in Roman traditions and consider myself more Roman than the barbarians in Britannia. I promised him that I would do his bidding as client king."

"What about the marital pact that Cunobelin and Amren negotiated?"

Marrock laughed. "It is a dead fish out of water."

"You are so clever, my king," Agrona cooed.

Marrock gave a broad grin while lifting his shirt to rub his belly. "Do you have anything else to eat besides those snake skins?"

Agrona nodded. She then retrieved a linen bag set against a giant oak and sat next to Marrock on a fallen tree. She pulled out moldy white cheese from the bag and offered it to him. He bit off some cheese and washed it down with ale from an animal pouch. He looked at Agrona.

"Do you have any meat?"

She handed him some salted pork rinds that he gobbled down. He moaned with delight, "Mmmm … better than snake skins," and let out a couple of belches, his raw breath making Agrona recoil. She gave him an appalled look.

Marrock did not appear to be bothered by her reaction as he casually remarked, "When I visited you in my wolf form a fortnight ago, I was surprised to see Catrin's beauty."

Agrona shifted uncomfortably under Marrock's piercing stare as he continued, "I found it odd that I fell asleep when you performed the ritual on Catrin. When I awoke, all I could feel was unadulterated hate for the wench after dreaming her black-feathered friends pecked out my eyes. By the way, how does she and her odious raven fare?"

Agrona gulped the ale in her mouth. "Stubborn as a rock."

"Have you entered her mind yet?"

Agrona gave Marrock a steely look. *You fool. Your failure to transform Catrin into a wolf altered my curse.* She nevertheless kept a straight face to hide her anger, so she could use him to carry out the curse and slay Amren.

"Answer me!" Marrock demanded. "Could you see Catrin's thoughts that night when I was with you in my wolf form?"

"I saw her vision of fire-breathing eagles destroying Durovernum."

"Does Catrin know what the eagles represent?"

Agrona shrugged. "She never said."

"I know what it means," Marrock haughtily proclaimed. "Eagles represent Romans. They will help me overthrow Father's kingdom as you fated in your curse."

"What makes you think the eagles symbolize the Romans?" asked Agrona.

"Look at their eagle standards. Surely, the raven revealed to Catrin that it is my destiny to become king of the Cantiaci. Did she see me in her vision?"

Agrona nervously scratched her chin as she closely regarded Marrock's eyes probing her for the truth like a scalpel. She finally admitted, "I saw you slit the throats of two children and transform them into wolves. You were about to do the same to Catrin, but the ravens attacked you and she escaped. Your failure to transform Catrin into a wolf altered the curse."

Marrock jerked his head back in anger. "We have already been through this. I did nothing to change the curse. You cast the curse; you fix it. I have thus far lived up to what the original curse foretold. My only purpose now is to lop off my father's head as you foresaw!"

Agrona lowered her eyes to avoid a confrontation. "I did see another vision that you should be aware of. Marcellus descends in a chariot like a sun god and rescues Catrin from the firestorm on the village."

Marrock's eyebrows perked up. "Marcellus, the senator's son?"

"Yes, you might say their love was born out of a curse," she quipped.

He mimicked a cut to his throat with a hand. "Why don't you just kill the wench for ordering her ravens to peck out chunks of my face and leave me for dead to drown in my own blood? That would be sweet justice, don't you think. I could cut her up and feed the pieces to her raven companions."

Agrona patted his arm. "Calm yourself. Remember, we still need Catrin to fulfill the curse."

Marrock pulled away. "No, we don't."

Agrona shrugged. "My original curse did say she would fly out as a raven and join you. Now the curse says she will fly out of Apollo's flames as a raven with the powers of the Ancient Druids."

Marrock unsheathed a dagger from his belt and extended it at Agrona. "She will fly out and meet my blade! So will you, if you do not drop the subject."

Lips quivering, Agrona gaped at the glimmering blade. "Forgive me, son. You are right. You must keep your eyes fixed on your destiny like a north star. We must now focus all our efforts on assuring the Romans support you. Two days ago, an opportunity presented itself that I should tell you. Rhiannon left the village, so she could plea for the Regni king's support if war breaks out. She left me in charge of everyday activities while she was gone. My next command will be to sentence Marcellus to death for defiling Catrin. Surely this horrendous act will force the senator's hand to ally with you and to destroy the king and his family. We must hurry, though, as it will only be a matter of time before the queen discovers the senator's mandate was a fake."

Marrock grumbled, "What can that idiot whore and her lover, Trystan, do to us?"

"Probably nothing," Agrona replied. "But I must make sure Marcellus meets a most horrible death to incite the senator's fury against Rhiannon."

"Will the people from the village follow your command?"

"After I announce the Romans slaughtered the king, the warriors will gladly paint their bodies with Marcellus's blood. Your task is to make sure Amren dies. Can you do that and fulfill that part of the curse?"

"You know I can." Marrock's brow lifted. "What about Catrin? The raven did reveal a different fate for her than what you foretold in the original curse."

Agrona did not answer, wondering how she could break Catrin down and travel to the Wall of Lives, so she could gain more powers from the Otherworld.

Marrock tapped her on the shoulder and asked again, "What do you plan to do with Catrin?"

"For now, I will keep her as a prisoner." Agrona stared at Marrock. "You must stay the course on your pathway to greatness. Continue your masquerade of allying with both the Romans and Cunobelin, so they will help you bring Amren down. Afterward, you can avenge Cunobelin for his treachery. As for the Romans, I saw a golden eagle fly out to sea and never return. This is a sign they will leave our homeland after they help you overthrow your father."

Marrock rose from the log and placed the dagger in his belt. "Again, I ask, how will you counter Catrin's vision that she will be rescued by Marcellus?"

Agrona quickly conjured a prophecy to assuage Marrock's concerns. She stood and tilted her head back to look into his eyes. "Oh! I almost forgot. The other night, I dreamt that Catrin fell out of the chariot as Marcellus drove the horses over the white cliffs. Just before she smashed on the jagged rocks, you transformed her into a silver wolf. This is a sign that Marcellus will abandon Catrin, so she can join your wolf pack and mate with you."

Marrock squinted at Agrona as if he did not quite believe what she had said. She placed a hand on his chest to reassure him. "I have put everything in place for you. You are the legitimate king. Go forth and claim what is rightfully yours."

And what will ultimately be mine.

39

CLANDESTINE MEETING

This was a bad omen that the clandestine meeting she had set up with the senator might be a trap.

The ride to Camulodunon was long and hard. For two days and nights, Rhiannon had galloped incognito alongside her trusted guards, Trystan and Cynwrig. The diversion through Regni lands doubled the distance, but the rapid pace of their horses across estuary marshlands, dense forests, and rolling farmlands made up for lost time.

The queen rode with one objective in mind—win Amren's release.

In retrospect, she should have heeded Marcellus's warning that traitors within her circle had most likely forged Senator Lucius Antonius's letter that said Amren was imprisoned, but what reason did she have to believe Marcellus was telling the truth? As far as she was concerned, he was a scoundrel who had deflowered her daughter to gratify his lust. Only after he gave Catrin the Apollo amulet did she go raving mad, as if she was cursed with the god's evil spirits.

Rhiannon's anger did not stop with Marcellus. She wanted to banish Catrin for recklessly sleeping with the Roman enemy and betraying her family. The queen wasn't sure who to trust now. Certainly, she could count on the loyalty of the two guards riding beside her. Mor and Belinus were trustworthy, but she questioned their judgment. The Druidess concerned her. Had she made a mistake, leaving Catrin and Marcellus under Agrona's charge?

Galloping headlong into enemy territory, Rhiannon grew anxious when blood-red clouds began forming fangs in the molten sunset. This was a bad omen that the clandestine meeting she had set up with the senator might be a trap. She reined her horse to a halt on the wooded hillside east of Camulodunon and waved the men over. She asked Trystan, "Where is the senator's headquarters from here?"

He pointed northward, where fog was rolling inland from the coast and obscuring their view. "The senator's tent is located in the center of the encampment. I assume Amren is held in a cell near the back stables."

"How many soldiers guard the entrance?"

"Last week, when I was here, five or six guards were checking merchants delivering supplies at the entrance. More guards were posted at towers around the encampment. I estimate about six hundred legionaries in the camp."

Rhiannon glanced at the darkening woods. "We'll set up camp here tonight. No fire."

Trystan dismounted and helped her off the horse. Cynwrig took the reins of all the horses to hobble them at a nearby tree.

After the long ride, Rhiannon's legs were sore. She lumbered to the covering of tall grass to relieve herself. When she finished, she noticed honeysuckle vines nearby and ambled over to smell the sweet citric fragrance. As she whiffed the blossoms, a tap on her shoulder startled her. She turned to find Trystan with a big smile on his face and a handful of the trumpet-shaped flowers. He said, "I remember these are your favorite."

Rhiannon glanced around to confirm that Cynwrig was setting up camp at a distance from them. She took the flowers from Trystan and inhaled the sweet fragrance. She gave him a wistful smile. "When we were younger, life seemed simpler and full of joy. Now, I can only smell blood and rotting flesh if war breaks out. I regret sending the threatening message to Senator Antonius."

"You made the choice based on the threat presented," Trystan said, gently touching her arm. "It was only a matter of time before Amren's negotiations fell apart."

Rhiannon leaned closer. "Tell me again what Amren told you last week when you informed him about what happened to Catrin."

Trystan shifted his weight and looked down for a moment. "Amren took the news badly. I could tell by the way his eyes blazed that he would surely confront the senator about what Marcellus had done. He confided to me that he had grown to mistrust the senator. He called him a forked-tongue snake for secretly meeting with Marrock behind his back."

"Did I make the right decision about making Catrin go with Agrona?" Rhiannon asked, her heart sinking with remorse. "I was so angry. I wanted to disown her … banish her. I never thought I could ever feel that way, but there you have it. I did."

"Your decision is made. Leave it at that." Trystan yanked some leaves from a birch tree and dropped them on the ground. "Right now, you need to keep your focus on gaining Amren's release. Let him pass judgment on Catrin when he returns."

Rhiannon sighed ruefully. "I know you are right. Nevertheless, Catrin is my blood, and it tears at my heart that she may ultimately carry out Rhan's original curse."

Trystan lifted her chin. "We don't know that yet. Amren told me he wanted to inspect the dagger before making any conclusions that Catrin altered the curse. Leave it at that. There is nothing more we can do."

Rhiannon nodded with resignation. Her knotted stomach ripped a loud growl. She pressed a hand against her abdomen to stop the grumbling before Trystan gave her another scolding about not eating. Another gastric rumble soon followed.

Trystan looked at her with concern. "You need to eat and regain your strength. I'll stand guard tonight, so you can sleep and gather your wits before meeting the senator tomorrow."

"I am fine," she said stiffly. "Salted pork strips won't settle my stomach." She clasped the bouquet of flowers tighter. "I'm worried about you. Are you sure you want to approach the senator alone at the break of dawn? His demand that we meet him in his quarters may be a trap."

Trystan adjusted the belted sword slung on his back. "That is why I will demand he meet you here. If he decides to strike at me, I am expendable. We cannot lose our queen."

Rhiannon paused, considering what he said. "What is your plan?"

"I will present my fake credentials as the emperor's courier to gain entry. After I am presented to the senator, I will then say who I am and demand he show me Amren before we talk further. Only after I confirm the king is alive will I tell him of your stipulation that you will only meet him outside the camp without any Roman guards. I will return after that. Wait for my whistle before you present yourself."

Rhiannon's throat clutched with emotion. "What if … you don't return?"

"If I am not back by sunset, assume the worst," Trystan replied sternly. "Leave immediately and prepare for war."

Misty-eyed, Rhiannon cautioned, "Be careful. I could not bear to lose you, too."

Trystan shot an arrogant grin. "I've been in far more dangerous situations. Cynwrig will stay and protect you. He can handle half the Roman army, while I take care of the rest."

"I can protect myself," Rhiannon said, touching her sword's hilt.

"I have no doubt." Trystan grinned. "Let's get back before Cynwrig becomes suspicious about us. We can go over our plans and give him final instructions."

The ground fog dissipated under the red glow of the sunrise the next morning. Unlike the previous evening, Rhiannon could now clearly see wagons and chariots rolling on the gravel road between the hill fort of Camulodunon and the Roman encampment. She turned to Trystan and handed him the two rolled parchments. "Give these to the senator to press our demands."

Trystan tucked the scrolls under his belt. Clean shaven and hair freshly shorn, he embodied an imperial courier in his red-striped toga and military cloak. He mounted the king's cherished black stallion and looked at Rhiannon and Cynwrig. "Make sure you wait for my signal before you present yourself. As for you, Cynwrig, make sure nothing happens to the queen or I'll have your head."

Cynwrig gave an arrogant grin. "You need only worry about your head. You can be assured the queen is in most capable hands."

Trystan chuckled and reined his horse closer to Rhiannon. She stroked the stallion's thick mane as she gazed at him. With a lingering dread that he might not return, she wanted to kiss him good-bye, but dare not with Cynwrig nearby. She instead stepped back and told Trystan, "May the gods protect you."

Trystan smiled at her and kneed the horse through the white-barked trees without looking back.

Rhiannon and Cynwrig took cover behind some tall bushes as they watched Trystan descend the hillside. At the bottom, he merged into the current of several open wagons streaming to the Roman encampment.

Rhiannon and Cynwrig then settled in. It would be a long day.

Rhiannon spotted a windowless carriage rolling up the hillside. Next to the vehicle was a rider whose chest armor glinted from the gold light of the setting sun. She assumed he was a Roman officer. Her heart rattled when she did not see Trystan. She shifted her eyes to Cynwrig. "What do you think?"

"From here, I can't tell if Trystan is with them." Cynwrig waved for her to stay put. "I'll take a closer look."

"No. I am going with you," she insisted.

Cynwrig opened his mouth as if ready to argue, but she stubbornly arched a stern eyebrow. He grimaced and pointed to a gigantic oak in the pasture. "Move over there."

Staying close to Cynwrig, Rhiannon scurried out of the woods to the cover of the oak. She peeked around its gnarly trunk and studied the approaching riders and carriage. The vehicle appeared large enough to hold four to six soldiers. She turned to Cynwrig. "Do you think it is a trap?"

Cynwrig shrugged. "Not sure. Let's wait a little longer. I now see another rider beside the carriage." He squinted. "I'm not sure if it is Trystan or not."

The next moments were heart-wrenching as Rhiannon listened to the squeaky, click-clacks of the wheels growing louder and louder until a man's gruff voice shouted, "Whoa there!"

She again peered around the tree, but the carriage blocked her vision of the riders. With the loud chatter of birds in the forest, she held her breath and listened for Trystan's distinct partridge call. A warbler's trill pierced the air—the signal for them to hide.

Heart pounding, she rushed alongside Cynwrig to the cover of the hedgerow bordering the roadway. She cautiously spread the thorny stems of the bush apart. All she could see were shadows growing, then shrinking, around the carriage. When she glanced at Cynwrig, he brought a forefinger to his lips. "Shhh." He drew a battle-ax from his belt. In turn, she unsheathed the sword at her side. Breathing quietly, she listened intently for Trystan's signal.

When the crunch of twigs could be heard nearby, they both turned their heads sideways toward the direction of the sound. A shadowy figure appeared behind some thick trees.

Trystan or Roman soldier, she wondered and glanced around for movement of other soldiers.

The forest was deathly still.

The shadow stretched toward them, stopped in its tracks, and looked all around. Unable to discern who it was, she held her breath.

A few heartbeats later, she heard the distinct scratchy call of a partridge. She exhaled the breath she had been holding when Trystan appeared through the trees under the sun's fading light. He waved for Cynwrig and her to follow him deeper into the forest.

In a grove of thick beech trees, they huddled together as Trystan discussed the next steps.

"The senator has agreed to meet the queen in the carriage. Cynwrig, you stay put. The Romans don't know you're here. Give an owl hoot if you see anything suspicious while the queen and I speak with the senator."

Cynwrig nodded. The tattoo of the lightning bolt appeared to strike down his arm as he shifted the battle-ax in his hand.

Rhiannon followed Trystan to the wooden-framed carriage where the tribune, whom she recognized as Decimus from their first meeting, opened the door. Stepping in, she noted the red-cushioned passenger seats that lined both sides of the lamp-lit coach. With the senator seated at the rear, she bent her head and seated herself on the front cushion. Trystan then pulled himself through the doorway and sat next to her. When the tribune lumbered in, the coach bounced as he struggled to sit in the narrow space next to the senator. Although the outside air was brisk, the windowless coach was stifling.

Adjusting her eyes to the dim light, Rhiannon acknowledged the senator with a slight nod. "Greetings, Senator Antonius. Thank you for meeting me—"

Lucius rudely interrupted. "Why did you refuse to meet me at my headquarters?"

"I wanted to meet on neutral ground," Rhiannon replied sharply. "I assume you read the scrolls."

Lucius's stare pierced at Rhiannon. "I did and have met all your demands. Your commander here agreed that my tribune can stay with me."

Rhiannon met the senator's steely-gray eyes. "Likewise, Trystan will stay with me. Did you verify whether the scroll we intercepted was written by you?"

"No. It was not written by me," Lucius said with a grated voice. "If you had shown this to Marcellus, he would have told you it was a fake."

"He did see it," Rhiannon admitted. "I did not believe him when he said it was a forgery."

Lucius frowned. "What made you change your mind?"

Rhiannon glanced at Trystan. "Trystan, beside me, arrived from your encampment after I had already ordered my courier to deliver my message to you. Trystan confirmed that my husband was free when he visited your encampment last week."

"Unfortunate, you did not wait for your commander's return," Lucius said. "It was only after I received your threat that the king was imprisoned. The young courier who delivered your message was beheaded."

Rhiannon winced and clenched her hands. She closely watched the senator when he turned to Decimus, as if seeking advice. The tribune arched an eyebrow and Lucius looked at her again. "Before we continue, I want proof Marcellus is not harmed."

"He is alive," she declared. "I also want to see that my husband has not been harmed."

One of Lucius's eyelids twitched closed, unnerving Rhiannon. "I can't do that," he said. "We risk discovery by Cunobelin if I allow that. Your commander with you saw the king today. He can vouch for his health."

Rhiannon turned to Trystan for a response. He grimaced. "My queen, the king yet lives." She could tell by the tension in his voice that Amren had been harmed, making it even more urgent she negotiate the prisoner exchange. She regarded the senator's face for any intimation of trickery. The sweat on his forehead made his skin sheen as he fiddled with the cuffs of his tunic.

"We are both victims of unfortunate events," Lucius said. "Someone stole my insignia ring which may have been used to seal the forged message. Most likely, it was a traitor in your inner circle."

Rhiannon leveled her eyes at the senator. "Tell me, how did this traitor get past your guards?"

The tribune interjected. "I strictly monitor all visitors. I can assure you that only Cunobelin and his closest advisors meet with the senator."

"Is not Marrock one of Cunobelin's advisors?" Rhiannon asked, raising an eyebrow.

"Well, yes ..." Lucius said, his eyes flitting to the tribune. "I showed Marrock my signet ring. That was all."

The senator confirmed Rhiannon's suspicions that Marrock had most likely forged the message. She added, "Marrock is versed in Latin. Did you ever consider that he might have stolen the ring and wrote the fake message?"

Lucius leaned forward and said with a graveled voice, "Even though what you say may be true, I am deeply disturbed that you made no attempt to contact me before shackling my son and hurling your threat at me." Lucius's jaw clenched as he shifted back in his seat and said through gritted teeth, "Despite this, I am ready to take the next steps to get my son back. What do you propose?"

Without any hesitation, Rhiannon rolled out her demands. "There must be utmost secrecy on where the prisoner exchange will take place. No word of what we say here gets back to Cunobelin or Marrock. Only a small contingency of your soldiers can escort the king. After the exchange is made, I will send you instructions for exchanging Vala for the Roman soldiers we captured."

"Agreed." Lucius pressed his lips into a firm line. "but only on the condition your commander remains here as a guarantee that you will adhere to our agreement. Further, only your youngest daughter escorts Marcellus to the designated spot. No other warriors can be with her. After my son is released, Trystan will be released at the same time as the king."

Rhiannon glanced at Trystan for affirmation that he would stay. He lightly touched her arm and nodded. She took a deep breath and unfurled her next stipulations. "My commander agrees to stay, but I will not concede that only Catrin escorts Marcellus. A small number of my warriors will escort him instead. Further, you must give me written assurance that your emperor will drop his support of Marrock's claims."

Lucius smiled thinly. "Only the emperor can make that decree, but I can speak on your behalf. As for Catrin, I was deeply disturbed that your husband accused Marcellus of raping her. I asked myself if this was the real reason that you threatened to butcher my son like an animal, this punishment done without a trial. Marcellus has the same signet ring as me, so the forged letter you presented me could have been written by anyone, including you."

The senator's cold stare sent a shiver down Rhiannon's spine. "What are you insinuating?"

"I am not insinuating anything," Lucius said, his eyes fixed on Rhiannon. "I demand only Catrin accompany Marcellus."

The queen knew then he would not budge from this condition, even at the risk of his son's life. She sensed that beneath the senator's scaly demeanor was a cold-blooded reptile that would sacrifice his own young to get his way. She had no other option now but to concede to his demand to save her husband's life.

She shot him a piercing stare. "I accept your condition. If anything goes wrong, I promise we will meet again."

40

SENATOR'S REVENGE

"Senator, I am indebted to you, but what happens to me if the emperor finds out what we have done here?"

Late that night, Lucius Antonius paced like a wild animal in his tented quarters, the image of the queen's pontifical mien rattling in his brain. He gawked at the two scrolls in his hand and an uncontrollable rage sizzled through him. He hurled the parchments against the tapestry divider. His outburst then ignited into a firestorm. He lashed out on all the objects within sight, sweeping his arm across the writing table. Ink bottles, quills, and parchment flew off, landing with loud thuds on the red carpet. The black ink splattered all over the rug's fibers.

His eyes next focused on the wax tablets and scrolls set on the elongated table. Off they flew, one-by-one. His anger coiled so tight he was ready to snap. Shrieking and cursing, he rammed his shoulders into the solid table. The pointed edge spiked his shoulder and the stabbing pain forced him to his knees. He roared in frustration that his own furniture had brought him down in humiliation.

Groaning loudly, Lucius felt powerful arms wrap around him and restrain him. Decimus's commanding voice echoed in his ears. "What has caused this uproar?"

How could Lucius explain the hurricane forces swelling inside him since he was a young man, at the time he was unjustly maligned and banished for his father's sins? Nothing on this trip to Britannia had gone right. Everyone who Lucius believed he outwitted had outmaneuvered him. And now, he must meet the outrageous demands of a barbarian queen to save his son. Shaking with rage, Lucius glowered at Decimus. "How can I remain calm, when a woman, a woman spews orders at me as if I am a dog? I am the grandson of Mark Antony, a brutal general who made fodder out of worthless shit such as her. Yet here I am, groveling to this bitch, a beast that insults me and threatens to kill my son."

Decimus held Lucius's arms tighter. "No one is more enraged than me. Yet in all wars, at one time or another, we must retreat and regroup before we can strike again."

Lucius yanked away, the pain shooting from his shoulder to his arm. He hardened his stare at Decimus. "Who am I to trust? Someone stole my ring to seal a forged letter that ignited this inferno. Everything the queen says points a finger at Marrock, but Cunobelin could have directed these events."

"Senator, you have achieved your primary objective," Decimus said with a firm voice. "You have divided Cunobelin and Amren. Unfortunately, the queen holds Marcellus prisoner and has pressed us against the wall. We must make sure your son is released before we make final agreements with any of these barbarians."

"The gods shit on me!" Lucius cursed, lifting his eyes to the ceiling. "Why must Marcellus keep tormenting me like this?"

Decimus winced. "Sir, I do not understand your meaning."

"Every time I try to steer my son onto the right path, he turns everything into a catastrophe."

"Sir, you should give your son some credit for his courage to volunteer as a hostage. His action helped ease a tense situation at our initial meeting with Amren."

"Give him credit!" Lucius bellowed. "Before that bitch queen sent her nasty note, Amren confronted me, telling me that Marcellus had raped his youngest daughter. I know my son. This is an outlandish lie. He is too smooth for that."

"Isn't that what you instructed?" Decimus said. "Seduce her to find out more information."

"My directive was not for him to get caught!"

"Senator, your anger toward Marcellus is misplaced. Right now, our first priority should be to get him back to Rome alive. As you said, we cannot trust anyone. You knew that when we arrived in Britannia. We must now think as Julius Caesar did—divide and conquer."

"What do you suggest we do?" Lucius said, rubbing his achy shoulder.

"Do as the queen demands for the prisoner exchange," Decimus said. "Make sure only a few of our most trusted soldiers are involved to prevent any misunderstandings."

"How can I trust that fucking queen?" Lucius snarled as he gingerly lowered himself onto a chair. The throbbing pain in his shoulder had become almost unbearable. "Did you see the scowl on her face? She might attack our soldiers out of spite and rescue the king. She could keep Marcellus and make further demands."

"Let me remind you, we still hold Amren's eldest daughter as leverage. I will personally take charge of the prisoner exchange. I won't release Amren until I see with my own eyes that only the king's daughter escorts him to the site."

"How can we get Amren and his commander out of camp without Cunobelin and Marrock knowing?" asked Lucius.

"We'll transport them at night," Decimus suggested. "We can tell Cunobelin later that our hands were forced to exchange them."

"What if Cunobelin turns against us and attacks us for our betrayal?"

"He won't, not if you offer him recompense—wine, luxury goods, whatever it takes."

"You're right," Lucius agreed. "We could offer Cunobelin our Roman forces to help Marrock overthrow Amren."

Decimus's eyes widened. "How can you say that? The emperor ordered all our forces out of Britannia. That goes against his mandate."

The tribune's hesitation provoked Lucius. "Tiberius did not give us a timetable. I am not leaving this island with my tail tucked between my legs without teaching that arrogant boar and his sow queen a lesson. No one threatens me and lives!"

"Sir, I will not defy the emperor," Decimus argued. "Praise the gods if we get Marcellus out of here alive. I do not have enough soldiers to defend us against the various factions if they all turn against us."

Lucius roared, "Do not defy me, Decimus! You already failed me when your soldiers allowed themselves to be captured like stupid little girls. Now we must barter for the release of those idiots." Decimus opened his mouth to speak, but Lucius pounded his fist on the table. "I told you not to defy me!"

The tribune's jaw clenched. "What do you want of me?"

Lucius said with a commanding voice, "This is my charge to you. When Marcellus is released and out of danger, you will retake the king as prisoner and capture Catrin. When they are brought into camp, I want that pompous king to watch every soldier taking a turn with his beloved daughter. If Marcellus needs something to soothe his wounds, he can take that wench back to Rome and pillage her at will. When he is done, he can sell her off to a brothel." Lucius stared coldly at Decimus. "If you confront me again about this, remember that I was the only senator who defended you when the others wanted to strip you of rank. I did this, even though I believed you committed an affront to the empire when you divorced your Roman wife to marry a whore from Gaul."

Decimus swallowed hard and looked down. "Senator, I am indebted to you, but what happens to me if the emperor finds out what we have done here?"

"What you have done," Lucius said bluntly. "And pray, my friend, I do not tell him."

41

MELD WITH THE RAVEN

She realized then, the divine creature was offering her the key for unlocking these supernatural powers.

Asleep, Catrin felt herself levitating over Marcellus's headless body that was burning on a pyre. Horrified, she dropped like a rock and her arms flung up. Disoriented, she thought she heard Marcellus cry out, "Help me, Catrin!" and then something sharp clawed her chest.

Rousting out of her nightmare, she opened her eyes, finding her raven's beak within inches of her face. Startled, she whacked the bird off and glanced around to confirm where she was. The hearth-lit hovel was disheveled with various cauldrons, stringed bird bones hanging from the beams, and jars of strong smelling herbs strewn across two tables. Smoke from an open hearth was filtering through the thatched roof. Nothing had changed. She was still in Agrona's lair with her ankles chained. Having been isolated and shackled for at least a month, she had lost track of time, the hours and the days merging together.

Catrin again heard Marcellus's cries for help, the urgency in his voice making her heart shudder. She couldn't go on like this, helpless and desperate, not knowing what had happened to him or transpired at home. Loneliness had mired her in gloom. Frustrated that she could not return home was devouring her. There had to be a way for her to escape. If she did, what would her parents do to her if she could not convince them of the dangers that Agrona posed?

Every time Catrin gazed into Agrona's eyes, Rhan was lurking there. Fiery red braids slithered around Rhan's ashen face and her bluish lips contorted into a grotesque smile. Agrona's eyes glowed like the mammoth red wolf that had accompanied her on the day the Druidess had entered Catrin's mind for the first and only time. Successfully blocking Agrona's further attempt to control her made Catrin realize that her power was at least as strong as Agrona's.

The word "power" resonated in Catrin's mind. She said "power" out loud. The words "power, power, power" ran together in a mantra. She stretched out her hand to summon the powerful forces into her fingertips. The energy entered her like a hot fluid and flowed through her arm, down her body, and all the way to her toes.

The raven's loud shriek and sharp jab at her ankle broke Catrin's trance. Annoyed, she pushed the raven aside and complained, "I hate being locked up in here as much as you."

The raven tenaciously hopped back to Catrin, and it gurgled, wildly bobbed its head, and took another swipe at her leg. This time, she paid attention and asked, "What are you trying to tell me?"

The raven cocked its head, its eyes pleading for her to connect with it. She recalled the altered curse foretelling she would rise out of Apollo's flames as a raven with the powers of the Ancient Druids. She realized then, the divine creature was offering her the key for unlocking these supernatural powers. She extended an arm on which her raven perched and stroked the bird. Red sparks emitted from her fingers the harder she stroked the feathers.

Hearing footsteps to her back, she stopped and turned.

Belinus appeared in the open door with a belted sword at his side. He set a rusty-colored bowl on a table near the entrance and walked to the back wall where Catrin was shackled. He grinned and opened his hand to reveal raspberries. "Mor asked that I bring these to you."

Catrin took a couple of berries to eat, but the bitterness of not being able to see her sister made the fruit's sweetness sour in her mouth. She looked sadly at Belinus. "Why can't Mor come? Why do you chain me like this? I am a princess, not a criminal."

Belinus frowned. "As I already said, Agrona has ordered me to chain you until she lifts your curse."

"Is this what Mother ordered, that I be chained like a crazed beast?"

"No, that is what Agrona mandated." Belinus looked at the raven gawking at him. "Are you conjuring spells with that raven?"

Perhaps I should, Catrin thought, but she instead said, "No, it keeps me company. I still do not understand why I can't go home. Has Mother said anything about you marrying Mor?"

"Yes, but she told me not to tell anyone." Belinus's jaw tensed. "There is something I should say … Mor says I can't keep this from you … no matter what Agrona ordered—"

"Spit it out," Catrin said impatiently.

Belinus said, "Senator Antonius has taken your father prisoner!"

Catrin felt her throat clutch. "What about Vala?"

"No one knows where Vala is being held," Belinus said grimly. "The queen imprisoned Marcellus in retaliation. A week ago, your mother and some warriors left the village to gather support from the Regni king if war breaks out. They have yet to return."

The bad news confirmed Catrin's premonition that Marcellus was in grave danger. Now concerned for her entire family and people, she asked, "Who has been left in charge?"

"Agrona."

A sense of dread crawled over Catrin. She said, "Mor should have been granted this authority. You have to believe me that Agrona is working against us. That is why she keeps me chained up, so I will not tell anyone. She wants everyone to believe I have gone insane."

Belinus regarded Catrin for a moment. "The king ordered that Agrona be second-in-command before he left to meet with the senator."

Catrin staggered to her feet, but the chains restrained her from taking a step. "Father does not know the threat that Agrona poses. Gods above! We are in a desperate situation. Marrock was here last week in the shape of a large wolf."

Belinus raised his eyebrows. "You expect me to believe that?"

"Yes, I do. Marrock is conspiring with Agrona to destroy Father, to destroy our kingdom. You need to let me go, so we can stop this!"

He shook his head. "You know I can't do that."

Catrin realized that she would not be able to convince Belinus to go against Agrona. She had to find another way to escape. Calming herself down, she said in a more tempered voice, "At least give me some dignity and take off my shackles. Allow me to walk around the room and eat at the table."

Belinus paused. "All right, but no tricks."

He pulled out a straight key from a pouch, unlocked the shackles, and helped Catrin unwrap them. Her ankles felt sore and swollen as she followed Belinus to the table and sat across from him. He handed her some cheese from his pouch and gestured toward the red bowl of porridge. "I'm only unshackling you because Mor asked me to treat you more kindly."

Catrin took the block of cheese and broke it in half, giving one piece to Belinus. As she nibbled on the tangy cheese, she nervously watched him pull a knife from his belt and examine the blade. He said, "There is something else I should tell you. Five Roman soldiers were captured near our village. Even though they refused to talk under torture, the queen assumed they were sent to help Marcellus escape. She suspects the Roman knew of the plan before he was held as hostage." Belinus spat on the surface of the knife's blade. "That Roman lover of yours cannot be trusted."

Catrin swallowed the cheese in her mouth and gulped water from a cup. Her throat still dry, she rasped, "He helped me when I was stricken with the falling sickness."

"You mean the falling sickness he cursed you with. Don't let your affection for the Roman blind you. The only reason he still lives is that we can use him as leverage to bargain the king's release." With the tip of the knife, Belinus cut a thin line on his forefinger. "If I had my way, that good-for-nothing scum would already be dead, and I would make sure he died slowly."

Belinus set the knife down and licked the blood off his finger. Catrin glanced at the weapon, wondering if she could steal it. She said, "It would be foolhardy for you to kill him. I believe he could help us negotiate a release for Father."

Belinus sneered, "That Roman help us? Agrona is right. You have lost all reason and gone mad with Apollo's curse."

Catrin's stomach knotted. "Is that what you think, that I'm crazy?"

Belinus waved two fingers in front of his eyes as if he was trying to ward off evil spirits. "You will be if Agrona cannot lift your curse."

Catrin was not making any inroads with Belinus. At this point, the only trick she had up her sleeve was her raven. She quietly communed to the raven. It flew to her and its talons emitted prickly heat into her arm. A light flashed in her mind, signaling she had forged with the raven's essence. This time, she was determined to direct the raven's actions like a charioteer driving horses. She would coordinate her human form at the same time she controlled the raven's action. Before, she could only control one physical form at a time.

Coordinating the movements of her human body and the raven concurrently was dizzying. She concentrated harder, telling herself step-by-step what to do next.

See through the raven's eyes.

Her vision switched to the raven's eyesight.

Move my human head. Speak to Belinus with my mouth.

The raven's eyes fixed on Belinus while she tilted her human head toward him. Looking at Belinus through the raven's eyes, she said, "Tell Agrona that I'm now willing to train with her."

"This is a sudden change in attitude," Belinus replied, suspicion in his voice.

Catrin could not tell if she was hearing his voice through human or raven ears. Turning her human head toward the raven, she still saw Belinus through the raven's eyes. She told Belinus, "I've been considering this decision the last few days. Will Agrona be visiting me this morning, so I can start training?"

"No, but I am to meet her after I leave here." Belinus leaned over the tabletop and gaped at the raven. "The light must be bad in here. I swear the bird's eyes have turned blue."

Curious as to whether her eyes had also changed color as a result of entering the raven's mind, Catrin asked, "What color are my eyes?"

Belinus studied her face. "Blue … no wait." His eyes grew bigger. "They look almost black in the dim light."

Catrin directed the raven to look at her. When the bird tilted its head, the room appeared to whirl until she saw herself through the bird's eyes.

"Are you all right?" Belinus asked. "Your eyes look strange … hollow."

Catrin steered the raven's head to look at Belinus. "I am not sure what you mean."

He did not respond, his eyes darting back and forth between the raven and hers. She turned her head toward the raven and directed it to raise its leg. It did as instructed. She then wondered if she could see through both her human and raven's eyes at the same time.

She could!

But seeing images of Belinus and herself at the same time was disconcerting. She lurched out of the raven's mind and switched completely to her human senses.

Belinus leaned over the table. "I can't believe it!"

"Believe what?"

"Your eyes! They switched from blue to amber, and now they're blue again."

The fear in Belinus's eyes gave Catrin an idea on how to play with his mind, so she could escape. "You must be seeing the eyes of evil spirits that live inside me. Go tell Agrona I need to speak with her. Tell her to hurry, so she can purge these demons from me. On your way out, leave the door open, so any ghouls hiding in here can also leave with you."

Belinus flinched. "What ghouls? You know I can't leave the door unlocked."

"Oh, I forgot," Catrin said.

Belinus flinched when the raven on her arm arched its wings and shrieked. He asked in a quivering voice, "Is that creature putting a curse on me?"

The raven answered his question by flouncing onto his head. Belinus froze, his eyes rolling up. "Get this thing off me!"

"Do not show the raven any fear," Catrin warned, lowering her voice. "Its talons might shred your head like cabbage leaves!"

Belinus was as motionless as a statue as the raven raked its beak through his lime-bleached hair. Then the bird hopped onto the floor.

Eyes and mouth both gaping open, Belinus muttered, "I need to go now!" He picked up his knife from the table and opened the door, the raven waddling out behind him. The door slammed shut and the bolt clicked.

Hearing Belinus leave, Catrin leaned against the door to budge it. Nothing.

Again she pushed. Still nothing.

Frustrated, she pounded on the door for several moments and then lowered herself on the ground in despair after realizing she had lost her chance to escape. The image of Marcellus's headless body rolled into her mind. Panic struck her like a whirlwind that not only could he be killed, but also her father. What could she do? Even if she escaped, who would believe that Agrona was the embodiment of Rhan?

42

HUMAN SACRIFICE

Apollo has given that Roman the power to destroy us. To counter his god, we must offer him as a human sacrifice to entreat our gods to lift Apollo's curse off Catrin.

Calm down, Catrin told herself. *Think. Think.* She then recalled what her father had told her: *Know your enemies better than your friends. Learn to think like them. Counter them by anticipating their next moves.*

An idea nested in her mind. The raven was at her beck and call. Through the raven, she could follow Belinus and find out what Agrona was up to. She could then learn how to counter the Druidess. *Take one step at a time,* she reminded herself, *and find a way to save Marcellus and my father.*

Sitting cross-legged on the hard earthen floor, Catrin melded her thoughts with the raven that was just outside the door. Through its eyes, she could see Belinus striding deeper into the woods. She instructed the raven to follow him.

A cool breeze under the raven's wings lifted her up to the treetops, where she had a bird's eye view of the forest. When she saw Belinus walking through a clearing, she directed her raven to soar over the green canopy of the woods and follow him.

Several moments later, she noticed smoke spiraling through the treetops directly ahead. She ordered the raven to descend, so she could confirm if the smoke was emanating from a campfire that Agrona had started. The leaves appeared like green eddies as the bird dived between the dense trees. When the bird landed behind a pile of wood, the twigs snapped beneath its feet. On the mossy ground nearby, a stiff mouse came into view.

The sudden motion of the raven's beak thrusting into the vermin's bloated abdomen made Catrin's head spin. She overpowered the raven's urge to eat the carrion, so it would follow her next instruction to move around the woodpile.

The stubborn raven finally obeyed her and waddled around the logs. A black cauldron over a campfire came into sight. Standing next to the black pot was Agrona, humming as she stirred a coppery slime bubbling over the top. Through the raven's nostrils, Catrin inhaled the ghastly odor of burning skin from the brew. Her human stomach roiled from the disgusting stench. She directed the raven to move closer to Agrona.

The Druidess lifted her head and called, "Who is there?"

Thinking the Druidess was calling out to her, Catrin felt her heart pound in her chest, but then she realized Agrona was talking to someone else.

Belinus then appeared beside the Druidess with a white dove cupped in his hands. He held out the stiff bird and said, "I brought this for the ritual."

Agrona sniffed and gave a crooked smile. "Good. Not quite dead. The last ingredient for my potion."

She clasped the dove as she plucked out its tail feathers and dropped them into the cauldron. The concoction oozed over the rim and skittered down the black metal. Using a knife, she sliced the dove's abdomen open, spread the tissue apart with her fingers and scooped out its entrails. After she tossed the guts into the mixture, she looked at Belinus. "I will now entreat the gods to give me a sign of what we should do with Marcellus to appease them."

Catrin shuddered.

Pacifying the gods required a human sacrifice.

Agrona stirred the mixture in the cauldron with a long ladle, at times licking the green coating of the metal surface, then lifted her arms to the heavens and chanted, "Taranis, God of Thunder, I beseech you to show me a sign of what I must offer to appease your anger."

Catrin's connection to the raven disrupted when she heard crackling noises. Everything before the raven's eyes disappeared into nothingness and she could not hear a thing. Not sure what happened, she called out to the raven to reconnect.

An instant later, brilliant light flashed in her mind and she heard Agrona asking Belinus in a croaky voice, "How did Catrin appear when you left her?"

"Not as defiant," he answered.

"In what way?"

"She is now willing to accept your training."

"That is a step forward," Agrona said leaning closer, scrutinizing his face. "I can see that something troubles you."

Belinus looked down and shifted his feet. "Something odd occurred when I was with Catrin earlier. I am not sure if it was real … or if she and the raven had cast a spell on me. At one moment, Catrin was as motionless as a rock. Then her head jerked and the color of her eyes turned to the color of amber."

Agrona lifted her brow. "What was her raven doing?"

Belinus shook his head as if he could not believe what he was saying. "Its eyes switched colors, just like Catrin. At one moment, it was stiff as a tree and then at the next, its head bobbed."

"Did Catrin say anything while this was occurring?"

"Yes, she stared blankly as she spoke, her voice flat. After a few heartbeats, her eyes again brightened and she seemed back to herself again."

Agrona stroked her chin. "Hmm ... strange. Did you leave her raven inside the cottage when you left?"

Belinus mumbled, "Well ... I'm not sure."

"Not sure?"

"I was distracted and—"

A gusty wind roared through the forest, muffling the conversation. Soon after, lightning webbing across the sky was followed by ear-shattering rumbles. Catrin only heard bits of the conversation between cracks of thunder.

"We have angered Taranis," Agrona yelled. "To remove curse ... looming ... must offer human sacrifice."

Belinus's mouth flung open. "Sacrifice Catrin!"

"No, you idiot! Marcellus!"

Catrin's heart raced as she struggled to hear the voices through pounding rain falling in sheets.

Belinus shouted, "We must wait ... the queen could start a war ... bloodbath vengeance!"

Agrona pointed to herself. "You forget ... I take orders from the gods. Sacrifice Marcellus ... appease the gods ... cut his throat ... offer blood ..."

Catrin's heart felt as if it was ramming against her ribs. She kept telling herself, *Stay with the raven, stay with the raven.*

After several more moments, the raging storm finally quieted, and Catrin could then clearly hear Belinus say, "Romans do not have that kind of sorcery—"

Agrona interrupted. "They pray to Apollo, a god who rules the sun. Look at his power to drive the sun across the sky."

Belinus tilted his head back to look up. "Still, the thought of burning Marcellus alive makes me cringe."

Agrona dug her fingernails into Belinus's arm like a wolf pulling down its prey. "You idiot! Apollo has given that Roman the power to destroy us. To counter his god, we must offer him as a human sacrifice to entreat our gods to lift Apollo's curse off Catrin. You must return to the village and double the guards watching Marcellus. Tomorrow, we offer him to the war goddesses. In return, they will embolden our warriors for battle. Meanwhile, I will return to my lair and see what Catrin is up to."

As Belinus and Agrona rushed off in different directions, Catrin was faced with a dilemma. She had never been in the raven's mind so long. She feared being stricken with the falling sickness again if she pulled out too quickly. So this would not happen again, she focused on transferring step-by-step all of the raven senses back to her human form.

First, wiggle my fingers.

Next move my arms.

When she moved her hands and arms, it felt as if a thousand needles were pricking her skin. Ignoring the sensation, she focused on regaining her vision.

Look through my human eyes.

For a few moments, the walls bounced in conjunction with the raven's hopping on the ground. The sensory assault of being in both minds was too dizzying. She made one final leap.

Get out of the raven now!

As Catrin somersaulted out of the raven's mind, her stomach felt as if it had jumped to her throat. Head spinning, she collapsed on the floor and her chin slammed hard on the earthen floor in Agrona's lair.

Dazed, she lay on her back and gazed at the wooden beams swirling above as she floated into black sleep.

43

MAGIC OF ANCIENT DRUIDS

"I can see your love for him burns hot inside you. He diminishes your powers while I can accentuate them. If you willingly sacrifice him …"

Waking up, Catrin wiped cold sweat off her forehead, wondering how long she had been lying there. The sobering realization that the Druidess would soon arrive cleared the fogginess in her head. She crawled to the table and grasped its edge for support as she staggered to sit on a three-legged stool. Placing her head on the tabletop, she struggled to gather her wits. A light flickered in her mind—a signal from her raven to meld with it, but she did not have time to connect. The door clicked open and Agrona walked through the doorway, the raven waddling discretely behind her.

"Morning, my love," Agrona said, her eyes flitting around the room. "Clumsy of Belinus to leave you unchained."

"Did he tell you I'm ready to train with you?" asked Catrin.

"Yes, he mentioned it," Agrona said, again glancing all around. "Where is your feathered companion?"

The raven immediately announced its presence with a blood-chilling shriek that made Agrona jump. When the Druidess looked down, the bird cocked its head and peered at her with beady amber eyes. She asked, "How did you magically appear?"

The raven answered with several jabs at Agrona's feet, whereupon she jumped back and shrieked, "For the love of gods! Catrin, get that thing under control!"

Catrin smirked and extended her arm on which the raven then perched. As the bird settled, Catrin watched the Druidess sit down across from her. She noticed Agrona's black-painted, curled fingernails, bright crimson lips that appeared to be smeared with blood, and eyelids shaded the same icy blue as the veins on her hands.

The Druidess first glanced at the raven, then looked at Catrin. "I can see your pet raven and you are good friends. Have you yet connected with it to gain the powers of the Ancient Druids?"

Smiling thinly, Catrin stroked the raven's ebony breast. "As you can see, the raven and I are now forged as one. As such, it has disclosed dark secrets about you."

Agrona arched her eyebrows. "What did it reveal?"

Catrin leaned over, gambling her instincts were right. "You do not have the mystical powers you claim to have. It is a delusion."

"Is not all magic a delusion," Agrona chuckled, "a trick of the hands?"

"No, my magic is real."

"My clever girl, you are mistaken." Agrona's right eyelid began twitching. "Like you, I am a soul traveler who can enter other living beings."

"Then enter my raven's mind," Catrin challenged, "and let me see you do this."

Agrona pointed to a spider spinning an intricate lattice overhead. "Why would I do this when you and the raven can instead enter my domain?"

Recalling her father's words that Agrona knew how to trick her enemies, Catrin realized she had to take on this same trait to outmaneuver the Druidess. Remaining stone-faced, she said, "My raven has opened my eyes to the webs you entangle your enemies with. I want you to teach me how you do this."

Agrona regarded Catrin for a moment. "Are you playing mind games with me? You are nothing more than a newborn playing with wildfire. Only through me can you learn how to control the magic of the Ancient Druids."

Catrin laughed. "I can already do that."

"Is that so? Then tell me how you draw these powers."

"From the portal dividing the mortal world and Otherworld."

Agrona curled one side of her mouth into a half-smile. "I have already travelled there with you in the raven's mind."

"I know." Catrin smiled. "Do you want to do it again?"

"Yes, if we work together, we can combine our magic. I can teach you how to meld with the raven as painlessly as blinking an eye. You will have none of the ill effects which you have previously suffered. Are you willing to join me on this journey?"

Catrin regarded Agrona's smug smile. "I will join you, but you must tell me more about the gateway into the Otherworld."

Agrona cocked an eyebrow. "Why should I tell you?"

"Because only my raven can travel to this portal," Catrin said, suspecting Agrona could not travel to the portal by herself. She rubbed the raven's beak with a forefinger. "Only through me can you access the magic through the Otherworld's portal."

"And what magic is that?"

"Do you not know?" Catrin mocked, "Are you not the master of such things?"

Agrona pulled out a dagger from her belt and circled the blade over the candle flame. "Do not play me for the fool. I know how such things are done. I know how the wheel turns, but I need you to spin the magic for me."

The raven's talons pressed into Catrin's skin, and it cawed three times. Intuitively, she understood the bird's meaning that Agrona did not have the ability to enter her mind. Still, Catrin was uncertain how much power the Druidess still retained and thus mined her for more information. "The raven tells me you have only performed one feat of magic. You defied death once, but your soul became entrapped in Agrona's head. Once her body dies, your soul also perishes. You need me to take you to the Wall of Lives, so you can again rejuvenate your powers and resurrect your soul into another living being."

Agrona's eyelid twitched again. "My child, you underestimate my abilities. You must do my bidding, or you will suffer great pain when you call on these supernatural forces. To tame your raven's powers, you must forge your mind with mine and sacrifice what stands in your way."

Catrin hesitated. "What is that sacrifice?"

Agrona said coldly, "Marcellus."

A breath clutched in Catrin's throat. "How can he possibly stand in the way?"

Agrona thrust the tip of the dagger through the candle flame. "I can see your love for him burns hot inside you. He diminishes your powers while I can accentuate them. If you willingly sacrifice him, I will show you how to permanently merge with both the raven and me to summon god-like abilities of prophecy, shape-shifting, and calling on nature's forces from the Wall of Lives you have described. Together, we can overcome Marrock."

The only reason Catrin could surmise that Agrona wanted to overcome Marrock was to keep all the power for herself. Catrin must be a key for the Druidess to regain her mystical abilities. It now made sense that the Druidess thought killing Marcellus would break down Catrin's final barrier for merging with her. Agrona could only harvest the powers of the Ancient Druids through the raven spirit. She stared at Agrona. *I will not let you do that.*

The Druidess did not flinch, confirming she had not heard Catrin's thoughts.

Catrin finally said, "I abhor human sacrifice, and my parents forbid it."

"Your parents are probably dead!" Agrona snarled, baring her teeth. "I now stand as ruler of the Cantiaci. You must pay homage to me."

Catrin's stomach clenched like a fist. "Why do you believe my parents are dead?"

"The Romans most likely killed your father. Your mother left over a week ago. Nobody knows where she is, so I also assume she is dead. You and I must now join forces to protect the kingdom against Marrock."

A distrustful shiver crawled down Catrin's spine.

You mean destroy my family, so you can take over the kingdom!

The urgency of escaping became foremost in Catrin's mind. Eyeing the dagger in Agrona's hand, she said, "You are right. Like you, I only want to protect our kingdom from enemies ready to devour us. Tell me what I need to do to make this happen."

When Agrona's irises switched from green to shimmering gold in the candlelight, Catrin sensed a gray aura shrouding her like a corpse. She averted her eyes from the deadly stare that was drawing her in, then suddenly felt Agrona's grip around her wrist.

"Go back with me to the village," Agrona demanded. "Proclaim your fealty to me and join me in offering Marcellus to the war goddesses. After that, you must allow my soul to enter you, so we can combine our magic. Together, we can avenge your parents' deaths by destroying Cunobelin, Marrock, and the Romans."

Agrona's sinister scheme was now clear to Catrin. The Druidess intended to carry out the curse by inciting the Romans to seek vengeance for sacrificing Marcellus. The fire-breathing eagles in her visions that would destroy her village were the Romans. She had to find a way to stop Agrona. She pounded her fist on the table, shaking the raven off her arm. "I will do it! And further ... I will hold the knife that slashes Marcellus's throat. Now take me home, so we can prepare for the sacrificial ritual."

When the raven fluttered to an overhead raft, Agrona tightened her grip around Catrin's wrist. "We must first seal our bond with blood."

Not sure what commingling their blood would do, Catrin quickly fused her thoughts with the raven as the Druidess cut the palm of her hand with the blade.

The raven dived at Agrona with outstretched claws, slicing her face. In defense, the Druidess crossed her arms to shield herself from its further assault, all the while keeping a tight hold of the weapon.

Catrin hurled herself across the table and rammed her head into Agrona's chest. The next instant, she found herself on the ground, alongside Agrona, the table toppled on them. The dagger was loose, but just out of Catrin's reach. She lunged for the weapon, but Agrona's knee hammered into her chest and forced her back, flat on the floor. Then lethal hands gripped Catrin's throat, cutting off air.

Fighting for her life, Catrin quickly reconnected to the raven.

Attack!

The raven again swooped at Agrona. A few screeches later, Catrin felt Agrona's hand slack around her throat. Catrin peeled the fingers away and rolled to face her foe. When she saw the raven's black wings flapping at Agrona's face, she swiftly kicked the Druidess in the stomach, the force slamming Agrona on her back.

Catrin jumped up, scooped the dagger into her hand, and pressed it against Agrona's belly. "Get up!" she demanded.

The Druidess staggered to her feet and slowly backed away. Taking no chances that she might use one of her tricks, Catrin brandished the weapon and warned, "Do not even think of escape."

Agrona's lips pressed into a firm line as she continued backing away. Catrin stepped forward and pushed the dagger harder into Agrona's belly.

"Not another step!"

Agrona's eyes widened with fear. "Put your weapon aside. I'll do whatever you say."

Releasing the pressure on the handle, Catrin ordered, "Put the shackles around your ankles."

Agrona kept her eyes fixed on Catrin as she walked to the back and wrapped the shackles around her ankles. Catrin inserted the pin to lock them, and she mocked, "Let me see you use your magic to get out of these."

Agrona rattled the chains. "You will regret this, sorceress! The gods will curse you for what you have done!"

"I think not," Catrin said, taking one last look at Agrona's blood-soaked face. She considered killing the traitorous Druidess, but sensed a powerful force holding her back.

With dagger in hand, Catrin jarred the heavy door open and let the raven and herself out. Outside, she sprinted toward the direction of her raven's flight over the forest canopy. Melding her thoughts with the raven, she ordered it to find her mother.

44

QUEEN'S MANDATE

… but her rage finally boiled to the surface and she bitterly blasted, "Then it was you who ordered Marcellus killed!"

Catrin followed her raven through a maze of unfamiliar woodlands. Several times the raven disappeared into thickets, but then appeared above the trees. Unfamiliar with the landscape, she feared backtracking to Agrona's lair. She looked around to get her bearings. Vines snaking over tree branches appeared eerily similar to where Marrock had taken her that fateful day. The fear she felt as a little girl of not being able to find her way home disquieted her again. She needed an aerial view, so she could locate her village and possibly find her mother.

She summoned the raven that was flying overhead. It swooped down and landed on her extended arm. Sitting cross-legged behind the cover of scrubby bushes, she entered the raven's mind. Step-by-step, she switched to its eyesight and took control of its movements. Through the raven's eyes, she confirmed her motionless human body was safely hidden from predators. She then directed her raven to fly above the verdure canopy of the dense woods. Spreading the raven's fingertipped wings, she felt a cool breeze lift her above the patchworks of forests, pastures, and farmlands. With the aerial view, she determined Agrona's hut was halfway between the village and the white cliffs. The road near the river meandering around her village was congested with people and farm animals. She flew lower to discern the riders, but could not find her mother. Sensing that her mother was nearby, she circled the dense forest where she had left her human form. She finally spotted her mother riding the black stallion. Next to her was Cynwrig astride a gray gelding.

Excited to find them, Catrin lurched out of the raven's mind and burst through what appeared to be green aureoles swirling around her. When she returned to her human form, her head felt as if a stake had rammed through it.

Groggy, she crumbled to the ground.

When she slowly came to her human senses, she heard a woman say, "Answer me. Answer me." Then her mother's face came into view, Cynwrig beside her.

Unable to speak, Catrin struggled to wiggle her stiff fingers. As sensation returned to her muscles, it felt as if her skin was ripping apart. The queen placed a hand on Catrin's forehead and asked if she was all right.

Her tongue still numb, Catrin garbled, "Wha ... hap ... pen?"

"We were on our way to Agrona's hut to fetch you," Rhiannon said, "but we halted when we saw your raven hop behind these bushes and shriek. Then something strange happened." The queen widened her eyes at Cynwrig.

Mouth agape, Cynwrig shook his head as if he couldn't believe what he was saying. "The raven disappeared just as you appeared."

Though what Cynwrig observed confounded Catrin, her most urgent priority was to warn them of Agrona. Her tongue felt as thick as honey as she uttered, "Do ... do not ... take me back." The rest of the words stuck in her throat, and she gestured for water.

Cynwrig brought an animal-skinned bag to her lips from which she drank. As she sipped, the water drooled out of her mouth. She clasped his arm and grunted, the words refusing to roll off her tongue.

Cynwrig gave her a bewildered look and then turned to the queen. "Something is not right."

The queen looked at the sky now darkening with billowing clouds. "Let us seek shelter at the cave nearby. There I can care for my daughter."

Cynwrig nodded. "It should be stockpiled with everything we need."

Without a further word, he hoisted Catrin up. Dangling off his shoulder, she became woozy with blood rushing into her head. His jolting strides exacerbated her dizziness.

After several moments of bouncing, Catrin was pulled off Cynwrig's shoulder and leaned in a sitting position against the cave's wall close to the entrance. The stone wall was hard on her back, and drops of water from a lichen-crusted ceiling annoyingly dripped on her face. Looking around, she saw an arsenal of spears, shields, and swords stacked against the wall across from her. Outside, near the cave's entrance, her mother was hobbling the horses.

The queen then stepped inside the cave and placed a hand on Catrin's forehead. "Do you feel better?"

"Yes," Catrin muttered. Although relieved to talk again, she nonetheless felt fatigued and feverish. "Where are we?"

"In a cave. Near the river."

It finally dawned on Catrin that this was where she had left Mor and Belinus before her liaison with Marcellus. Shivering from what she assumed were the ill effects of connecting so long with her raven, she thought it strange that the cave was now stockpiled with weapons, foodstuff, and strong-smelling sacks of medicinal herbs.

When the specter of Agrona loomed in Catrin's mind again, she urgently told her mother, "Don't take me back to Agrona! She wants my powers! She shackled me, drugged me. I had to escape."

Rhiannon gripped Catrin's arm. "Slow down, you're not making any sense."

Catrin began shaking uncontrollably and her teeth clacked. "Agrona ... she said ... the Romans killed Father. You were dead."

Rhiannon creased her brow into a deep furrow. "Your father yet lives, but he is a Roman prisoner. I left home over a week ago to negotiate his freedom. Marcellus is to be exchanged for him. That is why I came to fetch you."

"Does Agrona know this?"

"I never told her."

Catrin felt her heart seize in her chest. "Oh, gods! Agrona plans to sacrifice Marcellus tomorrow! Mother, you can't let her do this. She is evil."

Rhiannon tensed. "That can't happen! We need Marcellus alive."

"Why did the Romans take Father prisoner?"

Rhiannon told Catrin everything that had happened after her warriors discovered the forged message from Senator Antonius on a dead Catuvellauni courier. Fearing that the king would be executed, she admitted threatening the senator that she would sacrifice Marcellus, unless Amren was returned.

The words "sacrifice Marcellus" hooked in Catrin's mind. Anger burned in her chest that it was her mother that ordered Marcellus sacrificed, not Agrona. She half-listened to her mother continue the story, but her rage finally broiled to the surface and she bitterly blasted, "Then it was you who ordered Marcellus killed!"

The queen quickly replied, "Only if I did not return. That is why I raced back to get you. Only you can escort Marcellus to the prisoner exchange."

"Me, me ..." Catrin stammered, fighting for composure. "I don't understand."

"That was what the senator demanded. He also retains Trystan. Right now I don't know who to trust from our village."

"Agrona is a traitor!" Catrin exclaimed. "When you forced me to go with her, I saw Marrock in the shape of a wolf at her lair. I'm sure they are conspiring to start a war between the Romans and us."

Cynwrig interjected. "My queen, I agree that Agrona can't be trusted. She mustn't know we have Catrin and that we've talked with the senator."

Rhiannon paused and lifted her eyes. "I agree. We'll only tell her that we spoke with the Regni king who has agreed to aid us. We'll play along that we support her decision to sacrifice Marcellus—"

Catrin broke off her mother's words. "No! You cannot do that!"

"Let me finish!" Rhiannon snapped. "With everyone focused on the sacrifice, this is a golden opportunity to make it appear as if the Romans helped Marcellus escape. Catrin, you could bring him here to hide until the prisoner exchange."

Cynwrig added, "I could remain hidden in the trees during the actual exchange. If there is any hint of Roman treachery, I will unleash fury."

"This is a bold plan," Rhiannon said, tapping her chin. "It might work. That way, no one from the village will suspect the prisoner swap is taking place. Afterward, Amren can deal with all the traitors in his inner circle."

The queen turned to Catrin. "When you make the exchange, tell the Romans you will not hesitate to kill Marcellus, if there is any suggestion of treachery. Once your father and Trystan are freed, run like a deer to the cover of this cave. If a conflict breaks out, do what you must to save yourself, even if that means killing Marcellus."

Catrin gasped. "I could never kill him! I love him."

Rhiannon's jaw clenched. "What did you just say?"

"I love him," Catrin repeated.

Rhiannon snapped her eyes at Cynwrig. "Leave us!"

When he left the cave, Catrin met the fiery stare of her mother.

Rhiannon lashed, "Why must you force me to question your loyalty? Your family comes first, not this Roman you hardly know. You are naïve to believe he loves you. He would not hesitate to sacrifice you to save himself. Your blind loyalty to him will not only destroy you, but it will destroy our family."

"I will never kill Marcellus," Catrin proclaimed. "I know in my heart he is not the enemy. We pledged ourselves as husband and wife before Mother Goddess."

"Dreams! Visions! Pledges!" Rhiannon snarled, pacing back and forth like a wild animal. "Are you really that stupid? Having sex does not constitute a marriage. Almighty gods, what am I to do with you?" She gripped Catrin by the shirt and yanked her closer. "The only way you can be with that Roman is to be his whore. Is that what you want? Cater to his sexual needs? He deceived you. Once he is through with you, he will dump you as a trollop."

Enraged, Catrin shoved her mother back. "The raven has shown me a vision that Marcellus will save me from a firestorm at our village. He is not the traitor; Agrona and Marrock are!"

Rhiannon drew in a furious breath and roared, "Did you not hear a word I said?" She backhanded Catrin across the face so hard, the force propelled her against the cave's jagged wall.

With the air knocked out of her lungs, Catrin gaped in horror as her mother raised a fist. She shrunk back, crossing her arms to defend herself from her mother's fury.

"Gods no, Mother! Gods no, don't hit me!"

Rhiannon shook her clenched hand at Catrin's face. "You will not defy me. You hold your father's life, your family's lives, and our kingdom in your hands. You will not betray us—not now, not ever!"

Catrin defiantly staggered to her feet and met her mother's seething glare. "I do hold my family close to my heart; I am not a traitor!"

The queen gripped Catrin's arm and yanked her outside the cave's opening, where they continued hurling venomous words at each other. When Cynwrig walked out of the trees with a handful of firewood, they quieted. He asked, "What are you two shouting about?"

"I am having a discussion with my daughter," Rhiannon said sharply and gestured for him to go into the cave. "Start a fire for the night."

Cynwrig's eyes flitted to Rhiannon, then Catrin, and back to the queen again. He shook his head and disappeared into the cave, leaving the women alone to continue their heated argument.

The pain of being accused as a traitor ripped through Catrin's heart, and she choked back angry tears to tell her mother, "Why won't you believe me about Agrona? I suffered at her hands because of you. Why did you allow her to take me? She is the traitor—not me, not Marcellus."

Though Rhiannon did not say a word, Catrin withered under her mother's oppressive glare as gentle rain began falling. Chilled, she looked away, so her mother would not see the tears mixing with the raindrops on her face.

After a few moments, Catrin felt the light touch of her mother's arm on her shoulder.

"I do believe you. Let us go back inside and discuss this with quieter tongues."

Catrin followed her mother back into the cave, now illuminated with torches that Cynwrig had lit. Shivering, Catrin retrieved some woolen blankets from supplies in the back and gave one to her mother. They both cocooned inside their blankets as Cynwrig placed more tinder and logs on the fire. The flames shot higher as they huddled near the fire's heat to warm their hands.

Waiting for her mother to initiate the conversation, Catrin apprehensively gazed at the flickering orange flames. Her mother said in Latin, "I will now speak with you, but I don't want Cynwrig to know what we are saying."

Catrin turned to her mother. "I understand."

Rhiannon's face turned grim as she said with a somber voice, "Although I have no doubt that what you said about Agrona is true,

I still think Marcellus misled you. First love is often most cruel. This is especially true when you can't bind it with a marriage that both families accept. Believe me when I say love is a hot flame that will burn out, and this is true for Marcellus. The only true love is what you hold for your family. With everything that has happened, you must take on the mantle of a warrior and defend our family and kingdom from the scourge of our enemies."

The queen then hardened her eyes into cold steel. "Great rulers are forged in the hot fires of sacrifice, duty, and honor. I saw the hate the senator had for me. He will never allow you to stay with Marcellus, except as his slave whore. In Rome, Lucius Antonius is the paterfamilias. Do you know what that means?"

Catrin shook her head.

"A Roman father has complete control over his family—wife, children, and slaves. If they disobey him, he has the power of life and death over them. This is not true for you. A woman can own property and be a ruler, a warrior, a Druidess, a mother. You are judged by the people for your actions. Heed my warning. If the Romans ever capture you, they will brutally rape you before they kill you, or far worse—sell you into slavery to defile your body. That is what Romans do to people they conquer—men, women, boys, and girls. This is their way to demonstrate their domination."

Though her mother's words stung with truth for others, it did not hold true for Catrin. She insisted, "Marcellus is not like this. I am sure once he is released, he will help us find a way to make a truce with his father. It is Marrock who has turned the Romans against us."

The queen blew out an exasperated breath. "No doubt Marrock is a despicable man—cunning and ruthless as a wolf. Nonetheless, the Romans barter with any predator that serves their purpose. If Marrock ever captures me, I fear what he might do. He blames me for his banishment."

Catrin said, "Father banished Marrock, not you."

"Marrock blames me!" Rhiannon said bitterly. "I accused him of trying to rape and to kill you when we were in the presence of your father. Marrock pulled a knife on me, but Amren grabbed his wrist and turned the blade on him. The only reason Amren did not kill Marrock was because Agrona intervened and advised him to banish his son instead. A mistake I fear we will regret for the rest of our lives."

Surprised by the revelation, Catrin said, "Mother … why did you … not tell me?"

"Because you were dealing with your own nightmares from what he did to you. That has now changed. You must now prepare yourself to confront that monster and fight him to the death. If either Marrock or the Romans capture us, they will do unspeakable things. Life never presents us with clear choices. If the Romans resort to treachery at the prisoner exchange, you will have to fight for your life. If that means killing Marcellus, then you must do it. And if you are captured, you will receive greater mercy by turning the blade on yourself than what your captors will do. Do you understand?"

Believing in her heart that Marcellus would never betray her, Catrin said, "I understand. I will do what is necessary to save everyone I love."

45

PERILOUS ESCAPE

Without some kind of tool to snap the chains from his shackles, it would be impossible to escape. If I am to die, he resolved, I will go down fighting.

The rumble of pig grunts shook Marcellus out of his afternoon snooze, and the stench of dung rudely greeted his nostrils. Sitting in an open entrance stall, he stared at his shackled ankle. His muscles ached, and it took all his strength to stand. He could only take a couple steps before the chain constrained him. Through the wall's cracks, he saw the hogs wallowing in the muck. He grumbled to himself, "I am a Roman nobleman, yet I am treated worse than those pigs!"

His legs were caked with dirt, straw, and who knew what else. They itched incessantly from gnat bites that tormented him more than the occasional kicks from his guards. At that moment, he longed to luxuriate in a steam bath, to shave off his facial hair, and to crawl into a soft bed. His only raw emotion was hate for the barbarians making him rot next to the pigpen. The rattling of the chain reminded him that he could be butchered as easily as the swine bathing next to him. The gruesome image of one of his guards chopping off his head and throwing it to the pack of boars for them to fight over made him shudder. The sun now sinking in the western horizon was an intimation of what could possibly be his fate on this forsaken isle.

Marcellus clasped his hands and prayed, "Almighty Apollo, I beseech you. Give me the strength to endure my suffering and the insight to recognize my pathway to freedom. In return, I will offer you a bull and serve in the Roman Legion with the same distinction as my great-grandfather, Mark Antony. Your likeness will be emblazoned on my chest armor in remembrance of the mercy you shine on me today as I slaughter my enemies as an offering to you."

At that moment, Catrin's image floated into his mind. Her hair hung almost perfectly on her shoulders, the thin braids weaving through her golden tresses, except for the rebellious strand she kept pushing back out of her face. Her blue-green eyes sparkled. It had been more than one month since he had last seen her. For some reason, her image lifted his spirits and gave him hope.

But his optimism faded when he saw Belinus and another guard approaching, both of them with chains in hand. His contempt for these painted savages boiled to the surface. He knew his acerbic tongue could be met with a fist to his jaw, but unable to contain his words, he sneered, "Please take me to the queen. I wish to personally thank her for my new quarters."

Belinus snorted, "Enough of your pig shit!"

Marcellus blurted, "You are right. I do have enough. Let's bring some to the queen for her bath."

Belinus grimaced and barked to the other guard who Marcellus tagged as "the Lion" because his disheveled coppery hair and beard was like a mane around his face. The barbarian cranked Marcellus into a head lock. Infuriated, Marcellus gripped the warrior's arm and used it as a brace to kick Belinus in the groin. Marcellus's delight at hearing Belinus scream in agony was quickly replaced with his own agony as the other guard, grabbing him by the hair, ripped clumps out of his scalp. The Lion then hurled him headfirst into a wooden beam.

Stunned, Marcellus saw dots flash before his eyes as he lost consciousness.

Gasping, snorting, Marcellus thought he was drowning in a tumultuous sea when he awoke. With water all over his face, he was bewildered to find himself lying on his back and gazing at a domed roof. His skull felt as if a spear had been pierced through it. Groggy, he wondered if he had been cursed to the bowels of the Underworld. If so, who paid his passage across the River Styx?

To his consternation, the chained shackles around his ankles restrained his movement as he sat up. Looking around, he wondered why he had been moved to what looked like one of the thatched-roof round houses. It was barren of furniture and the central hearth was dead with cold ashes. His heart shuddered. This could be the final spot for his execution. Without some kind of tool to snap the chains from his shackles, it would be impossible to escape.

If I am to die, he resolved, *I will go down fighting.*

The sudden movement of a shadow overhead startled him. He blinked several times as the winged figure swooped over him and landed near the central hearth. Shocked to see the raven, he cursed, "Damn the gods in Hades! Not that thing!"

Anticipating the raven might peck at him, he flinched when it hopped over. To his pleasant surprise, the raven cocked its head and gurgled softly. When he noticed that the raven's eyes were the same blue-green color as Catrin's, he wondered if he was hallucinating. He recalled the tribune saying, when they first landed at Britannia, that the Druids could shape-shift into animals.

Is it possible that Catrin also has this power?

He extended his hand in a welcoming gesture to the raven. It waddled next to him and nuzzled against his side. Relaxing, he allowed the raven to perch on his crossed legs. As he stroked its iridescent plumage, soothing warmth radiated into his fingertips.

"Is that you, Catrin?" he asked. "Where have you kept yourself these past weeks?"

The raven bobbed its head and cawed.

Marcellus chuckled. "How stupid of me to think I could actually talk to a bird."

The raven pressed a claw against his belly. Looking down, he noticed a tiny scroll adhered to the bird's leg with a metal band. He pulled the message out.

It read: "Be ready."

Be ready for what?

His heart rattled as questions rumbled in his head.

Did Catrin write the message? If so, is she working with the Romans?
What if she did not write it? Am I being set up for a trap?
What in Hades am I up against?

The raven suddenly plopped against him and stiffened. Alarmed, he examined the bird's eyes which now appeared as black beads. He pulled on a wing, but it remained limp. Then he fixed his eyes at the entry door, readying himself—for what, he wasn't sure.

The entry door clicked open.

The listless raven suddenly sprung to life and darted to a ceiling beam.

Senses heightened, Marcellus crouched and focused intently on the door. He squinted, but couldn't make out the shadowy figure coming through the entryway—friend or enemy?

He only had a brief moment to imagine how relieved he would be to see Catrin when Belinus strode through the entryway with a plate of food. The raven then dove at Belinus with outstretched talons, its shrieks slamming off the walls.

Belinus flung the platter, scattering food all over. The raven's talons viciously jabbed at him as its black wings flapped around his face. He threw a punch at the raven, but it averted the blow and swooshed through the doorway. Screaming indiscernible words, Belinus also dashed through the entryway and disappeared into the darkness.

Marcellus, panicking, yanked hard on his chains to pull them out of the wooden post.

No luck.

When he heard shuffling feet and clanging noises outside, he again stared at the entrance.

No motion.

Drums beating in the background mixed with what sounded like a scuffle. He assumed the crazy savages were in a mock fight as part of the celebration.

He heard a loud thud. Then Catrin suddenly appeared in the entryway armed with a shield strapped to her shoulder. In her hand was a helical key.

The excitement of seeing her made Marcellus's heart race with excitement. He embraced her, but she pulled away and said, "I need to get you out of here!"

"Good idea," he said, smiling.

With a steady hand, Catrin inserted the key into the manacle, twisted it, and unlocked the spring mechanism. Marcellus helped her unwind the cuffs from his wrists. Legs cramping, he staggered to his feet as she steadied him.

"Can you run?" she asked.

He nodded.

She motioned for him to follow her.

Outside, near the doorway, Marcellus noticed Belinus lying motionless on the ground. Looking around, he thought it odd there were no other guards. He glanced at Catrin in bewilderment, and she pointed toward the town's center. Between the thatched structures were people dancing around a raging fire. A woman, whose head was covered with a wolf pelt, was interweaving between the revelers.

Marcellus assumed it was Agrona inciting the natives.

Unfamiliar with the village's set-up, he looked to Catrin for her lead.

He trailed her, both scurrying from one structure to the next. His senses on alert, he darted his eyes all around for any unexpected motion before bounding to the next structure. After passing several dome-roofed houses, they at last reached the outer spiked wall where some wooden planks had fallen, leaving a narrow opening.

Catrin shoved her shield through the gap, then squeezed herself through the opening. Marcellus did the same, forcing himself between the splintered wooden planks that ripped his trousers and scratched his legs.

On the other side of the walled fortress, he saw the silvery moon escape the cover of clouds and illuminate a raven swooping down an escarpment.

Catrin tapped him on the shoulder. "We need to follow that raven."

"You go first," he said, his voice rasped from rapid breaths.

He watched Catrin sprint down the hillside and leap over a rock as gracefully as a deer. He quickly surveyed the shadowy hillside, wondering how he could ever navigate the unfamiliar landscape at night.

Am I crazy?

No time to ponder.

He chased after Catrin and clumsily maneuvered the first concentric ditch surrounding the hill fort. He reassured himself. *Only two ditches to go!*

His stamina weakening, he urged his metal-heavy legs forward to keep up with the light-footed princess. With the drums and wails quieting from the village, his gasps grinded in his throat as he climbed over the second trench.

Just one to go!

His lungs burned as if they were on fire when he dashed to the final ditch. When he reached the embankment, his legs gave out and he flung over the top, rolling down several feet before his head slammed against a boulder. Momentarily stunned, he gazed at the stars streaking around the full moon.

Then he felt Catrin's arms wrap around him. "Move!" she ordered. "My people will soon know you have escaped."

46

UNLOCKING ANCESTRAL POWERS

Resisting the pull from her ancestors to join them in the Otherworld, she cried out to the raven, "Let me go back, so I can shift the future."

Catrin's legs ached from fatigue as she scrambled through thorny bushes toward the raven's shrieks. Lagging behind her was Marcellus whose breathing grated louder and louder with each step. With his head injury, she wasn't sure how much further he could move without collapsing. Ahead, through the trees, the river's surface lit up from the reflection of the full moon. Her people must surely know by now their human sacrifice had escaped. Her mother was still in the village convincing Agrona and her people that the Romans had helped Marcellus escape. She anticipated Cynwrig would join them at the cave by dawn. She stopped to wait for Marcellus to catch up and dropped her heavy shield on the ground.

He breathlessly staggered to her and gasped, "How much further?"

"A short distance from here is a cave. We can hide in there."

"Then what?"

Catrin felt her throat clutch. Now was not the right time to tell him about the prisoner exchange. It would take too long to explain, maybe later at the cave.

Marcellus touched her arm. "Why don't you answer? What will your people do if they discover you've helped me?"

"I don't know," Catrin said, wondering if any villager had yet found Belinus who Cynwrig clubbed and left unconscious.

Marcellus gripped her shoulders. "If you take me to my father, I can protect you from harm."

Catrin looked at him in bewilderment. "What harm?"

"Vengeance from your people for helping me to escape. I could take you back to Rome."

"Rome?"

"I could find a place where you could hide, and we could secretly meet."

For some unknown reason, the invitation tempted Catrin, but she hesitated remembering her mother's warning that she would be nothing more than his whore. "I would never leave my homeland."

"But you may not have a choice."

Catrin pulled away, drew a dagger from her belt, and handed it to him. "Take this. We need to move. Now!"

Marcellus inspected the blade and tucked it under his belt. "Will your people search for us tonight?"

Looking above, Catrin cringed at how fast the storm clouds were shrouding the moon. "They will most likely wait until dawn to begin their search. A storm is coming. We need to seek shelter."

"Which way?"

Catrin pointed toward the river.

Marcellus waved his arm. "Lead the way."

With the silvery moon disappearing behind thick clouds, she ran toward her squawking raven that was now guiding them through the shadowy maze. When they reached the dense woods, they descended a steep slope, Marcellus touching Catrin's shoulder as she stretched her hands for unseen obstacles. The chill of the impending storm hovered over them.

Moments later, a light drizzle compounded the danger of their moving downward in the dark. Feet slipping on mossy rocks, Catrin could barely discern the trees. When lightning webbed overhead, a shiver bolted down her spine. Conditions were becoming deadly.

A fierce gale roared through the forest. Rain slapped horizontally into her eyes, obscuring her vision. As she took her next step, her feet were caught in a mudslide. She grabbed for an exposed tree root to stop her fall, but her hands slid over the slick surface and she fell into a torrential mud flow.

"Help me! Help me!" she cried out, panic setting in.

Marcellus appeared above her. He extended one hand while anchored by a tree branch with his other.

"Take it!" he shouted.

Catrin clasped his wrist. He leaned back and jerked her hard. She felt as if her arm would pop out of her shoulder blade when he dragged her over the jagged rocks. He pulled her up to his chest. They then struggled to higher ground under the pelting rain until they found shelter under a gigantic oak.

Raindrops blasted against Catrin's face as she sat against the tree. Cold water streamed around her and seeped into her trousers. Shivering, she could not stop her teeth from rattling. Marcellus cradled her head against his chest. She could feel him tremble as he shielded her from the downpour. She snuggled closer for his warmth, but the chill from her drenched clothing numbed her. Tighter and tighter, they held each other against the warring factions—earth, sky, and water—an omen of what was to come with the various political factions against the king.

Above them, lightning flashed the image of a skull. Claps of thunder rumbled through the forest as tentacles of bolts streaked closer and closer through the treetops. One bolt struck a nearby tree, splitting its trunk in half. Electrical charges skipped over the ground, zigzagged around Catrin's fingertips and bolted up her arm. A burning charge weaved its way through her body and jolted into her head. She was then immediately transported to a deeper realm of the raven's mind where a powerful force yanked her into a tunnel of brilliant light. Ancestral souls stretched out their arms and pulled her toward the portal into the Otherworld. Plummeting, she braced herself to burst through the black vortex, but was startled when she somersaulted off its flexible wall. As she careened up the convoluted surface, she saw images of humans flash as they entered the Otherworld. She realized death was waiting to snatch her, but the thin barrier was somehow barricading her entrance to the Otherworld.

She floated up to the rainbow archway where Marcellus's life-thread lined up and fitted together like pieces of a puzzle. In one image, he was cradling her, rocking back and forth during the raging thunderstorm after the lightning struck. In another image, he was walking ahead of Cynwrig who was carrying her over his shoulder. The next moment, she held a sword against him as the Romans released her father and Trystan. The final images became surreal as the Roman soldiers transformed themselves into eagles and attacked a raven. As the raptors dragged the raven to a nest of ravenous eaglets, she saw Cynwrig shoot an arrow at Marcellus, the shaft piercing deep into his breastbone. Seeing his image dissolve into the black portal, she reached for his life-thread and pulled him back.

The surface of the multicolored wall rippled, extending the image of Marcellus for a short distance into the future where he was killed by a red wolf that Catrin recognized as Marrock. Marcellus's image again dissolved into the Otherworld's portal. For the second time, she pulled his life-thread from the portal, extending his life only a short time when he was struck dead by a cobra. This time she waited to see what would happen. His life-thread yanked back to its original position where he was originally slain by the death arrow.

Perplexed as to why the life-thread had returned to its original position, she asked the raven, "Why can't I change his fate?"

The raven said, "Only the gods and goddesses have been divined the ability to weave human lives, but you have inherited other god-like abilities from your father that differentiates you from other mortals."

"What are these?" Catrin asked.

"Your soul is a liquid essence that flows into other physical forms while you are yet alive. You are what Ancient Druids call a soul traveler. By merging with other physical forms, you leave bits of your soul in other living entities."

"Is that what happened when I made love to Marcellus?"

"Yes, you left part of your soul in him," the raven croaked. "That is why you are still connected to him spiritually. The bond is so strong that you can never love another."

She curiously asked, "What other mystical powers do I have?"

The raven said in a man's deep voice, "You can only unlock god-like abilities and universal truths at the time you most need them on your lifetime odyssey."

"Right now, I need to save Marcellus from certain death at the prisoner exchange," Catrin said, heart pounding harder. "I need to unlock the power to change his future."

"As I told you," the raven shrieked, "changing the future is a mystical power only for the gods and goddesses."

Catrin paused, giving consideration on how to present her argument to the raven. "I was able to manipulate Marcellus's life-thread on the Wall of Lives. I extended his life-thread into the future when he again faced death two times. Both times, I was able to save him, but then something strange happened. His life-thread returned to the original moment when he is killed at the prisoner exchange."

The raven cawed three times, then croaked, "Mortals cannot change the future from the past. Mortals can only change the future at the exact time it occurs in the present. If you do so, you distort and reshape the Wall of Lives' curvature. This could result in dire consequences on others in the future."

Still hovering near the portal leading into the Otherworld, Catrin was resolved to escape death's clutches and return to the mortal world, so she could save Marcellus from dying young and break

Rhan's curse. Now that she understood the secret of changing the future, she studied Marcellus's life-thread for a way to save his life. She saw they would never make love again before he died. She wondered if adding another sexual encounter, something she most desired, could lead to another pathway for Marcellus to complete his life's journey. Still, he had to defy the gods two more times to escape death.

Resisting the pull from her ancestors to join them in the Otherworld, she cried out to the raven, "Let me go back, so I can shift the future."

The raven tilted its head and ruffled its feathers. "Be careful what you wish for."

Catrin proclaimed, "I accept the fate of my decisions."

"Then let it be," the raven thundered.

A light flashed in Catrin's mind and she returned to her physical world. Disoriented, she could barely discern Marcellus holding her in his arms.

47

DARK INTRUDER

Suddenly a sword-wielding man was striding toward them. Fight instincts heightened, Marcellus quickly reached for his dagger.

Stunned, Marcellus found himself slumped over Catrin, his arms tightly wrapped around her. With rain still drumming against him, he was chilled from his wet clothes. The last thing he could remember was the raging storm. He wasn't sure if his dizziness, the buzzing in his ears, and the burning pain on his arms were the aftereffects of a lighting strike. Of more concern, Catrin appeared dead. She was cold and limp in his arms. He raised her wrist to feel a pulse, but could not detect a beat. Placing an ear over her mouth, he heard faint gurgles. He then placed two fingers on her neck and was relieved to find a weak pulse. As he nestled her in his arms, he tried to focus his eyes into the darkness, so he could find some other shelter from the tempestuous night.

From overhead, flashes of lightning illuminated the forest with pulsating light. A short distance away, a figure appeared through the trees. Marcellus shuddered when the shadow disappeared into the darkening woods. The loud thunder and the smashing of raindrops made it impossible for him to hear any approaching footsteps. Anticipating a potential attack from this phantom, he leaned Catrin against the tree trunk, so he could maneuver about more easily.

Suddenly, a sword-wielding man was striding toward them. Fight instincts heightened, Marcellus quickly reached for his dagger, but his hand slipped on the wet hilt. He did not get a second chance to grab his weapon when a sharp tip pressed into his neck. He froze. Anticipating the fatal blow, he felt his chest heave in panic. The sword's tension eased as the warrior pointed to Marcellus's dagger. As instructed, Marcellus slowly pulled out his weapon and handed it to the warrior.

The warrior mumbled something in Celtic, giving Marcellus tenuous reassurance he would not be immediately hurled into the bowels of the Underworld. He nervously watched his foe kneel beside Catrin and place a couple of fingers on her neck. With sword still in hand, the warrior deftly swung Catrin over his shoulder, stood up, and muttered a hissing curse.

Marcellus shook his head in confusion and shrugged.

The warrior gestured for Marcellus to stand.

Marcellus pointed to himself. "You want me to get up?"

The man gave a slight nod.

Marcellus gave the warrior a thin smile and staggered to his feet. Keeping a close watch on his adversary, he thought humorously, *Good news! I will be executed elsewhere.*

But seeing Catrin slung over the warrior's shoulder shot Marcellus back into the grim reality that they both could be executed at the village. A sick feeling roiled in his stomach.

The warrior motioned for Marcellus to stay at his side as they descended the precarious slope in the pounding rain. It was through sheer fortitude that Marcellus was able to force himself forward on cramping legs. A couple of times, he considered making a mad escape, but without any familiarity of the land, it would be futile and downright stupid to make such an attempt. Besides, he could not leave Catrin to the mercy of this man.

After a few more minutes, the rain stopped as they walked off the river trail and climbed up a hill to a spot where light flickered through some shrubbery. With Catrin still on his shoulder, the warrior pulled a loose bush away and motioned for Marcellus to do the same. Working alongside him, Marcellus helped clear the remaining bushes until the entrance of a dimly lit cave was revealed. He recalled this was the same cave where he and Catrin had dropped off Mor and Belinus before they had made love.

Following the warrior inside, Marcellus ducked under tree roots hanging from the olive-green ceiling. About halfway inside was a campfire that dimly lit the approximately twenty-foot cave. Glancing around, he could see that some of the cave had been dug out to store pelts, clothing, and bagged food. Most disconcerting was the stockpile of weapons near the entrance. An ominous shiver ran down his back that there may be others who would soon join them.

When the rain-drenched warrior set Catrin on a silver pelt near the fire, Marcellus recognized him as Cynwrig, the last Cantiaci fighter he would ever want to combat. With the assortment of weapons, he wondered why Cynwrig had made no attempt to bind him. Why was he brought here instead of the village? The only person who could enlighten him was Catrin, unconscious and shivering spasmodically. He anxiously stared at her until he was startled when rolled garments were thrown at him. He looked at Cynwrig, who pointed to a water bucket near the entrance.

Marcellus looked into the metal-rimmed container and was aghast by his reflection on the water's surface. A bristly beard shadowed his jaw. A purplish eyelid on his face was swollen almost shut. Fighting for composure, he pulled his soaked shirt off to splash cold water on his face and chest. Goose bumps erupted all over his skin and his teeth chattered so hard, he thought they might break. When he again glanced at Cynwrig, he was dismayed when the warrior removed Catrin's leather chest armor and undershirt, exposing her bluish-tinted breasts. He puffed out his chest and glared. Cynwrig gestured for him to turn around. Marcellus held his ground, eyeing the weapons against the wall.

Cynwrig, appearing to read his mind, set Catrin on the pelt and drew an axe from his belt with deadly silence. An icy chill spiked down Marcellus's spine. Having seen this fierce warrior's skill in axe-throwing, he hesitated and waited for the warrior's next moves.

Cynwrig pointed to Catrin with an exaggerated shivering motion. Then he mimicked taking off his mail-armor shirt and waving his hand over the fire.

Marcellus relaxed, now understanding the warrior's intent to treat Catrin. Yet he continued watching Cynwrig closely as he walked toward the back of the cave to take off his stinking shirt and breeches. He unrolled the garments Cynwrig had given him and was surprised to see his freshly cleaned Roman tunic and toga that he had believed discarded after his drunken first night at the village. The white fabric was no longer stained and had a light sweet fragrance. After he was dressed in the knee-high tunic, he watched Cynwrig cover Catrin with a woolen cape before discretely removing her trousers. After that, the warrior washed her face with a wet cloth warmed in a metal pot above the fire. Her violent shivering calmed after he covered her with a sheep pelt.

Vexing questions haunted Marcellus. Why would one of the queen's most trusted guards give him his Roman clothing back, unless there was some kind of plan to release him? If there was a plan to release him, wouldn't the queen have done so? Besides, Catrin wouldn't have helped him to escape. But now she was lost to his world when he most needed her. At least this time she did not appear to be suffering from the effects of the falling sickness. He turned to Cynwrig and barked, "Hey," to get his attention and pointed to the fire. "Can I sleep there? Get warm."

Cynwrig nodded and grunted.

Marcellus sat near Catrin to assess her condition. Breathing even, she appeared at peace, a rosy color returned to her face. He was tempted to stroke her hair, but with Cynwrig closely watching him, he decided it would not be prudent. Yet desire consumed him as he gazed at Catrin, lying naked under the pelt. Though he had been brutalized by her people, he still felt a strong bond with this foreign woman. A waft of lavender scent from his tunic reminded him of making love to her. Though she had been an ill-at-ease virgin, he had never expected her to respond so amorously to his touch. Her strength almost matched his as she lifted her hips to meet him. He ruefully sighed. How could he ever go back to Rome after Catrin had turned his Roman beliefs upside down regarding his father's plan to invade Britannia? His soul had joined hers, and without her, he would never be whole.

He drew in a long breath. Nothing made sense any more, his reasoning blurred with powerful emotions.

With profound fatigue overtaking him, Marcellus looked at Cynwrig and gestured that he wanted to sleep close to the fire. Cynwrig retrieved a pelt and put it on the ground for him to sleep on.

Marcellus collapsed on the soft pelt and sank into a deep sleep.

48

LURE OF THE SIREN

She was now that Siren luring him into her perilous waters.

The sound of splashing water awoke Marcellus from his erotic dream. His chest was dripping with hot sweat. Drowsy, he was at first disoriented as to where he was. He struggled to leave his sensual muse for the grim reality of where he was. With his precarious situation, he had to focus on an escape plan and not be distracted by his full erection. When he looked around the cave, his eyes landed on Catrin washing her naked body.

Gods above, am I dreaming?

Suddenly recalling Cynwrig, Marcellus darted his eyes all around. He could not believe the fierce warrior would leave them alone. He again gazed at Catrin and saw a nimbus of sunlight encircling her as a goddess. He shook his head with disbelief.

I must be dreaming.

He slapped his forehead. The pain was real. It must be happening.

When Catrin bent over to reveal all her womanly beauty, a lusty gasp caught in his throat and his thoughts oddly jumped to the tale of the Greek hero Odysseus and his encounter with the Sirens. Odysseus had been warned about the enchantresses whose spellbinding voices lured sailors to shipwreck off their rocky shore. Though his soldiers plugged their ears with wax, he had them tie him to a mast, so he could listen to the Sirens' songs. When the ship passed these alluring women, Odysseus tried to rip off his bonds and jump headlong into the dangerous sea. It was wise foresight on Odysseus's part that his men neither heard the songs nor their leader's pleas to unbind him.

With the tale still in mind, Marcellus thought he must be under Catrin's spell as he watched her wrap a cape over her shoulders and walk toward him. He closed his eyes, pretending to be asleep. When he felt a soft touch on his forehead, her warmth radiated into him, taking away all his physical and emotional pain from his ordeal. When he opened his eyes, he was drawn into Catrin's sea-blue eyes as she sat next to him.

"Your face is swollen," she said. "I am afraid to ask what happened."

"I think you know. The last month has been difficult." Marcellus refrained from saying more about the brutality he had endured. Fighting to keep his wits, he asked, "I'm confused. I thought you had helped me to escape. Last night, Cynwrig found us in the thunderstorm and brought us here to safety. Where is he now?"

Catrin smiled and rubbed a finger over his mouth. "I told him to go ahead and scout out the Romans. Soon they will arrive for the exchange."

Marcellus widened his eyes with surprise. "What exchange?"

Catrin clasped his hand. "You are to be traded for my father. Only a few of my people know. We suspect traitors from our village."

Disconcerted that Catrin had not told him this previously, Marcellus said, "I told your mother about possible traitors when she showed me the forged message that said your father had been imprisoned. Yet she refused to believe me."

"My mother is now well aware."

Marcellus shook his head in confusion. "If the exchange has already been set, why did you pretend to help me escape?"

"It was a setup to divert traitors from our true plans. My mother agreed to your father's demands that only I escort you to the exchange. Cynwrig is here to protect me in case anything goes wrong."

Marcellus knew his father had no compunction for avenging himself against any person who insulted him. Yet the queen had also bared her teeth when she believed the king's life was endangered. He leveled his eyes at Catrin. "Can I trust you?"

"Yes. Of course. I asked Cynwrig to leave us, so I could speak with you privately. My raven will warn us when he is returning. In the meanwhile, there is something I must tell you. I sense you are in danger—not only today, but also in your future."

"And how is that?" Marcellus asked, nervously lifting his brow.

"Last night, during the storm, I was pulled into the raven's mind for a revelation ..." Catrin gazed at the fire as if she was envisioning something.

Marcellus nudged her shoulder. "Go ahead and tell me what you saw."

Staring vacantly at the fire, she revealed, "The raven took me to a place that divides the mortal world and the Otherworld."

A prickle clawed at Marcellus's neck as he recalled Decimus saying that Catrin was a sorceress. Her eyes reflected the fire's crimson flames as she continued her story.

"My raven showed me your past, present, and future on the Wall of Lives where souls emerge and reincarnate into other living beings. I had three visions. In the first, an arrow pierced your heart during the prisoner exchange, mortally wounding you. As you slipped through the portal, I grasped your life-thread and pulled it back from the Otherworld. In the second vision, a red wolf that I believe is Marrock attacked you and ripped your heart out. Your life-thread again disappeared through the portal, but I pulled it back. The third time—"

Marcellus interrupted, "Gods beneath me! There cannot be another grim prophecy?"

Catrin removed her cape to reveal her naked body.

Marcellus gasped, "What are you doing?"

"Hear me out," Catrin said firmly. "In the third vision, a poisonous serpent strikes you in your neck when you are with your Roman lover." She placed Marcellus's hand on her breast, the softness plunging him into tempestuous desire. As she pulled his hand down over her abdomen into her sexual danger, he could hear his heart pounding.

She said in a sultry voice, "The only way I can save you is for us to join."

Breathing erratically, Marcellus rasped, "What do you mean?"

"You must enter me, so I can save you."

Flabbergasted, Marcellus blurted, "Gods above! Here? Now? What about Cynwrig?"

Before he could say another word, Catrin covered his mouth with hers. She was now that Siren luring him into her perilous waters. He was plunged into that raw state where lust overruled reason. He fervently pushed Catrin down by the fire and kissed her, his tongue searching for hers. The exigency to dive into her deepest depths heightened his senses. He was a doomed soul drowning in her turbulent waters and giving over his sanity to this goddess. Body flushed with hot sweat, he flamed into her as she wrapped her powerful legs around his hips, driving him still deeper. All his frustrations and rage plunged into her heat—their souls and bodies forging into steel.

In what must have been only a blink of an eye, he drove everything he had into her and cried out, "Heavens above! What have you done to me?" Still burning in her heat, he was loath to leave her fire as he heard her say in his mind:

Our souls are now wedded and will never part.

Silently, he made his love request.

Come back to Rome with me.

A light flashed in his mind as her thoughts disconnected from his. He rolled to his back and pillowed his head on bent elbows as he stared at her. Her face was a brilliant pink as she brushed some unruly tresses of hair away from her sea blue eyes. Yet several golden strands still teasingly covered her breasts. Not yet ready to end the moment, he pulled her next to him again.

"I feel as if I'm Apollo inside you." He snuffled her hair and inhaled the intoxicating earthy fragrance.

Catrin tilted her head back to look at him and smiled. "You are my Apollo."

Suddenly uneasy, Marcellus cocked an eyebrow. "Can I ask you a question?"

"Of course."

"Did you like it this time?" Marcellus struggled for words. "Last time … when we made love … I tried to be careful … not to hurt you, yet today, I was so swept away by you … I may have been too rough again."

Catrin's eyes sparkled with amusement. "I like when you let go of your restraints. The first time we made love, I could not share in your final pleasure because the raven robbed me of those joyous moments afterward."

He grimaced. "What do you mean 'robbed'?"

She averted her eyes from his. "I thought our act of love would destroy us."

Marcellus recalled that he had been perplexed by Catrin's aloofness, particularly after her vigorous response to his touch. She kept staring at the bloodstained pelt on which they had made love. He thought she was confused about losing her virginity. It was only after she told him about Marrock that he understood that was not the reason. He said, hoping he remembered it wrong, "What was the meaning of the reflection of the white raven on my eyes? You said you saw the same thing on Marrock's eyes."

"You set me on a silvery wolf pelt just like he did." Catrin paused. "When I saw the reflection of the white raven disappear from your eyes, I took this as an omen that our love was doomed."

"Did you envision that today?" Marcellus asked warily.

Catrin's eyes glinted from the crackling fire as she traced the curvature of his eyebrow with her finger. "Today, I only thought of you and the joy you brought me. The memory will last a lifetime after we part and go our separate ways."

The words "go our separate ways" seared in Marcellus's mind. Swallowing the pain that he would soon lose Catrin, he lifted her chin. "I wish we had more time to know each other better. If everything goes right today and I survive that omen of yours, I promise to find a way for us to be together."

Sadness washed over Catrin's face as her eyes filled with tears. "I could never willingly leave my home. The only promise I can now keep is that I will always be with you in spirit." She suddenly pulled away from him and wrapped herself inside her cape. She stood and reached for some stacked garments nearby. Marcellus was surprised when she lifted the leather-stringed Apollo amulet that he had given her, placed it around her neck, and bowed her head in prayer. "Apollo, let my soul walk with Marcellus Antonius on his life's journey."

Marcellus said, "I thought your mother had taken that amulet away from you. She accused me of cursing you with it."

Catrin smiled. "The raven stole it from her and returned it to me. I put it back on, so it would protect me."

In the bittersweet moment, Marcellus watched Catrin wash off the vestiges of their lovemaking. Had he been a fool for succumbing to her sexual danger? Was this Apollo's cruel trick to send this Siren to seduce him and to capture his heart like no other woman? Could his first instinct that she would lead him to his destruction be true?

As Catrin donned her crimson and red-plaid trousers and chain mail shirt, transforming her into a warrior, Marcellus felt emptiness stab into his soul. He rose and clutched his hand to his chest. "Why must it come to this? Just when we find each other, the Fates pull us apart. I don't know what kind of mystical powers you have over me, but I again ask, will you return with me to Rome? I fear what might happen to you." Guilt-ridden, he dropped his eyes, recognizing that he never told Catrin of his father's sinister plan to invade Britannia.

"Do not make this any harder," she said with a somber tone. "What I did … I did for you. And if anything goes wrong …" A sob caught in her throat. "I must fight to save my father."

From her pained grimace, Marcellus knew she would kill Roman soldiers to protect her father. *Would she kill me if ordered to do so?* Staring at her, he asked, "Could you do that? Hurt me after making love to me?"

She shook her head, tears streaming down her face. "No, but I need your help to make sure my father is released and I am not taken prisoner. Otherwise, I foresee that Cynwrig will release an arrow that kills you."

The tribune's warning that Catrin was a sorceress again rattled in Marcellus's mind. How could he completely trust this mystical woman who had just strangely lured him into another dangerous encounter at the risk of Cynwrig returning any moment?

Masking his growing mistrust, he stepped over to Catrin and pulled her into his embrace. As he stroked her hair, his thoughts switched to his father, a man with the pride of Jupiter, who would readily betray any agreement for revenge. He kissed Catrin for what possibly could be the last time and said softly, "This moment will be forever etched in my memory."

49

PREPARATIONS FOR THE EXCHANGE

"For us to defy the gods today, I must know exactly what you saw in your vision before I am to be killed. If we do everything exactly the same, it might be easier to change that one moment in time."

Catrin left Marcellus in the cave and scanned the area for Cynwrig at the entrance. Cynwrig had departed at the break of dawn to place weapons at the Ancient Oak, close to the designated site for the exchange. Before she caught sight of Cynwrig, the raven's screech warned of his approach.

He strode out of the woods, his wet hair hanging like coiled wool over his shoulders. In his hand was a freshly killed rabbit.

She asked him, "Did you see the Roman camp?"

Joining her at the cave's entrance, he replied, "Yes, as you foresaw in your vision, there are more Romans than what the queen had agreed to … at least, fifteen soldiers, maybe more. Your father's and Trystan's ankles were bound." He looked around. "Where is the Roman prisoner?"

"Inside the cave, by the fire." Watching Cynwrig closely, she flinched when he pulled a knife from his baldric. "What are you planning to do with that?"

He sliced a hole through the rabbit's shoulder and muttered, "Prepare this, so we can eat."

When he cut and ripped the fur away from the rabbit's body, she shuddered, recalling rumored tortures that Romans inflicted on their prisoners. "How did Father look? Bruised or battered?"

"From a distance, he looked mean and hungry to escape," Cynwrig said, snapping the ankle joint of the rabbit's foot. "Have you talked to that Roman about our plans?"

She winced at the sound of his cracking the rabbit's bones. "He knows what is expected of him."

Cynwrig pulled the fur down the rabbit's legs like he was removing socks. Slicing the underbelly with his knife, he grunted, "Do not let your heart for that foreigner get in the way. If your vision holds true, I will unleash the fury of the gods on any Roman who betrays us and tries to capture you and retake your father." He scooped out the slithering guts with his hand and set them on a rock. "Does the Roman know that I will kill him if he even thinks of betraying us?"

Familiar with Cynwrig's ferocity, Catrin could feel her heart pound more rapidly. "He's assumed that by your presence. He will also feel the sharpness of my sword against his throat until my father is released."

After Cynwrig crammed a sharpened stick through the pink-fleshed hare, Catrin followed him inside the cave to the fire. He set the spitted meat on a tripod over the fire. She glanced at Marcellus, who tensely nodded his acknowledgement.

Cynwrig unbuckled his baldric and placed it on the ground. Frowning at his chain mail shirt, he grumbled, "This armor hinders me from moving quick as a fox." He gripped the bottom of his metal shirt and uttered, "Help me take this thing off."

She yanked the shirt over his head and his sweaty chest blasted a pungent odor into the cave. The blue tattoos on his chest and arms reminded her of the lightning bolts that the thunder god Taranis had hurled at them the previous night. Scrunching her nose, she turned to Marcellus to see him gagging, too.

After clearing his throat, Marcellus asked, "What did Cynwrig say?"

"The Romans are camped close by. There are about fifteen soldiers." The outer corners of Catrin's eyes creased as she said bitterly, "Your father broke his word. Only five guards were to escort my father."

Marcellus grimaced. "I'll do what I can to make sure everything goes smoothly. Are we to wait here until then?"

"Yes, that will give us a chance to discuss our plan and eat. Be forewarned: Cynwrig will not hesitate to kill you if he suspects you or any other Roman of treachery. Unless you do exactly what I say, I may not be able to save you today."

Cynwrig snarled in Celtic. "What are you saying to that Roman?"

"I told him his people are already here." Catrin gestured toward the back of the cave. "Check through the weapons while I speak further with him."

Cynwrig grunted and did as she commanded.

Turning to Marcellus, she again described the prisoner exchange that was projected on the Wall of Lives. She concluded by saying, "You must convince your people to leave peaceably. If they do not, Cynwrig has been ordered to kill you. I am telling you this, so we can thwart the gods' fate that you will die today."

Marcellus regarded her for a few moments, then said, "I don't understand your mystical powers. If the gods have fated me to die today, how can we counter them?"

"As I told you, we shifted the future when we made love; this was not shown on the wall. It is hard to explain how everything works. Just know that if I alter a moment in your life, then I can change your fate of when you die. I am not sure how this change will affect my future or others, but I cannot bear to see you killed today."

Marcellus creased his brow. "What if ... you cannot defy the gods and change my fate?"

"I can do this," Catrin proclaimed, "but this must happen the instant Cynwrig releases an arrow at you. What I fear most is my concentration will be disrupted if the Romans attack me."

"How will I know when this is about to occur?"

"Listen for my voice. It may come to you in your mind. I may shout it out. You must instantly hurl yourself on the ground to avoid the death arrow."

Marcellus rubbed his jaw as if he was mulling over everything she had said. "If I am slain, what will happen to you?"

"My father and I escape. After that, I fear your father might use your death as an excuse to destroy my family and to elevate Marrock to the throne."

With a dagger in hand, Cynwrig walked out of the cave's shadows. "You have talked a very long time to that prisoner. What are you saying to each other?"

"He knows of your reputation for being a brutal warrior," Catrin replied. "He says he will try to convince his people to let my father go without incident."

"You have put a lot of trust in that foreigner." Cynwrig spat on the dagger blade. "Remember, he will do anything to save himself, and that means killing you."

"I am well aware," she said, knowing in her heart Marcellus would never turn against her.

Cynwrig picked up his baldric and glanced at her. "Please help me adjust this."

Catrin buckled and tightened the leather straps around his bare chest. He told her in a hushed tone as he put the dagger in the belted scabbard, "Make sure you keep an eye on the Roman. Do not let him overpower you while I'm gone to make final preparations."

"I can handle him," Catrin said firmly. "Besides, if he had wanted to escape, he would have already done so. He is smart. His only chance for survival is for the exchange to take place."

Cynwrig shook his head as he placed a couple of swords in his baldric and grabbed two spears. Striding away, he glanced over his shoulder. "I'll make sure there are no other Romans hiding in the forest. Get yourself armed, so we can move quickly after we eat." Without another word, he swaggered out of the cave.

Catrin knelt by the fire to inspect the roasting hare. The meat was browning nicely. The aroma of dripping juices sizzling in the fire made her mouth water. When she looked at Marcellus, he appeared troubled, his eyes languishing on her.

"What is wrong?" she asked.

Marcellus sighed loudly. "Just thinking. I know we've already discussed this, but I don't believe I was meant to go back to Rome without you. Perhaps, the gods fated me …" He looked down, shaking his head.

"Say it," Catrin urged.

He looked at her with doleful eyes. "If we cannot be together, perhaps it is because of the gods' mercy that I am fated to die young. Somehow, I've always known this. Now that you are part of me, I can sense your thoughts and feel you"—he pointed to his heart—"here."

She reached for his hand. "For you to live, we must both accept that we may never see each other again, but you still must escape two deathtraps set by the gods. I can help you today, but after that, you must listen to your own instincts. My gift to you is for you to rewrite your own legacy."

Marcellus embraced Catrin with a kiss. "Thank you, sweet love, for giving me courage. For us to defy the gods today, I must know exactly what you saw in your vision before I am to be killed. If we do everything exactly the same, it might be easier to change that one moment in time."

Catrin pressed her hand against Marcellus's throat. "I put a blade against your neck and cut the skin to make it bleed. Only after I threaten to slash your throat does the scar-faced commander let my father and Trystan go."

"Was the commander the tribune at our first meeting?"

Catrin nodded.

"That is Decimus. I assume they still have your sister Vala."

"Yes, your father did not agree to let her go until you were released. We are holding some Roman soldiers captive in the village. My mother plans to barter them for my sister's release."

"Decimus is loyal to his soldiers," Marcellus said. "Knowing this, I can reason with him not to do anything rash that could cost my life. What else did you see?"

"After I release you, two Romans chase after me while others run after my father and Trystan. That is when Cynwrig shoots an arrow at you."

"You can only change one predetermined moment at a time?"

"Or add another moment that was not on the Wall of Lives."

Marcellus gripped Catrin by the shoulders. "Do everything exactly as you saw in your vision. I will try to reason with Decimus that we need to leave peaceably."

Catrin gave a self-assured smile. "I can do that."

He did not return the smile.

50

GROWING DOUBTS

Binding my hands makes me feel like a sheep being taken to slaughter."

After the morning meal, Marcellus warily watched Cynwrig help Catrin strap a sword at her side. He handed her a dagger and knife, which she placed underneath her belt. With his fingertips, he painted blue arched wings on her forehead—a ritual Marcellus assumed was performed to embolden her. In the span of a few minutes, she was transformed from a young woman into a fierce warrior. As they conversed in Celtic, Cynwrig's feral eyes remained fixed on Marcellus, leaving no doubt the fierce warrior would take great pleasure in slaying him.

Twice that morning, Cynwrig had left the cave with an armload of swords, spears, and arrows. Uneasy that Catrin had not been forthright about other warriors hiding nearby, Marcellus approached them and asked, "What are you and Cynwrig talking about?"

Catrin turned to Marcellus. "Cynwrig is placing more weapons near the exchange site for my father and Trystan to use should the Romans attack."

Marcellus wondered, *Why would they need so many weapons for so few men?* He stared at Catrin. "It looks like Cynwrig is preparing an army for battle. Is there something I should be aware of?"

"I have already told you everything," Catrin said sharply. "We must be prepared for any ambush. The Romans cannot be trusted."

A twinge of panic sliced into Marcellus when Catrin mumbled some orders to Cynwrig in Celtic. The warrior grunted and walked to the back of the cave. She motioned for Marcellus to join her outside.

When Marcellus walked out of the cave to join her, he found the forest eerily still as wisps of fog hovered over the treetops like ghosts. He had hoped to see a favorable omen after last night's storm. He glanced over his shoulder, but didn't see Cynwrig come out of the cave. He turned to Catrin, "Isn't Cynwrig going with us?"

"He is taking a different route, so he is not seen by the Romans."

Everything that she was saying was raising the hairs on the back of his neck like hackles. "Why are you making such moves?"

"Precautions to counter any Roman ambush," Catrin replied sharply. "Now turn around, so I can bind your wrists and blindfold you. Do not say a word until I tell you."

Marcellus nervously shifted. *Why does she keep belaboring the possibility of a Roman ambush?* He dubiously raised an eyebrow. "Don't you trust me?"

"Of course, I do, but Cynwrig doesn't trust anyone."

"Binding my hands makes me feel like a sheep being taken to slaughter. Didn't you tell Cynwrig that I would help ease the tension at the exchange?"

Catrin snapped her eyes at him. "I did. Still, he ordered me to blindfold and restrain you. Don't argue with me. He is watching. Put your hands behind your back."

Uneasy with her explanation, Marcellus hesitantly put his arms behind him, so she could tie his wrists together with leather straps. After she placed the cloth over his eyes, she grabbed his arm and led him up a steep slope. Sure-footed as a goat, she told him when to step around a rock or over a fallen branch. He cautiously walked on the muddy ground, occasionally slipping on slick spots. A raven's croaks loomed over the chatter of other birds in the forest. The odor of decaying leaves and mold added to his dread.

After several minutes, she called a halt and told him they needed to wait a little while. She untied his straps and removed the black cloth from his eyes. Rubbing his wrists, he adjusted his eyes to the light filtering through the thick woods beside the river's edge. "After everything we have gone through," he said bitterly, "I thought you had more trust in me."

"I do," she snapped, "but I could not show this in front of Cynwrig. He is already leery that I may not fulfill my part in this."

Marcellus held out a hand. "At least, give me a dagger to defend myself in case anything goes wrong."

She yanked a knife from her belt and slapped it in his hand. "Now do you trust me?"

Still skeptical, he quietly flipped the knife in his hand.

"Much good that will do you," she said with a sarcastic bite to her voice. "I've been ordered to keep your wrists tied during the exchange."

Marcellus said, voice grating, "I need to draw a weapon to defend myself if anything goes wrong. If it would make you feel better, I will hold my hands up at the exchange."

Catrin blew out an exasperated sigh. "I will not tie your hands."

"Where to?" Marcellus asked, hiding the knife under his belt.

"We will wade a short distance down the river. Cynwrig spotted some Roman scouts along the pathway. He does not want any surprises."

Marcellus tensed. *Surprises from whom?* Trying to maintain a stone face, he decided to keep a close eye on his surroundings for any hidden warriors. He gave her a disingenuous smile. "Makes sense, lead the way."

Catrin stepped into the shallow water while he followed. She was as quiet as swimming minnows while he splashed in the water. After a few hundred feet, she hoisted herself onto the riverbank. Feeling grimy, Marcellus stayed in the river to splash water on his face. He frowned at the reflection of his swollen eye now rippling on the surface. He recalled Decimus telling him that nothing is ever what it seems. With the tribune's words loudly echoing in his head, he was beginning to wonder whether Catrin was truly how she appeared to him—his lover and friend. Taking such an arduous route added to his uneasiness.

He joined Catrin on shore and said, "I thought you said the exchange site was a short distance from the cave. We have walked at least a mile."

"As I told you, Cynwrig fears you could lead the Romans back to the cave." She stared at Marcellus and her shoulders tensed. "You have declared your love for me, but have not yet told me the real reason Rome is here."

Though he was aware that Catrin had been charged by the king to exploit him for information, he felt anxious that her love for him had been a facade. Yet he was reticent to express his doubts and did not answer her.

Catrin said, "If you ever meet Marrock, you would clearly see how evil he is. Why would Rome put him on the throne to replace my father?"

The pit of Marcellus's stomach clenched, making him queasy. "You are asking me to betray my own people."

Catrin jerked her head back and glared. "I have already been accused of this because of my steadfast loyalty to you."

"If you are an oracle as you profess," he retorted, "you should already know this."

She regarded him for a moment. "My visions are flashes of the future, but I don't always know how to interpret them. My images of your future have been the clearest. I sense your father is an embittered man harboring deep grudges and can be cruel if it serves his ambitions."

"You are describing characteristics of all powerful rulers," Marcellus said sardonically. "This is also true for your parents. Your mother had no compunction about sacrificing me if that would save your father's life."

Marcellus regarded Catrin for any inflection in her face that she was deceiving him. Unsettled that he might have been blinded to what she really was, he said with forlorn hope, "I want to believe your heart is pure and you are loyal to those you love. And that you are but a white raven in the midst of black ravens feeding on the carrion of their enemies. Before I answer your question, you must first answer mine. Did you lie with me, so you could obtain this information?"

A teardrop formed in Catrin's downcast eyes. "I did this to show you my love and to change your fate to die young."

"Did you bewitch me when we made love?" he asked, not sure if he wanted to hear the truth.

"What I did was out of true love," she said, her glistening eyes meeting his. "I cannot control how you feel about me. Only your true heart can do that."

Marcellus took a deep breath. "Right, I will answer your question. I am not sure how this will help your family avoid the dangers looming ahead. The emperor sent my father to determine which rulers would aid Rome if they invaded Britannia. My father believes Marrock will not resist an invasion if Rome agrees to support his claims to your father's throne. All I know is my father had planned to negotiate a separate agreement with Marrock. Beyond that, I don't know if this ever took place. Knowing your father, he would never agree to aid my father's plan to invade Britannia. Further, the emperor suspects Amren allied with a Germanian prince in a rebellion that annihilated three Roman legions. This happened about fifteen years ago, but the emperor has a long memory. Your father is considered anti-Roman, and that does not bode well for him."

Catrin looked at Marcellus with pleading eyes. "Could you persuade your father to help my father and not Marrock?"

Marcellus hesitated. "Even if I argued on your behalf, I may not be able to change his mind. He takes little credence in what I say. Ultimately, only the emperor can make the final decision on whether to invade or not. I don't want to see you harmed. That is why I asked you to go back to Rome with me. I will find a way to hide you, to protect you."

Emptiness throbbed in his heart as he stared at her. *If you truly love me, you will come with me.*

Catrin looked away and gazed blankly across the river toward the east. "My mother warned me that your father would never allow you to take me back, except as your whore. From what you have told me, I know it is impossible for us to be together. It is better that I die by the sword defending my homeland than to lose my honor by agreeing to go with you to Rome."

Marcellus felt as if his heart had been ripped out. He turned his head the other way with the agonizing realization that he had just betrayed his own people for the love of this foreign woman. He vowed not to go down the same path as his forefathers.

51

BETRAYAL

The wrenched pain on his face tore at her heart when he growled with hate, "You betrayed me."

As Catrin silently sat next to Marcellus, she gazed at the billowy clouds which were similar to those in last night's storm. Even though the last moments with Marcellus were heart-wrenching, she could not bring herself to say good-bye knowing she would never see him again. Cold wind sweeping across the waterway made her tremble. Perhaps it was her anxious energy as she reviewed every image on the Wall of Lives in her mind.

After a few moments, she heard three scratchy partridge calls, Cynwrig's signal the Romans were approaching the exchange site. To emotionally distance herself, she avoided looking at Marcellus when she told him it was time to go.

They walked together up the hill in dead silence and continued on the footpath beside the river way. After a few hundred feet, she heard approaching footsteps, but the thick hedges obscured her view. She halted and told Marcellus, "Get in front of me." She drew her dagger and pressed the tip against his back.

A few minutes later, three Roman soldiers appeared on the pathway. When Catrin did not see her father and Trystan with them, her stomach clenched. The Wall of Lives had shown that her father and Trystan would be escorted by the tribune and four other Roman soldiers when they first met. In front of her was a brawny commander wearing a helmet that had what looked like a red rooster's crown on top of it. He displayed a warrior's demeanor with uplifted broad shoulders as he strode toward them. The bright sun escaping the cover of clouds was also unexpected as the sky had been gray on the Wall of Lives. Cynwrig's latest report that there were at least fifteen soldiers in the entourage concerned her.

She whispered to Marcellus, "Something is wrong. It was the tribune I saw in my vision."

"That officer is a centurion by the name of Priscus Dius," Marcellus said. "He is a former gladiator who Decimus recruited to carry out his most dangerous assignments. This is not a good sign."

Senses heightened, Catrin raised the dagger blade against Marcellus's throat when the centurion came within a few dozen feet of her. "Halt! Identify yourself."

The centurion, ignoring Catrin's command, took a few more steps.

She sliced Marcellus's neck with the blade and shouted, "Halt or he dies!"

Marcellus gasped, "Gods above!"

The centurion stopped and motioned for his men to do the same. When blood began dribbling down Marcellus's neck, Catrin pulled the blade away.

"What are you doing?" Marcellus rasped. "I would like to leave with my head."

Catrin's heart stung for the pain she had inflicted on him. She swept the remorse from her mind as she again demanded, "Identify yourself."

"I am Centurion Priscus Dius dispatched to deliver two prisoners. Who are you?"

"I am Catrin, daughter of King Amren. Where are my father and his commander?"

"They are not far from here," Priscus said, hardening his stare. "My orders are to escort Marcellus to our camp before I release them."

Catrin remained adamant. "I will not release my prisoner until you release my father and his commander."

The centurion kept eyeing the hedges beside him. Fear was rising in her chest that she had inadvertently altered the future as a result of making love to Marcellus. She continued threateningly, "If you do not return your prisoners to me first, I will cut off his head."

Marcellus blubbered, "Do what she says! I'm bleeding!"

Priscus hesitated and again glanced at the hedges. A swarm of ravens began circling over the treetops to his right. When Marcellus tilted his head toward the thick woods, Catrin also turned to check, but could not see anything. She then turned her eyes on the bushes.

About ten Roman soldiers brandishing their weapons rushed into the open. Among them was Tribune Decimus, barking orders, "Surround Marcellus and the girl!"

Dismayed that she had not foreseen this, Catrin gripped Marcellus by the arm, pulled him closer, and pressed the blade against his neck.

"Stand back! Or I slash his throat."

"Do what she says!" Marcellus cried out.

Catrin again demanded, "I want to see the king now."

The tribune held up his hand to halt the men. "Did you bring any other warriors with you?"

"As you can see, I am alone," she said. "I have met my end of the bargain. Now meet yours."

Decimus glanced at Marcellus. "Are you hurt?"

"No, but I will be if you don't stop this hostility."

The tribune waved one of his soldiers closer and they huddled together. A rivulet of sweat streamed down Catrin's face as she nervously waited for the tribune's next move.

Decimus finally ordered Priscus to bring forth the prisoners. Priscus saluted and left with two men down the path.

Catrin breathed a little easier. Her arm twitched with fatigue as she held the dagger against Marcellus. Noticing he was struggling to swallow, she pulled the blade back a tiny bit from his skin.

A few minutes later, both her father and Trystan appeared, unshackled, walking alongside five Romans down the path. She again pressed the blade against Marcellus's throat. "Stop there! Only my father and his commander move forward."

The soldiers looked to Decimus.

"Do as she says," he grunted. "Release the prisoners."

Leaving their guards, the king and Trystan strode swiftly toward Catrin, frequently glancing back. When they reached her, the king demanded in Celtic, "I want you out of here now!"

Catrin shook her head. "Cynwrig has weapons ready for you at the Ancient Oak. I will stay until I hear your signal that you are safe."

Trystan interjected, "It makes more sense that I stay with Marcellus. We cannot risk the Romans taking either of you prisoner."

"I am staying," Catrin said firmly. "If we're attacked, our best line of defense is for you to be fully armed. Cynwrig is now ready with bow and arrow."

The king reluctantly nodded. "As soon as you hear our signal, release the Roman and run for your life."

The king and Trystan dashed to the woods as she kept a steady blade against Marcellus's throat.

"Could you take the pressure off," Marcellus rasped. "You are hurting me."

Noting the pained grimace on his face, she allowed the blade to drop to his collarbone.

After a few moments, a warbler's whistle shrilled through the forest, Trystan's distinct order to attack. Panic clawed at Catrin that he had foolishly signaled for an ambush with only three men and herself. They would surely all be slaughtered.

Catrin then noticed Marcellus gawking at the woods near the Roman soldiers. When she turned her head in the direction of his eyes, she was shocked to see several Cantiaci warriors charge through the trees like a tidal wave.

The sudden grip of Marcellus's strong hand around her wrist further shocked her. She momentarily froze as he quickly pivoted to face her and grabbed her other arm. She eyed the dagger still in her hand that he was forcing to her neck. Terrified, she pushed against his arm with all her might as the shimmering blade inched closer and closer to her.

When the cold steel finally pressed against her throat, she gasped and stared into her executioner's cold blue eyes that glinted in the sun. The wrenched pain on his face tore at her heart when he growled with hate, "You betrayed me."

With the weight of the Apollo amulet pressing against her breast, she rasped, "You are my Apollo. You promised to protect me."

He hesitated, uncertainty written all over his face.

The blade shook against Catrin's throat and began to cut into her skin.

A pained anguish sheared through Catrin that her true love was resolved to slay her. She stared into his eyes and could feel her pounding heart reaching for Marcellus.

His eyes turned misty and she felt the blade release. He pushed her back and his voice cracked with emotion. "Go! Save yourself!"

Momentarily stunned, Catrin watched him bolt away with the sword that he had taken from her belt. He sprinted into the melee of Roman soldiers and war-painted warriors clashing head-on with the clang of swords and shields.

In the distance, she observed more Roman soldiers marching quickly to join the battle. With betrayal on both sides, there must have been all together fifty soldiers and warriors in brutal combat.

Catrin paled when Centurion Priscus ran out of the chaos straight at her. Realizing she was unarmed, she wheeled on her heels and pumped her arms hard up and down as she dashed to the cover of dense woods.

Just as she reached the trees, Priscus caught and tackled her to the ground. He picked her up and shook her like an empty sack. Then he slammed her to the ground, knocking the breath out of her, and kicked her in the stomach.

She curled into a ball and writhed, unable to draw air into her lungs. Nausea waved over her until a breath grated through her throat and she gasped.

The next instant, the centurion came within inches of her eyes. All she could see was the scar that stretched from his mouth to his ear like a macabre smile. With the strength of a bull, he again picked her up and hurled her on the ground like a slab of meat, knocking her unconscious.

52

DEATH ARROW

A blurry line suddenly blocked his vision and what felt like hot metal shot into his chest and sharp pain burned deep into his ribs.

In the midst of the battle, Marcellus thrust his sword into the belly of a blurred warrior catapulting at him. His hand jerked back when the blade pierced the abdomen and they both slammed on the ground.

Lying flat on his back, Marcellus saw dots flash before his eyes. With the warrior's weight on him, he could hardly breathe. He pushed the broad-shouldered man off and rolled to his side for a closer look at his foe.

King Amren!

Panic spliced through him. With other Cantiaci warriors closing on him to protect their king, Marcellus sprung to his feet. Before he could escape, a vice-grip hand clenched his arm and stopped him. He turned to strike his opponent with his sword, but pulled back when he recognized Decimus.

The tribune barked orders to the soldiers, "Line to formation. Get Marcellus out of here now!"

Two soldiers with shoulders the size of bulls grabbed Marcellus and shoved him through a blur of clashing soldiers and warriors. One guard, upon reaching the edge of the fray, released Marcellus to fight off a blue-faced warrior armed with a spear.

A strange force compelled Marcellus to look at the pathway in the distance. There, Priscus had Catrin pinned on the ground.

Whatever betrayal Marcellus had felt switched to raw emotions that gripped his heart. In that split second, he had only one thought in mind.

I must protect my true love!

He yanked his arm away from the soldier guarding him and charged like a raging boar toward Priscus. Everything seemed in slow motion when he saw Priscus's hands clenched around Catrin's throat. A flash of anger rushed into his blood, yet he could not move his legs fast enough as he watched Catrin buck Priscus and knee his groin. The centurion jackknifed to the ground, his hands clasped over his crotch.

Marcellus had to make sure Priscus did not get up again. Reaching the centurion, he roared, "Get off her," and nailed a hammer fist into Priscus's temple, followed by a crunching fist to his jaw.

The assault hardly seemed to faze the maddened centurion. Rallying swiftly, Priscus jumped up and blocked Marcellus's next blow with his forearm. Priscus rammed his head into Marcellus, and they both crashed on the pebbly path. Before Marcellus could throw another punch, the centurion wrapped his arms around to restrain him.

Priscus yelled, "What in god's name are you doing?" With the aid of another soldier, the centurion yanked Marcellus up and planted him on his feet. Fighting against the men's restraints, Marcellus again felt Catrin's essence, and he frantically darted his eyes around for her.

When he caught sight of Catrin, she was staring at him with fear-struck eyes, as if trying to warn him.

His heart shuddered.

A blurry line suddenly blocked his vision and what felt like hot metal shot into his chest and sharp pain burned deep into his ribs. The force knocked Marcellus against Priscus, who then staggered backward and loosened his grip.

Legs crumbling, Marcellus fell on the ground beside the centurion. He cried out as the pain radiated over his chest like thorns jabbing him. Rolling to his side, he struggled to pull the death arrow out, but something was in the way. He groped at a feathery creature pressed against his chest.

What in Hades?

Perplexed at what he felt, he lifted his hands to his face.

Blood! So much blood! Oh, gods, I am mortally wounded!

Fighting to retain his wits, he again reached for the embedded arrow to pull it out. His head throbbed from the sounds of clacking metal, gruff men's voices, and whizzing arrows all around him. Becoming frantic about what had happened to Catrin, he pushed himself up to a sitting position, the arrow still lodged in his chest. To his horror, a soldier mounted her limp body. He roared, "Get off her," but the pain clawed at his ribs again.

Nausea from the excruciating pain clamped his stomach and he collapsed on his back. Above him was Decimus looking down. A spasm of agony ripped through Marcellus's chest as the tribune yanked the arrow free. His thoughts still on Catrin, Marcellus forced words through gritted teeth. "Call your men off Catrin!"

"Have you lost your mind?" Decimus growled, pushing cloth deep into his wound to staunch the bleeding. "That sorceress led us into an ambush."

Breathing becoming ragged from the searing pain in his lungs, Marcellus looked up when the blood scene suddenly darkened with fast moving shadows.

Like demented demons, ravens dived and attacked the Romans. Several of the creatures swarmed the soldier on top of Catrin, punishing him with their beaks and claws. The soldier tried to roll into a ball as the birds shredded his face with their razor talons. His blood-curdling screams chilled the air as the ravens pureed his tongue and gouged out his eyeballs.

When several birds darted at Decimus, he jumped up and scurried away from the avenging ravens, screeching, "Gods above, have mercy … have mercy!"

Spared from the aerial assault, Marcellus again pushed himself up and gagged at the sight of the soldier's corpse now covered with several ravens ripping flesh away from bone. Close to the mutilated body were several birds huddling protectively around Catrin while others continued attacking the remaining Romans.

Just then, Cynwrig rushed out of the dense woods and trampled through the feasting hoard to kneel beside Catrin. He swung her over his shoulders, and the ravens took flight massing into an arrow formation aimed at the sun.

Marcellus knew then, Catrin had unleashed her fury through her army of black-feathered warriors, a force of nature that alarmed him. Thoughts that she had misled him roiled through his mind again.

Am I mistaken? Is Catrin a Sorceress, a Siren who lured me to my death with her sweet promise of life?

What else can explain what just happened?

Did she truly love me? If so, why did she break her promise to save me from the death arrow?

Or had she?

Impulsively, he looked down at the creamy-colored creature that had been impaled into his chest with the death arrow, but was removed by Decimus. He then realized the white raven had sustained the brunt of the arrow's force and thus shielded him from death's grip. Catrin must have called upon the pristine raven to sacrifice itself for him. She had, after all, kept her promise and saved his life.

Marcellus watched Cynwrig carry Catrin over his shoulders and dash toward the woods. At the forest's edge, the warrior stopped and set Catrin down on her feet. A mist swirled around her and rose in the form of a raven into the sun's crimson glow. In his mind, he heard Catrin say, *Good-bye, my love,* before she disappeared into the gloom of the forest like a star at dawn.

Heart-broken, he slumped on the ground. Floating into oblivion, he again heard Catrin's voice. *No one dies. Our souls live in a circle* of *death and rebirth. Dreams are glimpses into our souls as we fly over life's currents.*

The revelation that Catrin had given him the gift to complete his life's journey and to steer his own destiny over life's deep oceans overwhelmed Marcellus. Tears shed from his eyes, but hope filled his heart. If he escaped his fate once, could not the future shift and they meet again?

Acknowledgments

I am indebted to many people who inspired and helped me on my odyssey of writing this book. My beloved mother introduced me to mythology and encouraged me to follow my passion. My devoted husband, Tom, an English teacher and coach, supported my dream to write this epic series. He always gave me his honest opinion and was my go-to person for demonstrating moves in fight scenes. I experienced the vicarious thrill of disarming him. His favorite quote was "Warriors don't cry."

My special thank you is extended to my friend Bob Underwood with a gift for language and self-deprecating humor that I tried to pass on to Marcellus. During memorable coffee shop moments, Bob would read my drafts aloud with a Shakespearean voice in the midst of coffee drinkers. He gave me the building blocks for becoming a better writer.

My writing coach, Doug Kurtz, helped me realize my dream of completing the first book by helping me to fine-tune the story and develop the characters. Judith Briles, The Book Shepherd, and others from AuthorU provided invaluable advice and services on my journey to independent publishing. I am also grateful to Kate Anderson and Tom Goodfellow for their insightful suggestions and for encouraging me to write this story from multiple points of view. Rebekah West provided a vision of Catrin through her photography that inspired me. And finally, special thanks are extended to Theresa Snyder and to everyone in the TaxiWriters group for their input and support.

Author's Note

The *Apollo's Raven* series is historical fiction/fantasy based on a blend of history and mythology of southeast Celtic tribes in Britain before the invasion of the Roman Emperor Claudius in 43 AD. The biggest challenge in researching this project is that the ancient Celts left almost no written records. Historical events had to be supplanted by Greek and Roman historians and medieval writers that spun Celtic mythology into their Christian beliefs. Archaeological findings from this time period also help fill in some of the gaps.

The political background used in this series is based on my research on southeast Celtic tribes in Britain which evolved differently than those in Wales, Scotland, and Ireland. After Julius Caesar's military expeditions to this area in 55-54 BC, there was strong Roman influence over the politics and trading. Powerful Celtic kings expanded their territories and minted coins. Many of the rulers were educated in Rome and adopted many of the Romans' tastes for luxury goods. To support their extravagant lifestyles, pro-Roman kings warred with other tribal territories to supply the Roman Empire with slaves. Although there is no written account of any Roman expeditionary forces sent to Britain before Claudius's invasion in 43 AD, there are recorded incidences that pro-Roman rulers pleaded for Rome's help to intervene on their behalf. Archaeological evidence now supports that Claudius's invasion was nothing more than a peacekeeping mission to halt the expansion of the anti-Roman factions led by Cunobelin's sons, Caratacus and Togodumnus. There may have already been a Roman military presence that protected the areas of Britain vital to trading with the empire. The tribal names in this novel are based on Ptolemy's map of Celtic kingdoms generated in 150 AD.

The Celtic characters in this novel are fictional except for Cunobelin, referred as the King of Britannia by the Romans, and his son Adminius. Several Celtic characters in the novel spoke Latin either through formal training in Rome and Britain, or through interactions with Roman merchants. Although the Celtic society was becoming more paternalistic, women were still held in high regard and could rule. The most famous warrior queen was Boudica who united the Britons in 61 BC and almost expelled the Romans. She was also known as a powerful Druidess who Romans claimed sacrificed some of her victims to the war goddess Andaste.

The Roman characters are fictional except for Lucius Antonius, the son of Iullus Antonius and grandson of Marcus Antonius (Mark Antony). Very little is known about Lucius Antonius except that he was banished in 2 AD to Gaul after his father, Iullus Antonius, was accused of treason and forced to fall on his sword. It is unclear whether Lucius had any children, but it is coincidental that another famous Roman general, Marcus Antonius Primus, was born in Gaul about 30 AD.

The fantastical elements in this novel are based on mystical powers of heroes and heroines from the Celtic legends in Ireland and Wales. Most interestingly, ancient historians, including Julius Caesar, write the Celts believed in the reincarnation of the soul. This philosophy is consistent with the Greek philosopher, Pythagoras, in 500 BC. I have freely expanded on the concept of the soul as a way to explain Catrin's mystical powers. There are more than three hundred documented names of Celtic gods and goddesses, but only a few of the more popular names referred by the Romans are presented in this story. Also of note, several Celtic healing sites are named after Apollo, probably a consequence of the blending of religious beliefs.

It should be noted that "cathos" means detestation or hatred in the ancient Celtic language.

About the Author

Linnea Tanner is a native of Colorado where she attended the University of Colorado and earned both her bachelor's and master's degree in Chemistry. She is pursuing her lifelong passion to write historical fiction/fantasy based on her love of ancient history and mythology.

The *Apollo's Raven* series is inspired by the history and rich mythology of the ancient Celtic and Roman civilizations. Catrin is inspired by historical accounts and legends of Celtic women warriors, while the legacy of Mark Antony and his tragic love story with Cleopatra sparked the creation of Marcellus.

Linnea has done broad research and traveled extensively to the United Kingdom and France. She is a member of the Historical Novel Society, Lighthouse Writers, Pikes Peak Writers, Northern Colorado Writers, and Rocky Mountain Fiction Writers. Currently, she and her husband live in Windsor, CO, and have two children and six grandchildren. Her interests include ancient and medieval history, action movies, flamenco dancing, and gardening.

EMPIRE'S ANVIL
BOOK TWO IN THE APOLLO'S RAVEN SERIES

Follow Catrin and Marcellus in their epic Celtic tale of love, magic, adventure, intrigue and betrayal in Ancient Rome and Britannia. Don't miss Book Two in the *Apollo's Raven* series coming soon:

Linnea Tanner's
EMPIRE'S ANVIL
See the following pages for a preview ...

War looms over 24 AD Britannia where rival tribal rulers fight each other for power and the Romans threaten to invade to settle their differences. Princess Catrin is accused of treason for abetting her Roman lover, Marcellus. To redeem herself, she must prove her loyalty to her father by forsaking all men and defending their kingdom, even to the death. Forged into a fierce warrior, Catrin must overcome tribulations in her quest to break the curse that foretells their kingdom will be destroyed by a great empire. She is tested and her mettle hardened on the brutality of the Roman Empire's anvil. Yet, when she again reunites with Marcellus, she must face her greatest challenger that could destroy her life, freedom, and humanity.

To keep up-to-date with the latest news on the development of the *Apollo's Raven* epic series please visit and sign up for the FREE e-Bulletin:
linneatanner.com

You can also follow us on Facebook:
facebook.com/apollosraven

I

TREASON

The only reason her father would order warriors out of hearing range was to reprimand her. He must know about her relationship with Marcellus, a Roman hostage who had been put under her charge.

August 24 AD, Southeast Britannia

All around Princess Catrin were warriors carrying the casualties from the conflict that broke out at the prisoner exchange. Her heart still pounded from the fierce fighting as she ran alongside the king's commander, Trystan, to the hillside cave—a haven where the injured were being placed. Some of the warriors claimed her father had been retaken as prisoner, but with the chaos of battle he could as well have been among the wounded … or that was what she hoped.

When they finally reached the rocked façade of the cave, tree roots dangling over the entrance like snakes obscured her vision of the inside. She weaved through the entangled roots into the cavern's dank womb. The heavy stench of feces, blood, and vomit filled her nostrils, and the warriors appeared as bustling shadows kneeling and tending the injured.

Trystan placed another burning torch in a sconce that clearly illuminated motionless bodies on the muddy floor. Catrin's heart quickened when her eyes landed on her father lying prone against the back wall that was stacked with weapons. She rushed to his side and turned him over. A chill sliced down her spine when she saw her father's blood-smeared face. Fearing that he may have already succumbed to his wounds, she placed a shaky palm on his forehead.

His skin was hot and clammy which gave her momentary relief that he was still alive. She then scanned his torso for injuries. Noticing the dark streaks on his red tunic, she rubbed the sticky fabric and observed her blood-stained fingers under the light of the torch. She flicked her eyes at Cynwrig, a warrior renowned for his skill with the battle-ax, and ordered, "Help me remove the tunic. I need to stop the bleeding!"

Cynwrig supported the king as Catrin cut the fabric away from his chest. Seeing the crisscross cuts on her father's chest and deep gash in his stomach made her cringe. She scrunched her nose from a waft of rotten egg odor.

King Amren, aware of Catrin, fidgeted under her stare. He rasped, "Fetch Agrona."

Catrin gave Cynwrig a wary look, but Trystan quickly replied, "I will get her now."

"No!" Catrin snapped to stop him. "There are traitors in our village. Agrona may be one of them. We can't risk letting anyone know we have rescued the king. I will care for him. There are herbs in satchels next to the wall which I can use for swelling and festering." She bent down and clasped her father's hand. "Trust me on this."

Amren regarded her for a moment and then ordered with a weak voice, "Do what my daughter says."

The flaming torch reflected on Cynwrig's hazel eyes as he pointed toward the entryway. "I'll ignite a fire there and heat my dagger blade to seal the wounds."

She looked at Trystan. "I need water from the river to wash him."

The commander motioned for one of his men to do what Catrin instructed. She then rummaged through several pouches, smelling each to discern the herb it contained. When the warrior returned with a bucket of water, she soaked several strips of willow bark in it, then pinched some powdered blackberry, borage, and sage into a ceramic bowl and poured in some ale. After she finished preparing the paste dressing, she asked Cynwrig if the dagger was hot enough to seal the wounds.

He pulled the blade from the fire and inspected the fiery red surface. "It looks hot enough for me to proceed."

"No. Let me do it," Catrin demanded.

Cynwrig put a stick in the king's mouth to muffle his cries and restrained his arms as Catrin pressed the hot metal on each wound, methodically moving right to left then downward. The king writhed with agony from every touch of the red-hot blade, his wild eyes reminding her of a wounded animal as he fought against Cynwrig's restraint. The king's jaw clenched so tight, she feared he might break one of his gritted teeth. Concentrating on her task, she swallowed the acrid taste in her mouth, but the ghastly stench of sizzling pus and burning skin finally made her gag and her stomach recoil. She handed the dagger to Cynwrig to reheat the blade, retched what little was in her belly, and broke into a cold sweat. Becoming light-headed, she leaned her head into the hard wall to brace herself before continuing.

After her stomach settled, she smoothed green paste over her father's reddened wounds. With her every touch, his muscles flinched. Seeing the agony in his face, she placed a blanket under his head and gave him chamomile and poppy in water to make him more comfortable before she proceeded. As she placed bark strips on the criss-cross cuts on his chest, the sudden grip of her father's hand around her wrist startled her.

Amren said, "We need to speak about Agrona and Marcellus."

Catrin winced. "What about?"

King Amren closed his eyelids for a moment and breathed deeply. He then waved Trystan over and whispered into his ear. The commander nodded and ordered everyone away from the king.

Catrin shuddered. The only reason her father would order warriors out of hearing range was to reprimand her. He must know about her relationship with Marcellus, a Roman hostage who had been put under her charge.

A slight growl vibrated in her father's voice as he spoke. "Trystan told me, when he was imprisoned with me, that Cynwrig had found you delirious in Marcellus's arms. When he brought you back home to be treated by Agrona, she found an amulet of Apollo around your neck. She warned that Marcellus's patron god inflicted you with the falling sickness and made you go mad. She took you to her lair to lift the spell. I want to know what happened there."

Throat becoming parched, Catrin could hardly swallow, afraid to upset her father in his weakened condition. She said sweetly, "You should rest now. We can talk about this later."

"I want to know now!" Amren demanded.

Catrin said, her voice cracking, "The amulet never cursed me. Agrona drugged me to make it appear that I was mad. She is not who you think. She embodies a Druidic spirit from your past."

"Get to your meaning," Amren snapped angrily.

"I had a vision of the day you executed your former queen," Catrin said. "Under a blood moon, you walked a pathway of red-hot rocks around a towering fire. A woman with a wolf pelt draped over her shoulder walked toward you between two lines of people chanting, "Rhan, Rhan, Rhan.""

The king frowned. "What did this woman look like?"

"She had coppery hair and wolf eyes, the color of amber like Marrock's. He was also there, a few feet behind her. He looked only about eight years old."

A lump moved down Amren's throat. "What did you see next?"

"You accused the woman of treason and cut off her head with one swing of your sword. Her head flew off and slipped through the hands of a little girl standing next to Marrock. When the girl spoke, her earth-brown eyes glowed."

"The girl is Agrona," Amren said with a faded voice. "How do you interpret this vision?"

"Rhan did not die that day. Her essence possessed Agrona because of touching her severed head. Rhan's soul now lives in Agrona. When I confronted Agrona about this, she drugged me and melded my thoughts with hers. I resisted her evil attempt at possession for a time, but then she succeeded in breaking me down." Catrin paused, recalling the slimy feeling of Agrona's thoughts crawling in and out of her mind like a maggot. "She wanted my magical powers. Why did you not suspect that Rhan possessed Agrona?"

Amren muttered, as if struggling to comprehend what Catrin had just told him. His words became crisper as he uttered, "I believed the gods spoke through Agrona. She had been mute since birth, but spoke for the first time at Rhan's execution. She declared me to be the king of truth and light. Agrona told me things that only Rhan could have known. I completely trusted her."

"She tricked you," Catrin exclaimed, "like she did with me."

"I am not so sure about that ..." Amren squeezed his eyelids shut and moaned, "Give me poppy for my pain."

Catrin whiffed each pouch at her side until she found the poppy's distinct spicy scent. She pinched some of the brown powder into a cup of water, then returned to her father and held his head so he could drink it. A few moments later, he relaxed and asked her to help him lean against the stone wall. Though the pacing of his speech was slower, his voice became stronger as he continued, "Trystan told me Cynwrig found you naked with Marcellus in the woods. Your mother questioned Marcellus about what he had done to you before you were stricken. He finally confessed that he had pledged his love to you before Mother Goddess ... that can only mean that you consummated what you believed was marriage."

A sob clutched in Catrin's throat when her father glared at her. "Yes, I love Marcellus."

"You did this knowing I was negotiating your betrothal to Cunobelin's son?"

Catrin dropped her eyes. "Yes. I felt you betrayed me by doing this without my permission."

"What in the name of the gods have you done?" Amren said, raising his voice. "The queen showed Trystan the dagger on which I inscribed Rhan's curse. The blade was glowing as if it had been pulled out of a furnace. Words were melting away and being replaced by others. Your mother quickly put the dagger in the case and locked it, fearing the curse was transforming again."

The revelation stunned Catrin.

Amren proclaimed, "I believe your act of love altered the curse."

She shook her head in denial.

No. No. This can't be. Our love is blameless. Something else caused this to happen.

"Find your tongue," Amren demanded.

Catrin knew that no matter the repercussions, she had to tell her father the truth. "This has nothing to do with Marcellus. It was during this time when my raven sent me a vision that explained how my Druidic powers worked. It said that I always had these abilities, but didn't know how to use them correctly."

"And what are these abilities?" asked Amren.

Catrin drew in a long breath and exhaled slowly to steady herself. "I can travel to other realms in my raven's mind. One place is a transitional barrier where the mortal world and the Otherworld of the spirits meet. The raven called this the Wall of Lives. On its surface are life-threads of every living human being. The threads weave into a fluid tapestry that flows through the portal into the Otherworld. It is where the past, the present, and the future merge into one. I discovered that I could shift the future by manipulating the threads."

"How is that?"

Catrin explained, "I can change when someone dies by pulling a person's life-thread out of the portal and reweaving it into other strands in the tapestry."

"No mortal has that power," Amren said, incredulous.

"I have that power," Catrin proclaimed. "When I pulled a life-thread out of the portal and rewove it into the tapestry, I extended a person's life. The only problem, though, is I don't know how the future changes for others because the tapestry then rippled out like water."

"Whose life did you extend?" Amren asked. "Mine?"

Catrin's voice cracked with emotion when she burst out, "I saved Marcellus!"

"Cursed gods above!" Amren's blue eyes blazed from the torch flame when he pointed to his abdomen. "The slash in my belly is from your lover's blade. By saving an enemy, he almost killed me!"

Horror sheared into Catrin's heart. *Marcellus could not have done this! He knows how much I love him ... my father. Why had I not foreseen this?* She tore her eyes from her father's burning stare and shrilled, "Oh gods no! I wanted to save Marcellus, but I never meant to harm you."

"Nothing good came out of this!" Amren snarled. "I saw Marcellus fall from an arrow shot into his chest."

"No, father, he is alive! I summoned a white raven to take the brunt of the arrow before it could pierce his heart."

Amren's fingers clawed into the cave's dirt floor like a crab's pincers. "This is the disloyal act of a stupid girl blinded by love—not a noble princess I raised to put family and kingdom first. I must now go to war against my own banished son and rival king. The Romans will likely join their cause after we killed so many of their soldiers today. Just when I needed your magical powers, you let me down. Far worse, you betrayed me and my people when you slept and abetted the Roman enemy. And finally, your actions altered the curse by changing the future. In what way, I can't be certain until I inspect the dagger's inscription. You've left me with no choice but to charge you with treason and put you on trial for your crimes."

Catrin felt as if a mule had kicked her in the stomach. She gasped, "Father, you cannot mean this."

"I always mean what I say," Amren said coldly, then shifted his eyes toward the back of the cave and called out, "Trystan, come here!"

The commander walked out of the shadows and presented himself. The pallor of Amren's face turned leaden as he ordered, "Detain Catrin as prisoner until she is tried for treason."

The king's lips abruptly turned ice blue, and he crumpled on the cave's muddy floor.

Conflicting emotions of shock, fear, love and hate whirled inside Catrin like a storm as she pressed trembling fingers on her father's neck for a pulse. When she could not feel a heartbeat, she gasped and pressed harder.

Then suddenly, the king's hand swatted her fingers as if they were flies on a corpse. Startled, she lurched back and filled with terror when his eyes froze on her. He barked at Trystan, "Do what I said. Take her as prisoner."

Catrin gaped in horror at Trystan. He flinched, but then he clenched her arm and the floor seemed to sweep underneath her feet as he forced her up. She pleaded with her eyes for him to show mercy.

He showed none and dragged her away like a carcass through the cave's entrance. Outside, he ordered a warrior to tether her to a tree until they could return home the next morning.

In the night's dark gloom, unforgiving rain washed tears of remorse from her face that she had lost her father's trust and was branded as a traitor for loving Marcellus.

2

BETRAYAL

"Two of my soldiers were not killed in battle. They were pecked to death by those demonic creatures."

At times feverish, Marcellus languished during the arduous five-day wagon ride to the Roman encampment near the Catuvellauni capital of Camulodunon. Today, he took the tribune's advice and told the driver to distance their wagon from the Roman troops and two wagons full of injured soldiers. The constant jostling aggravated his chest pain. The soldiers' open contempt that he had betrayed them by saving Catrin at the prison exchange grated like salt into a festering wound.

The first soldier who treated his wound spat on the bandage before covering the dressing on his chest. At the time, Marcellus tried to humor himself. *Undoubtedly, he gave me an offering for the healing process.*

Another cavalryman with two swollen black eyes offered him another round of sputum on his bandage and said contemptuously, "Why would you save a Celtic cunni after she led our men into an ambush?"

If the wound in his chest had not hurt so much, Marcellus would have knocked the foul-mouthed horseman off his mount and whip-fisted him. Weakened and his mobility limited by stabbing pain, he only had enough rage to grumble, "Keep your nose out of my affairs."

The badger-eyed horseman then contorted his face into the ugliest scowl Marcellus had ever seen and said, "The other day, I buried five of my friends. Two had their eyes gouged out by those damn ravens. I reckon that is my concern." As the cavalryman left, Marcellus overhead him mumble, "Traitor."

The word "traitor" still resonated in Marcellus's mind. Even now, he couldn't explain what he was thinking when the centurion hurled Catrin on the ground and began stomping her abdomen. All he knew was his heart was torn with the horror that she might be raped and possibly killed. Love can make a man lose all reason.

With the dark clouds billowing above, his mood now spiraled into a vortex of gloom. Not only did his chest stab with pain, his head throbbed with the constant clack, clack of the wagon wheels on the rough pathway. A pang of loneliness dug into his soul. At the moment he had lost all trust in Catrin to change his fate to die young, she proved him wrong. The white raven that she had summoned took the full force of the death arrow before it could pierce his heart. He had believed himself invincible, but death almost claimed him in Britannia. And now he must face two more attempts on his life that Catrin had prophesied. The first attacker would be her half-brother, Marrock—a shape-shifter who would take the form of a red wolf. A serpent would then strike him when he returned to Rome and reconnected with his married lover. To prevent this from happening, he resolved never to see her again.

Marcellus drew in a grated breath. Not until he met Catrin did he realize how he had frittered his life away. His happiest moments were when he was a boy at his family's villa that was nestled on a wooded hillside between the Saone and Roane Rivers. He play-acted as his great-grandfather, Mark Antony, on a quest with Julius Caesar to overcome the Celtic hoards at Alesia. Yet this whimsical role-playing never erased his resentment that his forefathers were considered traitors by Rome. Even his grandfather, Iullus Antonius, was branded a traitor for committing adultery with Augustus's daughter, Julia, and was forced to commit suicide by falling on his sword. As a consequence, Marcellus's father, Senator Lucius Antonius, was banished to Gaul.

At age twelve, Marcellus recalled his father's excitement announcing that Tiberius had pardoned him and they were moving back to Rome. Much to his chagrin, the sounds of the countryside that had been music to his ears was replaced by the urban clamor of shoppers in the Roman forum. Even with the approximately one million inhabitants scurrying in and out of multi-storied insulae in the city, loneliness plagued him. A gangling and unrefined boy, he never quite meshed with his more sophisticated peers.

That all changed when he immersed himself in weapons training, military strategy, and oratory. He ultimately caught the eye of the consul's wife almost twice his age. An exotic, dark haired beauty, she invited him over to her villa so they could read poetry together. In her bedchamber, she would undress him and stroke his manhood in elegiac couplet as she read Ovid's **Ars Amatoria**:

Woman cannot resist the flames and cruel darts of love, shafts which, methinks, pierce not the heart of man so deeply. Pluck, then, the rose and lose no time, since if thou pluck it not 'twill fall forlorn and withered, of its own accord.

She likened lovemaking to military service. He lustily obeyed her every command. How could a young man resist such a duty? Yet she taught him the darker side of erotic pleasures that sometimes ended in opium-induced oblivion. He was at her every beck and call to satiate her needs … and, of course, his too.

Once, her husband, a drooling silver haired ex-commander with crippling gout, almost limped in on them when his legs were entwined about his lover. The panic of getting caught made his heart leap to his throat as he scrambled to hide behind a large vase. At the time, he gave little thought of his mortality and the vengeance the consul might have exacted.

Drawing out of his reverie, Marcellus lifted his eyes to the sun that was peering through thick clouds. He prayed silently.

Apollo, show me how I can rise out of my ashes and ascend to the heavens.

The name "Catrin" whispered into his mind and he released a long rueful sigh. At the moment he realized he had found his true love, Apollo snatched her away. He knew their relationship was impossible. Would she ever forgive him for stabbing her father?

He then remembered the king lunging at him in the melee of battle. He had to defend himself or die. It was never his intent to harm him—the possibility that he had killed Catrin's father gnawed at his every waking thought. Though she had changed his fate to die young, he never expected the future might shift in unpredictable and deadly ways. And soon, he must face his own father who surely must know the soldiers had branded him as a traitor.

No longer able to tolerate the clicking of the wooden wheels, Marcellus shouted to the driver, "Stop. I need to get out!"

"No need," the driver replied. "We're almost there."

Marcellus pulled himself up against the wagon's side to look over. Ahead was the rectangular Roman encampment on top of a rolling hill. Riding beside the wagon was Decimus whose scarred face wore a perpetual scowl. The close-lipped tribune was an enigma to Marcellus. Rumors abound in Rome that his political career had floundered when he married a Gallic wench who died giving birth to their daughter—a tale of caution, his father Lucius told him, for any nobleman considering marrying a foreigner beneath his status.

Lucius never seemed to give this gossip much credence as Decimus was the only man who could confront the senator and steer him to a steadier path. Marcellus had to admit he had grown to respect the commander's rock-solid demeanor since their initial confrontation with King Amren. Yet the tribune's silence on the trip to the Roman camp had roared disapproval of what Marcellus had done.

Tribune glanced at Marcellus and reined his horse closer to the wagon.

He said, "You look pale as a corpse. What did those savages do to you back there?"

Marcellus hesitated. Exposing what he had been through as a prisoner could disrupt the political balance and endanger Catrin. He replied dryly, "Nothing much. The bleak weather has put me in a bad mood."

"Weather?" Decimus quipped. "The bruises on your face tell me otherwise."

Marcellus looked away. "It happened at the fight during the prisoner exchange."

"Those bruises were there before the conflict broke out," Decimus said. "I'm still baffled why you attacked Priscus, so you could save that Celtic wench."

Marcellus stiffened. "Catrin helped me to escape."

Decimus spat on the ground. "Those Cantiaci warriors at the prisoner exchange who were ready to ambush us tell me otherwise. As I recall, you are the one who shouted the alert."

Marcellus gripped the side of the wagon as it bumped over a rough area of the road. He told Decimus, "Catrin didn't know this would happen. Besides, the Romans were ready to do the same thing."

"You mean ambush?"

Marcellus nodded.

Decimus' jaw tensed. "As commander, I must prepare for any surprise. Don't fool yourself. That wench knew exactly what she was doing. She lured us into a trap. It is best we got you away from her wiles. What else could explain why you turned on Priscus to save her, except that she bewitched you?"

Marcellus glared at the tribune "She did no such thing. I protected her because she helped me. *Quid pro quo*. I betrayed no Roman."

Decimus fidgeted with his reins and stared at Marcellus. "I warned you that Catrin was a sorceress. What about those ravens that attacked our soldiers when the conflict broke out at the exchange? I've never seen such numbers swoop down like that. Two of my soldiers were not killed in battle. They were pecked to death by those demonic creatures. There is something evil about Catrin as there is Marrock."

"Her half-brother," Marcellus's voice spewed with disgust. "You lecture me about Catrin. Yet Father and you bargained with that monster. Marrock ignited the firestorm when I was held hostage. He must have stolen my father's insignia ring and used it to imprint the wax seal on the fake message addressed to you, which was conveniently discovered on a dead courier. It was only after Queen Rhiannon read that Amren had been imprisoned and the Romans would soon attack her kingdom did she threaten to kill me. Didn't you think of that when you broke the agreement at the prisoner exchange?"

"Of course, I knew," Decimus grunted, "but anyone could have sent that letter."

"It was Marrock," Marcellus insisted. "You are a reasonable man. I am surprised you support my father in his dealings with Marrock."

"As a loyal servant to your father, I do what I am told," Decimus said with a bitter tinge to his voice. "Between the two of us, this cursed island should sink in the ocean along with its brutal warriors and sorcery. We should not be dealing with any of them."

"Oh, I see. You are of the same mind as me," Marcellus said, suspecting a falling-out between his father and Decimus. "Has something happened that I need to know about?"

Decimus pressed his lips together and glared straight ahead at the Roman encampment. "Let me just say that I now understand your father's friendship to me solely depends on my services to elevate his political standing. If anything goes wrong here, it will be me who takes the blame."

A sudden pain from his chest wound made Marcellus flinch, diverting his attention from the conversation. Grabbing the edge of the wagon side, he cursed, "Damn the gods! I can't let father see me helpless like this."

"Perhaps a good meal and some wine will put you in better spirits," Decimus said with a lighter tone.

"I almost forgot how I missed Roman comforts." Marcellus grimaced, trying to ease his discomfort by leaning on the wagon's edge. He asked, "Is there a horse I can ride into camp? I would like to present myself as a nobleman, not a barnyard cat."

Decimus cracked a smile and barked at a nearby cavalryman, "Give this man your horse."

A lanky horseman climbed off his black-spotted gray pony that could not have been more than fourteen hands high. Marcellus gingerly crawled out of the wagon and lumbered to the pony. As he mounted, he again felt a sharp pain in his chest. For good measure, he cursed the gods again when he reined his horse close to the tribune.

Decimus sniffed and scrunched his nose. "It looks like you'll need fresh clothes. You are starting to stink like piss and shit."

Marcellus was not sure how to take the tribune's comment. He decided to keep the conversation cordial to find out more about the possible disagreement between his father and Decimus.

Rubbing his bristly beard, Marcellus said casually, "I need a shave. Have any other envoys joined my father at the headquarters?"

"Senator Marcus Crassus Frugi is there." Decimus's smile turned downward into a grimace. "He has the same mind as your father regarding Britannia."

"Which is?"

"Now is the right time for Rome to invade this god-forsaken island."

The prospect of Catrin being slain in the invasion brought on a wave of pain and nausea in Marcellus. He said with a grated voice, "Invasion is a bad idea. The sooner we leave the better."

"I've argued this exact point with your father," Decimus grumbled. "His response is that I am here to serve him. He can as easily bring me down just as he raised me up."

Lucius's father's harsh words to Decimus disquieted Marcellus. "Did you openly tell him that we should leave?"

"Yes, I confronted Lucius. I also learned from him that the emperor had the same mind as me," Decimus said, creasing his brow. "Ask your father about the letter that Tiberius sent. Right now, I could use some of your support."

Marcellus gave a bewildered look. "What support?"

Decimus shook his head. "Forget it. I don't want any further troubles with your father."

Without saying another word, Decimus abruptly kicked his heels into the horse's side and galloped ahead of Marcellus to the encampment.

3

CHIMERA

A creature with wide-opened jaws and eyes that glowed like red embers bounded into the room. Twice the size of a timber wolf, the beast was not of this world.

When Marcellus and the troops reached the Roman encampment, the main tower's sentry waved them through. At the center of camp, Lucius and Decimus were waiting outside the palatial tented headquarters surrounded by banners emblazoned with the gold image of Apollo in his chariot. Marcellus dismounted and embraced his father.

Lucius stiffly pulled away and said coldly, "Thank the gods, you are alive. Your mother would never forgive me if I left you dead in Britannia." He then looked at Decimus. "I need to talk with you before I speak with my boy."

Marcellus shot his father a seething glare. *Boy! You still call me boy after what I've been through!* Fuming, he followed his father into the receiving chamber, sparsely furnished with two tables, foldable stools, and multiple shelves. Behind the elongated table was a scarlet tapestry with an embroidered gold eagle.

Lucius pulled back the tapestry to reveal a smaller bedchamber. "You can clean up in here while I speak with Decimus."

Marcellus avoided his father's eyes as he entered the sleeping quarters, about half the size of the main chamber. There were two beds on each side, end tables, and corner shelves on which scrolls were piled high. He eyed a large copper bowl of water on one of the tables and took off his torn tunic to inspect the bandages. When he touched the pink-tinged linen over his chest wound, he winced from the pain and grumbled, "Son of a bitch!" He then rinsed the cloth in water and carefully lifted his bandage to wipe the swollen area.

With his appetite returning, Marcellus noticed a platter of cheese, bread, and berries that had been set on another table. He gobbled the food down and searched the room for fresh garments. His eyes landed on a corner shelf with a sundry of folded clothes, brushes, strigils, razors, and jars of cleansing oil. Rummaging through the shelf, he found a scarlet military tunic. As he slid the garment off of the shelf, a scroll dropped at his feet. He picked it up and looked at the broken wax seal. It had the intaglio portrait of Emperor Tiberius. It was a mystery as to why his father had placed such an important document with his personal effects. Upon further consideration, he wondered if the message had something to do with the discord between his father and Decimus. Curiosity aroused, he unrolled the parchment on the table and read:

Immediately cease all diplomatic negotiations in Britannia and return to Rome. The cohorts under the command of Tribune Decimus Flavius should report to the military fort at Gesoriacum, Gaul, for further assignment.

He wondered why his father and Senator Frugi were still discussing an invasion if the emperor had clearly recalled them. Defying the emperor was treasonous. The ramifications of his father disobeying an imperial mandate rattled in his head. Senators had been banished ... even executed for such acts. No wonder Decimus was upset.

A sudden movement of the tapestry divider captured Marcellus's attention. He hastily rolled the parchment and tucked it under his sleeve. He winced when his father walked in.

Lucius regarded Marcellus for a moment and then said, "It looks like you found something to wear."

Marcellus readjusted the sleeve to conceal the scroll. "Yes, but most of my belongings are still at King Amren's villa."

"I will have my body slave find you some other clothes." Lucius rubbed the back of his neck and grimaced. "Tell me everything that happened to you when you were held hostage."

Marcellus bristled. "No warm greetings … just an interrogation?"

"You expect a warm greeting after your antics," Lucius sneered.

"Antics?"

"During my mediations with Amren," Lucius said with a grated voice, "he confronted me with news that one of his warriors had found you naked with his youngest daughter. He accused you of raping and leaving her half-dead. Then he ranted that Apollo had cursed her with the falling sickness."

After his ordeal with the Cantiaci warriors and their unwarranted accusations, Marcellus was in no mood to reasonably defend himself again with his father. He snapped, "That is a lie!"

Lucius creased his brow. "Did you seduce her to get the information I asked for?"

"No, I befriended her," Marcellus answered sharply. "That is all it took to learn that Marrock is a debauched man whom you should not be dealing with."

Lucius shot a scathing glower at Marrock. "I deal with any barbarian who serves my ambition! Why did you help Catrin escape? It was my intention to capture her after you had been released."

Marcellus blazed. "I thought the exchange was to calm the political fire between you and the Cantiaci? It sounds as if you never intended to honor your agreement with Queen Rhiannon."

"Did she not betray us?" Lucius retorted. "Decimus described how a conflict broke out at the prisoner exchange when the queen's warriors ambushed us. Even with this treachery, you assaulted a centurion, so Catrin could escape. You did this without any regard for the safety of our legionaries. The men accuse you of betraying them!"

"I betrayed no one," Marcellus said, stepping closer to his father. "Priscus was trying to kill Catrin. She had no knowledge that her mother had planned the ambush."

Lucius huffed. "Do you think I am an idiot to believe that? That Celtic tramp lured us into a trap!"

"If the queen had trusted you, none of this bloodshed would have occurred."

Lucius grabbed Marcellus by the arm. "I bargained to save your life. After that, no one threatens my family and lives!"

Angered, Marcellus pulled away, but his father continued ranting, "That bitch queen, she wanted to butcher you, sacrifice you to her war goddesses. I swear that witch will pay dearly for threatening me and my boy, do you hear me Jupiter?"

"What do you plan to do?" Marcellus asked.

Lucius clenched his hands. "I want vengeance! I want that pompous king and all his family to suffer. They must die for threatening me and you!"

"The queen acted like any prey cornered by a predator," Marcellus argued. "You would have done the same—defend your family any way you could."

"You idiot, I had to grovel like a mangy dog to that mad bitch—an insect I should ground beneath my heels! Why did I do this? Let me tell you why." Lucius stomped his foot. "To save your ungrateful arse!"

Marcellus knew then that his father was determined to stay in Britannia and destroy King Amren, despite the emperor's orders. The rage in his father's eyes reminded him of another incident in Rome. After his father had a heated dispute with a political rival, the aristocrat's bloated body was found a few days later floating in the Tiber. At the time, Marcellus believed his father had no connection to this man's death, but now he was not so sure. Before him was a three-headed chimera speaking from whichever head served him the best.

Desperate to thwart his father from going down a destructive path, Marcellus pulled the scroll out of his sleeve and waved it in front of him. "Tell me about this! How can you stay in Britannia when the emperor ordered you to return? You can't ignore his mandate, so you can avenge King Amren."

Lucius angrily grabbed for the scroll. "Where did you get that?"

Marcellus pulled it away from him. "It was in plain sight with your personal effects."

"You impudent boy!" Lucius said through gritted teeth. "I brought you here so you could learn about dealing with foreign kings, but you threw it all away on a sorceress whore."

Marcellus shoved his father in the chest. "She is not a sorceress! I owe her a debt for saving my life."

Lucius lashed, "And you paid that debt by fucking her! Don't think that you were her first. Marrock claims she bewitches men."

Marcellus put his face within inches of his father. "Why does that monster's opinion matter? The issue is Tiberius. If you defy him, you could be charged for treason."

Eyes ablaze, Lucius slammed Marcellus into the table, knocking off scrolls and goblets all over the red-carpeted floor. He shouted, "You ungrateful bastard! You know nothing of my plan to convince Tiberius otherwise. Do not challenge me!"

Marcellus furiously raised his clenched hand. "Back off! Or I will lay you flat on the floor."

Lucius acted first and threw a hammer punch into Marcellus's chest, the pain from the blow ripping into his lungs. Gasping, Marcellus stumbled backward and landed hard on the floor, the scroll flying out of his hand. His father hastily picked the scroll up and placed it over a burning candle on the table. The edges of the parchment charred quickly and smoke filled the room. The fumes exacerbated the burning pain in Marcellus's lungs. He pushed himself up and hacked until he spewed some bloody mucous.

A sudden blood-chilling growl from the adjacent chamber startled Marcellus. He turned toward the movement of the swaying tapestry. When large red-furred paws suddenly appeared underneath the fabric, he shuddered. The next instant, loud barks and snarls mixed with the clamor of footsteps and banging metal.

Marcellus sprung to a defensive stance, his fear overcoming his pain.

Lucius shouted, "What is going on?"

The paws disappeared beneath the tapestry and were replaced with leather-strapped boots shuffling back and forth. The emblazoned gold eagle on the crimson tapestry appeared to be flying as the fabric whipped back and forth.

A soldier yelled, "Jupiter's balls!"

Another shrieked, "Look at the size of that wolf!"

Marcellus recognized Decimus's voice. "Corner him ... spear him now!"

When the creature's red-furred muzzle squeezed under the tapestry, Lucius tapped Marcellus on the arm and handed him a dagger.

Marcellus scanned the room for a more deadly weapon.

Nothing.

He snapped his eyes at his father. "I need a spear."

Lucius scrambled to retrieve a spear at the back.

A growl rumbled into the chamber as the tapestry shot up. A creature with wide-opened jaws and eyes that glowed like red embers bounded into the room. The massive beast was not of this world and twice the size of a timber wolf.

Panic tore into Marcellus when the mammoth wolf leapt at him as a red flame of fur. The next instant, he was under the beast's heavy paws. Sharp pain again ripped to his lungs. Gasping for air, he almost passed out.

Then time slowed to a crawl when a powerful force entered him as a burning bolt through his arm. His hand had a will of its own, thrusting the dagger blade into the beast's underbelly.

The wolf's jaws snapped within inches of his face.

Staring into the creature's glowing red eyes, Marcellus thought he was looking into the soul of a demon. His hand again stabbed the wolf's underbelly and then stabbed one more time.

He heard Catrin shout in his mind. *Get away now! It is Marrock.* This was the second attacker that she had predicted would attempt to take his life—the Blood Wolf foretold in Rhan's curse.

No time for him to ponder.

Just as the beast's fangs lunged for his throat, the creature was hurled back as if caught in a whirlwind.

With new life springing into his legs, Marcellus bounced to his feet.

About ten feet from him was the wolf, appearing dazed, struggling to get up as two soldiers and Decimus surrounded it.

A soldier threw a javelin into the creature's side. The direct hit did not stop the beast. It rose on its paws. Before any other man could throw another weapon, the wolf leapt up and disappeared into a vortex of multicolored flashes of light.

Bewildered, Marcellus asked the soldiers, "What just happened?"

He then looked up and saw a vision of Catrin floating over him like a translucent cloud. At that moment, he realized her second prophecy that he would escape Marrock in his shape-shifted wolf form had been fulfilled. He reached for her hand, but she faded into a cool mist.

Remember to keep up-to-date with the latest news
on the development of the *Apollo's Raven* epic series.
Please visit and sign up for the FREE e-Bulletin:
www.linneatanner.com